WICKED

WEIRD &

WILY

YANKEES

WICKED WEIRD & WILY YANKEES

A CELEBRATION OF NEW ENGLAND'S ECCENTRICS AND MISFITS

STEPHEN GENCARELLA

Globe
Pequot

GUILFORD
CONNECTICUT

Globe
Pequot

An imprint of The Rowman & Littlefield Publishing Group, Inc.
4501 Forbes Blvd., Ste. 200
Lanham, MD 20706
www.rowman.com

Distributed by NATIONAL BOOK NETWORK

British Library Cataloguing in Publication Information Available

Library of Congress Cataloging-in-Publication Data

Names: Gencarella, Stephen Olbrys, 1971– author.
Title: Wicked weird & wily yankees : a celebration of New England's eccentrics and misfits / Stephen Gencarella.
Description: Guilford, Connecticut : Globe Pequot, 2018.
Identifiers: LCCN 2017051050 (print) | LCCN 2017053577 (ebook) | ISBN 9781493032662 (pbk.) | ISBN 9781493032679 (ebook)
Subjects: LCSH: New England—Biography. | Eccentrics and eccentricities—New England—Biography. | Eccentrics and eccentricities—New England—History.
Classification: LCC F3 (ebook) | LCC F3 .G45 2018 (print) | DDC 974—dc23 LC record available at https://lccn.loc.gov/2017051050

♾™ The paper used in this publication meets the minimum requirements of American National Standard for Information Sciences—Permanence of Paper for Printed Library Materials, ANSI/NISO Z39.48-1992.

Printed in the United States of America

For all those with the courage to keep things weird

CONTENTS

INTRODUCTION
Let Us Now Praise Eccentric Folk ix

1. THE LORD
Timothy Dexter (MA and NH) 1

2. THE SECRET KEEPER AND THE SEER
Joseph Moody (ME) and Horace Johnson (CT) 15

3. THE UNRULY WOMEN
Mary Webster (MA) and Hetty Green (VT and MA) 27

4. THE HERMITS
John Smith (MA) and English Jack (NH) 41

5. THE HEALERS
Elisha Perkins (CT), Sylvester Graham (MA),
Robert Wesselhoeft (VT), and F. C. Fowler (CT) 55

6. THE SETTLER
William Blaxton (RI) 71

7. THE POETS
Sarah Helen Whitman (RI) and Frederick Goddard Tuckerman (MA) 83

8. THE MESMERISTS
John Bovee Dods (ME and MA) and Phineas Parkhurst Quimby (ME) 97

9. THE FORTUNE-TELLERS
Moll Pitcher (MA) and Mary Scannell Pepper Vanderbilt (ME) 111

10. THE PROPHET
William Sheldon (MA) 121

11. THE REFORMERS
The Smith Sisters (CT) 133

12. THE VAGABONDS
The Old Darned Man (CT) and the Leather Man (CT) 147

13. THE BANDIT
John Wilson (VT) 161

14. THE WEALTH SEEKERS
Edward Norton (NH and VT), Samuel Bemis (NH),
and Phineas Gardner Wright (CT)   173

15. THE BENEFACTORS
George Beckwith (CT), Joseph Battell (VT),
and Isabella Stewart Gardner (MA)   185

16. THE CASTLE BUILDERS
William Gillette (CT) and Antoinette Sherri (NH)   199

17. THE GREAT AMERICAN TRAVELER
Daniel Pratt (MA)   213

18. THE VISIONARIES OF THE ORDINARY
Joseph Palmer (MA), William Henry Harrison Rose (RI),
Elizabeth Tashjian (CT), and William Johnson (ME)   227

19. THE LEGENDARY ECCENTRICS
Charles Dunbar (MA and ME), Tombolin (MA), and Tom Cook (MA)   241

ACKNOWLEDGMENTS   255

BIBLIOGRAPHY   257

INDEX   271

ABOUT THE AUTHOR   281

INTRODUCTION

LET US NOW PRAISE
ECCENTRIC FOLK

"In its insistence on the sacred right of the individual to be a character, New England may have bred eccentrics rather than heroes." So wrote the distinguished folklorist of the previous century, Benjamin A. Botkin, in his popular collection of the region's folklore. The wisdom of Botkin's observation is undeniable, but his examples of eccentrics were few, for the pages of his treasury demanded attention to countless folk narratives of equally important measure. I offer this present collection in the hopes of extending his insights and of reminding New Englanders of our long and honorable tradition.

There is perhaps nothing more eccentric than attempts to define eccentricity, but that has not stopped good people from trying. The psychologist David Weeks has written eloquently on the matter, ruminating on the gift of eccentrics and compiling a list of characteristic traits that apply to virtually all of them. The anthropologist George Marcus offered a similar case, arguing that wealth and eccentricity had a unique relationship. And the historian Rémi Brague has gone so far to suggest that entire cultures could be eccentric.

I applaud these attempts to give shape to the elusive idea of eccentricity. My contribution here, however, takes a slightly different approach, one informed by the study of folklore. Rather than attempting to settle the question of whether an individual is or is not an eccentric—and whether eccentricity is or is not an inherent quality—in this book I highlight people who were called eccentrics by storytellers in their day or sometime thereafter. From my perspective, eccentrics are made, not born, and they are made by the tales people tell about them.

This is not the first book to focus exclusively on eccentrics and social misfits—not even of those who populate New England. Many of the predecessors, however, winked as they retold their stories, sometimes gently and sometimes smugly mocking the subject. I hope to avoid that tendency in the pages that follow. I have aimed for a collection that would be neither chatty nor erudite, neither gossip nor research. I hope to be respectful of the eccentrics and to understand them on their own terms.

Occasionally that is not an easy task. Many of the eccentrics in this book held beliefs or lived lives that challenge my own sensibilities, but that ultimately is why they are important. And as Samuel Lorenzo Knapp, a biographer of the eccentric Daniel Pratt, once quipped, "No one can be said to have a thorough knowledge of human nature, who has only examined a few of the good and wise." (I will remain quiet on the question of who among us could ever fit the conditions of the good and the wise.)

My attempt to appreciate eccentrics and eccentricity influenced who I included in this book. I tried to steer clear of any correlation between religion and eccentricity, a decision that distinguishes this book from several previous publications. This also proved more difficult than it would seem, as New England has for centuries been a hotbed for experiments in religious ideas that has produced fascinating characters. This means that preachers such as William Miller, Lorenzo Dow, Jemima Wilkinson, Jones Very, William Scales, and John Humphrey Noyes do not appear except in an occasional mention. I could not ignore religion entirely, however—many eccentrics held robust religious ideas, and the chapter on fortune-tellers directly engages Spiritualism—but I hope that these essays show deference to the many ways in which people address the ultimate questions of the cosmos.

I also sought to avoid cases in which eccentricity was a euphemism for mental illness. Amy Archer-Gilligan, for example, the serial killer whose story inspired *Arsenic and Old Lace*, qualifies as an eccentric for many, but the violence her eccentricity manifested and the inner turmoil that produced it was not something I thought should be exploited. Finally, I elected not to include living eccentrics, as the term still may be used to disparage people and harm their livelihood. As a result, I have held back telling stories of remarkable individuals or of recent historical groups (such as "The Republic of Nayaug" in Connecticut or the Renaissance Community of Massachusetts) whose nonconformity enriches contemporary society.

Readers will note a pattern. Many of the eccentrics in this book are white men, several from the nineteenth century. There are reasons for this, and it is not because they have a claim to New England or to the Yankee character more than others. Regrettably, the stories of women and nonwhites were too often buried or treated as something other than eccentricity—hysteria, rabble-rousing, or outright threats to social order—and painted with a meaner veneer. And although as a term, *eccentric* has been around for centuries in the language of astronomy, it was not until the 1800s that it became popular as a noun to describe unusual people. I will happily correct these gaps in the future if readers encourage me to do so.

Indeed, the most difficult and most humbling aspect of writing this book was leaving out people whose stories deserve attention. There is Joseph Holden, who believed that the earth was flat. And Guy Kidder and Maggie Little, true free spirits. And Sal Verdirome, the inspired builder of the Sanctuary of Love. And William Coperthwaite, the yurt maker. And Louise Shattuck, the artist and dog lover extraordinaire. And "Wild Bill" Ziegler of Middletown, Connecticut, and Eva Van Cortland Hawkes of Bar Harbor, Maine. And the list goes on without end.

I welcome you to contact me. If you have tales or corrections to add to these chapters or suggestions for other eccentrics whose stories must be told, please reach out to my e-mail at solbrys@comm.umass.edu or ctfolklorist @ctrivermuseum.org.

And above all, stay weird, folks!

1

THE LORD:
TIMOTHY DEXTER

In August 1794 the Philadelphia-based *Gazette of the United States* published a most unusual item, a reprint of an advertisement appearing days before in Newburyport, Massachusetts:

> To mankind at large—to in Corege the finding out A white Devel, or black one or coper one or bleu Devel in this hellish world, Twenty Dolors Rewarde that broke said Dexter's windows—If this is Equality, Damn Equality, good by, N. Port for me to pay one Dolor A Day to support my parron and Cant Ride without so much grinning fare you well

This missive was signed "Timothy Dexter." The editors, unsure of its meaning, ventured to guess the writer was upset that people laughed at him and his new carriage. And so it would be for Timothy Dexter throughout his life, a man so often laughed at by the public for his eccentricities.

Dexter was born in Malden, Massachusetts in 1747. Several full-length books chronicle his life—and deservedly so. He was one of the most interesting misfits in New England history, perhaps in the United States, and known for questionable fame even in his own day. In 1801, for example, a political primer presented a list of honorable people. Thomas Jefferson was "the first man," and the New England Revolutionary War hero Ethan Allen was "the strongest man." Timothy Dexter? He was, simply, "the strangest man." When he died, a newspaper in Greenfield, Massachusetts, summarized the opinion of many contemporaries and announced that his "ignorance was almost without a parallel in the United States of America." A more charitable account in a Newburyport paper exclaimed him "perhaps one of the most eccentric men of his time," whose "singularities and peculiar notions" had become proverbial.

The previous biographers of Dexter are, thankfully, generally united concerning the particulars of his life. They differ regarding dates and motives and reactions, and as time passed on after his death, legendary material replaced or accompanied genuinely substantiated claims. Dexter himself had a hand to play in confusing matters as an unabashed self-promoter and rumormonger. It is a point of agreement, however, that he was not born wealthy and that his early education was not extensive. Coupled with his convoluted writings, these humble origins gave rise to the belief that he was, in the words of one biographer, a "feeble intellect who gained wealth by luck." As a teenager he apprenticed in Charlestown, Massachusetts, then a center for the leather industry, and made his way to Newburyport via Boston around 1769.

Early biographies of Dexter contend that he was thrifty in his career and had amassed a respectable income by the time he married Elizabeth Lord Frothingham, a widow, whose first husband provided well for her. Dexter opened a shop in Newburyport and purchased some properties. He and his wife were the parents of a son, Samuel Lord, and a daughter, Nancy. It appears that Dexter did not fight in the American Revolution, but events leading to the creation of the United States were integral to his success, as he speculated on Continental currency when it depreciated to a remarkably low price. After the American Revolution, a debate ensued concerning the national debt, which included the fate of the "continentals," those debts owed to people like Dexter. Default was an option, but Alexander Hamilton proposed they be paid with interest in order to bolster the new country's creditworthiness. When Hamilton won the argument, Dexter became an incredibly wealthy man—and seemingly overnight.

So endowed, Dexter continued to speculate throughout the 1790s and invested in overseas trade. He had two merchant ships, the *Mehitable* and the *Congress*, built for this purpose, and in 1792 he became the largest stockholder for a bridge over the Merrimack River and Deer Island. On the Fourth of July, 1793, Dexter presented a speech at the Deer Island toll house celebrating the nation. Perhaps as a preview of the eccentricities to come, he elected to deliver it in French, despite—in his own words—the "small chance I have had to learn French." He compensated for his lack of knowing the language, apparently, by mimicking the gestures of Frenchmen. Still later he published a translation of his toast, which to its credit did wish "good nature, breeding, concord, benevolence, piety, understanding, wit, humor, Punch and wine" upon those assembled.

Dexter also purchased a magisterial house on State Street following his immediate wealth in 1791. Today it is the Newburyport Public Library. In this act, biographers spy a sincere attempt to enter into high society. The town, however, was reluctant to embrace him and rejected his numerous offers to pay for the construction of public and civic buildings (reportedly with the condition they bear his name). In the early 1790s daughter Nancy married and gave him a grandson, who died in his first year. Soon thereafter she abandoned her marriage, leaving Dexter's granddaughter with her ex-husband, and returned to her father's estate. Samuel became involved in his father's business, but by many accounts became an irresponsible product of sudden wealth, given to gambling and its accompanying problems. And Dexter himself demonstrated an appreciation for alcohol that may have further kept him from the company he sought.

According to Samuel Knapp, his first biographer, Dexter was in Boston when the citizens learned of the execution of King Louis XVI during the French Revolution. He sped back to Newburyport and bribed the sextons of the local church to toll the bells at an unusual hour, which summoned the town residents and allowed Dexter the opportunity to reveal the news. A group of boys began to debate the character of the French king and whether his death was just. The crowd that favored the monarch decided to thank Dexter for speaking well of him—Dexter was fond of the French royal family and reportedly encouraged them to flee to his own home, even purchasing provisions for their arrival—and gathered in front of his house. He invited them to drink. They declined, but not before their cheers of "long live Dexter" filled the street. That day, Knapp writes, was the happiest of Dexter's life. And although the veracity of this tale is questionable, it underscores Dexter's wish for acceptance and the public's exploitation of that desire.

In 1796, wealthy but unsuccessful in his attempt to be recognized as a member of the elite, Dexter moved his family to Chester, New Hampshire. Chester, although rural, was home to many prominent political families and their mansions; the home that Dexter purchased, for example, was an intimidating hip-roofed Georgian. And here, as in Newburyport, he attempted to impress the citizens, again to little avail. Local tradition records a similar pattern of generosity with strings attached. Dexter offered, for example, to pave one of the main roads as long as the town named it "Dexter Street." The gift was promptly declined.

The Dexter family returned to Newburyport in 1797. The motive is not entirely clear, but several accounts hint at gathering embarrassments in New Hampshire. Knapp, for example, recounts an event in which Dexter, prone to chase women, took his flirtation too far and "assailed" a girl at Hampton Beach. A young man came to her rescue, seized Dexter, and proceeded to deliver a spanking "as school-masters used to do [to] unlucky urchins who stole apples." Arthur Livermore, the son of the esteemed judge and congressman by the same name, penned a letter in 1897 relating a similar family tradition. Therein, he explained that Dexter "found a great deal of pleasure in the committal of assault and battery, and was quite willing to purchase the enjoyment of it at the moderate cost of the fines or damages awarded by magistrates." He eventually gathered the nerve to try Judge Livermore, who responded, if one reads between the lines, by knocking Dexter senseless with his cane. (The younger Livermore decided the story was too good to imperil by inquiring into its truth.) Dexter himself noted this ill-treatment, but interpreted the matter differently, arguing that Livermore was jealous that the people had declared him Lord Dexter, king of Chester.

The appellation "Lord Dexter" stuck, whether granted by the people of Chester or not—and if it were, whether in jest or sincerity. Or to be more precise, the title remained, as Dexter adopted it for the remainder of his life. Back in Newburyport, he purchased another grand home and nourished his eccentricities. He added minarets to the roof and a golden eagle to the cupola, imported furniture from France, built a clock collection, and constructed a library stocked with an enormous number of books. He then transformed the garden into a "museum" with statues of important men in history (forty in total) perched high on arches throughout the grounds. The chosen ones included Biblical figures, saints, politicians, and businessmen. And on a statue of himself located near the front fence for passersby to see, Dexter inscribed the honorific, "I am the first in the East" or "I am the greatest man in the East" (biographers disagree on the exact wording, but concur on the sentiment). Later Dexter described himself as "First in the East, First in the West and the Greatest Philosopher of all the Known World."

One arch, called the Royal Arch and prominently positioned at the entrance of his home, held a statue of George Washington at the center, with John Adams to his right and Thomas Jefferson to his left. Adams, apparently, was sculpted without a hat, as Dexter deemed no man should hold the dignified position at Washington's right hand without showing proper respect to the Father of the Country. But the story concerning Jefferson is a classic statement of Dexter's eccentricity. Retold by Knapp, it becomes almost a comic scene. Dexter had employed a favorite painter to adorn the partially unrolled scroll in Jefferson's hand with the words of his most famous document. The artist "measured out his letters, 'The Declaration of Independence,' and while penciling it, Dexter, from the ground, could not distinctly see the letters, but as soon as the painter had reached DEC, Dexter called out to him, "That is not the way to spell Constitution."

"You want," returned the painter, "The Declaration of Independence."

"I want the Constitution, and the Constitution I will have."

As Knapp continues, a quarrel broke out among the two men as to the legitimacy of this request, until Dexter settled the matter by firing a shot from his pistol. And so, for as long as the statue stood, Thomas Jefferson held the proud honor of being the author of the Constitution.

This incident raises a point that few previous biographers have examined directly: Dexter's inclinations toward violence. Most have depicted him as a wily figure, whose good luck in business compensated for his lack of intelligence and whose success was a foil to the elites who ignored him. His aggression has often been framed as a sign of roguishness, or uncouth origins, or intoxication, and frequently made a humorous element of his eccentricities. There is another rumored occasion, for example, in which Dexter fired a pistol at an onlooker to his museum that he ordered away, and was forced to spend some time imprisoned for this act. Those who have mentioned this legendary example have tended to focus on how he rode to jail in an elaborate coach rather than lament the hostile temper brooding under the surface of his skin.

There is no better example of this hostility than the story of his mock funeral. In the garden of his home, Dexter constructed a tomb—another elaborate work he called the Temple of Reason—and then designed an equally impressive coffin, painted (as he himself boasted) white and green, "with brass trimmings, eight handles, and a good lock." It was stocked with tobacco, pipes, a trumpet, and reading material. And to give his impressive resting place a test of sorts, he staged a mock funeral, complete with a procession and eulogy. Citizens of Newburyport attended in throngs. Dexter was reportedly pleased by this affair except for two things: The town did not toll the bells in his honor and his wife did not shed tears. Indeed most versions of this story conclude with the guests discovering his ruse when they heard cries from the kitchen and discovered Dexter beating his wife for her poor showing of grief.

It is important to recognize that Dexter's life story is a study in hearsay and that the degree of truth in any of these episodes is questionable. We can no more readily prove or disprove them, and I would urge caution in assuming that even well-known stories asserted as biographical fact are factual without historical corroboration. But folklore, even when it is not historically accurate, often gets to the heart of the matter about someone's reputation. Dexter may not have been a man prone to menacing outbursts, but people told stories that he was, so it is important to ask why and what impressions they correspond with.

Dexter, for example, was not satisfied that his grandeur had been proven by ostentatious displays of wealth, so he wrote a book that would leave no doubt. He had previously published letters in newspapers that willingly (in the words of one of them) "amused the public with the comical ebullitions of Lord Dexter's genius." This text, *A Pickle for the Knowing Ones, or Plain Truths in Homespun Dress*, is a holy writ of eccentricity. The first edition appeared in 1802. To call it rambling is to do a disservice to the word *rambling*. It is written in the tortured style of the letter that opens this chapter, or as a contemporary described it, it is "a jumble of letters promiscuously gathered together." Dexter creates his own orthography, uses no punctuation, spells words as he sees fit, capitalizes letters as if by random, and shifts concepts mid-sentence. It has, thankfully, been "translated" by an aficionado.

A Pickle begins with the declaration of his lordship. "IME the first Lord in the younited States of A mericary," he commences, "Now of Newburyport it is the voise of the peopel and I cant Help it and so Let it goue." Dexter places himself in a train of dignitaries who follow George Washington, promises wonders at his museum, commands "pease and the gratest brotherly love," and explains how the United States, Great Britain, and France will lead the world. And all this is contained within the first paragraph. In the second, there is an echo of a concern that haunted Dexter his entire adult life. In his own words: "Unto you all mankind Com to my hous to mock and sneare whi ye."

That is, he wants to know why so many people come to his house to mock and sneer at him. In response, Dexter explains his intentions in a passage that is among his most quoted lines. "I wans to make my Enemys grin in time," he confesses, "Lik A Cat over A hot pudding and goue Away and hang there heads Doun Like a Dogg bin After sheep gilty."

Dexter then details the grounds of his mansion, including the Royal Arch, the Temple of Reason, and his tomb. He abruptly turns to local affairs in Newburyport, and complains about the number of church meetings that occur. Indeed, much of *A Pickle* is laced with commentary critical of formal religious worship and admonitions against those who are "so preast Riden"—that is, priest-ridden. He takes umbrage with clergymen who seem to work one day of the week and even then do something that does not appear to be work. He considers this "a cheat" of sorts, and wonders why he has never seen an immortal soul that clergy receive money to save. He then expresses incredulity at the beliefs people hold concerning the afterlife. (Dexter himself, according to reports that circulated after his death, was inclined to believe in the transmigration of souls and thought he would return as a devil's needle, a dragonfly.)

His critique is not reserved for the clergy alone. Dexter is resolute that college learning is a potential scam, especially considering the amount of money required to send children to esteemed places of education. When one reckons the cost, Dexter asserts, "see houe many houndred thousand millions of Dolors it would com" only for the purpose "to make Rougs and thieves to plunder the Labering man that sweats to get his bread." Good common learning, he recommends, is the best education. Certainly, Dexter has his own life history in mind when he makes this pronouncement, but he also contemplates how it can be that humans are at once the best animal and the worst—and really like the Devil—and the role education plays in promoting the wicked.

Honesty is a major theme throughout *A Pickle*. Dexter bluntly states that he is "a frind to all onnest men," and wishes fire and brimstone upon liars in this world. His examples of truly dishonest men include, by name, his assailant Arthur Livermore. And as he closes his ruminations, he praises the Deer Island bridge, offers his opinion on the growing population of Newburyport and the local turnpikes, complains about the lack of a good watch in the town, describes the earth as a large living creature upon which we humans are but mere fleas (even as we are masters of the beasts of dry land), and reminds his readers to be cognizant of humanity's tendency to be bad.

A Pickle saw several editions. In the second, Dexter added an Addendum in response to the complaints by fellow Knowing Ones that he did not use punctuation. In a show of generosity and solidarity, he decided to include it—but all at once, allowing his readers to "peper and solt it as they plese." And hence:

,,,,,,,,,,,,,,,,,, ,,,,,,,,,,,,,,,,,,, ,,,,,,,,,,,,,,,,,, ,,,,,,,,,,,,,,,,,,,, ,,,,,,,,,,,,,,,,,,

,,,,,,,,,,,,,,,,,, ,,,,,,,,,,,,,,,,,,, ,,,,,,,,,,,,,,,,,, ,,,,,,,,,,,,,,,,,,,, ,,,,,,,,,,,,,,,,,,

. . . .

,,,,,,,,,,,,,,,,,, ,,,,,,,,,,,,,,,,,,, ,,,,,,,,,,,,,,,,,, ,,,,,,,,,,,,,,,,,,,, ,,,,,,,,,,,,,,,,,,

. . . .

. . . .

. . . .! ! ! ! ! ! ! ! ! ! ! ! ! ! ! ! !. . . . .

. . . . ! ! ! ! ! ! ! ! ! ! ! . . . .

. . . . ! ! ! ! ! . . . .

. . . .! . . . .

. . . .

, ,

. . . .????????????????????????????. . . . .

Later editions included letters, ruminations, and speeches inserted by editors. They are random in their revelations, even more so than the original, but include such gems as his criticism of his ex-son-in-law; his explanation of why he never joined the Freemasons (a ghost forbade him because he possessed too much knowledge); his willingness to stand for Emperor, especially after the fall of the Pope; his brief and unexplained claim to be Quaker, perhaps a roundabout way to express an opinion against bloodshed; his pursuit of a good housekeeper and maid—among the many qualifications necessary, she must know when to speak and when to be silent; his belief that schools should teach proper manners and foreign languages to assist with global trade; his boasts about women and thoughts about what fashion they should wear; his opinions on national debt; his query whether angels have wings; and his confirmation of some personal history as well as his dealings with gout. Other observers have focused on Dexter's claim that on the day he was born a great storm arose and Mars and Jupiter (it is not entirely clear if he means the planets or the deities) signaled that he would become a great man, but another passage hints again at more personal motives: "thay all Caled me a foull forty years;" Dexter writes, "Now I will Call all foulls but onnes men."

In an early and telling passage in *A Pickle*, Dexter explains, "I found I was very luckky in spekkelation." He summarizes how he made money in a single paragraph, invoking whale bones, warming-pans, and Bibles. These examples would lay the foundation for folklore about him that lasted well beyond his death. As later storytellers fancied, Dexter was continually lucky despite his lack of intelligence. In the case of the whale bones, he decided to amass all the remains of these creatures just before they became necessary for women's fashion, whereupon he made a sizeable profit. In the case of the warming-pans, he was tricked into sending a vast quantity of these tools (used to warm beds in cold climates like New England) to the West Indies, but made a fortune when people repurposed them for molasses production. And in the case of the Bibles, he sent them out for sale at the very moment missionaries needed them for conversion efforts. Later stories depicted him sending mittens to Africa just as it opened trade with Baltic nations, shipping cats to the West Indies in time for a rat infestation, and literally selling coal to Newcastle.

Closer inspection of *A Pickle*, however, demonstrates that Dexter revels in his shrewdness rather than in his luck. The incidents he mentions may simply be inventions of his imagination—again, he was not above creating a lore he thought profitable to himself—but his boasts reinforce that he understood the benefits of cornering a market and monopolizing commodities that others did not initially see as valuable. He also brags about employing cunning men as runners and encouraging them to "act the fool" in order to accumulate wealth when others were not looking—or were openly laughing at him for his odd investments. (Knapp also mentions that Dexter utilized this same business technique to corner the market on opium in the region for some time, an idea that dropped out of later anecdotes.) The desire to have the last laugh seems to have illuminated every important decision he made.

This perspicacity, however, was not strictly rational. Dexter consulted, apparently with some frequency, astrologers and fortune-tellers, including Moll Pitcher (whose story is told in another chapter of this book). He kept a retainer of eccentric people in his train. One of these, Jonathan Plummer, was a fish seller by trade but also an amateur poet who became Dexter's laureate. The first stanza of his best known poem is often excerpted, but the entire piece is noteworthy for its lauding of his patron:

> Lord Dexter is a man of fame;
> Most celebrated is his name;
> More precious far than gold that's pure,
> Lord Dexter shine forevermore.
> His noble house, it shines more bright
> Than Lebanon's most pleasant height;
> Never was one who stepped therein
> Who wanted to come out again.
> His house is fill'd with sweet perfumes,
> Rich furniture doth fill his rooms;
> Inside and out it is adorn'd,
> And on the top an eagle's form'd.
> His house is white and trim'd with green,
> For many miles it may be seen;
> It shines as bright as any star,
> The fame of it has spread afar.
> Lord Dexter, thou, whose name alone

Shines brighter than king George's throne;
Thy name shall stand in books of fame,
And Princes shall his name proclaim.
Lord Dexter hath a coach beside,
In pomp and splendor he doth ride;
The horses champ the silver bitt,
And throw the foam around their feet.
The images around him stand,
For they were made by his command,
Looking to see Lord Dexter come,
With fixed eyes they see him home.
Four lions stand to guard the door,
With mouths wide open to devour
All enemies who dare oppose
Lord Dexter or his shady groves.
Lord Dexter, like king Solomon,
Hath gold and silver by the ton,
And bells to churches he hath given,
To worship the great king of heaven.
His mighty deeds they are so great,
He's honor'd both in church and state,
And when he comes all must give way,
To let Lord Dexter bear the sway.
When Dexter dies all things shall droop,
Lord East, Lord West, Lord North shall stoop,
And then Lord South with pomp shall come,
And bear his body to the tomb.
His tomb most charming to behold,
A thousand sweets it doth unfold;
When Dexter dies shall willows weep,
And mourning friends shall fill the street.

May Washington forever stand;

May Jefferson by God's command,

Support the rights of all mankind,

John Adams not a whit behind.

America, with all your host,

Lord Dexter in a bumper toast;

May he enjoy his life in peace,

And when he's dead his name not cease.

In heaven may he always reign,

For there's no sorrow, sin, nor pain;

Unto the world I leave the rest,

For to pronounce Lord Dexter blest.

All things came to droop in October 1806, when Dexter passed away—although, perhaps fittingly for someone who longed for celebrity as he did, reports of his death were greatly exaggerated in April that same year. Announcements and obituaries appeared in newspapers throughout New England and as far away as Ontario, Philadelphia, and Trenton. In his will, he left some monies to both Malden and Newburyport, the latter for the benefit of the poor.

Newburyport did not permit burial in the tomb beneath the Temple of Reason, so his body was placed in the local cemetery under a sedate tombstone. Countless memories of his eccentricities, however, lived on. Several editions of *A Pickle* followed, as did biographies and reminiscences, and in 1874 Henry Ames Blood penned a comedy entitled "Lord Timothy Dexter, or, The Greatest Man in the East." By the 1880s, rumor credited him for the invention of—or the inducement in his will for the production of—a short clay pipe, which was stamped "TD." (This is pure folklore; the first pipes of this kind were British imports before the Revolution, although the name of the original maker remains subject to debate.)

In 1891, Oliver Wendell Holmes Sr. saw fit to mention Dexter in his commentary *Over the Teacups*, favorably comparing him as a more adventurous writer than better-known literary successes. Holmes also summarized the predicament of his eccentricity admirably. "If the true American spirit," he writes, "shows itself most clearly in boundless self-assertion, Timothy Dexter is the great original American egotist." In a celebrity and popularity-obsessed culture such as ours, where vanity and braggadocio stand in place of wisdom, we would do well to wonder if we are not living in a world that Dexter made.

2

~

THE SECRET KEEPER AND THE SEER: JOSEPH MOODY AND HORACE JOHNSON

The relatively short life of Joseph Moody—spanning 1700 to 1753—was eventful in a deeply mysterious way. His eccentricities were noteworthy enough to inspire a storytelling tradition that still thrives, especially in collections dedicated to the so-called haunted elements of New England. And his tale seems as set in stone as his gravesite in York, Maine. Moody was born to Samuel Moody, a prominent and fervent Puritan preacher in the garrison town of York. After graduation from Harvard, the younger Moody returned for a career in civic affairs, serving nobly as a lawyer, then as Registrar of Deeds and Town Clerk, and then as a judge. At his father's behest and against his own wishes, Moody abandoned this life for one of the pulpit, accepting the charge of the Second Parish of York. He was studious, admired, and successful in this position until tragedy struck in the death of his wife.

Melancholy seized Moody, and with it the ghosts of his past—and an unpardonable sin. Driven by gloom, in 1738 he adorned himself with a black handkerchief, tied around his forehead and suspended over his entire face. He never explained the meaning of the veil to his parishioners. At first they accepted his unusual garb and changing demeanor with sympathy, but in time they grew tired of their endlessly morose pastor. They began avoiding him in public, and Moody, in return, drew further into a reclusive state, taking walks under cover of darkness or on the lonely beach. When he appeared among them to eat, he turned his back to face the wall and he preached in the same manner. Eventually the townsfolk asked him to leave his ministry and he retreated into the relative solitude of a colleague's home.

Moody recovered from his malaise well enough to serve in his father's stead in 1745, when the elder Moody participated in the Siege of Louisbourg. But the handkerchief remained. Indeed, it never left his face, a constant reminder of a secret he would not share—that is, not until his dying day. As he lay in his deathbed, Moody explained to an attending minister the reason for covering his face in guilt and in shame: He had, on a hunting trip years before, accidentally shot and killed a close friend. The death was blamed on a hostile Indian and Moody never confessed to the sin. In doing so with his final breath, he released his burden and found a solace that escaped him in life. When the townspeople finally lifted the handkerchief, he was smiling with the serenity of salvation.

It's a fine story, but hardly a lick of it is true. And although this has become the most popular version told today, it was not the definitive tale told in the nineteenth or twentieth centuries. In the 1920s, for example, newspapers often ran with the line that Moody was injured as a soldier and donned the handkerchief to conceal disfigurement. In the 1940s, *Ripley's Believe It or Not* introduced the idea that he wore the veil after his cousin Mary Hirst rejected him in love. By the early 1970s, speculation arose that his eyes were damaged by long hours of study for his sermons and left him unable to experience direct sunlight without pain. And all of these explanations stood under the shadow of Nathaniel Hawthorne's story, "The Minister's Black Veil," first published in 1832 and which adapted certain facts and rumors about Moody that had likely been in the oral tradition for a century.

The real Joseph Moody was a secret keeper, however, in that he penned a diary in coded Latin. A few lines were published in the 1800s, but it was not until 1981 that Philip McIntire Woodwell undertook a complete translation of four years of the journal (from 1720 to 1724) and made an invaluable contribution for understanding this complicated man, whose story is no less compelling than the fictions composed about him. And as with other examples throughout this book, Moody's transformation from an actual person with a few unusual habits into a folkloric figure of preternatural behavior demonstrates how eccentricity is not an inherent quality but one always partially imposed from the outside, from the society that demarcates and gazes upon the eccentric.

Moody was, indeed, the son of a minister known and respected for his faithfulness to Puritanism and his lengthy sermons. Samuel Moody—also known as "Father Moody"—was instrumental in the development of York at a time when hostilities between colonialists and the indigenous people resulted in frequent war and atrocity. Among his contributions to the town, he founded a grammar school that would employ his son early in his career. Father Moody was recognized as an eccentric man himself and his reputation for both passionate and unusual behavior grew over the centuries. For a brief period he was as familiar a figure in storytelling as his son, and some anecdotes about the father became attached to Joseph Moody. Many of these tales depict Father Moody as a longwinded preacher, with a stormy temper, who did not suffer fools or sinners.

Father Moody and his first wife, Hannah Sewall, gave birth to two children, Joseph and Mary. Through their daughter, they became the great-great-grandparents of the philosopher Ralph Waldo Emerson. But it is their son Joseph who entered into the folklore of New England as a congenital eccentric—and the same was said of "Master Moody," Joseph's son Samuel, who became what a Boston newspaper in 1865 described as "an eccentric but admirable teacher" at the Dummer School (now The Governor's Academy) in Byfield, Massachusetts. (Among the quirks belonging to the third Moody was his encouragement of learning by reading aloud, which produced a cacophony of education.) Given this nineteenth-century predilection for ascribing eccentricity to the males in the family, it is not surprising that Father Moody's habits would have a role to play in narratives about "Handkerchief Moody's" tendency to brood.

Indeed, it is Samuel rather than his son Joseph Moody who appears in two important collections of regional folk narratives, Benjamin Botkin's *A Treasury of New England Folklore* and Richard Dorson's *Jonathan Draws the Long Bow*. He emerges in both in stories—Dorson calls them "Yankee yarns"—concerning the tendency of parishioners to fall asleep during his sermons. In the Botkin collection, Moody awakens a member of his flock by yelling "Fire!" and, when asked by the suddenly invested auditor where the flames were, replying, "In hell, for sleeping sinners." In the 1850s, several newspapers confused a story about Father Moody and Handkerchief Moody, ascribing another anecdote about a lengthy sermon, in which he fooled the congregation into staying by offering to preach first to the sinners and then to the saints, dismissing the former when he was done. No one in the church was, of course, willing to leave and self-identify as a sinner.

The popular explanation in the 1800s that Joseph Moody was a faithful son to an ill-tempered and overbearing father who forced him to abandon his life of public service is not well founded. It seems to originate in a genealogy composed in 1847 by Charles Moody, but this work itself may reflect family stories and a broader narrative tradition. The translations of Moody's journal, furthermore, show unequivocally that he had always intended upon the career of a minister. His work in public service was only supplemental to this desire, which was realized in 1732 with his becoming pastor of the Second Congregational Church, also known as the North Parish or "Scotland," due to the influx of Scottish immigrants.

Moody's hope to become a minister contradicts the old explanation that his depression erupted on account of having to fulfill his father's demands. So, too, should the incident of his accidentally taking a life—an historical event that did mar his youth—be taken as the originating haunting memory only with a grain of salt. The sad event was not a hunting trip. Moody was eight years old at the time and the boyhood companion, Ebenezer Preble, was of similar age; the death occurred when the boys investigated a loaded pistol in the house. There is, however, no reference to this incident in his journals, and, as Woodwell has evidenced, there is no outside support for any claim that his adoption of the veil was penance for something that happened thirty years prior.

The romantic explanation that rejection in love drove him to don the veil is also spurious. It is true that an affection for his cousin, Mary Hirst, awakened in Moody and that he sought permission to call off his engagement with Lucy White. His journal is replete with powerful emotions and a concurrent sense of religious alarm. "I almost hate Miss Hirst," he wrote in an entry in December 1721, and resolved to seek God within the depth of his soul for aid, but in early January 1722 he confessed, "I do not love Lucy with conjugal affection." Soon thereafter he approached his father to discuss the possibility of leaving White for Hirst. "Father did not approve" was the blunt response. Moody accordingly went through with his marriage and Hirst wed William Pepperrell, a friend and relative of the Moody family. Only later did a tale arise that Hirst left Moody for Pepperrell, breaking his heart and leading him to forever hide from the world.

There is a passage in Moody's journal from 1723 that has not received the attention it deserves. "I questioned our Flora," he writes, probably in reference to a family slave, "to some extent about the customs of her nation. She told me that among her people there were certain old men who were able to bring dark matters into the light. They cover their faces with a disc, bound by a leather thong above; they walk about, repeatedly plunging their hands in water, and clapping with their palms. At length, the bond being loosed, they make clear the secret matters." In all likelihood, this is a description of a divination practice and it certainly cannot be taken as the originating idea for Moody to wear a handkerchief. But it is also not merely coincidental, as nothing recorded in Moody's diary occurs by happenstance. The passage may reflect his very early ruminations on the relationship between secrets and a veil and of someone knowingly capable of penetrating the mysteries of both.

Woodwell also observes that there are no accounts from Moody's contemporaries that he ever wore a handkerchief. The earliest reports come from people decades later, who were not present and who heard the story from relatives. This does not mean the tale is wholly untrue, but it should invite the question. The Moody family became the subject of a cycle of folkloric tales, so any claim that stretches the boundaries of the normal needs to be considered skeptically. Indeed, in 1744 the English evangelical clergyman George Whitefield visited Moody. In his journal, Whitefield remarks on Moody's melancholy and dejected spirit, comparing him to Job, but does not mention the veil. It is probable, then, that if he wore the handkerchief it was only for a brief time.

Presuming he did wear the veil and if the typical reasons said for doing so were not accurate, what is the most likely explanation? It is, sadly, quite likely the very melancholy that had been treated as tangential to more fantastical stories. Moody was deeply introverted—his journals are clear on this—and may have suffered from depression throughout his life. These tendencies, coupled with incessant demands from others, physical exhaustion, and the sudden death of his wife in childbirth in 1736 (leaving him with four children ages three to ten), may have led him to collapse inward. His piety and his moral principles only heightened that sense of responsibility and fueled an impending sense of doom and failure that plagued his days.

Moody's journals testify to an inner uneasiness, although how much of it is personal psychology and how much conformance to a Puritan mind-set is difficult to ascertain. Throughout the entries, he expresses alienation from God, a heart gone astray, deep distress, and worries about his miserable or wretched soul. He confesses routinely to "defiling" himself and to the shame associated with it. He also punishes himself for being too frivolous and, other times, for being "insensible" and not feeling enough or in the way he should. Some lines seize the reader with pathos. Moody cries out, for example, "What shall be done concerning my soul?" in one entry, decries his "undeserving, dull, and impious" heart in another, and confesses to the weight of his soul "oppressed by the unspeakable burden of the damned" in yet another. At the close of 1720—when he was only a young man of twenty—he laments spending another year "wholly in sin, surely in the worst manner" and two years later he fears that he has "drank damnation."

If mental health issues were behind Moody's erratic behavior, the storytelling traditions of the 1800s did little to sympathize. Hawthorne's story, which of course is purely fictional (and technically about a clergyman named Hooper), ignores any hint of a wounded psyche in favor of symbolizing and critiquing an underlying Puritanism that would produce inner misery. Hawthorne is at least a deft writer, but Moody was not so lucky in later accounts. Newspapers in the 1860s, for example, had no pangs running stories about "the crazy minister" and his "nervous disease" with little regard for people who suffered in this manner, but that should not compel us to continue the tradition today.

—~—

Although the name Horace Johnson has slipped into obscurity since his death a century ago, at the time of his passing, *The Sun* of New York asserted that no one who claimed to love New England could be ignorant of "Uncle Horace." He was ninety-two when he died and best known then as a weather prognosticator whose forecasts were regular features in newspapers throughout the region, the Northeast, and even the nation. But over his long lifetime, Johnson managed many remarkable careers and found numerous ways to share his erudite knowledge with the world and with it his unique perspective. Extroversion and eccentricity combined in a most interesting way in his mind, and despite the mutual enjoyment he and the media shared in one another, he never received the biographical treatment he deserved.

Born in the village of Middle Haddam (now in the town of East Hampton, Connecticut, and then called Chatham) in 1824, Johnson was the son of a family of shipbuilders. This was one of the most important industries in the area, but Johnson did not pursue his father's calling. Instead, he made his way to Hartford to work in dry-goods stores and as an auctioneer, the latter occupation a sign of his willingness to entertain audiences and be the focus of attention. He holds the unpleasant distinction of being one of the first people in the United States—if not the first, as newspapers later reported—to make a claim on an accident insurance policy after being injured in a collision of railcars in 1864.

Johnson was already a public figure at the time of this incident. Having returned to Middle Haddam around 1855, he continued to amass a fortune in real estate deals that stretched from Hartford to Block Island. In February 1860, he announced his intention to renovate a former church in Hartford and lease it for businesses. The announcement speaks volumes about his personality, as it broke all conventions for advertising and opens as if a letter to an old friend. "I can assure you," Johnson wrote, "it gives me no little pleasure to feel that I am soon to be again in the midst of my old and tried friends, to share with them in their joys, to bear with them their sorrows, and to enjoy with them that mutual interchange of feeling which endears us to each other, lightens our burdens, and makes smooth what otherwise would be the rough and thorny paths of life." All of this, essentially, from someone looking to become a landlord!

By 1863, Johnson's reputation had grown throughout the region as a supplier of sundries to river tourists. He was rewarded for investments in steamboats used to transport goods between Boston and New York during the US Civil War and demonstrated a patriotism that earned the nickname "Big Gun"—that is, he flew a large flag and fired a massive cannon to the exhilaration of visitors. Any appreciation of that contribution, however, should not preclude taking note of an acerbic editorial in the *Hartford Courant* published February 1864. It was in response to one he published in the rival *Hartford Times*. The editorial capped a heated debate that concerned—there is no diplomatic way to express this—Johnson's support for slavery, a belief epitomized by his expressed wish that "the war would continue until every damn abolitionist in the North was killed."

It is a difficult exchange to read, especially Johnson's rhetoric laced with racist terms now considered beyond the pale. Although an egregious example, this case bears witness that many of the eccentrics highlighted in this book thrived at a time when slavery and related oppression was a normalized institution. Rather than ignore this for more likeable and salutary elements in the person's biography, I think it is better to contextualize them and to recognize the limitations of all humans as creatures of a specific historical period and of ethical choices made in the face of the norms of their times. In this manner, eccentrics such as Johnson have as much to teach us in their failures as they do to celebrate in their successes that challenge the conventions and traditions of a staid society.

Johnson remained a fixture in the Hartford newspapers following the war, and increasingly began to appear in and contribute to others in Middletown and in Norwich, Connecticut. In time, virtually every newspaper in the state found space for his antics, a decision followed by the other New England states and New York. In 1870, for example, the *Courant* relished conveying a story in which he was dragged out into the Connecticut River in an attempt to save the detached wheelhouse of a boat and required rescue after a seven-mile drift. Johnson also flirted with a political career, serving as one of the youngest Councilmen of Hartford and joining the short-lived Greenback Party (and serving as temporary chairman of the state convention in 1878), but involvement in his businesses—to which he had then added investments in railroads—kept him from running for office.

Johnson's widespread claim to fame, however, arrived in 1888 when, as a man in his mid-sixties, he turned his attention from speculating in business to speculating about the weather. In February of that year, he sent numerous warnings of an impending blizzard to strike sometime between March 12 and March 15. When the Great Blizzard roared from March 11 to March 14, burying the Northeast from New Jersey to New Brunswick, Canada in as much as sixty inches of snow, Johnson was hailed as a "weather prophet," a moniker that lasted the remainder of his life. In the decades that followed, his predictions included forecasts of storms, floods, droughts, frosts, thaws, seasonal changes, and even earthquakes. Among the many correct "prophecies" he scored, Johnson warned William Howard Taft of a blizzard for his inauguration in 1909 and claimed awareness of the earthquakes that struck the earth in 1906.

Johnson taunted the National Weather Bureau and routinely challenged its leaders (especially Willis Moore, who penned a lengthy editorial in the *Courant* dismissing Johnson as a quack) to predict more accurately than he, betting up to $1,000 on his prowess. This confidence, perhaps not surprisingly, was a welcome burst of excitement for journalists as far away as Washington, DC, and various newspapers, individuals, and communities either rallied behind Johnson or wallowed in his mistaken forecasts. And, to be fair, he had many failures, most notably predictions of tidal waves that never came and, in 1907, the complete and utter destruction of Manhattan by earthquake. He was not the only prognosticator, but his rate of success and his other eccentric habits made him the darling of the New England press, especially as local rivals such as Richard Lamont of Middletown, "R. Rho" of Farmington, "Farmer Beebe" of Salisbury, Wilbur Stillman of Voluntown, or "Dr. Baggs" of Westerly, Rhode Island, went down in flames, or when he proved a better guide than the government and gave citizens a reason to rail against taxes used for weather predictions.

Johnson's technique for revealing the secrets of the weather was novel. It included typical meteorological information and mathematical analysis of patterns, but had an additional reliance on astronomical knowledge. To be clear, Johnson had no interest in astrology; he considered his work scientifically sound. But he was adamant that Earth's atmosphere could be influenced by the movement of Mars, Venus, and other heavenly bodies. Accordingly, he spent evenings gazing upon the night sky. (He also intended to construct a large observatory with a massive telescope, but this never manifested.) The beauty of this approach was that it provided a clever escape for errors, as Johnson could claim that the prediction was correct but that the location on the earth or the timing of the event was off due to problems of scope in employing planetary orbits to determine local weather.

Johnson was a fixture in New England by the 1890s. It is unclear, however, the degree to which his predictions were taken seriously or as a reason to smirk. Many organizations pretended that he could control the weather and would ask him for a favorable prediction for fairs or other public events. At other times, his suggestions were taken as sensible precaution. In 1893, for example, the Boston Globe published a lengthy article on him that included a forecast of a hurricane and tidal wave to strike the city "with a force powerful enough to shake Bunker Hill monument to its very foundation." The wave never came, but before dismissing this as evidence of tongue-in-cheek indulgence, it bears notice that when he offered the predication, seven hurricanes had slammed the United States that season, including a brutal one in New York and the "Sea Islands Hurricane" that crippled the East Coast. Five more occurred that year, and although none tore through Boston, the region was anxious for months.

He was, furthermore, often depicted positively for relying upon natural phenomena that professional meteorologists, professors, and other "learned" people rejected as salient information for weather prediction. In 1890, for example, Johnson made headlines across the region by forecasting a very difficult winter ahead. He had utilized astronomical data, but additionally courted elements of folk wisdom such as the thickening of crab shells and what he took to be the fattening of animals in the region. Throughout his life, he promoted the notion that certain animals served as "natural barometers," and humans were not an exception. Indeed, Johnson claimed that he could feel the weather in his bones, only then to confirm his hunches with scientific data. His status as an eccentric folk hero makes sense, then, at a time of rapidly changing technologies and the rise of experts distanced from a populace that relied upon them.

And for a man who lived vigorously well beyond the expected life span, the elderly Johnson took on qualities of a seer. "Uncle Horace" stories proliferated in the early twentieth century alongside his forecasts. Among the more popular were tales of his unusual collections of antiques and Bibles, his leasing of land for a feldspar mine, his challenge at age eighty-five to anyone eighty or older to a marathon, and his claim that he technically invented anesthesia while working with his friend, the dentist Horace Wells, to whom the honor is conventionally bestowed. A more gruesome tale, reported in the *Hartford Globe*, suggested that a man from Bangor, Maine, plotted to murder Johnson in revenge for one of his predictions of an earthquake, which the conspirator said drove his wife to such a state that she died of fright.

As Johnson aged, his views on war also mellowed, and by the close of his life, he was an ardent advocate against humanity's ready resort to such violence (although he also volunteered to join the army in the First World War should his services be necessary). Johnson penned a poem dedicated to peace and in interviews and letters to editors regularly advised against activities that he regarded as designed to foment conflict. He also critiqued a dominant two-party system in the United States as an instigator of internal division that would compromise national interests and put parties ahead of sensible individuals and ideas. In addition, Johnson continually tinkered with inventions or proposals to reduce flood damage in the Connecticut River Valley and to improve boating safety, but he also landed himself in court over land disputes and an occasional nuisance lawsuit. He was, simply, everything the media and its readers could want in a local character.

In 1916, one year before he died, Johnson was a featured in a lengthy celebration that ran in the *Hartford Courant*, the *Boston Globe*, the *New York Times*, and numerous ancillary papers. When he passed, eulogies poured in, noting that he always "meant well by his fellow man," or that he was "much misunderstood" but forever good-natured, or that he was very serious that the key to being happier was the study of astronomy and meteorology rather than theology. But in many ways, Johnson's life could be summarized by a conciliatory article in the *Courant* from 1908, which praised him for having a mind that "ran along a different channel from others." And although the young and ambitious "Big Gun" Johnson may not have taken his own advice, it seems that by the close of his life, "Uncle Horace" had learned enough that, when asked the secret to living a long and good life, he could reply, simply, "Live decently."

3

THE UNRULY WOMEN: MARY WEBSTER AND HETTY GREEN

"Witches" were the original eccentrics in New England at the unfortunate time when radical deviation from societal expectation could result in capital punishment. The New England colonies imported beliefs from old England about the material existence of the Devil and about those in league with him who could do harm to others. This led, unfortunately, to the accusations of several hundred people throughout the seventeenth century across the entire region, and the subsequent deaths of several dozen in public executions or in jail. The accusations began in earnest as early as 1645 with the first official execution taking place in 1647, when Alse Young was convicted in Hartford. A witchcraft panic struck that city in 1662, an event eclipsed by the infamous Salem Witch Trials thirty years later. And although widespread accusations rapidly came to a close after 1697, a case occurred as late as 1724 in Colchester, Connecticut. Given the condoned violence against them, it is almost callous to number the victims of these accusations among New England eccentrics, but they represent an important moment in history when people thought to be unusual were regarded as misfits whose existence threatened the community.

And while it is true that the preponderance of accused witches were found not guilty or had their guilty sentences overturned, there is another aspect to this troubling history that bears inclusion in this book: The accused were frequently women and often of lower economic status—easy targets as scapegoats for the ills suffered by a community. Many, furthermore, were women depicted by their contemporaries as outspoken, ill-tempered, or otherwise unconventional with regard to societal norms, even as those norms may have been absurdly repressive or deleterious in their rigid expectations of "proper" gender roles. In other words, while imaginary witches threatened New England communities throughout the 1600s, the real women who suffered the afflictions of those accusations formed a sorority who drew attention to the very need for society to change its ways.

Although every person accused of witchcraft in New England, female or male, bears a compelling story deserving attention, there is perhaps no tale more unusual than that of Mary Reeve Webster of Hadley, Massachusetts. She was an original unruly woman. The paucity of information about her life makes it difficult to separate fact from fiction. No personal testimony of hers survives, so her identity is too often subsumed under the impressions she made on others, but the force of her personality does come through even against these odds. Born in Springfield, Massachusetts, in 1670 she married William Webster, a son of one of the founders of Hadley, Massachusetts, where she went to live with her husband. Town records demonstrate that the couple were not wealthy and occasionally required assistance from the community.

It is not clear whether the couple's financial troubles were considered a burden on the town, and records do not exist by local contemporaries clarifying Webster's personality and behavior, but documents that have survived—written by men who did not know her personally—assert that she was prone to be brash and quarrelsome. Sylvester Judd, in his *History of Hadley*, published in 1863, observed that her "temper, which was not the most placid, was not improved by poverty and neglect, and she used harsh words when offended." A tour guide from 1890 maintained this tradition, contending that the poverty she faced "did not sweeten a temper, under which other conditions would perhaps have proved of average amiability." The author of the guide, Charles Forbes Warner, continued in this manner, depicting—without supporting evidence—Webster as a woman who fretted and scolded people frequently and who became unpopular "from the exhibition of certain eccentric traits of character."

It is worth pausing to consider what is happening in these passages, both of which were composed roughly two hundred years after Webster lived. Judd's depiction likely influenced Warner's, and Judd admits that he gathered his information from an active oral tradition. Whether that tradition preserved stories for two centuries is unclear, but it certainly provided ample opportunities to sully her name. In no case should either of these accounts be considered accurate regarding anything but a tendency of people in the nineteenth century to speculate wildly about women in the seventeenth century. And while they may reflect accounts of stories shared about the so-called "Witch of Hadley," they also rob Webster of her own voice. Judd and Warner, put simply, tell us nothing about Webster's personality but much about what the nineteenth century expected from "well-behaved" women.

This is not the first case of folkloric tales of an eccentric person supplanting attempts to understand the motives of the actual person, and it is one of the more frustrating aspects of giving these individuals their due. In the case of Webster herself, Judd and Warner were following—and expanding upon—a tradition that had roots in Webster's time and the accusation made against her. That accusation took place in March 1683, when she was brought before the magistrates in Northampton, Massachusetts, for an initial investigation of "being under strong suspicion of having familiarity with the devil, or using witchcraft." The court records note that "many testimonies" were "brought in against her," but otherwise provide scant detail and do not name the people involved in the accusations. The magistrates decided to send the case to the Court of Assistants in Boston.

Imprisoned there, Webster was formally indicted in May by a court whose attendees included Governor Simon Bradstreet. The language of the indictment is chilling. Webster was accused of "not having the fear of God before her eyes, and being instigated by the devil," so that she "entered into covenant and had familiarity with him in the shape of a warraneage, and had his imps sucking her, and teats or marks found on her, as in and by several testimonies may appear." The warraneage is a reference to a wild animal, perhaps a fisher, and often translated as "black cat." It is a term from an Algonquian language spoken by an indigenous group in Massachusetts. The entire indictment, then, sutures together the things that Puritan men in New England feared the most: the Devil, the indigenous people, and unruly women—especially those whose sexuality did not conform to societal norms.

To be absolutely clear, I am not suggesting that Webster had any interest in the orgiastic along the lines of the indictment. We simply do not know what Webster thought of all this, except for her insistence in her innocence through a plea of not guilty. Again, we have only men speaking for and about her, and in doing so deliberately casting her as a misfit unworthy of society. Thankfully, the court acquitted her of the charges and released her from custody. Unfortunately, this occurred in September 1683 following six months of imprisonment. What toll this ordeal must have taken upon Webster can only be imagined, but it must have been nightmarish.

After her trial, Webster returned home to Hadley. Perhaps she would have lived in peace thereafter, following the pattern of so many of the falsely accused but acquitted in New England. This would not, however, be Webster's fate, and the second phase of her associations with witchcraft was, in a word, hellacious. It began in the winter of 1684 when Philip Smith fell ill. Smith was a well-regarded member of Hadley, having served as a lieutenant, justice of the peace, selectman, deacon, and member of the local court. He is named by Judd as one of the members of the original group in Northampton that heard Webster's accusation. His earthly decline included a descent into delirium, which raised suspicions—or an excuse—for people to think that Webster and the malevolent arts of witchcraft were behind his illness and death.

As with the first accusation, there are no local or contemporary accounts to provide robust details of this incident, but it crept into the writings of Cotton Mather, the fiery Puritan minister, in two books, *Memorable Providences* (an account of witchcraft published in 1690) and *Magnalia Christi Americana* (published in 1702). In these works Mather sought to explain how "pious and holy men" are sometimes made to suffer by "hellish witches." He unrepentantly empathized with Smith at the expense of Webster, whom he did not even dignify by naming but referred only to as a "wretched woman" before asserting that the death was an actual murder. Here lies the originating depiction of Webster as a wicked woman, for Mather asserts that with regard to Smith, she was "dissatisfied at some of his *just cares* about her," and "expressed herself unto him in such a manner, that he declared himself apprehensive of receiving *mischief* at her hands."

Mather describes in gory detail the end of Smith's days as he writhed in physical and mental agony. He identifies a litany of supernatural horrors unfolding at Smith's deathbed, all signs of the diabolical hand at work. During these fits the dying man named Webster directly as his tormentor. These elements were, in Mather's mind, proof of witchcraft. And if the Puritan minister is to be believed, so too was it proof to those in attendance of Smith's death, for in an attempt to relieve his calamity, young men "did three or four times in one night, go and give *disturbance* to the woman that we have spoken of: all the while they were doing of it, the good man was at ease, and slept as a weary man." That is, in order to bring some relief to the dying, people attacked the woman they thought responsible for his ailments and assumed the just nature of their action in that Smith was able to rest while Webster was subject to such violence.

Without substantiating evidence, it will remain uncertain whether Mather relayed information supplied to him by someone present in Hadley or simply invented a story about what occurred in order to bolster his own convictions about the threat of the satanic in New England. Mather does not explain the specific gruesome vengeance brought upon Webster, but Thomas Hutchinson, the Massachusetts governor, offered clarification in his *History of the Colony and Province of Massachusetts-Bay*. He asserted that young men seized Webster and hung her "until she was near dead," only then to cut her down, roll her and bury her in snow, and abandon her to the elements. But here again there is an anachronistic problem: Hutchinson published this volume in 1767 and provided no source for the tale. Although it spawned countless artistic interpretations of Webster's ordeal, the veracity of this account is in no way infallible.

Public records do indicate, however, that Webster lived until 1696 and that her husband likely passed around 1688. There are no records indicating children and she left only a modest number of items, but a Bible and other religious items were among them. By the nineteenth century, stories concerning Webster's diabolical actions were part of local lore. Judd recorded several of them. In one, cattle or horses refused to pass by her house until their drivers threatened to whip her. In another, she overturned a load of hay, but flipped it back to avoid punishment. In a third, her presence in a home caused an infant to levitate from its cradle. And in a fourth, a hen descended down a neighbor's chimney into a boiling pot, at which point Webster experienced a mysterious scalding on her body.

All of these tales belong to a greater body of folklore concerning witches in New England and were told about others presumed to be in league with the devil, so this list is a localized version attached to the Webster story. Samuel Gardner Drake, in *Annals of Witchcraft in New England*, adopted all of these narratives and inexplicably added a tale that Webster was thought to ride in the air, sometimes upon a broomstick. Regional newspapers further spread her tale throughout the late 1800s. By the twentieth century, these stories evolved to suggest that she survived the hanging by force of will, sometimes suffering through an entire night. Margaret Atwood's 1995 poem, "Half-Hanged Mary," for example, continues her legend, reinterpreting it as a testimony to fortitude and appealing to those who have suffered for their resistance to convention. It imagines Webster's inner dialogue hour by hour as she struggles to survive, and it concludes with one of the most striking testimonies to the conviction of an unjustly mistreated woman:

Before, I was not a witch.
But now I am one.

Hetty Green has long fascinated commentators on eccentricity. In Carl Sifakis's *Great American Eccentrics*, for example, she has the distinction of her own lengthy entry and of inspiring two others, those of her children, Ned and Sylvia. Regrettably, Sifakis adheres to an image of Green that he inherited from earlier biographers, namely the so-called "Witch of Wall Street," whose lust for money led to a life somewhere between callousness and villainy. Readers of this book may judiciously wonder why she is not in the chapter on the wealth seekers, for indeed much of Green's life was dedicated to amassing—and rarely spending—a fortune that, at her death in 1916, was reported to be between $100 to $200 million, which in today's amount would be in the billions. Green was, however, much more than the caricature of greed that has been passed down for a century, and recent rehabilitations of her life—most notably Charles Slack's *Hetty*—have gone far to flesh out this complex and unruly woman.

Portrait of Hetty Howland Robinson Green, c. 1897
LIBRARY OF CONGRESS

It is important to recognize, for example, that Green accomplished her wealth at a time when women were regarded as having an inferior mind with respect to finance and effectively prohibited from the arena of business. And, for that matter, she held tremendous political and economic influence—the City of New York often borrowed money from her—before women had the right to vote in the United States. Her reputation for being a vicious competitor, an epic tightwad, and an occasional oddball is well earned, but she has been falsely accused of a lack of humanity even toward members of her family that require correction. There is no doubt that she was eccentric, but her unusual behaviors were neither erratic nor demonic, and deserve a thoughtful exploration.

Folklore abounds with Green—rumors, anecdotes, tall tales, legends, and outright falsehoods. The proliferation of these scandalous stories and the disrespect for her gender that characterized much of her day (and the century following her death) further complicate matters of accuracy. It is certain that she was born in 1834 to Abby Howland and Edward Mott Robinson in New Bedford, Massachusetts. The Howland family were heirs to a whaling company established in 1755 that had arguably become the most important and profitable in the nation. Robinson joined the firm, soon thereafter married the owner's daughter, and within a relatively short period of time was in charge of the company himself. Both parents were of a Quaker heritage, and although biographers of Green were inclined to ignore or dismiss the point, she herself often explained her thrifty ways as due diligence to her faith.

Green spent her youth between her parents' and grandparents' homes; private schools in New Bedford, Boston, and Cape Cod; and a family estate at Round Hill, a coastal section of Dartmouth, Massachusetts. Apocryphal stories of her youth equate her with the love of money for which she would become famous. One of them imagined her screaming inconsolably in the dentist's chair until a shrewd servant thought to tempt her with a silver dollar in exchange for good behavior, which she promptly displayed. Another imagined that she read the financial section of newspapers to her father at a very early age. There seems to be truth in the latter, or at least agreement from Green herself, who confirmed the rumor in interviews. Her childhood was also regimented to the extent that she kept records of expenses and practiced saving money, perhaps a behavior slightly unusual for most children, but not for a family commanding the fortunes that hers did.

In her twenties, Green moved to New York, where she was expected to enter into the life of high society. In 1865, however, two events would change the course of her life: the death of her father and the death of her aunt Sylvia Howland within two weeks of each other (Green's mother had passed in 1860). Although their deaths and the subsequent inheritance made Green one of the wealthiest young women in the country in theory, in practice matters were far more complicated. Her father bequeathed her nearly a million dollars in cash but established the remainder of his tremendous gift in a trust headed by men—and by men whose management Green did not appreciate. Her aunt's inheritance proved even more exasperating to her and led to a legal battle, *Robinson v. Mandell*, which became national news. Both deaths also kept Green intimately tied to New Bedford while the affairs were settled.

Green's aunt Sylvia's final will bequeathed significant amounts to charities, servants, and others responsible for her welfare in addition to her niece; moreover, further monies would be distributed once Green herself had passed. Green challenged the will on the grounds of Sylvia's previous one, which was far more generous to her. During the trial, surprising evidence was introduced: a "second page" of the earlier will, presumably written by Sylvia, making clear her desire for Green to be well cared for and denying the legitimacy of any future wills. The defense immediately suspected forgery. Leading scientists and doctors skilled with microscopes (including Louis Agassiz and Oliver Wendell Holmes Sr.) and handwriting analysts testified on behalf of both sides. The case was eventually ruled against Green, a loss that she did not soon forget and that indelibly shaped her attitude toward inheritance and the legal system.

Even with these setbacks, Green commanded a greater fortune than most people could imagine. She was, however, still limited in her influence as a financier, but a promising turn came with her marriage to Edward Green in

1867. Rumors persist today that she forced him to sign a prenuptial agreement, but as Slack demonstrates, this claim is impossible to verify. More likely it is lore about Green, perhaps originating in her insistence that their respective wealth be kept separate or her convincing Matthew Wilks, her son-in-law, to agree to one with her daughter. What is not difficult to determine, however, is the radically divergent approach to spending money that Green and her husband upheld. As Hetty Green continued a personal policy of closed fists and haggling, Edward Green enjoyed the privileged life and its favors.

One such indulgence was the ability to move in 1874 to Bellows Falls, Vermont, where Edward Green was raised. Eventually they would purchase the Tucker House, a large home overlooking the Connecticut River and associated with his grandfather. By a twist of fate and unfortunate financial decisions, Edward Green would in time lose possession of this dwelling to his own wife, who continued an association with the town for the remainder of her life. But Bellows Falls was also one of the first places to produce copious stories concerning Green's eccentricities. Among the best known was her decision to wash only the bottom of her dresses in order to save money on soap or cleaning fees; her forcing her children to resell in the afternoon newspapers that she had read in the morning; her incessant haggling with store owners and inexhaustible attempts to thwart full prices; her reuse of materials that most people would discard; her customary meal of oatmeal or onions; and her dressing herself and her children in shoddily made and poorly fitting but cheap clothing.

One of the representative anecdotes of Green's miserliness concerns the pursuit of a two-cent postage stamp, for which she reportedly enlisted numerous servants to retrace all the steps she had taken before realizing her loss, only to discover that the stamp was safely stored away in a pocket. Perhaps the most damning rumor—and the one frequently cited as the quintessence of her irrepressible greed—was that she essentially allowed her son Ned to lose the lower half of his leg after a sledding incident rather than to pay for medical care. This story is laden with error and with an intention to depict Green as nefarious, emphasizing "witch" tendencies in her personality.

The truth is that the precise nature of her son's injury is unknown, but it was considerable enough to cause him to limp in his youth and ultimately required amputation and replacement with a cork leg. But that result came after years in attempts to save it, which included home remedies (drawn from the Quaker tradition) and frequent medical aid by highly regarded specialists. The basis for this story, it seems, lies in the verifiable reports that Green occasionally disguised herself as a pauper and brought her children to free clinics rather than to the same doctor's private office that would require payment, and that on one occasion she was outed in this practice and sought another surgeon, but that is a far cry from the ghoulish rumors of neglect.

Green and her husband separated after an economic fiasco in 1885 that led to the collapse of the financiers John J. Cisco and Son. Rumors that the company was becoming unstable prompted her to remove her money from their management, but the request was met with the shocking news that her husband was their largest debtor and that they expected her to cover his debts. She refused, but Green was eventually forced by the courts to pay the loss, a decision that strengthened her resolve to separate from her husband. It also made her famous in the New York and New England press, which took no time in detailing the unusual habits and unflappable business acumen of the richest woman in the United States.

Chemical National Bank became the recipient of Green's wealth and in return she maintained an office there to conduct her business, which increasingly added mortgages, railroad stocks, federal bonds, and Wall Street investments. She also began a long process of changing residencies, oscillating between New York (usually Brooklyn) and Hoboken, New Jersey. She maintained a connection to Bellows Falls, however, regularly summering there. This practice, too, led to wild speculations and rumors about the conditions in which she lived. Storytellers, both in her time and after her passing, relished imagining her in the most wretched of hovels or living in dilapidated tenements in order to save her money. Again, these rumors say more about the motives of the press and of her adversaries than Green. In reality, she often lived in modest circumstances and occasionally would rent out a swankier location, including a gorgeous building near Central Park.

By the turn of the twentieth century, Green was a celebrity throughout the Northeast. Newspapers regularly ran stories—oftentimes invented—of encounters with her or of her legendary money-saving activities. In a similar vein, she was increasingly subject to character pieces that described her as wicked or vengeful, as spiritually unhappy and unfulfilled despite her wealth, and as she aged, as uglier. All of these comments should be understood today as a convention of gender expectations that men simply would not tolerate. This does not, however, exonerate Green from a ruthlessness she seemed very capable of enacting or a desire for litigious action or a lack of philanthropic interests, but it does help contextualize how her eccentricities were in no small measure the result of a remarkable and strong-willed woman under conditions designed to be almost entirely against her.

It would be too much of a stretch to consider Green an icon of women's rights, but she opposed the norms of her day that encouraged men to become interested in economic matters and women to become inclined toward the domestic, and she was willing to offer this critique of society in numerous interviews. Her essay, "Why Women Are Not Money Makers," is still cited today for that very argument—indeed, it has in many ways become more relevant as social expectations have altered. And more recent assessments of Green's life have discovered ample evidence of her responding to the needs of others, of being a good neighbor, and of encouraging children to save money by presenting them with the opportunity to earn a dollar from her. Furthermore, in lending money to religious organizations, she did not gouge them with interest and often asked for a return under the going rate. She even took the side of striking trolley workers on the grounds that they should have an opportunity to become wealthy, and she did not lord opulence or ostentatious displays of wealth over those less fortunate in society.

Yet the representation of Green as the wicked miser continued unabated for decades. Even in her death, a rumor persisted that she suffered a stroke while arguing with a servant about the use of skim milk instead of a heavier cream in a recipe. While this tale had no truthfulness except the stroke, it confirms a perverse morality that wanted to punish a woman for succeeding in a man's world; in it, her death literally becomes a strange morality tale, when no similar narrative treatment befell her male counterparts. And in the end, Green was buried beside her husband (with whom she had a reconciliation of sorts) in Bellows Falls. She did not leave gaudy memorials to herself plastered on statues or buildings, but rather testified to an inward strength of conviction that certainly was eccentric, but only because it was sincere.

4

THE HERMITS: JOHN SMITH AND ENGLISH JACK

New England has seen its share of eccentric hermits from its earliest days. Town histories and local newspapers are filled with stories of these men and women who literally set themselves apart from the crowd. Too often these passages leave us wanting more. There is, for example, regrettably little known about David Wilbur, the "wild man" of Westerly, Rhode Island, who made a name for himself with weather predictions and scratching odd markings into pumpkins, or Benoni Wright, an early settler of Bradford, Vermont, whose claim to fame included a stint as a hermit in which he attempted to fast for forty days in a cave. Like so many other hermits in the region, their stories hint at Yankee ingenuity and New England individualism taken to its extreme.

At times, the hermit is genuinely reclusive. The sad tale of Sarah Bishop, the so-called "Atrocity Hermitess," who fled Long Island to the border of New York and Ridgefield, Connecticut, falls into this group, along with Robert Voorhis, a fugitive and former slave, who lived near Providence, Rhode Island, and later Seekonk, Massachusetts. Other times the hermitage is only a passing phase, such as Henry David Thoreau's retreat to Walden Pond. And at still other times the hermit seeks to resist social expectations—including paying taxes—such as the recent case of Bill Britt of Chestnut Hill, Massachusetts, whose story became a national affair. Finally, there are the "professional hermits," those individuals who play the part of an eccentric, solidary figure to the delight of their fans.

John Smith was such a professional. His celebrity erupted in the late 1860s, soon after he was discovered living in a cave in Erving, Massachusetts. By 1874, he and his cave—christened "Erving Castle"—appeared in the *Gazetteer of the State of Massachusetts*, a travel guide that described him as "a man of some intelligence" who receives "visitors with a kindly spirit." Smith's fame rose precipitously in the decade that followed, drawing thousands of summer visitors to his woodland abode. He welcomed them as a source of company, conversation, and income, selling items that he knitted, photos with him, and no fewer than two pamphlets written about his life.

The first of these pamphlets appeared in 1868. Entitled *History of the Hermit of Erving Castle*, it was essentially an oral history narrated by Smith to George Warren Barber, a student at Andover Theological Seminary and a resident of Orange, Massachusetts, a town adjacent to Erving. The second pamphlet, authored by Smith himself, appeared as *The Hermit of Erving Castle* in 1871. It reads like a novel and includes several poems composed by Smith or in his honor. Both provide an illuminating—if occasionally contradictory—glimpse into his storied biography.

Taken together, the two pamphlets assert that Smith was born in 1823 in Perth, Scotland. His mother died when he was a child and his father was absent, so his grandmother and her confidant, Tibby Scugle, raised him. Although his mother was reportedly a maid to a Lady MacDonald of Keppeth Castle—a woman who showed kindness to him throughout his life—his early years were difficult and he became a peddler by the time he was fifteen. In one of his peddling trips through the Highlands of Scotland, he met—or was rescued by— the daughter of a wealthy farmer. The second pamphlet calls her Betsey (or Betty), but in both accounts, she is Smith's first love. Then the stories become a little less agreeable with each other.

In the earlier version, Smith claims that he failed to confess his love too late and lost her to elopement with a cattle dealer in England. In the later version, he weaves a more elaborate tale of heartbreak, beginning with his taking on

Photograph of John Smith, c. 1870
ERVING PUBLIC LIBRARY

a supplemental career as a stage actor. This work led him to a company head-lined by Fanny Tysdal, the sister of "one of the leading actors of the day." Smith invited Betsey to attend a performance of his in London, but failed to inform her that his name on the bill would be a pseudonym. When Betsey discovered the false name and the man she adored on stage in the arms of another—a love scene—she fled the theater and never spoke to him again.

In the first pamphlet, this failed romance threw Smith into despondency and chased him into a life of solitude. In the second, it edged him nearer, and when he suffered through the death of an adopted son, he became "tired of a busy world" and adopted the hermit's life. Throughout the first account, Smith names the many nobles who protected his hermitage for two decades, pepper-ing each entry with gossip and an occasional hint of a ghostly haunting. In the second account, he skips these wanderings altogether, electing instead to tell the tale of a reunion with a rich uncle, who promised a sizeable inheritance if Smith would marry his caretaker and who raged when his nephew refused the offer.

The pamphlets generally agree on the next chapter of his story, when he crossed the Atlantic in 1866 under turbulent storms, feared for his life, and after many hours of prayer and meditation upon Jonah, was delivered to New York City. Smith eventually made his way to Boston, stopping at Springfield and other towns along the way. There, he found some comfort with other Scottish families and learned of the chance to make a living by picking berries and chestnuts in western Massachusetts and selling them in the east. So began Smith's new life in the United States, walking the three-and-a-half days and nearly one hundred miles between Leverett and Boston for a mere four dollars of profit. In other months he sold wreaths or knitted stockings, but he never made enough to purchase land of his own.

Property mattered little to Smith, however, as he learned from his days as a hermit to survive in the woods. And in March 1867, he moved into a cave in Erving he discovered months earlier when fleeing a group of "rowdies." The cave was adjacent to a natural spring, and this sign assured Smith that he had found the right place for hermitage. He lived there for several months in what he described as the happiest time of his life, reading and composing poetry and enjoying the calm life of contemplation. In time, he christened the local geography with Biblical terms: The spring became Moses Rock; a ledge became Pulpit Rock; and a natural incline even became the Devil's Staircase.

Smith's seclusion came to an abrupt close in November 1867, when Samuel Dirth, a local man employed with a road construction company, discovered him. When Dirth returned days later with two other crew members brandishing axes and spades, Smith feared they would chop him to pieces. His anxieties were unfounded, however, and their inquiry blossomed into a friendship. Soon he was presented with charitable gifts and company from the community, and he returned the hospitality to a growing number of guests. The owners of the property (initially a lawyer or two lawyers from Springfield and later a local man) granted Smith permission to remain on the grounds.

And as might be expected for someone who earned his living telling stories, Smith was willing to alter elements here and there based on his audience. In an article in the *Boston Globe* in 1892, for example, he identified himself as a native of Moore Green, Nottinghamshire, in England, who moved to Perth. That alone is hardly a contradiction, but the other claims are problematic to reconcile with the early pamphlets. Smith gave his birth year as 1818 and claimed his father was a farmer who died young. And in this account, he always wanted to be an actor and was quite successful at it—even performing in a troupe before Queen Victoria—until he failed to profess his love for the leading lady of his company and lost her hand in marriage to a gambler, a loss that launched his life as a hermit and sent him across the ocean for solace and solitude.

These inconsistencies should not, however, indict Smith as a liar, nor should later accounts that argue his true name was not John Smith. While the truth of the matter is that none of these accounts are likely wholly true, they reveal a man with the wherewithal and wiles to tell a good tale. They suggest, furthermore, that he may well have had training as an actor and was practiced at employing those skills in order to keep audiences coming back for more. And come back they did. A newspaper account in 1874 reported that he saw ten thousand visitors in the previous year, and that estimate mushroomed to fifteen thousand in 1875. Among them, so the rumors go, were dignitaries that included Prussian nobility on tour in the United States, but most were summer tourists enjoying railroad trips between western and eastern Massachusetts.

Smith accommodated with good cheer. As early as his first pamphlet, he mentioned his intention to give the cave a "picturesque appearance" for visitors, and other newspaper reports noted his addition of picnic tables, gardens, and walkways for their enjoyment. He also welcomed many pets. He recalled a rabbit, for example, that joined Smith—that is, until he accidentally killed his companion and, after properly grieving, ate him. He wrote fondly of Frisky the mouse, whom he taught many tricks that delighted audiences. And he eventually played host for many cats, up to twenty at a time, with names such as Rodney Hunt, Princess Royal, Dolly Varden, Toddier, Colonel Fisk, Lady Ann, and the Ripper. One of his favorite cats, Toby, died in 1873, and an admirer paid for a small headstone to grace his grave.

In 1874, with the encouragement of an H. H. Turner of Orange (whose name adorns the list of Civil War soldiers on the town monument), Smith began a lecture series throughout the area. Advertisements of his public talks depict a man traveling throughout Massachusetts and New Hampshire, including Springfield, Holyoke, Boston, Westport, Keene, and Chesterfield. Here as well the numbers were impressive, with the Springfield event boasting a thousand in attendance. For these talks, Smith dressed in the garb of the "red and white guild," a rumored order of hermits who took their colors to represent loss in love. He regaled audiences with stories of his life in Scotland, his broken heart, his retreat to America, and his life as a hermit. He became, put simply, a celebrity.

Occasionally Smith suffered rude guests, and a few newspaper reports noted boys throwing stones into his cave or vandals attacking his home, and he once felt threatened by a man who turned out to be an escaped convict. He survived the Great Blizzard of 1888 (an incident that was one of the few times he expressed a wish to have had a wife for company) and often wept at the loss of another feline companion. Surely he labored to keep the stone stairways, gardens, and paths in order for the tourist season, and from the reports that survive, he dealt with rattlesnakes often enough. But his main rivalry came when, sometime before 1888, another hermit moved to within one-eighth of a mile at the same ledges and cave.

This man, Charles Thatcher, was described in the *Springfield Republican* as "a decrepit war veteran" who "thoroughly eschews all attempts to live a civilized life." A later report described him as a "brave soldier" who hailed from the 4th Vermont Infantry, and who, as a pensioner, could afford the nicely furnished abode he constructed on the mountain. But the same report makes clear that with respect to visitors, Thatcher "has no use for them and if they would come to him one at a time, he would throw them out the window." He also, apparently, practiced the habit of firing his revolver several times at midnight. If the media invented Thatcher's caricature as a foil to Smith's genteel nature, Smith confirmed the tension in an interview in 1892, claiming that Thatcher drove him from his home. Presumably, Smith meant from his cave proper, as he did not leave the property per se, but eventually erected a shack—or improved one left by road-builders—with (as the rumors went) driftwood he collected from the nearby Millers River.

Smith's final days came in 1900. He died in the nearby town of Montague while convalescing from an illness. He was buried in the Erving Center Cemetery, his headstone bearing the title "The Hermit" on its top and on its face the simple message:

Of Erving Castle.
John Smith
AE 82

The headstone of Toby the cat was eventually moved beside his grave. And to this day, the home where they lived together is still known as Hermit's Mountain.

—⁓—

The Hermit of Erving Castle was a fascinating figure in the history of New England, but he was not unique in the formal sense of that word. Smith was only one of several professional hermits who appeared in the woods just in time to become an attraction for the tourism boom after the US Civil War, when changing economics, travel conditions, and social expectations allowed people of even more modest means to find summer recreation. Another such an individual was English Jack, the Hermit of Crawford Notch in the White Mountains of New Hampshire. And he, like Smith, quickly rose to prominence and profitability on account of his "secluded" nature.

English Jack appears in newspapers in the late 1870s, usually attached to travelogues. In 1877, for example, a correspondent for the *New Hampshire Sentinel* described a pleasant visit to the area, starting with lodging at the grand Crawford House "just under the shadow of Mt. Willard." Among the many events and sights, the view of the "Hermit" smoking on his pipe stands out, for "the brave old veteran modestly claims only one hundred and ten years as his age." Whether this is English Jack or another hermit cannot be determined, but a year later, a newspaper in Lowell, Massachusetts, briefly reports the appearance of a British sailor living as a hermit in a hut known as "the house that Jack built." It also described a peculiar habit, which the *New York Star* elaborated on in March 1879 with a striking title: "A Live-Frog Eater." This lengthy article describes a winter journey through snows, finding the sign for the hut, and ruminating on "Wild Jack," whom the correspondent met the previous summer when the hermit visited a local hotel with a pocket full of frogs.

"Without further ceremony," the article continues, "he put his hand in his blouse pocket and pulled out a frog, live and kicking lustily; took it by the hind legs, threw back his head, opened his mouth as wide as a fly trap, and ushered the frog head first down his throat. Another, and still another, followed and shared the same fate as the first, until half a dozen large-sized frogs were hopping around in his stomach together." One hotel guest claimed to have seen him swallow sixteen in one sitting. When the group from the *Star* arrived at his hut, he had no frogs on hand on account of the winter, but welcomed his guests with a story about his life and his retreat into a hermitage after seeing the seas as a sailor. The reason, put simply, was "all on account of a woman," his beloved Eliza.

Jack explained that his real name was Alfred Viell—other reports also suggest Viles or Vials—born in England fifty years prior, who ran away from home at thirteen and joined a crew of sailors. His travels took him around the world, but an ill-fated voyage in his twenties—just after he had met Eliza in Liverpool and she agreed to marry him when he next returned—found him one of only two survivors of a shipwreck in the Mediterranean, where they subsisted on rattlesnakes and frogs until their rescue. Ever since then, he was able to repeat this odd culinary feat if circumstances or profit called. And after a long journey to the East Indies, he returned home elated to see his beloved, only to learn of awful news. "They told me she had heard about the wreck of the bark I sailed in," said Jack, "and supposing me to be in the bottom of the sea, she had pined away of grief, and was dead and buried these three months." The despondency that struck led him, like Smith, to flee to America and start a new life, where he abandoned a box of trinkets he intended to give to Eliza in the Custom House in Portland, Maine, and never looked back.

These basic elements remain in other stories told by and about Jack at the time. A report in the *Hartford Courant* the same year, for example, identified twenty survivors of the shipwreck, all of whom died on the island during their exile except Jack and two others. This article mentioned his strange diet, but did not consider any of the tragic romance. Instead, it stressed that Jack was fond of making (and sharing or selling) his own beer, just as other articles observed his fondness for chew and, as he once joked, his preference for "oil o' whiskey" over oil of peppermint to treat sciatica. In these habits, he distinguished himself from Smith, an avowed teetotaler who refused to sell alcohol to his visitors. And while there is no reason to doubt the sincerity of heartbreak in Jack's decision to become a hermit, it is prudent to see how the oscillation from the novelty of frog eating to the story of a broken heart would impress a great number of diverse audiences.

This decision worked. Advertisements for a "Grand Autumn Excursion" in 1889, for example, promised a four-day tour of Franconia and the White Mountains. It began at the Crawford House, and offered among its earliest events "a call at the cottage of Jack, the Hermit of the Hills." Another travel report in the *Boston Herald* in 1890 bluntly explained that "Old Jack" was "one of the Crawford curiosities that everyone goes to see, and children find him a never-failing source of delight." By this time, the story of his shipwreck included the need to eat all sorts of wild game uncooked, including birds, rabbits, and squirrels in addition to snakes and frogs. The romance was absent in this account, but Jack playfully remarked that he was smarter than rich people who paid one dollar only for frogs' legs when he could enjoy the entire meal for free. This article, furthermore, suggested that he came to the area working as an engine cleaner for the local branch of the Portland and Ogdensburg railroad, the major route for tourists to Crawford Notch.

A similar article in a Chicago newspaper retold with amazement of a visit with Jack, in which for a dollar he fished a frog out of a tub and swallowed it whole. "About fifteen years ago," the writer continued, "he was shipwrecked, and lived for several years on an uninhabited island, where he had nothing but frogs and berries to eat. He was finally rescued and made his home in the mountains, where he lived for some time unobserved. But he was later discovered, and his frog eating he turned to the entertainment of pleasure seekers and to the art of money making." Again, the subtle alterations here may be more a marker of the author's memory than Jack's storytelling, but these changes also demonstrate the need to keep the story fresh and to entice different audiences with different tales.

In time, Jack and his hut appeared on postcards and he could earn a living selling himself and his stories. And just like Smith, Jack's story found its way into a souvenir publication for the pilgrims who visited him. In 1891, James E. Mitchell published *The Story of Jack the Hermit of the White Mountains*; it saw several editions. It is a lengthy poem of forty-nine stanzas, composed as if sung by Jack himself, and addressed to an ambiguous "Captain," whom Jack invites to hear his tale over homemade beer. It is a sensationalized account in which Jack is orphaned in London at twelve, befriends a five-year-old girl named Mary Simmonds, and is made a cabin boy on the ship of her father, Bill. Jack sails with Bill for eight years without incident. Then, in a fateful trip into the Indian Ocean on the *Nelson*, the crew is shipwrecked. Only Jack, Bill, and eleven others survive; fifteen bodies wash ashore, and the rest of the forty-two-man crew are lost at sea. They survive for two years on mussels, crabs, limpets, snails, and snakes—no mention of frogs appear in these lines—and their numbers dwindle to three; Bill himself is the last to die on the island and beseeches Jack to return to England and bring word to his family.

A week later, an American ship rescues Jack and his two companions. They die on the way home to England, but Jack returns to London via Liverpool. He discovers that Mary's mother had died, so he rescues her from poor working conditions and sends her to school. He leaves for a yearlong voyage to Calcutta and Hong Kong, promising to return with her wedding dress. But when he does return, "there came a blight / That crushed my heart and ruined every plan." Mary, he discovers, had died a month before. Heartbroken, he falls into a despondent disease, but survives that ordeal. Desiring death, Jack enlists in the British navy and volunteers for missions certain to bring his end: He fights in Africa to free slaves, joins Edward Augustus Inglefield's search for John Franklin in the Arctic, battles in the Crimean War, and puts down a mutiny in India—all to no avail in his search for an end to his life. So broken, he leaves England and finds his way to America, where he remains waiting "for death to sound my call." In the years ahead, many would consider this tale to be an accurate account and cite it as his biography—and Jack did nothing to discourage it, often indulging in those tall tales himself to a willing audience.

In 1893, an article written by G. P. Smith appeared in newspapers throughout the United States and its territories, stretching as far as Honolulu. Entitled "Dead to the World," it catapulted Jack to fame and added a few missing details, but remained close to the major details. How much his visitors believed his stories is open to interpretation. In 1894 the *Boston Herald* praised his ability to tell "fish stories," for example, and a year later the *Springfield Republican* concurred that he was adept at spinning romantic yarns. This admission did not, however, prevent those papers from printing a copious number of his stories, including episodes from Mitchell's booklet and Jack's additional tales of eating *all* the snakes on his secluded island, as well as a bear that he once tried to train as a pet before it attempted to eat him.

A similar exposé in the *Boston Herald* in 1902 celebrated his "talkativeness." By this late date, the interviewer was able to cull few new items of interest, including a few names of the governors who visited Jack and his response when asked if he considered himself an Englishman: "No, sir, I'm a Yankee," was his remarkable statement. "And I'm goin' ter die a Yankee."

It's not a line to toss aside, and the reporter also noted that Jack's keen acumen for turning a buck made him as much a Yankee as any statement of one's politics. Indeed, the same honor could be paid equally to John Smith: Yankees by attitude if not by birth.

And, perhaps like most shrewd Yankees, Jack also had a rival. As the *Boston Herald* explained in an article in 1905, "Hill Hermits Bitter Enemies," a certain Ben Osborne—a former mountain guide whose clients reportedly included Mark Twain, Artemus Ward, and Ulysses S. Grant—had moved to the area twenty years prior and competed with Jack for tourist attention and affection. Unlike the diplomatic John Smith, however, Jack had no difficulty in speaking ill of his competitor, and the reporter affirmed that Jack's abilities as a storyteller far outpaced those of Osborne. A poem in the *White Mount Echo* in the early twentieth century, "The Lonesome Life," underscored this idea. Purportedly composed by Jack himself, it retold the shipwreck story—now set in the Bay of Biscay—absent of the love affair, but tidying the connection to Crawford Notch, for his rescuers were an American crew of whalers who convinced him to come home with them and work on the railroad, a path that led him to his new home.

Jack's death came in the spring of 1912. He had been wintering for several years at a nearby house, but age finally caught up to him. His passing was noted in regional papers and especially in New York; the *New York Times*, *The Sun*, *New York World*, and the *Brooklyn Eagle* covered the event, and their collective reports were reprinted in countless papers across the nation. In them, one finds a complete embrace of Mitchell's fantastical story as if it were honest fact, and hence the man who early in his career mentioned a love for a lost Eliza was hailed as finally reuniting with his beloved Mary. But even in his passing Jack left newspapers with one more delightful pursuit: namely that he was fond of Edgar Allan Poe's poem "Annabel Lee," and would often recite it by heart, or at least the line he thought best captured his own mood: "We loved with a love that was more than love." He was buried at Straw Cemetery in Twin Mountain, New Hampshire, with a simple gravestone that raises as many questions as it solves:

The Hermit of Crawford Notch

John Vials

Died

April 24, 1912

AE. 85 YRS

English Jack and John Smith epitomize the intersection where history, biography, and folklore mix. (And they are not the only ones; there are several other examples of professional hermits in New England at roughly the same time and living roughly the same pattern.) Their industriousness, knack for dramatic tales, and adaptability for different audiences are the hallmarks of skilled performers, and even if we may never know the truth of their early lives—or their late ones, for that matter, as they made their livelihood in caves and shacks—we can rest assured that they entertained weary travelers and excited tourists on their own terms. And now, more than a century after both have passed beyond, we who still delight in them prove that against the passing of time, nothing stands better than a good story.

5

THE HEALERS: ELISHA PERKINS, SYLVESTER GRAHAM, ROBERT WESSELHOEFT, AND F. C. FOWLER

Can eccentricity be commonplace? This question seems illogical on first inspection, but there are cases in which peculiarity is the professional norm. So it is with so many healers—the doctors, homeopaths, health reformers, hospital founders, tonic makers, and outright quacks—who inhabit the strange and strangely compelling history of medicinal practices and their evolution over the centuries. As with many people who appear in these pages, the offbeat healers of New England deserve their own book, but this collection would be incomplete without consideration of a few of the more outlandish and influential contributors to that history. I have elected to highlight four men who span a range of eccentricities and who all share the quirky distinction of dying in their late fifties.

According to the medical writer James Joseph Walsh, our first example, Elisha Perkins, is deserving of no less a title than the "Prince of Quacks." Born in

Norwich, Connecticut, in 1741 into the family of a prominent doctor, Perkins was a man of honorable distinction for much of his life. He became a physician himself and relocated to Plainfield, Connecticut, where he had a successful practice, was a surgeon during the American Revolution, regularly served as Chair of the Windham County Medical Society, and mentored several students over the course of twenty years. A biography of Perkins penned three decades after his death observed that he "possessed by nature uncommon endowments, both bodily and mental." These included a height of over six feet, the stamina to ride horseback sixty miles a day, and the willpower to refuse alcohol and stimulants. He did, however, reportedly demonstrate a peculiar habit: Whenever he made a professional visit and felt overcome with exhaustion, he would immediately lie down and sleep, having handed his watch to an onlooker with orders to awaken him in precisely five minutes. He would, furthermore, automatically arise should his slumber continue to the sixth minute. "By this practice," the report continued, "he was enabled to perform his duties with three or four hours sleep in the night for many weeks in succession, though subjected to great fatigue." His early mastery of exhaustion, however, would foreshadow his early death.

Perkins was a founding member of the prestigious Medical Society of the State of Connecticut. In 1795 he attended their convention and made a rather shocking announcement that would in time simultaneously bring him fame and infamy. Perkins claimed to have invented metallic rods capable of remarkable therapeutic acts. He called these rods Tractors; they were nail-shaped instruments—that is, with a pointed end and a blunt end—about three or four inches long, one roughly the color of iron (or steel) and the other of brass. (Later proponents would suggest that one consisted of a combination of copper, zinc, and gold and the other of iron, silver, and platinum.) He further explained that his Tractors could draw out disease or pain from an afflicted person through a specific technique he had discovered and perfected, essentially stroking or passing the pointed ends over the body, stimulating electrical fluids, and luring the malady as if by a magnet.

The reception of these wondrous items at the convention was, to put it mildly, unenthusiastic. Fellow members urged Perkins to return with more evidence at their next meeting and raised concerns that his proposal was essentially a remnant of mesmerism, a practice then recently discarded by the medical establishment. Undeterred by the Society's skepticism, Perkins filed a patent for his Tractors in 1796 and soon thereafter set the general public in New England ablaze with debate, with some warmly embracing his presumed miracle and some criticizing him as a charlatan. Enthusiasm for his Tractors would soon migrate to Copenhagen and then to London, where his son, Benjamin, moved to sell them.

Much of the biographical information concerning Perkins was recorded by his son in a series of books—four volumes and an edited collection—used as promotional material, so it can hardly be considered a sober resource. Benjamin's accounts do, however, make for an interesting story and the depiction of his father as a tireless visionary inadvertently contributed to later assessments of Elisha as a crackpot. Elisha, these books asserted, came to his discovery by observing certain responses of human tissue during surgery and the use of a lancet to bring relief to various ailments. The then recently published writings by Luigi Galvani on animal electricity inspired him to investigate further, and after years of experimentation with various metals, he developed the correct mixture and method to accomplish the impossible. The earliest accounts offered relief from such infirmities as rheumatism, gout, inflammation, and some tumors, but within a few years promises extended to countless maladies ranging from burns to ringworm to epilepsy. Thus "Perkinism" and "tractoration" were set loose on the world.

Perkins's decision to file a patent in Philadelphia was, in all likelihood, motivated by shrewd business acumen. At that time, the city was the nation's capital, and he reportedly demonstrated his Tractors to an audience of government officials including President Washington himself, who, the younger Perkins contended, purchased a pair. Public excitement soon erupted. Perkins Metallic Tractors promised a way for laymen to avoid the medical establishment altogether and bring relief in as quickly as twelve minutes. But as the younger Perkins tells the tale, enemies on the Connecticut Medical Society took advantage of his father's absence to ruin him, just as rivals once tried to ruin Copernicus and Galileo. In May 1796, the Society condemned "delusive quackery" and demanded that any proponents of such practice should explain why expulsion was not a reasonable outcome. Perkins did not help himself by publishing collections of testimonies from satisfied customers and in response the Society expelled him in 1797.

In a stark pronouncement the Society ejected Perkins on the grounds that he was encouraging "the use of nostrums," a known ineffective medical treatment. Benjamin refuted this claim by trying to win on a technicality. He argued that as his father had filed a formal patent—that is, a public document—his invention could not be a nostrum, which in everyday parlance suggested a *secretive* medicine. Elisha took another route and published criticism of the Society in various newspapers. And both father and son took to advertising their endorsements far and wide. When Oliver Wendell Holmes Sr., the pre-eminent scholar and dean of the Harvard Medical School, took up the example of Perkins in his 1842 essay "Homeopathy and Its Kindred Delusions," he spent considerable ink analyzing those voices of support in order to reveal how few of them were medical experts and how those who were tended to be agents for sale of the Tractors.

The responses to Perkins, both for and against, are themselves a fascinating aspect of his unusual story. One of the earliest criticisms appeared in an anonymous and lengthy poem published in the *Connecticut* (now the *Hartford*) *Courant* in 1796. Written from the perspective of Perkins advertising his wares, the poem mocks their purported healing properties in increasingly absurd terms, promising to reverse the aging process and ultimately to banish sin and death and bring peace to the world. In 1803, at the behest of Benjamin, Thomas Green Fessenden composed a poem praising the Tractors and satirizing the Royal College of Physicians. Licensed agents often produced pamphlets or books to laud their product, whereas other physicians—notable among them was John Haygarth, a doctor well regarded for combating smallpox—wrote critiques. (Haygarth's response is an early contribution to understanding the placebo effect.) Visual artists soon joined the fray. In 1801, for example, the famed British caricaturist James Gilray published an image of a quack doctor employing Tractors to remove the ills of alcohol from a suffering inebriate.

Commentators have been divided as to whether Perkins was a sincere believer or a huckster. He did not live long enough to prove either assessment wholly right or wrong or to finish a theoretical work explaining the science behind the Tractors as his son promised he would do. In 1798 yellow fever struck New England, and Perkins set out to test whether a simple anesthetic, derived from common vinegar and muriate of soda—that is, marine salt— diluted in hot water, could remedy the disease. Benjamin claimed that his father had found success combating dysentery and scarlet fever with this cure. Perkins took it to New London but arrived just as the disease was subsiding. The same circumstance met him in Boston. Then, in the summer of 1799, an outbreak in New York provided him the opportunity to try again. The desperation and subsequent demands he found in the city brought exhaustion more powerful than even his trained stamina could sustain, and he died of the disease within a few weeks.

Benjamin continued the family business after his father passed. He remained in London and at the turn of the nineteenth century founded a "Perkinian Institute," a charitable organization meant to bring the benefits of tractoration to the poor. Its directors reportedly included members of the British nobility and William Franklin, the estranged son of Benjamin Franklin. Neither the Institute nor Perkins lasted long, however. Perhaps sensing a declining interest in the fad, Perkins left England a very wealthy man (estimates suggest an impressive sum of $50,000) for New York, where he became a bookseller until his own untimely death in 1810. Following his demise, Perkinism fell into oblivion, although individuals did continue the practice into the first decades of the 1800s.

No one could doubt the sincerity of our second example, the health reformer Sylvester Graham. There are numerous articles and full-length books dedicated to his life, so I will only sketch his contributions here. Graham was a highly polarizing figure in his day. Some considered him a delusional zealot or a loon—the philosopher Ralph Waldo Emerson, for example, in a passing comment in his journals wryly called him "worthy Mr. Graham! poet of bran-bread and pumpkins"—and some considered him an enlightened inspiration. His life story is rife with personal struggles, especially concerning his health. Graham was born in Suffield, Connecticut, in 1794 to Reverend John Graham, a man of seventy-two (some commentators confused his father with his grandfather and suggested he was ninety years old). His father died two years later. According to an early biographer, Graham's mother Ruth suffered from "a melancholy derangement" that necessitated other relatives care for him—no easy task, as Graham was often sickly in his youth. He moved regularly between Connecticut, New York, and Middlebury, Vermont.

At an early age Graham showed keen artistic inclinations for drawing and poetry. He was, by all accounts, restless. A favorable biography suggested that "he appeared a thoughtless, rattle-headed, crazy boy, cheerful, wild, and extravagant" to most people, but possessed a temperament for "deep meditations and philosophic reflections far beyond his years." In an obituary assessment, the *Boston Medical and Surgical Journal* was far less charitable, describing Graham's penchant for excessive vanity and obtrusiveness and stating bluntly that he "wore out everybody who listened to him." In his late twenties, Graham briefly attended a preparatory school in Amherst, Massachusetts, but left under a dark cloud; rumors suggest that he was falsely accused of assaulting a young woman.

His exile from Amherst again brought illness—the implications are mental as well as physical—and he ended up convalescing in Little Compton, Rhode Island. He would marry one of the women who nursed him, Sarah Manchester Earle, and began a career as a Presbyterian minister. In 1830 he joined a temperance society in Philadelphia and lectured on health issues throughout the 1830s, often commanding sizeable audiences. Eventually Graham relocated to Boston, where he enjoyed a number of productive years and saw the rise of "Grahamites," converts to his principles. (He also saw riots driven by people whose businesses were threatened by his ideas.) And in 1850 he was instrumental in the creation of the American Vegetarian Society. Yet all the while he continued to fight his own serious illnesses, and Graham eventually retired to Northampton, Massachusetts—the home he occupied is felicitously now a bakery and whole food restaurant—and died in 1851.

Graham's unique perspective shines through his writings. These works are too numerous to discuss individually, but in summary, he argued that diet and hygiene were essential for robust health and long life and could prevent or cure many epidemic diseases. His insistence upon regular bathing, exercise, and sleep—now standard medical advice—was considered odd at the time. And just as he advocated temperance against alcohol, Graham also campaigned against meat and white bread. In 1837 he penned *A Treatise on Bread and Bread-Making* that set down his recipe (essentially coarse wheat flour without leavening yeast) and exalted the resultant product in almost religious terms as a kind of salvation. That wheat, a European colonial import, rather than American corn was the basis for his diet is not inconsequential; he regarded whole wheat as a civilizing agent and the key to domestic happiness, akin to the digestive wellness someone who ate so-called "Graham bread" would experience. (The graham cracker of today, although named in his honor, barely resembles his design.)

His call for sobriety, however, extended even further into moral matters. From his earliest sermons and lectures Graham was a strong proponent of chastity and the control of sexual urges, which he also saw as contributing to poor health. These ideas appeared in several publications and culminated in his *A Lecture to Young Men on Chastity*, where he railed against the abuses of amativeness, especially the "self-pollution" of masturbation. The vegetarian and whole-wheat diet he recommended would, he argued, prevent an overstimulation of these desires, allowing sufferers to recover from illness and dedicate their time to more worthy pursuits.

Toward the close of the 1830s he published his magnum opus, *Lectures on the Science of Human Life*, and was busily assembling *The Philosophy of Sacred History*, a work meant to reconcile his dietary recommendations with Scripture, when he died. While the ideas he promoted in both may strike the

Wood Engraving of Sylvester Graham, c. 1870
LIBRARY OF CONGRESS

contemporary reader as hopelessly misinformed, much of his stitching together of physiology with religiosity was common in the nineteenth century as the underpinning for much folk religion and medicine. In the same work in which he discussed brain anatomy, the nervous system, and the operation of the organs during hunger, Graham also contended that through moral weakness humans multiplied "artificial wants" that "impairs his mental faculties, and deteriorates his whole nature, and tends to the destruction of mind and body." Thankfully, Graham retorted, the Creator also endowed humans with moral and intellectual powers—*conscience*—that could realign them with eternal and proper constitutional laws.

Graham's eccentricity showed not in making this leap of reasoning, then, but rather in the sincerity and direction it took him. He argued, for example, that the comments of ancient writers (especially in the Judeo-Christian and Greco-Roman traditions) who purported humans living to be hundreds of years were correct and should inspire dietary changes in his time. "There is nothing in physiology," he wrote, "nor in any other known science, which proves that man cannot as well live a thousand years, as fifty." That people did not live as long as Methuselah was because, essentially, they were not trying. And worse, lives were cut short because people gave in to deleterious stimulants such as opium, tobacco, alcohol, coffee, tea, salt, pepper, mustard, and ginger. Graham's project, then, was to reeducate the world in the hopes of reversing the trend. I will leave it to the reader to decide what it means that he lived only fifty instead of a thousand years.

It is easy to dismiss Graham as a hopeless idealist, but it also pays to recall that his intentions were to promote self-healing in an age when vicious toxins and routine bleeding were the leading remedies for illness. Graham was often criticized for his own poor health by those who suggested that his eccentric ideas were precisely the cause of his frequent decline and early death. Against these accusations, he was even compelled to publish an apology and argued that he was still alive only thanks to his adoption of those principles. One thing is certain, however. When the aforementioned *Boston Medical and Surgical Journal* dismissed his fame as "a local one" and predicted that it "would not survive the lifetime of some of his disciples," nothing could be further from the truth.

⁓

Robert Ferdinand Wesselhoeft, our third example and a contemporary of Graham, may not precisely qualify as an eccentric personality, but as he was literally made a "mis-fit" several times during his life, he is deserving of a few pages. Born in 1796 in what is now Jena, Germany, Wesselhoeft trained as a lawyer while his brother, William, became a physician. Both led student protest movements in the city and revolutionary political organizations dedicated to a single German state under a republican government. With the tide turning against political dissidents, William left for the United States in 1824, but Robert remained in Europe.

He was arrested on several occasions, lost his position as a government official, and was eventually sentenced to imprisonment for fifteen years. He served seven before an amnesty release, when he joined his brother in the German enclaves of Allentown, Pennsylvania. While incarcerated, Wesselhoeft became interested in medicine. And although he wrote several works on politics and law in Germany, on this side of the Atlantic he shifted his attention to the promotion of homeopathy and especially to hydropathy. This latter movement, which began in earnest in Europe in the 1820s, promised that exposure to water, and to specific treatments with water, was curative. Immersion could stave off or reverse disease. Imbibing could relieve pains associated with headache or gout and extend one's life (an idea Graham also entertained). Cold wraps, properly applied, could heal broken bones.

The Wesselhoeft brothers moved to the Boston vicinity to practice homeopathic medicine in 1842. Careful readers will recall that was the same year in which the influential Oliver Wendell Holmes Sr. gave lectures against homeopathy, and the collision between these two physicians became legendary. In 1845, Robert Wesselhoeft left Boston for Brattleboro, Vermont (William joined him but kept his practice centered in Boston). A few commentators have hastily suggested that Holmes attacked Wesselhoeft in his "Kindred Delusions" essay and drove him from the Hub, but neither brother appears in that work. Instead, the direct antagonism arose when Robert published a series of seventeen letters, originally written privately to a friend, that were critical of Holmes.

Many of these missives reveal a nineteenth-century erudition that makes casual perusal difficult, but the gist of Wesselhoeft's critique was to turn the tables, suggesting that Holmes violated the same standard he demanded from others, namely a lack of expertise—in this case, in homeopathy and hydropathy. Wesselhoeft was particularly disgruntled by Holmes's suggestion that homeopathy bore any resemblance to Perkinism. His political leanings also peeked through. He noted, for example, that dogmatic devotion to conservatism had no place in the revolutionary art of medicine and concluded his spirited defense of hydropathy with populist slogans. He also confessed a concern that as a newcomer to the United States, his public opposition to a man as well connected and powerful as Holmes would lead to dire consequences.

These glimpses of immigrant anxiety—especially poignant from someone who lived through the turmoil of political detention—and his firm belief in the efficacy of homeopathy to heal in accord with nature and without the use of the "torture" of unnecessary medicine help to humanize Wesselhoeft, and by our contemporary sensibilities he strikes a very sympathetic figure. But in his time he would find himself caricatured by no less a writer than Nathaniel Hawthorne, whose 1844 short story "Rappaccini's Daughter" depicted a nefarious professor at odds with the sensible scholar Pietro Baglioni, a character inspired by Holmes. And Hawthorne would again return to the theme of a maliciously intended physician—Professor Westervelt—based on the Wesselhoeft brothers in *The Blithedale Romance*, his novel from 1852. Scholars still debate the reasons for these negative portrayals. Holmes took personal credit for them, but others have noted that Hawthorne's wife, Sophia, was a patient of William Wesselhoeft, who reportedly utilized hypnosis upon her in a manner that enraged her husband and inspired revenge through the literary pen.

Wesselhoeft's own stated reasons for moving to Brattleboro were much less scandalous. As he wrote in an editorial to the *New-York Tribune*, Brattleboro simply had what Boston did not: a constant supply of "pure, cold, never fading" water. In 1845 he opened the doors of the Wesselhoeft Water Cure on Elliot Street near Whetstone Brook. Treatments included wraps, spongings, plunge baths, running sitzes, and showers—all with cold water. A year later Wesselhoeft launched a journal, *The Green Mountain Spring*, in order to promote hydropathy and his business. Within a few years the institution was a remarkable success; the names of its visitors are rumored to include copious writers and politicians of the day from Martin Van Buren to Harriet Beecher Stowe.

While the water cure proved popular among elites who could afford it, it ran afoul of the mainstream medical establishment. *The Boston Medical and*

Surgical Journal of 1846, for example, offered a scathing criticism of Wessel-hoeft and his journal: "A constant devotion to the one absorbing thought of revolutionizing the public sentiment in regard to the cure of diseases exclusively by cold water would appear to have debilitated the mind, or at least so diluted the intellect that to some extent the dilution is actually perceptible to an unbiased reader." Wesselhoeft nevertheless continued his practice unabated, was featured in a promotional study in 1848 entitled *The Water Cure in America*, and fathered children who themselves would establish a multigenerational line of successful (and conventional) physicians. In 1850 Wesselhoeft suffered a stroke. He returned to Germany, presumably for treatment, and died in 1852. His widow continued the work of the spa for some time, but it closed permanently within a few years.

The name of my final example, Frank Chester—he went by F. C.—Fowler, has all but been lost to oblivion, but at the height of his prowess at the turn of the twentieth century he was a force to be reckoned with. In 1885 the *New Haven Register* dismissed Fowler in passing as the "chap who once swindled so many men out of money for mythical dogs," and who now "has gone into the quack medicine stamp swindling business." The *Connecticut Valley Advertiser* (the newspaper for Moodus, Connecticut, the town where Fowler was born and lived) explained this earlier scandal as the work of an impostor, but the negative perception clearly stuck. Yet in 1891 the *Illustrated Popular Biography of Connecticut* listed Fowler in its pages and praised how he had "achieved remarkable success in life for one of his years."

The intervening half-decade did prove extremely profitable for Fowler. As reported, in 1884 he assumed the title of Professor and developed a concoction he called "Dr. Rudolphe's Specific Remedy." His real genius, however, was in marketing. Fowler placed advertisements in virtually every major newspaper that existed in the country at the time. The wording evolved over the years, but in essence remained faithful to the earliest version:

PERFECT MANHOOD

To those suffering from the effects of youthful errors, seminal weakness, premature decay, lost manhood, nervousness, etc. I will send you particulars of a simple and certain means of self-cure, FREE OF CHARGE.

The particulars were a pamphlet on the Specific Remedy, which retailed for about three dollars, a hefty price.

Fowler obtained a medical degree and promoted himself as an expert on male sexuality. He opened a laboratory in Moodus and made a fortune through his mail-order business. Early estimates suggested that it grossed $300,000 a year and that for some time he personally pocketed $500 a week. By 1886 he was able to indulge a passion for buying and racing horses and by 1887 was doing the same for sailboats and yachts. In one month in 1889, for example, he purchased a stallion for $10,000 and then several fillies averaging $1,000 each. He kept them at his Oak Grove Farm, where he installed a racetrack and, in the words of the *Boston Herald*, "commodious buildings" for his stock. In 1891 Fowler was wealthy enough to retain the renowned horse trainer John Trout and his son at the farm. And in 1892 he added a kennel for prize Irish setters—the nationally recognized Dick Swiveler being his first purchased champion. By 1894 he had added a hotel in Moodus, as well as co-ownership of the *Connecticut Valley Advertiser*.

And in 1893 he purchased two thousand (some reports said three thousand) acres in the town and adjacent Colchester to create what one newspaper called "A Mammoth Deer Park." At the time, deer had been driven to near extinction in Connecticut, warranting laws that forbade their killing. Fowler, a sportsman, initiated efforts to repopulate the species, boasting an investment of $10,000 to capture and ship them from western states. In order to do so, he surrounded the entire reserve with fences that were twelve feet high in order to prohibit the game from escaping. In later years he would stock the ponds and streams of this private reserve with trout, import hundreds of pheasants and partridge, and develop several acres for duck hunting. Perhaps not surprisingly, fame and power followed money. Fowler served briefly in the Connecticut General Assembly, had a ferryboat named in his honor, and was often the subject of high society news.

He ran afoul of the US Postal Service in 1894, which instructed the Moodus office to cease assistance with his business, but when he relocated to New London in 1901, reports confirmed that he was still the major contributor there, employing hundreds of young women to open and stamp letters, type responses to his customers, and wrap the packages. (Some reports even suggested that his workers had a room in the post office for this bustling activity.) And in addition to this lucrative business, Fowler composed several pamphlets of medical advice, including one on syphilis. It is his 1896 book *Life: How to Enjoy It and How to Prolong It* that warrants mention here. It is an appropriate contribution to close this chapter, as it synthesizes several strands of alternative medicine, combining the moralizing of Graham's views against self-pollution (although not directly, as Fowler was not a proponent of vegetarianism) with an emphasis on naturopathic cures including cold baths, and just the faintest hint of swindling and untenable promises—Fowler claims, for example, to have been lecturing on the subject for thirty years, but he was only thirty-seven when he published the book—to be a descendant of Perkins's art of promotion.

By today's standards Fowler's book is ridiculous—except, perhaps, his opinion that Americans consume too much salt. His pronouncements in favor of ancient notions of personality types, his use of phrenology and his invention of a "physiognometer" to gauge one's sexual vitality, his claim that people in the Midwest were taller than New Englanders due to the lime in their soil and that married people live longer than the unmarried, his admonition that women could produce children with a second husband who looks like her first simply by thought projection, and his stance against Darwin—and, for that matter, against condiments on food—all raise a chuckle. And this is before his assertions that self-pollution and other abuses of amativeness could drive people insane, alter their physical appearance, and shorten the life span by depriving individuals of vital juices. Life lived well, in his opinion, is one deprived of bodily pleasures and of sexual energies redirected toward productive activities such as reading books about great men or joining temperance movements. Given his tendency to moralize throughout this work, it is difficult not to point out the irony that Fowler died at fifty-nine.

This is not meant to disparage Fowler, who lost his wife Enanntha the same year he published his book, and who, in a very telling paragraph, described his own struggle with what we would today recognize as a serious depression until, on a walk, he rescued children from a capsized boat and came to realize he "had found a way out of my trouble by trying to help others." (It also bears notice that, as he explained, half of the children born in the country at the time died before the age of twenty.) Like all of us, Fowler was a mixture of fortitudes and frailties, vices and virtues, and successes and failures. And in his own day he was not necessarily regarded as an eccentric or a misfit. Quite the contrary: He was the epitome of success in the social realm, and his medical advice was very much notable for its consistency with a slew of ideas percolating in the public consciousness at the time. In short, Fowler and his kin remind us that eccentricity is always a matter of contested perspectives.

6

THE SETTLER: WILLIAM BLAXTON

William Blaxton was, arguably, the first eccentric in America of European descent. At least that was the way numerous local histories described him in the nineteenth century. The terms have become familiar to the reader by now. Blaxton was "somewhat eccentric" or a "singular man" or a "strange individual" or a man of "marked peculiarities" or "peculiar interest and of singular eccentricity." Yet in many ways the most unusual aspect of his life is that he was called an eccentric without conspicuous reasons for the title. There is a hint of enigma here, then, which is appropriate for a man who seemed a mysterious figure to those writing about him more than a century after his passing in 1675. In telling the story of how Blaxton became the eccentric settler of both Boston and Rhode Island, we are reminded that one's reputation is always to some degree a mirror of the society that gazes upon the person.

Nineteenth-century narratives were fond of introducing Blaxton—also known as William Blackstone, but I prefer the name he used himself—as an almost spectral figure who shocked the Puritan settlers who were not expecting to encounter a fellow European living in the New England wilderness. The year was 1630, and the location was the present Charlestown neighborhood of

Boston. John Winthrop and a group of immigrants under the Massachusetts Bay Colony arrived on the ship *Arbella*. They discovered to their surprise (if the histories are correct) that the land opposite them on the Charles River was already occupied by a single and solitary figure, William Blaxton. When they could find no consistent source of freshwater, Blaxton invited them to Shawmut Peninsula, the area he had settled and what would in time become a city known as Boston.

It is unlikely that Blaxton's presence was completely unknown to those colonists. There were several individuals living on various islands that dotted the shoreline of eastern Massachusetts. To the south, the Plymouth Colony had existed for ten years, and Salem had greeted settlers since 1626. Numerous attempts to establish other colonies at the coastal regions had failed, leaving their settlers with the difficult decision to return to England or join another colony. But it does seem remarkable that one man could manage his life alone in what one dramatic author called—with apologies for the historical ethnocentrism—an "unbroken wilderness of woods traversed by savages, by wolves and by other wild beasts almost as dangerous," with others "too remote to be of help in case of need." This unusual circumstance was Blaxton's first step in his transformation into an eccentric, "the hermit of Shawmut" as another author christened him.

Aiding this characterization was the lack of information or confusion about how he first arrived in New England. Very early historical accounts simply confessed to having no idea. The surviving colonial records were not helpful, for although they referenced his activities, none seemed to define the route he took. This added to an air of mystery. Later in the nineteenth century, historians tended to agree that Blaxton arrived with Robert Gorges in 1623 as part of the Wessagusset Colony in what is now Weymouth, Massachusetts. This was a short-lived experiment—or more accurately, it was the second short-lived experiment of the Wessagusset Colony, the first having fallen apart only months prior to Gorges's expedition. Financial difficulties instigated a collapse of the colony by 1624, however, and Gorges returned to England.

Some immigrants from Wessagusset remained in New England, and Blaxton presumably was one of them. Regardless of the precise conditions of his arrival, he fell under the jurisdiction of the Plymouth Colony while he resided at Shawmut, at least until the area was incorporated into the Massachusetts Bay Colony. It was in this context, as a formal member of the Plymouth Colony, that Blaxton's name appears in 1628 when he was assessed twelve shillings to contribute to a fascinating and now largely forgotten campaign in New England history.

Thomas Morton was an English lawyer turned colonist who also happened to possess a libertine lust for life. Initially he resided with the Plymouth Colony, but he found Puritan morality too restrictive and in 1625 left to establish his own colony with his colleague Robert Wollaston and several dozen indentured men. They established themselves at a place they called Mount Wollaston, near modern Quincy and Braintree, Massachusetts (and also in the relative proximity of Weymouth). These colonists readily traded firearms and alcohol with the indigenous people for furs and soon ascended to an economic success far exceeding the Plymouth Colony. Tensions arose, however, between Morton and Wollaston, which led to an uprising that forced out the latter. The colony was then renamed Ma-re Mount, and soon became "Merry Mount" in the vernacular language.

In 1627 the Merry Mount community celebrated May Day with traditional European festivities including copious drinking and the raising of a maypole, an action that the Plymouth Colony found reprehensible in its immorality and paganism. Morton's willingness to consort with the indigenous people was also alarming to the Puritans. Following a second maypole celebration in 1628, the Plymouth Colony sent an armed contingent, led by Myles Standish, to arrest Morton and tear down the offending idol. Morton was exiled—he was too well-connected to be executed without irreparable consequences— and returned to England. In 1629 John Endicott led another group of Puritan colonists to raid the crops of what was left of Merry Mount and mowed down the remaining maypole structure. Compensation for the conflict and arrest of Morton became the responsibility of taxpaying members of the Plymouth Colony, including Blaxton. A few authors have suggested that he refused to pay any such tax, but others were certain he did so lest he suffer a similar fate.

Blaxton was not a libertine by any stretch of the imagination, but he was a nonconforming clergyman—or as one historian suggested, he was a non-conformist among noncomformists. The meaning of that word requires some unpacking. Essentially, it references someone who did not conform to the Church of England by disagreeing about the interpretation of Scripture, proper ceremonies, education, ordination requirements, or government involvement in religious matters. The term *Dissenters* can be used in the same way. Some nonconformists separated entirely from the Anglican Church—hence the name *Separatists* as applied to the Pilgrims at Plymouth—whereas others did not. *Puritan*, incidentally, was a term that originally had pejorative overtones, referring to someone who wanted to "purify" the Church of England from the influences of Catholicism.

Blaxton was an ordained minister in the Anglican Church, but for reasons that are not entirely clear to historians, he dissented in a manner serious enough to warrant his leaving England. Accounts suggest that he continued to wear the coat that signified his belonging to the Church when he arrived in New England—for some, this was a marker of his eccentricity—and to preach as an Episcopalian. His religious nonconformity, therefore, was not unusual per se. Quite the contrary: It was common at the time, and especially so in New England. What distinguished Blaxton was his commitment to religious freedom and to personal conscience in church membership.

His sentiment toward religious liberty placed Blaxton outside the norm, but his piety protected him from punishment for these convictions. In 1702, for example, Cotton Mather published *Magnalia Christi Americana*, a history of religion in New England. Early in Book Three, Mather turned his attention to pious men whose names deserve to be in his book even though they were not formally adherents to Puritanism. Among the "Godly Episcopalians" was Blaxton, "who, by happening to sleep first in a hovel, upon a point of land there, laid claim to all the ground." Mather continued with a telling comment. "This man was, indeed, of a particular humor," he wrote, "and he would never join himself to any of our churches, giving this reason for it: I came from England, because I did not like the Lord's bishops; but I can't join with you, because I would not be under the Lord's brethren."

This quote is in all likelihood the originating source for later representations of Blaxton's eccentricity. It certainly established him as someone of independent thought and of a willingness to be independent of society if necessary. And yet he was not condemned by the quickly judgmental Mather, emerging as an eccentric rather than a threat. In addition to living a principled life, Blaxton also seemed to live a prudent one and knew when it was best to leave. In his dealings with the Puritans of the Massachusetts Bay Colony, he eventually reduced his claim over the entire peninsula down to fifty acres. In time he sold all of these as well. With the monies from this sale, he purchased cattle and other necessities that allowed him, in 1635, to move south, returning to an area under the jurisdiction of the Plymouth Colony.

Today the place where Blaxton moved is the Lonsdale section of Cumberland, Rhode Island, near the river that shares his name, the Blackstone, and at the time called the Pawtucket. In the dialects of the indigenous people, the land was Wawepoonseag (signifying a place to trap geese), and to the colonists it was located in the Attleborough Gore. In 1645 the site became part of the town of Rehoboth, Massachusetts. Only in 1747, after a very lengthy border dispute, was it incorporated as a town in Rhode Island. For this reason many have argued that Blaxton never formally lived in what constituted Rhode Island during his lifetime, although he would travel there to visit Providence, the plantation established in 1636 by a fellow dissenter, Roger Williams. Nevertheless, this technicality has not dissuaded feisty Rhode Islanders from celebrating him as their first settler.

The specific land that Blaxton occupied took on a new name, Study Hill, and his abode became Study Hall. Nineteenth-century commentators hotly debated the precise location of this abode—as they did for his dwelling in Boston—but none disputed the meaning of the name, an honorific for Blaxton's dedication to the contemplative life. Blaxton's library was considerable; he left nearly 190 books upon his death including three Bibles, several books in Latin, and a few personal journals. These possessions helped secure his reputation as an eccentric, as they promoted the impression that he lived in the wilderness, away from the vicissitudes of human society, for the sake of the mind, the conscience, and the spirit.

The notion that Blaxton was a recluse, however, is wanting. He maintained business relations in Boston and was involved in a number of legal disputes. In 1659 he married, at age sixty-four, a widow by the name of Sarah Fisher Stevenson. She had children from her previous marriage—at least one of whom moved with her to Study Hill—and together they had one son, John. (Some early nineteenth-century historians erroneously thought they had a daughter as well.) Blaxton befriended Roger Williams and preached in Providence on regular occasions. As Williams was a Baptist, their friendship was one united in intellectual and political commitments to religious tolerance rather than to dogmatic agreement in faith. And finally, there was an alternative tradition that Blaxton had a servant named Abbott, after whom Abbott's Run, a brook in the town, was named. These are hardly the characteristics of a recluse, although they may well be the inclinations of a man intent on preserving a sense of freedom at a very contentious time.

Several writers have mentioned Blaxton's success in growing apples both at Shawmut and Study Hill. A very early history of Providence, for example, remarked that when the Massachusetts Bay Colony arrived in 1630, he had been there long enough "to have raised apple trees and planted an orchard." These apples—known as the Yellow Sweeting and nominated by one commentator to be "the richest and most delicious apple of the whole kind"—and the orchard in which he planted them are often credited with being the first in New England, or at least the first in Rhode Island. (Today many gardeners contend that the Rhode Island Greening or the Sweet Rhode Island Greening is the direct descendant of this fruit, but this may be a case of botanical folklore.) According to tradition, Blaxton found a unique purpose for these marvels of nature, taking them to Providence when he preached there and distributing them to children in exchange for good behavior.

Blaxton's trees reportedly survived into the mid-1800s, but his library did not fare as well. He died in May 1675 at age eighty and was buried on Study Hill next to his wife. Soon thereafter King Philip's War engulfed New England, pitting organized groups of indigenous peoples against colonialist settlers. While accounts agreed that Blaxton, like Roger Williams, was on relatively good terms with the Native Americans, his house—and much of Providence—was burned during the conflict, and his books were presumably lost in the flames. His reputation, however, continued to grow long after his death, and with it new elements of his peculiar nature came into focus. By the early nineteenth century, newspapers were very fond of telling a story that seems all the more incredible to readers today.

This tale first appeared in print in 1765, in a history of Providence composed by Governor Stephen Hopkins. Hopkins wrote, simply, "It is said that when he was old and unable to travel on foot, not having any horse, he used to ride a bull which he had tamed and tutored to that use." (Hopkins was also the source for information about the Yellow Sweetings and their distribution to children.) By 1827 the *Salem Observer* popularized this anecdote, and one year later the *Worcester Aegis* reiterated that "when he was advanced in life, and unable to travel on foot, he tamed a bull, and with the strange steed performed his journeys." By this time Blaxton was well established as a "learned but eccentric man," and his decision to ride such an unusual creature underscored his peculiarity.

As tends to happen when history yields to folklore, this oddity began to grow in dimensions through the course of a century of retellings—and always without any substantiation of fact. By the later decades of the nineteenth century, the bull had identifiable features of color (although the color was different depending on the storyteller), and by the twentieth century—and continuing even to this day—the bull became his primary mode of travel throughout his life rather than toward its close. Late nineteenth-century reports, for example, imagined Blaxton riding his bull on routine trips to Boston. Today it is not difficult to find stories circulating on the Internet purporting that he rode the creature around the nearly eight hundred acres of Shawmut Peninsula as his other cattle grazed in a meadow that became Boston Common.

The claim also ignited debate as to his motive. A history of Rehoboth published in 1836 explained the matter as one of convenience, namely that horses were rare in the late 1600s, so he used what was at his disposal. A later history from 1880 changed the beast from a bull to a steer—no small feat, and one that in neutering the animal could go far to explain it becoming tame enough for a saddle. And by the turn of the twentieth century, genealogists had changed the tune to suggest his taming of the bull was anything but unusual or uncommon, citing one other notable occasion, the 1621 wedding of John Alden and Priscilla Mullen in which the groom "covered his bull with a handsome piece of broadcloth, and rode on his back—but on his return he seated his bride on the animal and walked by her side, leading the bull by a rope fixed in his nose ring." This account, from an essay on cattle husbandry, actually lamented the decline of such transportation.

I will not attempt to decide whether Blaxton regularly rode a bull and whether that constitutes a sign of eccentricity, but I will point out that the seeming oddity of the act to nineteenth-century minds, coupled with his independence of thought and his ability to rattle Puritan expectations of decorum, granted Blaxton a certain cachet with writers of that time. In addition to a few poems composed in his honor, Blaxton emerged as a character in three fictional stories composed in the 1800s. He played a role in the now obscure *The Humours of Eutopia,* a satire of colonial life penned by Connecticut-born author Ezekiel Sanford in 1828, as the father of its heroine, Mary Blaxton. In those pages, Blaxton appears as a sensible man whose impulse for dissent and for intellectual pursuits runs in his family bloodline. This work also initiated the rumor that the Puritans tried to oust him but were prevented from doing so by his oratorical prowess.

In 1832 Blaxton surfaced in Nathaniel Hawthorne's short story "The May-Pole of Merry Mount." This story revolves around the incident with Thomas Morton and imagines two young people, Edith and Edgar, celebrating their wedding by dancing around the maypole. They are interrupted by the arrival of the Puritans under Governor John Endicott, who orders that the attendees be whipped and that the newlyweds conform to Puritan dress and hairstyles.

As the story opens, an English priest stands beside the maypole, "canonically dressed, yet decked with flowers, in heathen fashion, and wearing a chaplet of the native vine leaves" who "seemed the wildest monster there."

When Endicott descends to disrupt the celebration, he identifies this "priest of Baal" as Blackstone, "the man who couldst not abide the rule even of thine own corrupted church, and hast come hither to preach iniquity, and to give example of it in thy life." In a footnote, the author of the story—that is, both Hawthorne and the narrator—includes an intriguing comment. "Did Governor Endicott speak less positively," it reads, "we should suspect a mistake here. The Rev. Mr. Blackstone, though an eccentric, is not known to have been an immoral man. We rather doubt his identity with the priest of Merry Mount."

Blaxton certainly was not the attending priest at Merry Mount, and this is not the only act of poetic license that Hawthorne takes with him in the story—the author makes him a graduate of Oxford rather than of Cambridge, which is no small concession between those rivals. This would, furthermore, not be the last time that Hawthorne invoked him. In the seventh chapter of *The Scarlet Letter*, Hester Prynne (the woman forced to wear the titular mark of adultery) and her three-year-old daughter, Pearl, visit the estate of Governor Bellington to learn if the rumors were true that the leaders may separate mother and child. The two wait in a stately but oppressively controlled room. Pearl then spies rosebushes outside, "and a number of apple-trees, probably the descendants of those planted by the Reverend Mr. Blackstone, the first settler of the peninsula; that half mythological personage who rides through our early annals, seated on the back of a bull." Literary scholars have long debated the meaning of that allusion, but it is generally convincing to see that Hawthorne regarded both Blaxton and Pearl as children of nature and of resistance to intolerance.

Blaxton occupied a significant role as the hermit of Shawmut in John Lothrop Motley's novel *Merry Mount, a Romance of the Massachusetts Colony*, published in 1849. As the name implies, the novel revolves around two lovers, Henry Maudsley and Esther Ludlow, and is set in the early colonial period between the 1620s and 1630s. Historical figures turn up as characters. Sir Christopher Gardiner, an actual knight who fled England and, like Blaxton, reached New England under seemingly mysterious circumstances, is the villain of the novel, forever attempting to thwart the couple. Thomas Morton and the Merry Mount incident haunt the entire work, and the historical relationship that Gardiner, Morton, and perhaps Blaxton shared with the Gorges family inform the plot and the intrigue—although, to be perfectly honest, intrigue is lacking in this heavy-handed story. Motley was a well-respected historian and diplomat, but as one critic observed, imaginative skills were not his strongest suit.

In the novel, Blaxton serves as an intermediary between the hero and villain. Gardiner visits him early in the work to hide papers belonging to Gorges and his land claims. He warns Blaxton of the impending attack upon Morton and advises that the hermit find a way to avoid being forced to join the crusade. But when later treacherous acts by Gardiner leave Maudsley injured and dying, Blaxton rescues the hero and nurses him back to health. He later testifies to the General Assembly regarding all of the patents and land claims, and in doing so helps to secure the future for the two lovers. The novel concludes with his leaving Boston for more solitary circumstances.

Motley's characterization of Blaxton cemented his identity as an "eccentric solitary," a member of the fraternity of men "with no appointed place in the world," a person of "imaginative mind and nervous temperament," and a voluntary exile who turned his back on the world forever when tolerance became a crime. Motley imagined in ample detail the English cottage that Blaxton constructed for himself in the wilds of Shawmut and the cultivated garden to accompany it, all in an attempt to heighten the elegance and sagacity of the hermit's character. But Motley also depicted the clergyman delivering a lengthy speech to his library books as his "friends of solitude" and suggested that he conversed with them frequently. This, certainly, did no favor to rehabilitate Blaxton from a reputation for unusual behavior.

By the mid-nineteenth century, Blaxton's image as an eccentric was enshrined. In 1855, for example, a number of citizens organized the Blackstone Memorial Association, intending a proper commemoration of the man they regarded as the first settler of Rhode Island. Sylvanus Chase Newman spearheaded the campaign and presented a lecture at the founding meeting. In this talk Newman praised Blaxton as "a very benevolent, intelligent specimen of independent oddity" and a "pilgrim pioneer of liberty" whose mind was "one of eccentricity and boldness, and desirous of enjoying independence." Newman also took tremendous liberties in his exuberance. He imagined, for example, that Blaxton paid the tax for the campaign against Morton only under protest and even invented a speech he thought the clergyman would have delivered on the matter. Newman advanced the idea that Blaxton regularly rode a white bull and speculated on the ways his "bull-gine" would fare more nobly than the "engines" of their day. He continued the tradition that Blaxton resisted his ouster from the Massachusetts Bay Company with an impassioned argument and further implied that he was on excellent terms with the indigenous peoples. But Newman provided no supporting evidence for any of these celebratory remarks.

Despite the fanfare and promises by the Association to continue its work to completion, no memorial came out of these activities, and it would take events three decades later to reignite interest in his memorialization. In 1886 the Lonsdale Company sought to replace several deteriorating mills on the Blackstone River. The site for the new mill encompassed Study Hill and the presumed grave of Blaxton. In May of that year the gravesite—marked only by two weathered stones—was opened, revealing some human remains and coffin nails. Lorenzo Blackstone, a descendant, attended the disinterment. A report in the *Boston Post* explained that the remains would be reinterred in the same spot once the building was erected, albeit in the basement of the mill.

Company records from 1889 confirm the memorial's construction and that Blaxton's descendants asked to pay for it. It stood on the campus of the mill until the 1940s, when Lonsdale sold the building. In 1944 the monument was relocated to a small park, still tended by the town of Cumberland. There is some debate about the fate of Blaxton's remains—presuming, that is, that those disinterred in 1886 were his—but they are based on unsubstantiated memories by a few individuals. That said, even if Blaxton's physical ties to this world are now forever lost, we can take solace that he left a monument more lasting than bone or stone: a willingness to be an eccentric when toleration for others defined the height of eccentricity.

7

THE POETS: SARAH HELEN WHITMAN AND FREDERICK GODDARD TUCKERMAN

There are titans of eccentricity among the writers of New England. Emily Dickinson leaps to the fore, followed closely by the horror writer H. P. Lovecraft and, albeit somewhat erroneously, J. D. Salinger and Anne Sexton. Add the list of authors in the Romantic or Transcendentalist traditions and those who lived in the region long enough to be honorary New Englanders (such as Rudyard Kipling, Mark Twain, and Dr. Seuss), and it becomes a fool's errand to select a few representatives from this pantheon. But such folly is my task in this book. I have chosen, accordingly, to focus on two poets whose fame, once bright in their days, has long faded, but who well deserve another appreciative look: Sarah Helen Whitman and Frederick Goddard Tuckerman.

Whitman and Tuckerman offer a contrast of temperaments and achievements. She was, in the words of a thoughtful biographer, the seer of Providence, a woman deeply engaged in the ideas and social movements of her time, known for her charming abilities that attracted numerous admirers to her presence and to a very public life of letters. He was a solitary figure, drawn especially to nature, and increasingly reclusive as he aged, whose work was a commercial failure in his day and who once replied to Nathaniel Hawthorne that his one published book was not written to please anyone. Together they provide a telling look at the wide net of eccentricity as it merges with poetic creativity.

Sarah Helen Whitman is perhaps best known today as the woman who almost married Edgar Allan Poe, but the accomplishments of her productive life far surpass that single episode. Before venturing to tell her story, I need to offer a point of clarification. Whitman's younger sister, Susan Anna, was herself a talented young woman who was often described as "eccentric" in biographical accounts. In her case, however, the word is a euphemism for mental illness that she exhibited throughout her life. Out of respect for her and for the complicated matter of how people with mental health issues were treated in the past, I deliberately avoid this characterization. Sarah Helen Whitman—who went by her middle name—is an eccentric in the sense I embrace in this book, as an unconventional and idiosyncratic individual.

Whitman was born in Providence, Rhode Island, in 1803. She died in that same city in 1878 and lived much of her life there, but was in no means confined. Quite to the contrary, Whitman possessed a keen intellect with an international sphere of influence. Regrettably, there are very few sketches of her life outside her relationship to Poe. One of the earliest, written by Caroline Ticknor in 1916, has many virtues but nevertheless shows the tendency to eclipse her totality within that singular relationship; the book is simply called *Poe's Helen*. The most comprehensive work dedicated to Whitman remains John Grier Varner's massive dissertation from 1940, which was never published. Whitman was the subject of another dissertation in the late twentieth century and a recent book, but these excellent contributions are the exceptions that prove the rule of her general neglect.

The point here is that the near erasure of Whitman or her reduction to Poe's fiancée is a disservice to a woman who was regularly described in newspapers while alive as "much honored" and a "distinguished poet" and who possessed a strength of character such that, as the *New-York Tribune* eloquently stated in her obituary, "If she did not win a great name and fame among American writers, it was because she cared for neither." Helen Whitman's eccentricities combined many aspects of the unusual, but her most significant contribution was her independence of will and her ability to make the uncanny seem chic, at once intensely personal and profoundly human. In her gothic poem "Don Isle," for example, she drew upon Irish romance and her purported family history to retell the story of a nameless countess who defended a fortress against the incursion of Oliver Cromwell, perished in the assault, and forever haunts the ruins as a lonely but dauntless ghost. And this poem, as Varner noted, is an apt metaphor for her life.

Whitman was the second of five children of Nicholas Power and Anna Marsh. Her only brother died in his first year and a sister died at age three. That sister was originally named Susan Anna; Whitman's youngest sister, born in 1813, was honored with the same name. Her ancestors had been in Rhode Island since the founding under Roger Williams, and her grandfather, "Captain" Nicholas Power, was a man of considerable economic, social, and intellectual means. His influence was formative, but he passed in 1808, and the Power family moved to various locations in Rhode Island to accommodate the father's mercantile business. The War of 1812 and the accompanying blockades struck them hard, as they did so many families in New England whose financial means were tied to the sea, and in 1813, Whitman's father was captured by British soldiers. He was eventually released, but did not return home. Instead, for reasons still unclear, he stayed away from his family for another nineteen years, leading them to believe he had perished.

These were not easy times for a single mother and her daughters. Women did not have the right to sell their own property, which became the possession of their husband upon marriage, so the family was often forced to rely upon relatives for assistance. (Some people speculate that Nicholas Power only came back to lay claim to his wife's monies, as he did not live with the family upon his return.) Whitman was a precocious youth and enamored of fantasies, romances, and literature far earlier than her peers. Despite compromised financial circumstances and conventional attitudes against women, she received formal education and tutoring, although several relatives expressed unease with her intellectual interests in the strange and in "questionable" authors such as Lord Byron. Her delight in troubled men with troubling ideas may have led Whitman into her first marriage to John Winslow Whitman, who was a lawyer by training but a literary aspirant by temperament. They were engaged in 1824 and married in 1828.

The couple moved to Boston, which allowed Whitman to enjoy the company of literati and to attend lectures by some of the most unconventional free thinkers of that period. She befriended many spirited and creative women and kept correspondences with them throughout her life. These letters are a pleasure to read for many reasons, including the way they talked about so-called leading men of their day—not as gossip, but as insightful critique of writings now often considered untouchable works of American philosophy and literature. There is some debate as to whether Whitman was truly happy in her marriage. As with her early life, she felt the pangs of financial instability, but this was also the time when she launched her literary career. Her husband was an editor of the *Boston Spectator and Ladies' Album*, a short-lived magazine; Whitman's first poem appeared in those pages. It would be unfair, however, to think that her success was contingent on her husband's connections, for other editors quickly recognized her talents and recruited her contributions.

John Whitman died unexpectedly in 1833. Whitman returned to Providence to join her mother and sister, Anna—just in time for her father's return—and by all accounts shouldered months of mourning and depression. And yet she persevered. Her circle of friends grew to include virtually all members of the Providence intelligentsia, and her career as a poet flourished at this time. Very much in line with nineteenth-century trends, Whitman composed poems on flowers, cemeteries, walks in nature, moonrises, storms, Indian summers, and the changing seasons, and sonnets to various people. She also penned fantastical poems on enchanted castles, fairy tales, and other manifestations of the phantasmal.

"Evening on the Banks of the Moshassuck," written in 1839, offers a good example of her melancholic charm. The poem opens with a scene on this river in Rhode Island on a golden day in September. The river's "silver tide"

Reflects each green herb on its side
Each tasseled wreath and tangling vine,
Whose tendrils o'er its margin twine.

The poet recalls standing on the "velvet shore" with a beloved, and the poem continues with a juxtaposition of the beauty of the scene and the longing for reunion. It concludes

And beautiful her pearly light
As when we blessed its beams last night;
But thou art on the far blue sea,
And I can only think on thee.

One rich irony, perhaps, is that the Moshassuck River had been a site since the 1700s for industrial mills, slaughterhouses, transportation between Providence and Worcester via the Blackstone Canal, and sewerage. By the mid-1800s it was very heavily polluted and likely contributed to cholera outbreaks in the 1830s. In Whitman's hands, the river transforms into an idyllic state that had not been seen in some time.

The ability to find beauty in the broken animated Whitman's spirit, but her eccentricities extended far beyond that talent. First and foremost there was her indomitable dedication to the unconventional and to rebelliousness in defense of intellectual, creative, and political liberty—all summarized by her personal motto, "Break Every Bond." While she shared this attitude with many social reformers of her day, Whitman's repeated demonstration of these convictions was unusual, to say the least, in socially conservative Rhode Island—a state that, for example, still allowed only landowning men to vote even after the American Revolution—as was her rejection of conventional morality and religion. But for all her willingness to upend tradition and shock expectations, Whitman was an unashamed lover of her home state. She saw in Rhode Island the embodiment of nonconformity and wrote copious homages to its founding figures. Roger Williams was honored on several occasions, and her hymn written for the 1877 dedication of his memorial statue was sung by more than a thousand children. But that same year, Whitman also wrote a polemic essay in favor of tramps and against the movement to reinstate public whippings for vagrancy.

In many ways Whitman deliberately made herself a misfit to the norms of her society, and perhaps there is no better example of this impulse than her published defenses of poets considered immoral by many New Englanders, including Percy Shelley and Johann Wolfgang von Goethe. When Harriet Beecher Stowe, the abolitionist writer best known for *Uncle Tom's Cabin*, ignited a scandal in 1869 by publishing an account insinuating Lord Byron's incest with his half-sister and arguing that his works should be banished for fear of corrupting young minds, Whitman responded with a passionate defense in the *Providence Journal*. All of these essays, as well as her defense of Poe, are ripe with expressions of her individualism. "Whatever danger there may be in leaving man to decide for himself," she writes for example in praising Goethe, "there is surely far less than in any attempt to restrict the individual right of opinion through regard to expediency or respect for authority.

"The timid faith that fails to question," she concluded, "cannot satisfy us."

It should not be surprising that Whitman joined movements against slavery and for women's rights, composing numerous poems and essays for the cause. The admiration for the disruptive and unusual also led her to embrace many philosophical and spiritual movements that pushed the boundaries of the normal. She was an early adherent of Transcendentalism—that uniquely New England expression of idealism tinged with mysticism—and a strong proponent of mesmerism and occultism. After her brief engagement with Poe ended in 1848, she became an ardent supporter of Spiritualism, regularly hosting séances (often in attempts to communicate with Poe, who died in 1849) and writing detailed accounts for the *New-York Tribune*. Whitman remained a believer until her death and long after scientific critiques and exposures of fraud had far weakened public support and interest.

There is another eccentric element of Whitman that should not pass unnoticed, although in raising it, I am concerned that it may reduce this very complex individual to a stereotype of her gender. Her unique dress was well noted in her lifetime as a sign of her nonconformity and embrace of other-worldliness. Whitman always wore black or white dresses that were short sleeved and low cut on the neck. This was enough to raise suspicion, but the design was made the frequent subject of gossip by the inclusion of veils and scarfs. Further adding to the scurrilous fashion, "she also wore, thrown over her head and fastened under her chin, a soft, loose, white 'Shetland' shawl, completely covering her head—save her face—and shoulders." For some time, Whitman also adorned her neck with a black velvet ribbon on which a tiny wooden coffin was pinned. We may laugh today at the reaction of her generation to a look that approximates our contemporary gothic, but it is also lamentable that her case testifies to the overtired history of debating what women wear rather than what they think.

Her romance and tumultuous relationship with Poe has been the subject of many commentaries, studies, and even a drama composed in the 1980s by Norman George, so there is no need to expound on it here other than to relish in the tidbit that while once trying to determine if she would be in Providence and available for courting, Poe posed as an autograph collector. Some fans of Poe have upheld her as his true love, while others have criticized her for exploiting the romance to her own benefit. There are as many interpretations of this affair as there are seasons changing since it ended. When taken into the wider scope of Whitman's life, however, it confirms the patterns of her countercultural impulses and rebellious championing of broken and mysterious things.

Whitman was certainly no saint. Even supportive colleagues and later biographers noted, for example, her tendencies toward vanity, sarcasm, and stubbornness. Yet as her friend, the poet Sarah Jacobs quipped in a fitting tribute, "St. Helena," Whitman "was not good at hating" and furthermore

> Her creed in short was to believe
> Whatever she ought not to,
> A table rampart was her crest,
> Excelsior, her motto

And by these many oddities that stared down dull conventions, she found many admirers

in every far and every nigh-land
Throughout Europe, Asia, Africa, America, Hades, and Rhode Island.

Sarah Helen Whitman died in 1878. Her final poem was a memorial to her sister, Anna, and her final essay another heated contribution to the growing debates about Poe. Although she was included in occasional anthologies, only one book of poetry, *Hours of Life*, was published in her lifetime and another after her death. Her journalism, essays, and translations largely remain uncollected, waiting for someone—perhaps a reader of these lines—to return them to the prominence they once held for New Englanders, even as the woman who wrote them pushed against their most sacred held beliefs.

⚊⚊

If Whitman sought to be the center of attention—and change what it meant to be there, Frederick Goddard Tuckerman sought solace away from the crowds. Tuckerman has not suffered the same scholarly neglect as has Whitman—to the contrary, there is heated debate about his poetry and a new edition of his poems recently appeared—but he remains generally unknown outside academic circles and did not enjoy success in his lifetime. Explanations for his reclusiveness have ranged from a romantic temperament to sustained grief to lifelong shyness, and thankfully we do not have to resolve that issue here. Instead I would like to highlight Tuckerman's eccentric insularity as a fascinating counterpoint to Whitman's sociability.

Tuckerman was born into a wealthy and influential family in Boston in 1821. He was one of four children. His brother Edward would become a professor of botany at Amherst College (and, with his wife, a friend of Emily Dickinson). His brother Samuel was a musical composer and his sister Sophia a writer of poetry, fiction, and travelogues. According to a family genealogist, Frederick was named for a relative on his mother's side, Frederick Goddard, who was a companion of William Wordsworth and the subject of an elegy by the English poet when he died a young man by drowning in Lake Zurich.

Tuckerman's early life was one of considerable means, and his inherited wealth allowed him to pursue creative and intellectual interests throughout his life. There are also hints that he was far from a revolutionary. An early biographer, for example, captured a comment written in Tuckerman's journal when he was a boy of ten. "I promise to try to behave better at the table," it reads, "and to try and break myself of being so set and always wanting to have just what I like best all the time. This rule must be strictly observed by F. G. Tuckerman." This is a sentiment that surely could not have been written by Whitman's hand.

Tuckerman enrolled at Harvard in 1837 and left one year later, perhaps due to trouble with his eyesight. He returned to earn a law degree in 1842, but did not pursue a career as a lawyer or as a public figure in his family's tradition. Instead, in his mid-twenties, Tuckerman moved to Greenfield, Massachusetts. It was not a strictly rural town at the time; canals and the railroad made it an accessible and important stop, industry was thriving, and immigrants were coming in waves to work in the mills. But Greenfield was remote in comparison to Boston, and the surrounding farmlands and woods offered ample opportunity for retreats into nature balanced by the hours spent in reading. Once there, he took up an interest in astronomy, meteorology, and botany. In 1847 he married Hannah Jones, the daughter of a store owner in the town, and purchased a home. A daughter was born one year later, but she died stillborn or as an infant.

He began his life as a poet in 1849 with the publication of "November" in *The Literary World*, a New York magazine. It is marked by remorse, opening with the lines:

> OH! who is there of us that has not felt
> The sad decadence of the failing year,
> And marked the lesson still with grief and fear
> Writ in the rollèd leaf, and widely dealt?

He then describes in degrees scenes of natural desolation, until "all the world is harsh, and cold, and gray."

No one has suggested that Tuckerman initiated a poetic career in response to the passing of his daughter; indeed, until a few decades ago commentators were unaware that she existed. It is also notoriously risky to read biographical information out of creative works, and given that the remainder of the poem as well as his second publication—"April"—explore natural rather than human relations, this sad confession is a probable coincidence. The poem does, however, announce themes that appear again and again in his writings: nature and melancholy. As with Whitman, these were not unusual for their day. Tuckerman's eccentricities, then, came not from the subject of his work but from his decision to shy away from an active life of civic engagement, although he did pen a reverent hymn for the dedication of a cemetery in Greenfield in 1851.

Access to wealth allowed the young Tuckerman to travel. He visited Europe in 1851 and 1854. While there, he struck up a relationship with the poet laureate of Great Britain, Lord Tennyson. On this second trip, Tuckerman was invited to Farringford House, Tennyson's estate on the Isle of Wight, and the two corresponded occasionally thereafter. Tennyson thought fondly enough of his American guest to present him with the original copy of "Locksley Hall," a narrative poem that tells the tale of a rejected suitor. The meetings with Tennyson inspired Tuckerman; the years following his visits were among the most productive of his career. These were also the years in which his family grew with a son, Edward, and a daughter, Hannah.

Tragedy struck in 1857. A second son, Frederick, was born. Tuckerman's wife then died within a week, presumably from difficulties in childbirth. It is, again, unwise to speculate too broadly, but for a man who was already inclined toward privacy and a life directed toward his family rather than society, this loss surely had profound effects upon him. One commentator noted that in the cemetery where his family is buried, his wife's tombstone stands taller than his own and did so at a time when high stones were the prerogative of a family patriarch. He also inscribed upon it testimony from the Book of Lamentations:

To the memory of

Hannah L.

the beloved wife of

Frederick G. Tuckerman

this stone is placed by

her husband

"Behold and see all ye that pass

by, if there be any sorrow like

unto my sorrow"

All accounts concur that the gravitational pull of solitude grew stronger after his wife had passed. He continued to write, however, and the poems and sonnets reflect his grief.

In 1860 Tuckerman published a collection of his poetry at his own expense. The poems include sonnets and tributes to nature and the local landscape— "Picomegan," for example, salutes the town's Green River. His keen interests in botany illuminate the pages, in which there is as likely to be a reference to a flower or plant as to Greek myth or American history. There are also lengthy narrative poems dedicated to troubled lovers—including to Paulo and Francesca, the lustful couple sentenced to hell in Dante's *Inferno*—and to romances of legendary or invented figures from European and New England history. Tuckerman spends ink, furthermore, for a few outcasts and misunderstood figures—a schoolgirl whose mother's death left her to a family of men, a Mormon missionary who "saw the great world fume and foam on" and was threatened by a violent mob, an old beggar tossed aside by a selfish society (and to whom Tuckerman sees every reason to be the "arm and band" to his fading strength), and an epic fool whose life reminds the author of his own. It would be a mistake to see these as mere projections of his psyche, of course, but in a very quiet way, Tuckerman hailed those who do not quite fit in their world and gave them dignity through recognition.

He sent a copy of *Poems* to literati of his day, including his friend Tennyson, Nathaniel Hawthorne, Ralph Waldo Emerson, and Henry Wadsworth

Longfellow. They saluted his work and his promise. Hawthorne called the collection "remarkable" but wondered if it would enjoy readership as "their merit does not lie upon the surface, but must be looked for with faith and sympathy, and a kind of insight as when you look into a carbuncle to discover its hidden fire." He further suggested that Tuckerman's poems become more striking when they are read a second time—only then to lament "but who reads so much as once, in these days?" This encouragement provoked a response from Tuckerman, who wrote in gratitude a line that speaks volumes to his temperament. "For the book," he replied, "I claim little, but that it is New Englandy (I hope), was not written to please anybody, and is addressed to those only who understand it." Although the two did not continue a long conversation, they remained aware of each other, and Tuckerman considered purchasing The Wayside, Hawthorne's house in Concord, Massachusetts, when Hawthorne's widow put it up for sale.

The boldness of Tuckerman's declaration may be more a record of his eccentricity or sign of respect to Hawthorne than an actual desire *not* to be read. He had, after all, paid for the publication of the work, and he continued to seek out venues for other poems. His book was reissued in London in 1863 and in Boston in 1864 and 1869 and advertised heavily. And as it became clear that the collection would not be a commercial success, Tuckerman's creative output began to dwindle. Tragedy and sadness soon returned to him. His mother died in 1870 and his son Edward passed the following year at twenty-one. (He had also lost a close friend, for whom he wrote a loving elegy, in the Civil War.) Around that same time, Tuckerman moved into a boarding house in Greenfield, the American Home. His youngest son Frederick went to Amherst and was raised by his brother. And then in 1873 Tuckerman died of "disease of the heart."

When he passed, Tuckerman was already essentially forgotten. His brief obituary in the *Greenfield Gazette* only noted in passing that he "published several fine poems" yet did not fail to observe that "he lived a retired and secluded life among us." The notice did not mention that he had recently penned an ode for the dedication of a monument to Civil War soldiers at the behest of the town. It would take decades for his work to be rediscovered and, with it, for a number of unpublished poems—including his ode, "The Cricket," considered by many to be his finest work—to come to light.

But in that strange way that misfits often find their unappreciated gifts are welcomed generations after they have gone, Tuckerman left an unusual legacy to Greenfield. There is a trap ridge overlooking the town called Rocky Mountain. The views are striking, even today as the town has become a city. On this ledge there was a niche, a perfect location for a hiker to rest and drink in the scenery. It was, apparently, called the Poet's Inkwell as early as the 1840s. Tuckerman invoked the location in one of his poems, calling it the Poet's Rock, and in one of his herbariums he identified it as Poet's Seat. A tradition arose that he frequented the location. A wooden observation tower was installed there in the late 1800s and then replaced in 1912 by a sandstone tower. Rumor has occasionally suggested that the spot was sacred to many writers, but Tuckerman has become the sole poet identified with it. It was his memory that townspeople invoked to save the tower from demolition in the 1970s, and today there is now a plaque honoring their "gifted solitary poet."

Tuckerman was not exclusively a poet of misfits or eccentricity, but such figures and ideas find sympathy in his poetry. In closing, I think it is appropriate to mention that both Hawthorne and Emerson singled out one poem for praise, "The Stranger." It is another lengthy narrative, rich with imagery of Greenfield and the poet's encounter with that figure, who, like so many of Tuckerman's creative works, speaks to sorrow but also to the depths of a person who is not to be found among the crowd:

> And I have mourned for him and for his grief;
> Yet never heard his name, and never knew
> Word of his history, or why he came
> Into this outskirt of the wilder land.

8

~

THE MESMERISTS: JOHN BOVEE DODS AND PHINEAS PARKHURST QUIMBY

Leaving the train station in Old Saybrook, Connecticut, travelers can walk a short distance to a restaurant fronting Route 1, the Boston Post Road that plays such an important role in New England history. Today that restaurant is called the Monkey Farm Cafe, but it has gone through numerous incarnations and owners since it served as an inn during the late 1800s. For a brief period in the early 1950s, when it was still known as the Coulter House, the establishment boasted a most unusual owner: Sevengala the hypnotist. That is not a misprint for Svengali. Sevengala, or Sol Weinberger to his friends, was the second man to use that stage name; he received permission from the widow of the first, a prominent hypnotist and magician at the turn of the twentieth century. Weinberger hailed from the area of Southington and Bristol, Connecticut, where he opened the "House of Sevengala" lounge in the late 1940s before trying his hand in the summer resort town of Old Saybrook.

Advertisements for the Coulter House at the time emphasized Sevengala's unusual talents, as he performed shows throughout the week. "See the Impossible! The unbelievable actually takes place before your very eyes! You'll gasp for more!" exclaimed these promotions, promising, "One hour of chills and thrills!" When Sevengala gave up his ventures as a restauranteur to return to show business in 1952, newspapers as far as Hartford praised his "colorful" career and his entertaining, if odd, abilities, which were unique to the region. Today, when countless stage hypnotists perform throughout New England at casinos, comedy clubs, summer camps, amusement parks, colleges, and school auditoriums, it is easy to forget that trance entertainment once had a contentious past in becoming an acceptable form of amusement.

Part of that tension, both in the past and today, is generated by hypnotherapists and researchers chagrined at the use of trance states for nonmedical purposes. What is perhaps less known and underappreciated is the significant role that New England played in the history of this eccentric art and science. Mesmerism, an intellectual and practical forerunner of hypnosis, is a term honoring Franz Mesmer, the German physician who experimented with a phenomenon he called "animal magnetism" in the 1770s. The gist of this theory is that a naturally occurring force (often described as if it were a liquid), invisible to the human eye but possessed by all living beings, could be manipulated to induce trances capable of wondrous effects, including healing. For some time, it was all the rage among intellectual and medical circles in Europe and in the United States, with ample proponents and opponents in heated debate.

"Animal magnetism" and "mesmerism" crept into the parlance of the Northeast by the turn of the nineteenth century thanks to, on one hand, a few practitioners of its reputed medical use and, on the other hand, stage comedies, farces, and other related forms of entertainment that satirized or borrowed its tropes. A new wave of interest arose in the 1830s and 1840s, following a lecture tour by the Frenchman Charles Poyen, who arrived in Portland, Maine in 1834. Poyen was a young man at the time and made his way to Haverhill and Lowell, Massachusetts, where relatives had settled. As the story is told, in Lowell he met the mayor, Elisha Barrett, a physician who encouraged the mysterious lad to introduce magnetism to the wider public. Poyen began this quest in 1836.

Poyen's initial foray was, however, not well received, and he considered resigning from the tour and New England. Then, in September 1836, he was called to Pawtucket, Rhode Island, where he worked with Cynthia Ann Gleason, a young woman who proved an excellent somnambulist and agreed to accompany him as his entranced subject. With the encouragement of the editor of the *Providence Journal* and the president of Brown University, Poyen relaunched his tour, garnering increasing acclaim. Boston remained relatively unwelcoming ground, but Nashua, Lowell, Taunton, New Bedford, and Nantucket made up for it with successful lectures and sizeable audiences. Numerous people trained with Poyen or learned magnetism on their own. Providence, for example, emerged as a center of mesmerism. And by late 1837, interest in the practice spread to New York City and Philadelphia. So too did condemnation by medical journals and establishments.

In these early days, mesmerism was largely seen as a curative practice rather than as entertainment, although the dramatic elements and uncanny sights surely thrilled audiences. One particular skill that somnambulists purportedly exhibited while in trance seems preposterous today: the ability to see inside the human body as if with an X-ray. Gazing upon and within an afflicted person, entranced subjects were also thought to be able to diagnose the illness and proscribe proper remedies, even when they had no medical training. Similarly, the use of trances to heal or anesthetize people remained faddishly viable, even after ether became readily available. And when Spiritualism became a popular movement starting in the 1840s, it inherited many of the parascientific and parapsychological elements associated with magnetism, including the belief that mediums could spirit travel or communicate with beings beyond this world while in an altered state of consciousness. All of this was prelude to the influence of two eccentric individuals who left a captivating spell on New England.

John Bovee Dods, the first wonderworker, was born in 1795 in Florida, New York, and died in Brooklyn, but he spent several pivotal decades of his life in Maine and Massachusetts, earning a tangled reputation among New

Englanders that warrants inclusion in this book. His father died when he was a child and by his own admission, he believed that the spirit—or more appropriately, the apparition—of his parent visited him on numerous occasions in his youth. Other spirits of the dead, too, reportedly contacted him in his teenage years, directing him to his future endeavors. This was, of course, before the rise of Spiritualism proper, but not outside certain beliefs concerning ghostly visitations prevalent in the folklore of the Northeast.

Dods's first career (and his first claim to notoriety) was as a Protestant minister. Holding to my commitment not to treat genuine religious experience as eccentric, I am inclined to skip over this aspect of Dods's life, but it plays an essential role in his later and more unusual contributions. In March 1820, newspapers in Maine ignited with dramatic testimony written on behalf of the professors at the esteemed Bangor Theological Institute. It decried the actions of one John Bovee Dods—or Dods Bovee, as they took liberties with his name, not quite understanding Dutch American nomenclature—for a forgery of a letter of support to gain admittance to the school. The professors accused him of attempting a similar act at the seminary in Andover, Massachusetts, and resolved to expel him.

Dods, for his part, responded to the charges in the Bangor newspapers in November that same year, but could not persuade the seminary to reinstate him. Years later, a local history of the town of Union, Maine, recalled this "remarkable excitement" and a separate history of Penobscot County summarized the incident as staining Dods with the reputation of being "quite notorious" to such a degree that his attempts to rehabilitate opinions about him by opening a grammar school in Bangor failed utterly. It was, simply, not a fortuitous start to adulthood, especially for someone who prided himself on "uncommon piety" in his application to the seminary.

The young man's reputation may have been wounded at the time, but he recovered enough to become a minister in Levant, Maine, a village not far from Bangor, by 1823. One year later a supernatural event reportedly took place in his home. As he explained in the *Spiritual Telegraph*,

There was in winter of 1824 serious and unaccountable disturbances at my house, and continued almost nightly till the following March. I admit that the house was jarred, and at times shaken to its foundation, attended by a singular sound or noise, that continued sometimes all night at short intervals. These were witnessed by many persons, who in the course of the winter came out of curiosity, and remained all night. The whole country, far and near, was thrown into excitement, and while some believed the house was haunted, others believed and reported that I made the whole by some *underground, or concealed machinery!*

Dods insisted that no such chicanery was afoot and that, to the contrary, he had been personally visited by several "spirits of the departed" and held long conversations with them. Among the topics they discussed, the apparitions assured him that he would live to be eighty-four and that he would revolutionize the understanding of the spirit world. One of the spirits who appeared to him was a young woman who committed suicide by drowning. Dods assumed she would be eternally punished for her sinful act of self-destruction, but to his surprise he found a different result. The spirit had, Dods asserted, been in contact with him for years, evolving through four manifestations until she revealed her final, angelic nature in her "electrical and immortal body." When she visited him in this form, she playfully lifted off his hat, flew it over his house, returned it to his head, and wished him farewell until they met again in the afterlife.

These incidents led Dods to convert from more stringent Calvinist beliefs to Universalism, a Christian religious movement that stressed the eventual salvation of all people rather than the possibility of damnation. In 1826 he moved to Union, where he became a Universalist minister, although he maintained some relationship with Levant and expanded his reach into Rockland. In the 1830s and early 1840s Dods subsequently moved to Massachusetts, with ministries in Taunton, Provincetown (where he also founded a grammar school), and Fall River. His earliest publications during this time were book-length collections of sermons and copious—and lengthy—letters to the editors in newspapers from Maine to Rhode Island in conversation and response to critics on issues related to Christianity.

Dods's relocation to Massachusetts primed his awareness of mesmerism, although some biographers claim that he attended Poyen's lectures on the subject in Portland, Maine. Regardless of how he was introduced, once he learned of its potential, Dods experienced another conversion of sorts and trained as a mesmerist. As Sheila O'Brien Quinn noted in her study on the subject, mesmerism and evangelical revivalism often went well together, as both promised access to a benevolent force beyond the comprehension of human consciousness. Dods became instrumental in forging this link and did so at a time when he could capitalize on the growing interest among a sizeable populace, thereby inoculating himself against the dismissive charges of being a charlatan.

Boston had been a tough stage for Poyen when he began his tours, but by 1843 Dods delivered lectures on the subject to packed audiences—perhaps as many as two thousand—at Marlboro Chapel in that city. The publication of these talks, *Six Lectures on the Philosophy of Mesmerism*, sold well, in no small measure thanks to a robust advertising campaign that lasted for a half of a decade. The collection offers riveting insights into Dods's eclectic mind and to the marriage of disparate subjects spanning animal magnetism, "mental electricity," science, clairvoyance, the five degrees of mesmerism, and Jesus and the Apostles.

In Dods's estimation these topics share more features than that list portends. His major contribution to the discussion is an emphasis on electricity as the force bridging the spiritual and physical worlds, working through the nervous system of animate beings. (Commentators have noted, however, that Dods possessed expertise in neither the science of electricity nor neurology.) And following an argument once offered by Poyen, Dods argued that Jesus himself was a mesmerist and that his call to heal the sick—that is, to bring "the wonderful power to charm all pain"—was proof of his membership in this illustrious group.

Dods continued this theme in what is arguably his magnum opus, *The Philosophy of Electrical Psychology*, this becoming his preferred term rather than *magnetism* or *mesmerism*. This work, a collection of twelve lectures, is another glimpse into a rich hybridization of religion, science, and parapsychology. Dods recognized the inherently eccentric nature of his work, noting in Lecture Two that "such strange facts as I have stated are most trying to human credulity" and likely to "draw forth the sneers of mankind," but he promised to persist in their pursuit as the advancement of science and scripture would demand. *Electrical Psychology*, like its older sibling, navigates a striking array of topics at a rapid pace, from proof of the existence of a Deity to reasons for different-colored blood to the physics of volcanoes to the proper use of herbs. And as with *Six Lectures*, Dods holds all these examples together by recourse to electricity as the connecting force between mind and matter and "the body of God" itself.

Once this connection was fully appreciated, Dods argued, the cure of disease was relatively simple. Throughout *Electrical Psychology* he drew examples of people relieved of blindness, deafness, palsy, and paralysis through "electro-curapathy," the medical practice founded on these insights. While its pages are replete with comments that would be laughable today, there are passages of sweeping implications that extend far beyond the conventional understandings of his time. His notion that the mind and brain were intimately related, for example, has a contemporary ring in its foreshadowing of neuroscience, and even his idea that there are two brains—or as he said in later interviews, that the mind is double—and both voluntary and involuntary nerves, while askew in many ways, nevertheless presages psychoanalytic concepts about the unconscious.

In his eleventh lecture, Dods revealed the "secret"—his word—of electrical psychology, providing information for the layperson to practice mesmerism. This revelation, while laudable for its populist impulse, was also a promotional tool. Dods attested that the most efficient way to benefit from the wisdom of his book would be to visit him directly for training. And with respect to the split between medical and entertainment uses of trance, Lecture One fleshes out some of the sights that constituted his public performances. Dods revealed that he could control the motion of subjects, rendering it impossible for them to stand up or sit down. He could take away their power of speech, sight, hearing, or memory. He could, the essay continues, "change the personal identity of certain individuals, making them imagine for the time being that they are persons of color, that they belong to the opposite sex, or that they are some renowned general, orator, statesman, or what-not." He could, furthermore, "change the appearance and taste of water in rapid succession to that of lemonade, honey, vinegar, molasses, wormwood, coffee, milk, brandy; the latter producing all the intoxicating effects of alcohol" or make subjects experience thunderstorms as if they were under imminent threat.

All of these examples—here used as proof of electrical psychology and its utility for healing—are, of course, precisely the classic antics that attendees would expect at one of Sevengala's gigs. But in 1850, the year that Dods published *Electrical Psychology*, these routines inspired enough awe to secure him an invitation to speak to the US Congress at the invitation of distinguished politicians including Daniel Webster and Henry Clay. (Dods had, a decade earlier, similarly been invited to speak before the Massachusetts legislature.) That same year, he left Massachusetts for Brooklyn, where he established a practice and resided for the remainder of his life, although he returned to New England often on the lecture circuit and likely attracted New Englanders to train with him in New York.

Dods's appetite for conversion, however, had one more eruption. In 1854 he published *Spirit Manifestations Examined and Explained* (another book on immortality appeared between *Electrical Psychology* and this one) that debunked the rising tide of Spiritualism. Dods had wondered if the apparitions that visited him in the decades prior were simply hallucinations produced by mesmeric effects, and in this work he set out to critique misunderstandings of such experiences. He was, however, generally evenhanded and sympathetic to Spiritualists, whom he regarded as misguided about natural phenomena but sincere in their beliefs. By 1856 Dods had become a proponent of Spiritualism, albeit in the vein of his insights, a change of opinion that earned him yet another round of criticism for being an intellectual opportunist. He did not live to eighty-four, dying instead in 1872 at the age of seventy-six, having lived a life of changing but consistently eccentric interests.

—~—

Phineas Parkhurst Quimby is perhaps best known for his influence upon the New Thought movement and his work over several years with Mary Baker Eddy, the founder of Christian Science. Although he did not publish extensively in his lifetime, and the majority of his manuscripts were not made available until the death of his son in the 1920s, Quimby should not be considered an obscure figure, as his healing practice may have attended to several thousand patients during the two decades it was operational. Akin to Dods, Quimby possessed an inventive mind that synthesized and expanded upon the ideas circulating in his day, notably mesmerism and Transcendentalism, a philosophical movement associated with idealism and inner experience. Quimby, however, arguably went further than any of his contemporaries in pursuit of the mind–body relationship and its effects on health.

Born in Lebanon, New Hampshire, in 1802 to a blacksmith, Quimby relocated with his family two years later to Belfast, Maine, where he lived for the preponderance of his life. He followed his brother to work as a clockmaker and registered several patents related to this line of work. A pivotal moment came in the 1830s, however, when he attended one of Poyen's lectures. As the biographies written about him by admirers explain, he essentially gave up his career and followed Poyen's tour until he was himself capable of mesmerizing others. Once proficient in this skill, Quimby launched his own lecture tour, mostly in Maine and maritime Canada. And like Poyen, he benefited from having an accompanying somnambulist, Lucius Burkmar, travel with him. Although some dramatic accounts by his supporters suggested that Quimby was often subject to threats of mob violence or accusations of nefarious activity, the newspaper reports from his time denoted generally favorable reception.

These public "experiments" were, for all intents and purposes, akin to the demonstrations people would have seen throughout New England, although

Quimby was inclined to promote the potential health benefits of the practice. He became skillful at inducing a mesmeric sleep in Burkmar simply by staring at him—another trope that would cross into the comedy realm—and according to numerous accounts, the two could "communicate" without the use of language, making it appear as though the subject did what was asked of him automatically and telepathically. At the time, these strange performances confirmed the prevalent belief that a force akin to magnetism or electricity was at work animating the entranced body.

Quimby, like Dods and other mesmerists, had a repertoire of examples to demonstrate mesmerism and impress the crowds. In his manuscripts, he recorded a popular routine in which he handed Burkmar a six-inch ruler but instructed him to imagine it a twelve-inch one. "He would immediately divide the rule into twelve inches by counting," wrote Quimby of the performance. "I have first asked him to tell me how long it was," he continued, "and he would answer me correctly. I would then ask him to look again, and then I would imagine any length I pleased, and he would answer me according to the impression I produced by my imagination." This is a harmless example, and one that survives in stage hypnosis, but as with other tours, Quimby's lectures also included a routine in which Burkmar, deep in trance, became a medical clairvoyant capable of peering into afflicted people, examining their viscera, and recommending cures to the diagnosed diseases found buried within.

This practice, as amazing as it must have seemed to audiences, eventually led Quimby to question the basis of mesmerism as grounded in an exchange of some force between magnetizer and subject. Several stories, many apocryphal, arose to explain the evolution of Quimby's attitudes on the matter. In one tale, Quimby found it impossible to mesmerize his subject during thunderstorms, and he attributed the failure to alterations in the atmosphere interfering with the transfer of energy. When he was successful on an attempt another day and subsequently learned that a storm was in the area, he decided to recalibrate his beliefs on the role of external forces. In a second tale, Quimby observed that an herb recommended to a patient failed to cure when proscribed by a doctor but succeeded when the same herb was suggested by a somnambulist, a contradiction that led him to think the suffering person wanted to believe in the cure only under certain conditions.

In the third tale Quimby himself was the beneficiary of medical advice. As a child he suffered from tuberculosis and reportedly found a way to heal himself by occupying his mind with pleasurable activities that overcame the lethargy associated with illness. He was, it seems, always considering the role that the mind had in healing but needed a final push to make the intellectual leap. It came when Burkmar unexpectedly turned to him when in trance— something Quimby forbade on principle—and correctly identified an illness plaguing Quimby's kidneys. Burkmar then "healed" the organs by laying his hands on Quimby, who recovered from the pain. "Now what is the secret of the cure?" Quimby himself asks in relating this story, "When he could cure me in the way he proposed, I began to think: and I discovered that I had been deceived into a belief that made me sick." Quimby did not believe that Burkmar actually healed him, but that he allowed his body to heal itself by going with the performance rather than against it.

Quimby changed his opinion, then, from upholding that the mesmerist or somnambulist had an ability to heal the sick by manipulating a connecting energy. In replacement he became convinced that illness—and healing— resided in the mind of the patient. In effect he became an eccentric among mesmerists, who themselves were already an eccentric lot, and in time he dismissed magnetism as a "stupendous humbug." By 1847 Quimby parted ways with Burkmar and retired from the lecture circuit. He returned to Belfast and to his early skills with technology, opening a business producing daguerreotypes, the forerunner of photographs. He did not, however, abandon his interests in healing—and indeed, daguerreotyping, a process of exchanging impressions, shadows, and light to create a suggestive image, served as an apt metaphor for his ideas about the mind.

A few years later Quimby commenced a new career as a healer—he was, accordingly, called Dr. Quimby by those who consulted with him—first in Bangor and then, from 1859 to 1865, in Portland, Maine. Although he had moved beyond animal magnetism as an explanation for curative practices,

Quimby did rely upon mesmeric techniques to "control the mind" of the sufferer and put into it the idea of healing. The accounts of these sessions are, pun intended, enthralling. In an ideal encounter Quimby and his patient would sit in silence until he ascertained the afflicting illness, almost as if a clairvoyant himself. Then he would initiate a process of directed conversation—a talking cure, in the purest sense—in order to convince his consultant to adopt a new language and with it a new mind-set that rejected the deception of illness. Occasionally he would physically touch or massage the diseased part of the body, but admitted that this was only to help coax the person into believing in the healing process.

As commentators have noticed, Quimby practiced something akin to psychoanalysis or neuro-linguistic programming long before either was formally recognized. Others have argued that he was a successful proponent of the placebo effect upon a willing audience. The terminology of his therapeutic methods also has a strikingly contemporary ring to it, resembling much of the self-help industry. Quimby called his program "the Truth," for example, and although it drew upon conventional religious language of his day, he was decidedly critical of formalized religion as a source of self-doubt, guilt, and other determinants of psychological pain. But he also recognized that his unorthodox approach could earn him a reputation for eccentricity. "To be unpopular," he once wrote, "be honest in every act; treat others with respect; mind your own affairs and permit others to do the same. Then like an old fashioned person you will be out of society and no one will care for you."

Quimby returned to Belfast in 1865 and died the following year. His son, George, explained in a biographical essay in *New England Magazine* in 1888 that his father was utterly exhausted at the end of his life, having taken on so many clients and often at very little expense to them. He left behind a sizeable collection of manuscripts that were slowly reconstructed by his closest friends, clients, and other supporters, many of whom themselves went on to promote mind healing or related approaches to therapy. These writings, especially his letters to patients, reveal a man of genuine compassion and—perhaps quite unlike many self-help gurus of today—little attempt at self-aggrandizement or the promotion of cultist activity that would lead to raw financial gains.

It is not that Quimby was immune to hubris. In a letter from 1862, for example, he declared his method "entirely original" and boldly asserted that he never made "war with medicine, but opinions," and in comments in response to critics he professed willingness to be condemned as that put him in company with Jesus, a fellow healer of the sick. These outbursts were, however, rare in comparison with his tempered and humble concern for his patients and the relief of their suffering. In the end, the veracity of his ideas about healing and the mind must be left to the reader to accept or to deny, but there is another lesson to be drawn that does not require the resolution of that issue. Quimby reminds us, after all, that the weird will always prove attractive to people who want a better life.

9

THE FORTUNE-TELLERS: MOLL PITCHER AND MARY SCANNELL PEPPER VANDERBILT

The enigmatic fortune-teller Moll Pitcher has been the subject of countless newspaper articles, essays, a novel, a dramatic play, and several poems, many written decades after she passed in 1813, a sure sign of the lasting impression she made on New England. In many ways she is a prime example of an invented eccentric—that is, her reputation as a person outside the norm, while certainly part of her mystique while alive, grew exponentially in the century after she left this world. As someone whose story quickly entered the realm of folklore and literature, the facts about her life are difficult to substantiate and often contradictory. But all records agree that she was, as one newspaper neatly summarized, "no ordinary woman," whose name was known by all people in New England and by many throughout the globe.

Pitcher's life centered in Lynn, Massachusetts, where for several decades—some reports said half a century—she held court telling fortunes to visitors at her home near High Rock, an impressive hill then on the outskirts of the town.

The lore surrounding Pitcher so nears the speculative that her birth year is only guessed to be 1738 based on reports that she was seventy-five when she passed. Although her contemporaries neglected to record certain specific details of her life, her name did appear regularly in regional newspapers throughout the late 1700s, often as in a proverbial sense—"Old Moll Pitcher" being code for foreknowledge—or in a polite jest, as a number of advertisements for lotteries played off her fame by promising better chances than she could offer. Not infrequently these passing comments were meant to mock shortsighted politicians who did not possess an appreciation of the future as did the sibylline Pitcher.

There is no doubt that she was well-known in her time. The only question is how well-known. Some reports, for example, claimed that she was consulted by European nobility as well as countless people in New England. These exaggerations are not surprising given the preeminence of ships traveling throughout the world from ports near Lynn, and according to one commentator writing soon after her death, anxious seamen were among her regular consultants. Merchants favored her, too, as did those searching for lost possessions or missing people. Young people frequented her home in the hopes of discovering their fate in love. But even those who were not superstitious took an interest in Pitcher, who earned the nickname the "Witch of Lynn" and thrilled audiences with her mysterious gifts.

In 1829 Alonzo Lewis—himself known as "the Bard of Lynn" for his poetic works—published a town history that included considerable space on Pitcher. In his book Lewis established many details that became canon for her story. Most important among them was that her grandfather, John Dimond, hailed from Marblehead, Massachusetts, and "exercised the same pretensions" as she did. Maddeningly, Lewis also fell into the pattern we have seen too often, giving far too much attention to her physical appearance, although his description was generally sympathetic. "She had that contour of face and expression," he opined, "which, without being positively beautiful, is, nevertheless, decidedly interesting—a thoughtful, pensive, and sometimes downcast look, almost approaching to melancholy—an eye, when it looked at you, of calm and keen penetration—and an expression of intelligent discernment, half mingled with a glance of shrewdness." My reason for mentioning this description will soon become apparent.

Lewis offered other poignant information about Pitcher, calling her "benevolent in her disposition" and presenting as an example that she would walk two miles daily, before sunrise, to a mill in order to purchase meals for a poor widow and her children. Lewis was, put simply, a writer who admired Pitcher, and further argued that given her "influence in shaping the fortunes of thousands," not all of her prophecies could have been explained as guesswork. The picture that emerges from this account—which was reprinted in newspapers throughout the Northeast and became influential upon all future reports—was certainly not of a misfit or even an eccentric, other than in someone who was very skilled at reading the desires of her audience.

An alternative impression arrived in earnest in a poem composed by John Greenleaf Whittier in 1832 which, like Lewis's earlier account, was reprinted and anthologized in numerous papers across New England. It is a lengthy work of some nine hundred lines in three parts, and it lacks the generosity and admiration of Lewis in every way. From the first line, Pitcher is a cackling witch, who, standing on High Rock, appears as

> A wasted, gray and meagre hag,
> In features evil as her lot.
> She had the crooked nose of a witch,
> And a crooked back and chin,
> And in her gait she had a hitch,
> And in her hand she carried a switch,
> To aid her work of sin.

Whittier—who, as many have noted, never met Pitcher—was only warming up the dramatic tension with this unflattering description of her base features. The poem concerns the visitation of a young maiden, Adela, whose beauty is the counterpoint to Pitcher's ugliness. Adela has come to have her fortune told and Pitcher takes the opportunity for revenge against the maiden who had formerly doubted her powers. She spins a story of Adela's secret lover lost at sea with just enough of the facts correct to convince the young woman of the prophecy. The news breaks Adela emotionally and she wanders in despair from the beach to the forest where the two lovers would rendezvous. Then, in the final part of the poem, her lover Henry returns and reunites with her. The poem ends when Pitcher, years later, suffering alone on her deathbed, is suddenly approached by Adela and Henry's daughter, a moment that allows the witch to repent before she expires.

This poem, coupled with an anonymous story (attributed both to Nathaniel Hawthorne and Edward Everett), "The Modern Job" (which fictionalized Pitcher as a melancholic who lost her only son at sea), and Joseph Stevens Jones's play "Moll Pitcher; or, the Fortune Teller of Lynn" (which depicted her again as a witch along the lines of Whittier's portrayal), launched a literary rendition that dominated the second half of the nineteenth century. Jones's play, in particular, was popular for several decades and toured the nation. And while these works generated interest in Pitcher as an outsider to society and its norms, they also invited others to join in her transformation into a hopelessly eccentric character. A Newburyport newspaper, for example, ran a story of a man who consulted her after his chickens were stolen. When he took his neighbor to court and was asked for evidence, he produced a letter from Pitcher with the name of the accused. The judge, so the anecdote concludes, was not amused.

By the late 1860s, accounts explained her remarkable skills as mere chicanery: Namely that she would hide in her house when visitors came and recruited a daughter to inquire upon them in order to learn their secrets and appear prophetic. And with this turn so came a mild critique of her gullible audiences. As one newspaper from Boston explained, Pitcher "made a good living out of simpletons, whom she could read like a glass." By the 1870s more humorous anecdotes appeared in illustrious magazines such as *Harper's*, including a tall tale that when asked about the location of hidden treasure, she retorted that if she had the power to see such things, she would have done so to her own benefit long ago. By the late 1800s Pitcher was a regular feature in historical and literary magazines and folklore anthologies, and was the protagonist of yet another well-received work, Ellen Mary Griffin Hoey's novel, *Moll Pitcher's Prophecies; Or, the American Sibyl*, which popularized the notion that she aided Washington during the American Revolution.

As time passed, newspapers also began to characterize Pitcher in more negative terms as a con artist or thief and did so without substantial evidence. One anecdote, related in a Boston newspaper in 1879, overtly took this path in describing her "many eccentricities," which included wearing a dress with very large pockets into which she would drop pilfered items at a store. The tale is likely fictional and developed long after she died, but it conjures a memory about her motives, which was known in the community as early as Lewis's commentary. Pitcher's husband was a shoemaker, it seems, and the family was poor, so she supplemented their income and "supported her family by her skill." These impoverished circumstances certainly should not be ignored in favor of fictional depictions of nefarious behavior. After all, if doing what one has to do to help one's family survive is a sign of eccentricity, then it is to be hoped ours is a world of eccentrics.

In the case of Mary "May" Scannell Pepper Vanderbilt, there is a very clear line dividing her supporters who considered her an extraordinary medium and her detractors who thought her to be a swindler of the highest order. She was without question a woman of contradictions. Certainties about her are few. She was born Mary Scannell in Mansfield, Massachusetts, in 1867 and at some point in her youth moved to Rhode Island near Providence. She was not a child of wealth or privilege. A few reports, for example, suggested that her father was a broom maker, and still others paint a more tragic tale of her mother dying when she was three, at which time she was left in the care of an aunt. Her early adult life necessitated domestic work that was not glamorous as a cleaner, a washerwoman, or a dairymaid.

By the turn of the twentieth century, Scannell was one of the most popular lecturers and mediums in the Northeast, making regular stops in Hartford, Providence, and Boston, as well as the area comprised of Saugus, Lynn, and

Swampscott, then a hotbed for Spiritualism. In 1904 she became the pastor of the First Spiritualist Church of Brooklyn, known in the *New York Times* as the Fraternity of the Soul Communion Church. Although her home and base of operations had moved to New York, she remained thoroughly involved in her "beloved New England" through lectures, séances, and participation in various Spiritualist camps and resorts, especially the ones located at Lake Pleasant, Massachusetts, and Etna, Maine, where she served as a presiding officer. She regarded Etna as "the dearest spot on earth," and even today she remains esteemed as their "most famous medium." Scannell served seventeen years there and could bring crowds, according to reports, of ten thousand people.

Spiritualism is mentioned elsewhere in this book, and given the important role it has played in the conceptualization of eccentricity in New England, it deserves further explanation. March 31, 1840, is frequently cited as the originating date for modern Spiritualism, when two sisters, Margaret and Kate Fox, claimed to have established contact with a spirit in their home in Hydesville, New York, by means of rappings—that is, knocking sounds produced by the spirit to communicate with this world. Within a decade, Spiritualism became a prominent movement, especially in the Northeast. Typical Spiritualist events featured a medium in communication with a spirit through any number of means such as séances, trances, psychometry, or automatic writing. Groups of believers and skeptics attended these events to seek answers to questions or guidance for the future.

By the 1860s loose confederations of Spiritualists began to gather regularly, and in 1893 the National Spiritualist Alliance incorporated. In the Northeast, Spiritualism raged from the 1870s to the 1920s. Periodicals and countless books followed, as did the rise of Spiritualist summer camps that provided additional recreation for the upper- and middle-class families who vacationed there. In the twentieth century, Spiritualism both saw a sharp decline in membership (especially during the economic turmoil of the Great Depression) and moved toward formal recognition as a religious movement. Earnest practitioners of Spiritualism maintain active services, congregations, and camps to this day.

Unfortunately the history of modern Spiritualism was marred by the prevalence of fraud mediums and others who exploited sincere believers, and it is precisely this issue that Scannell was thrust into. From the time she emerged on the lecture and séance circuit, she was surrounded by controversy. Newspapers in New England routinely reported on her activities—at the time she was known as May Pepper, taking the surname of her first partner, George Pepper—and drew sizeable crowds. She was the darling example in the works of several true believers, including Isaak Funk's (of Funk and Wagnalls) *The Psychic Riddle* and William Usborne Moore's *Glimpses of the Next State*. Willy Reichel, in his *An Occultist's Travels*, recorded a detailed encounter with Scannell at one of her services. "Her Tuesday and Friday sittings are so frequented," he writes, "that her sister, who sits at the entrance as cashier (50 cents each person) simply closes the door when there are no more chairs vacant, and many people are thus turned away." Reichel then described how visitors would leave sealed envelopes with questions on a table, a number of which Scannell would select at her pleasure, tear off a piece, put the letter in her mouth, and then deliver her prophecy.

If Reichel's account is accurate, Scannell selected at random and did not employ stooge letters. He noted, for example, that she occasionally answered queries that were not asked or did not answer questions that were posed. This disconnect was explained, however, on the grounds that contact with the spirit world was imperfect. Reichel also reported that if audience members challenged her, Scannell could avenge herself by revealing dishonorable information about her antagonists. She was, for her part, equally condemned and routinely dared by Joseph Rinn, a professional magician and skeptic (and friend of Harry Houdini), to submit to tests of his choosing. Scannell never accepted Rinn's offer.

Oddly Reichel did not mention "Bright Eyes," the spirit who was most closely associated with Scannell. Bright Eyes was reportedly an Indian girl (sometimes of the Kickapoo people and other times from New Bedford or Newburyport) and sometimes a half-Indian and half-French girl. The story is told that Scannell once confronted a skeptic at a meeting by prophetically recalling that he was a photographer who had taken a picture of Bright Eyes on his travels, unbeknownst to him. The photographer reportedly consulted his collection, discovered the image to his surprise, and rewarded Scannell by sending it to her. Another devotee, however, told a story that Scannell and her husband traveled to the western regions of the United States where, struck by the abject poverty of the indigenous people, they rescued and adopted a young girl, Bright Eyes. She soon succumbed to illness, but returned as a spirit to her caregiver.

Similarly, Scannell and her supporters provided many tales of her first encounter with Bright Eyes's spirit form. In some accounts Scannell was a teenager whom the spirit approached when she was visiting friends of her family in Narragansett, Rhode Island. In this tale she initially refused to accept the call of responsibility to mediumship, but found the courage within a few days. Other stories maintained that she was several years older and still others that she was a young girl of nine years. Once the connection occurred, however, Bright Eyes and Scannell were loyal interlocutors and the spirit was, purportedly, keenly interested in her medium's welfare. A particularly rewarding tale, for example, explained how Bright Eyes once guided Scannell and a companion out from being lost in the winding streets of Boston!

The act of welfare that concerned many people, however, was Scannell's marriage to Edward Ward Vanderbilt, a wealthy lumber merchant, who began to attend her services following the death of his first wife. Bright Eyes gave him hope, and her messages about his wife's spirit apparently raised Vanderbilt from despondency. In time Bright Eyes recommended that Vanderbilt care for Scannell by purchasing numerous gifts—including an expensive apartment—and then encouraged him to marry her, which he did in June 1907. He was more than twenty years older than she. In July that same year, Vanderbilt's daughter, Minerva, and his brother and sister sued to have him found incompetent and reclaim all of his fortune, which he had signed over entirely to Scannell.

The trials that ensued gripped the nation. Over several weeks the courtroom filled with salacious details. Accusations arose that Scannell was not formally married to George Pepper, and that he abandoned his actual wife and child for her. Testimony was given by a mysterious and veiled "woman in blue" (later identified) that Scannell had several lovers and affairs. Letters were produced from "Bright Eyes" and "Mamma"—Vanderbilt's first wife, channeled through Scannell—encouraging him to marry his medium. Information about Scannell's life poured out, including her previous claim to have been a medium for the spirit of an Irishman—a "Dublin ghost," as the newspapers called him—who attempted to convince a young man in Providence to marry her.

An expert witness, a neurologist from Long Island State Hospital, testified that no sane man would be a Spiritualist, opening questions of religious discrimination. Vanderbilt himself testified and described occasions when "Bright Eyes" would call him on the telephone. And when Scannell took the stand, she explained that she had no memory of those calls or letters, as she became unconscious during her trances. At one point an attorney asked her to read a closed envelope, but Scannell again insisted that it was the spirits and not she who could determine when to engage in such activities.

Throughout these proceedings, Scannell continued to attend Spiritualist retreats and the lecture circuit, visiting her regular haunts. Indeed, on more than one occasion the court expected her presence and had to spend resources to locate her, only to find her among one of the groups in New England. And despite her announcement of retirement when she married Vanderbilt, as the outcome looked less promising for her, Scannell increased her visibility at locales where she found supportive audiences for her side of the story. At the end of the trial, Vanderbilt was found incompetent, but after a lengthy appeal and another costly trial, the decision was reversed and his marriage to Scannell was officially recognized. Scannell would pass in 1919 and Vanderbilt in 1926; in 1927 his two daughters reclaimed what remained of his fortune.

The affair made Scannell a pariah in New York City, but she found welcoming audiences in New England and spent the final years of her life actively involved in the administration of the Etna Camp, where her ashes were eventually buried. Two years after her departure from the world of the living, her closest associates published a hagiography, *Mary S. Vanderbilt: A Twentieth Century*

Seer, which included loving reminiscences, the text of a lecture she delivered in Hartford, and poems in her honor, one of which proffers the tender lines:

> Oh spirit rare! Who guided us so long,
> Along the rough and stony paths of life
> Who hushed our fears, and taught us right from wrong,
> Who dried our tears, and helped us bear our strife.

Was Scannell a believer in her own abilities, or, as Minerva Vanderbilt accused her, "an unscrupulous fraud" who aimed to bilk susceptible and earnest Spiritualists? This decision remains a matter of perspective, but no one can doubt that Scannell's life was extraordinary.

10

THE PROPHET: WILLIAM SHELDON

In the early summer of 1871, newspapers and journals throughout the country published an obituary on the passing of "an eccentric old gentleman," William Sheldon of Longmeadow, Massachusetts. Few could resist mention of his unique habit of wearing what a later recollection called an "antique costume." As the *Springfield Republican* explained, Sheldon could regularly be seen walking about town in "a bell-crowned hat of great breadth and height, a high standing collar sustained by a white cravat with ample bows and double frilled shirt bosom, and to complete the effect, a blue dress-coat with gilt buttons, and pantaloons of a cut too ancient for minute description." That is, he dressed in a manner befitting someone who upheld the station of an aristocrat prior to the American Revolution. And, furthermore, Sheldon would routinely admit his loyalist inclinations to England, despite being born in 1788—the same year that Massachusetts ratified the Constitution to become the sixth state of the union. Sheldon's admiration was, however, much more than a case of an extreme Anglophile. As a lifelong interpreter of Scripture, he believed throughout his life that the end-time was fast approaching and prophesized that England—and eventually New England—would play a major role in their events.

Our tale begins here, but in many ways Sheldon's story begins many generations before he was born. He was a direct descendent of John Williams, the well-known minister who was captured in the Raid on Deerfield in 1704 by Indian allies to the French, and could also claim the fiery Puritan ministers Increase and Cotton Mather in his family tree. Although *obsession* may be too clinical a term to describe his relationship with his ancestors, their past clearly inspired his imagination. His father, a descendent of an equally influential family in Hartford, was a merchant who moved to Springfield and became a "doctor"—a term applied at the time to those who were druggists—and eventually involved himself in local and state politics, serving as a selectman several times and as a representative to the General Court in 1812. As the child of such a powerful and wealthy dynasty, Sheldon was able to indulge his passions with abandon—or as the *Republican* noted in his obituary, "An ample income exempted him from labor and gave him leisure to cultivate his oddities." When his father died in 1818, he and his mother returned to her native Longmeadow. Sheldon was then a man of thirty, but as the *Republican* again notes, that did not prohibit his "fond mother" from "assiduously devoting her remaining days to that tender and indulgent care which, conspiring with his natural idiosyncrasies, developed a life so singular and original as to demand an obituary."

William Sheldon was an eccentric who took great interest in other eccentrics. Unlike many others in this book, his eccentricity is also bound up with his writings, which number nearly nine hundred pages. Many of them are now available online for readers who wish to indulge in the journey of reading them. The Longmeadow Historical Society also has a number of letters, daguerreotypes of Sheldon, and other items of interest. It is no easy task to read Sheldon's work on account of his tendency to ramble or to dwell upon obscure references. The following short sentence is typical in packing a wallop of information:

Odicism, or the science of od-force, confirms the testimony of Scripture, as to the nature of spiritual existence—that it is MATERIAL.

Science, pseudoscience, religion, and occultism all collide in Sheldon's prophetic writings. The difficulty they present for the reader, however, also provides a rich record of the mind of an eccentric and his curious habits, beliefs, and activities.

Little is known about Sheldon's personal life outside his writings. A brief mortuary notice in the *Lowell Daily Citizen* mentions that he suffered from feeble health at the age of thirty—coinciding with his father's death—and thereafter took to a "rigid dietetics" that included weighing his food for much of the remainder of his life. Such behavior was not uncommon among eccentrics of the day, and, although it may seem to many readers to be a sign of compulsive habits, there is no indication that this practice or the foods he consumed shortened his life: He lived until he was eighty-three, although he himself had apparently thought he would live to see a full century on Earth.

By his own assertion, he began the study of Biblical prophecy in 1827, when he was nearing forty. His first work, *Millenial Institutions: Being a Comment on the Fortieth Chapter of the Prophet Ezekiel*, appeared in 1833 and survives today online and in several libraries throughout the Northeast. But as far as prophecies based on Scripture go, Sheldon's subject matter and interpretation are strangely run-of-the-mill. The passage from Ezekiel that he focuses on depicts a vision in which the Biblical prophet sees a new temple in Jerusalem and with it the return of the Lord's presence. Even in early Christian times, this verse was invoked as a forerunner of millennial prophecy. The Book of Revelation, for example, cites Ezekiel often and many people seeking to unlock its mysteries interpreted it as prophetic of the end-time. In this, then, Sheldon was not particularly novel.

His unique contribution came in his interpretation of the passage as a map of the world. That is, Sheldon read the description of the new temple against what he took to be the known locations of the world at the time of its composition so that, for example, the reference to a particular gate would refer to a city or region of the world. Drawing up his plans, he was able to include virtually all of Europe and the Middle East and much of Asia and Africa. He was, furthermore, able to suggest a rough time line of events from the scripture, predicting key moments in 1865, 1897, 1923, and 1950, among others. The details grow erudite and complex and, as with all of Sheldon's prophecies, deserve a lengthier study, so I will not go through them meticulously here, other than to mention his essential revelation was that England would be the chosen kingdom to initiate the institutions of the new millennium—meaning the Second Coming and the new world to follow. In offering this suggestion, Sheldon not only predicted global events to come but also interpreted then recent events (such as July Revolution in Paris in 1830) as signs of the prophecy in motion.

The United States is almost an afterthought in Sheldon's first book, although there are clues to where he would later continue. He asserts, for example, that Americans could only enter the new millennial city by returning to a paternal government and by turning away from the individualism inherent in a nation that, on one hand, rejected class distinctions and, on the other, promoted cupidity in pursuit of earthly gains such as wealth or political power. To state it plainly, Sheldon was making the case for a world very similar to his imagined ideals of his ancestors: those reverend ministers such as the Mathers and John and Stephen Williams, who were subjects of England and who never knew (or in the case of Stephen Williams, who held in suspicion) the nation of the United States after its revolution.

This nostalgic desire inspired more than his literary works; it guided nearly every aspect of his life. It also seemed to bring him some early disappointment. By his own account, Sheldon sent a copy of *Millenial Institutions* (and two other works, including a musical composition) to England, presumably to the royal family itself, in order to inform them of the role to be played by that nation in the prophecy. The result, however, was not the warm embrace he hoped for, but a rejection of the work as "humbug" and additional neglect—and, in his mind, perhaps even an attempt to poison him in order to frighten him into silence.

His admission of belief that nefarious forces sought to silence him came in his next major work, *The Seventh Vial: Consisting of Brief Comments on Various Scriptures; and of Observations on Divers Topics*, published in Springfield in 1849 when he was just over sixty. The entire work is a masterpiece of conspiratorial eccentricity. Longing to explain why the British authorities rejected his earlier works and why his first book, although published in New York City, was never actually sold to the public, he came upon the ready solution that the Freemasons were at work in their league with the Devil. Sheldon was not the first person—or the last—to fault the Masons as diabolical illuminati responsible for deleterious global events in an attempt to enact their satanic machinations. In his particular version, however, they were at work in London, Paris, and the United States, undermining his attempts to inform people—and especially those in England—of his prophetic interpretations.

Those interpretations had not altered significantly in the sixteen years since *Millenial Institutions*. England remained the chosen locale to initiate the coming kingdom of heaven, and its constitutional monarchy represented the correct political configuration for the end-time (with an emphasis on the monarchy). Sheldon interpreted other Biblical passages literally, including Creation, the Deluge, and the existence of Hell, but he also utilized these images to comment upon contemporary circumstances. Similarly, he implicated world events in his reading of Scripture, which incorporated numerous books of the Bible. In this manner he extended his earlier practice into a much more sophisticated form and found ways to interweave New England history and folklore into his prophetic interpretations. The American Revolution, for example, ignited the process leading to the end-time, and the revolution in France in 1848 only hastened its progress due to its unrepentant adherence to republicanism (and what he considered a corrupt church).

Although Sheldon did not offer specific dates for the coming of the new millennium as with his first attempt, he did manage to incorporate ruminations on, among other things, meteor showers throughout the world and other cosmological events as signs of the end-time; the founding of Corpus Christi, Texas; the fire and sinking of the steamship *Lexington* in Long Island Sound; the nature of electricity; the status of cherubim; the appearance of a sea serpent in Boston Harbor; the American Constitution; scientific processes of crystallization; mesmerism; the fate of the bodies of those who perished in the Flood; and the sinking of Atlantis, the existence of which he did not consider fabled.

Along the way he explained that all animals are rational and accountable to revelation (making an implicit case for vegetarianism), suggested that two of Prince Albert's sons were not of Royal issue, and insisted that the fall from Heaven is echoed in the United States' fall from allegiance to England. The work is, in short, a tour de force of eccentricity, conspiracies, and erudition, culling together much of the folklore, rumors, and occult ideas of his day.

One year later, in 1850, Sheldon seemed to take a break from his frenetic prophesizing with the publication of *Aerial Navigation and the Patent Laws*, but this contribution was no less remarkable than his others, as it presented a case for inventions allowing manned flight. Unlike the previous two books, this one is relatively short, just under fifty pages, but it packs an abundance of ideas between its covers. There are two main thrusts of this book. The first is Sheldon's description of an engine capable of artificial flight through combustion of atmospheric air or a fuel such as anthracite, accompanied by several illustrations. In this section, he rapidly considers scientific matters such as furnaces, temperature regulation, condensation, lubrications, gunpowder, wind resistance, velocity, and the aerial navigation of birds that should influence mechanical wing design.

The second half of the book soon becomes what we may identify as classic William Sheldon. From its inception he registers his complaint that inventors in general and he in particular often lose their rewards by the "lawful plunder" of the current patent system. Although he believes that such an injustice will be remedied in the new millennium—that is, the kingdom of heaven—he proposes a simple solution for the current times, burdened as it is by a lack of morality as much as by inferior patent laws: the creation of a Department of Inventions. This governmental entity, he argues, would purchase inventions from their creators and then farm them out to paying applicants. In but a few sentences, Sheldon works out a means by which national debts would be ended and taxation no longer necessary under this system. And although he petitions the US government for recompense, most of his examples and suggestions relate to Great Britain.

Perhaps not surprisingly, the invocation of England allows Sheldon to advocate its role as the chosen kingdom and to lament that the American Revolution severed a proper relationship with the empire, of which he longs to be a member. His nostalgia also cuts the path for a final commentary, in which he recognizes that this contribution may strike the reader as off kilter in relation to his previous works, as it focuses on science and patent laws. But Sheldon does not miss a beat, and in the closing paragraphs explains why his air engine (and his desire to be recognized as the lawful inventor) is so pressing. Citing Scripture again, he considers passages in which the prophet Elijah and Jesus himself return to Earth from the heavens. In other words, Sheldon implies that he has the plans to build the very machine that allows these events to unfold or to allow mortals living at the end-time to ascend upward toward heaven.

Continuing his string of publications, 1851 saw his next contribution to prophecy, *Observations on the Theological Mystery, the Harmonial Philosophy, and Spirit Rappings; with an Appendix Concerning Freemasonry*. Written in Sheldon's inimitable style, this work delivers more of his quirky aims and continuation of worldview and his insistence, as he proclaims late in the book, that "the day of visitation" and the end of the world were at hand. It also reveals an evolution of his thinking based on his awareness and participation of new movements, including in the occult, that were rising in popularity in the United States and especially in the Northeast. These developments were incorporated into his overall program, and this work is peppered with references to the *Seventh Vial* and the prophetic interpretations offered therein.

The first section of this book is a lengthy explanation and demonstration of the existence of spirits, drawing support from his reading of Biblical passages. Sheldon's claims are hardly unique, but certain digressions are very satisfying, such as his explanation of haunted houses and the means by which "phantom automatons" leave their impressions on surrounding objects. Once he has established the existence of spirits to his satisfaction, he then turns to comment upon contemporary social and religious movements. Sheldon critiques the "harmonial philosophy" of Andrew Jackson Davis, then a very popular if eclectic faith healer, and recommends that his rival stop publishing until he has learned to read Scripture as keenly as did Sheldon himself. He embraces, however, the growing Spiritualist movement as confirmation that his own beliefs and prophetic understandings were correct. In a discussion regarding the relationship between spiritualism, mesmerism, and clairvoyance, Sheldon provides a detailed transcript of a séance he attended in January 1851, including the questions and answers that he posed to the medium, which only emboldened his belief that the end-time was approaching. And for good measure, Sheldon included an appendix dedicated to yet another swipe at his "dark and mysterious foe," the Masons.

Having hit his stride with three consecutive years of publications and likely bolstered by the support Spiritualism promised for his ideas, Sheldon attempted to take his message to the greater public in the late 1850s. These strivings were about as successful as his earlier attempts to contact the British royal family. The *Proceedings* from Longmeadow's centennial reveals the responses of two such attempts in letters written in reply to him by Lydia Huntley Sigourney, the popular Connecticut writer and socialite, and Nathaniel Parker Willis, the writer and editor of several magazines. Sigourney dismissed Sheldon very diplomatically, wishing him well and confessing her own inabilities to comprehend the occult materials over which he had mastery. Willis, however, was blunt:

> You very much over-rate the level which the *Home Journal* is obliged to grade its reading in supposing that your able scientific article is suited to our columns. I sigh to tell you that our subscription depends almost wholly on those to whom the originality and interest of your views would be a dead letter. But so it is. I re-enclose your manuscript to you with the money for the extra copies . . . and trust you will forgive my thus having an eye to business and catering for the many rather than for the few.

We may smile at the thought of Sheldon's attempt to publish his ideas in *Home Journal*—a magazine known today as *Town & Country*—but to give him his due, all indications point to a sincere desire for sharing the news rather than for profiting personally from them.

We can only speculate as to the topic of Sheldon's "scientific article," but his final work may provide a clue. *The Millennium: The Good Time Coming; with a History of Experiments on the Odic Force* appeared in 1862 and followed the pattern of his previous works: a consistent building upon the prophetic interpretations he introduced in the 1830s, complemented by his most recent excursions into eccentric and occult matters. Much of it is predictable, at the least to the degree to which anything Sheldon wrote came close to predictability. Early chapters focus extensively on the coming millennium. He turns his attention in several chapters to the meaning of "Babylon" in Scripture, identifying it more closely with the individualistic ideology that he critiqued in *Millenial Institutions* than a specific city or locale. He also sees certain contemporary events as fulfillments of prophecy or signs of the end-time, including the waves of immigration of Irish Catholics to New England.

In the second half, however, Sheldon offers yet another surprising contribution, namely his decade-long embrace of what is called the odic or od-force. The idea, which he learned of in a Spiritualist monthly magazine, was introduced by the European intellectual Carl von Reichenbach, who coined the term in honor of Odin, the chief of the gods in Norse mythology. Reichenbach described the odic as a kind of life force or vital energy, akin in many ways to the electromagnetic force or a current, but energizing and connecting all living things. In a series of works on the od-force, Reichenbach suggested that certain sensitive individuals could see it emanating from objects, much like the idea of an aura. For Sheldon, this concept—now long rejected as pseudoscience and even criticized in its day—proved too tempting to ignore.

Indeed the od-force became the key Sheldon used to confirm virtually all of his previous interpretations and to tie together all his many speculations. As a life force connecting all bodies, it could readily explain mesmerism, spiritualism, and demonic possession (although his regular possessed antagonists, the Masons, were essentially missing from this text). Having detailed the basics of this phenomenon, Sheldon spent a considerable number of pages explaining

Biblical passages as examples of the od-force at work and how it would play a pivotal role in the Second Coming and the restoration of humankind in the new millennium.

But perhaps of most interest to the readers of this book, Sheldon also provided detailed information of his own experiments with the od-force, which commenced in 1851. Several of these involved the use of a pendulum or ring in divination practices, but even more fascinating were his claims to have learned how to cure diseases ranging from the common cold and toothache to influenza, cancer, and tuberculosis. He recorded performing these cures on the citizens of Longmeadow, and especially upon his housekeeper and her daughter. Consultation with Sheldon's remaining papers at the Longmeadow Historical Society confirms that these two women often were subject to his curative activities or witnesses to them. And, even more striking, they did not cease with individuals only, but extended to geographical regions and nations. In *The Millennium*, for example, Sheldon claims to have cured or prevented cholera in a wide swath of the United States east of the Mississippi. His obituary mentions similar acts of staying epidemics, and the Longmeadow centennial proceedings reprint his notations concerning his prevention of cholera and plague in Great Britain in 1865.

Sheldon declared that he had accomplished these miraculous and long-distance cures through the use of "traction wands"—that is, square-pointed rods that he charged with positive odic force in order to draw out or otherwise neutralize negative and morbid odic forces. And if this ability were not enough, those other records suggest that he could similarly detect evil spirits lurking in people by suspending a ring over their open palm and reading its movement, and that he once detected through odic tests that a bushel of potatoes he purchased were infected with disease, having originated in the cellar of a man with typhoid fever. In short, the discovery of the od-force provided Sheldon with an inexhaustible fuel for his eccentric behaviors and beliefs.

Although *The Millennium* is scant on material specific to New England for most of its pages, Sheldon delivers in the final chapter of the main text. He turns abruptly from a discussion on possession and the od-force to one of the Psalms that invokes a river pleasing to the city of God. He then speculates as to its location. Ruling out the major rivers of the Old Testament and the ancient world and even those of modern times, he suggests that it is none other than the Connecticut River itself, the longest river in New England. As we have come to expect, Sheldon is skillful at matching elements of his proposition with both scientific and historical facts and with Biblical passages. He suggests, for example, that the sources of the river, being near the border of Canada, would have been under the dominion of England at the end-time had the American Revolution not severed their connection. He provides in great detail his own impressions at various points on the river as they match the images from the Psalm. And he incorporates folklore from the river valley into his prophecy for the end-time.

One of the most delightful pieces of evidence that Sheldon offers for his claim was the recent discovery of enormous "bird tracks" on the banks of the river. Today, of course, we know these to be fossil footprints of dinosaurs, but Sheldon wasted no time in ascribing them to birds who survived the Flood and seeing in this proof that the Connecticut is a biblical river. He also noted that he himself had penned all of his works on prophecy in a town resting on the banks of the river—surely a good sign—and recalls that an earthquake occurred in Springfield in 1860 soon after Prince Edward passed over the river during his American tour. These coincidences inspire Sheldon to close the main body of his text with a direct appeal to Queen Victoria herself. Convinced as he was that all the signs pointed to the imminent end-time and the new millennium, he appealed to her to abdicate the throne in favor of Edward, as he could find no support in scripture that a woman would be monarch when the Second Coming occurred!

The queen did not yield her throne, of course, nor did the end-time come in Sheldon's lifetime. He produced no other major works before his passing in 1871, but his name appears occasionally in the late 1860s advertising and selling land. The Springfield Republican printed a review of The Millennium, recommending the "curious work" as a source of wonder rather than as prophecy, but he otherwise did not receive widespread acclaim or fame for his ideas. This did not, however, mean that Sheldon was forgotten. As his obituaries made clear, he remained an active fixture in the community until his death, and as late as 1909 the local newspapers remembered him as "Longmeadow's most eccentric character," walking the streets with a predictable time and course. Indeed Sheldon's fame was so well established in the community that in 1937, the Works Progress Administration guide to Massachusetts identified him as one of only four notable people in the town, demonstrating his lingering influence nearly seven decades after his death.

There is much more to say about William Sheldon, including his reported habits of avoiding carpets, his belief in the immortality of animals, and his antiquated ideas about women's role in society. I will also only mention in passing the claim in his obituary that he was a daily opium eater for fifty years; if this were true, it may certainly explain some of his predilections for the odd. But I would be remiss to leave out that every remembrance of Sheldon also noted his genteel manners, his kindness to the poor and to those who often took advantage of him, and his respectful attitude toward servants. These latter characteristics are not, however, very surprising if we take Sheldon at his word and as a person whose idiosyncrasies all derive from a deep well of sincerity to share important news with his fellow humans. His nostalgic quirkiness, his conspiratorial instincts, his willingness to embrace the occult fads of his day, and his keen ability to intellectually force square pegs to fit into round holes all reveal an underlying motive to inspire others, and in these respects he was both a genuine New England eccentric and a man who tried to live by the principles he believed in.

11

THE REFORMERS:
THE SMITH SISTERS

In every chapter of this book, there arises an immediate problem of focusing on certain individuals at the expense of other eccentrics. The selection of reformers is a particularly thorny task, as anyone who willingly disrupts the status quo, challenges traditional political and social order, and resists commonly accepted opinions or beliefs becomes a misfit of sorts, and deliberately so. The history of New England has been marked—perhaps we could even say enriched—by these women and men who met their world and wanted something better. Abolitionists, suffragists, labor reformers, education reformers, environmentalists, and advocates for religious freedom, immigrants, prisoners, and the extension of basic rights have all earned a position for commendation. Even movements that by today's standards may have seemed seem ill-conceived (such as prohibition) or hopelessly idealistic (such as utopian communities) contribute to that illustrious tapestry.

Certain activists upset the carts of their fellow reformers as frequently as those who resisted change. The indefatigable Margaret Fuller comes to mind as an example, as does Isabella Beecher Hooker, both of whom were viciously mocked in print and in person for their beliefs. Other reformers lived less flamboyantly but still made enormous contributions to the betterment of democratic society. The Smith sisters of Glastonbury, Connecticut, are among this latter group. Although they are not as celebrated as other New England reformers, their story provides a compelling example of how the actions of a few dedicated people can create far-reaching and sustained change. In a celebrated act of civil disobedience, Julia and Abby Smith demonstrated that they did not fit with the social expectations of the time, and the rupture they caused further raised the question of whether those norms were just.

The remarkable story of the Smith sisters begins with their mother, Hannah Hadassah Hickok, an educated woman and talented poet born an only child in the decade before the American Revolution. She was learned in Latin and French and taught herself Italian later in life in order to read yet more classic literature. She was also interested in mathematics and astronomy, and early reports remark that she was so capable in the latter that she could tell the time at night simply by looking at the position of the constellations. Numerous accounts also contend that she became skilled at mechanics and was able to make clocks, an activity normally reserved for men. In her youth Hickok saw tremendous political and social upheaval, but the resolution of the war did not lead her to complacency. To the contrary, she did not accept the shortcomings of the new nation, especially its tolerance for slavery.

Hickok often lambasted this pernicious practice in her poetry, and her opposition led her to the abolitionist movement in its formative years, including membership in the Hartford Anti-Slavery Society. In one of her poems, written as a critique of Independence Day, she decried the pretense of freedom in a nation that held certain people as slaves and argued that the day would be better spent in pleading for their freedom than in celebration. The final stanza underscores the seriousness of her criticism:

And never more a banner wave
Inscribed with Liberty
Till we unchain the prostrate slave
And set the captive free.

Her outspokenness on this issue continued throughout her lifetime. In 1839, for example, when she was in her early seventies, Hickok organized a petition against slavery and solicited signatures by going door-to-door in Glastonbury. Over the course of several months, she and her daughters collected forty names—an impressive achievement—and sent it to John Quincy Adams, then a US representative, who read such contributions aloud to Congress. This would not be the only time she organized petitions (one of the few ways that women could have a voice in politics at the time), and in addition to this work she helped to distribute abolitionist newspapers and reportedly invited prominent figures to speak from her home.

In 1786 Hickok married Zephaniah Hollister Smith, who was described in a Yale remembrance as "an original character." (His wife, similarly, was called "a woman of marked ability and of much eccentricity" by the same account.) Smith had studied at Yale and became a Congregational minister in Newtown, Connecticut—Hickok notes attending one of his sermons in her diary—but his time at the pulpit was limited. In diplomatic language, after an "injudicious" administration of the parish "it became necessary for him to ask a dismission," but in colloquial terms, he quarreled with his parish and they dismissed him in an act that brought mutual relief. The source of the division appears to be Smith's embrace of certain tenements of a nonconformist religious movement known as Sandemanianism.

The movement was named for Robert Sandeman, the son-in-law of the originator, John Glas, who brought it from Scotland to New England in the second half of the 1700s. "Bare faith" aptly summarizes the aim and principle of their beliefs. That is, Sandemanians believed that understanding and acceptance of the Gospel alone was the sole requirement for salvation. As a consequence they generally considered ministers unnecessary and stood in opposition to churches whose power was enforced by the state. It was, essentially, an attempt to restore the originating Christian community, in which all people could be participants and leaders regardless of occupation or education. This notion flew in the face of orthodox religion in America, where the British government and later the states protected ministerial authority, and often demanded (as it did in Connecticut) membership in a religious community as essential for full citizenship. Sandemanianism was, in many ways, a very early expression in favor of the separation of church and state.

The movement also tended toward pacifism—many followers of Sandeman left what would become the United States for Canada during the Revolution—and was critical of the individual accumulation of wealth, especially by ministers whose sole occupation was religious leadership. Although Smith was not a disciple of Sandeman, he was clearly influenced by his ideas. He strongly agreed with the Sandemanian rejection of paying people to preach, and this partially justified his leaving the ministry. His family likewise adopted an unconventional approach to religion. They would, for example, attend church services only rarely, using the time instead for performing charitable work or visiting with friends, and they refused officiating ministers for burial services, preferring instead a ceremony directed by surviving relatives and friends. While these activities were not regarded as unacceptable to Glastonbury residents, they certainly were outside the norm.

After Smith left the ministry, he trained as a lawyer and enjoyed tremendous success in that career. He also served as a justice of the peace and represented Glastonbury in the Connecticut legislature for several years. By these activities Smith became well-to-do—not excessively rich, but comfortably middle class—and while that financial advantage was perhaps not entirely without irony in the eyes of zealous Sandemanians, it did adhere to their principle of earning a living through a profession that did not have religious authority over others. That said, the Smith family were wealthy enough to purchase a large farm—known as the Kimberly Mansion for its originator, Eleazer Kimberly, a Connecticut secretary of state—on Main Street in Glastonbury, not far from the town hall.

Hickok and Smith would need money, too, as they raised a family of five daughters and were determined that each would benefit from the best education that could be found for women at the time. The five Smith sisters each distinguished themselves against the prevalent opinion that females were created for the domestic roles of becoming nurturing mothers and wives. None of them married, with the exception of a single unconventional relationship very late in life. This intimate sorority held together at the family estate in Glastonbury throughout their lives—and held the estate together, as they and their mother were responsible for its management beyond the normal chores expected of women. And despite the family reticence to participate in conventional worship, the sisters were exemplary Christians with regard to their charity in the community. They dedicated a great deal of time, for example, tending to Glastonbury residents who fell ill or into poverty, and they associated with freed slaves and African American activists.

The eldest daughter, Hancy Zephina (whose unconventional name was a tribute to her parents) was gifted in music and in mechanics. According to a local historian, she designed an improvement for shoeing cattle that the local blacksmiths gratefully adopted, and she may have built a boat by herself. More fanciful (and less exacting) biographers reported that Hancy designed a grindstone windmill powered by a pig on a treadmill and a potato peeler that was rejected because it removed too much of the skin for thrifty Yankees. She learned to play the piano, and, again according to reports more speculative than studious, she owned one of the first instruments in the state and practiced playing on wooden blocks before it arrived. We know the least about the second daughter, Cyrinthia Sacretia, but one of her embroideries from her days as a student at the Litchfield Female Academy survives. The subject, "A Cottage Girl," re-creates an image from James Thompson's poem *The Seasons* and depicts a virtuous young man reduced to poverty. She was, reportedly, also a skilled horticulturalist and rumored to have experimented with creating her own varieties of fruit. Both Hancy and Cyrinthia were involved in the abolitionist and charity work that characterized the family.

The third sister, Laurilla Aleroyla, was inclined toward the arts, and there are charming but imaginary accounts of her showing her mettle by painting colors upon the white houses of neighbors when she was a child. More accurate assessment of her art is found in a surviving painting, also from her schooldays at Litchfield, in which she painted a watercolor entitled "The Sons of Tippoo Saib About to be Delivered as Hostages to the English," presumably at the age of thirteen. This scene was popular in the visual arts. It depicts a moment in the life of Tipu Sultan, the ruler of Mysore, a kingdom in Southern India, who resisted British colonization in a series of wars and who in 1793 was in defeat forced to hand over two sons as ransom until reparations were paid. Many representations of this scene focus on the handover to Lord Charles Cornwallis. Fewer represent the family in grief saying their farewells without any imagery of the victors. Laurilla chose the latter.

She signed the painting "Laurilla A. Smith," but when she fully engaged the abolitionist cause she published a few striking essays under the name "Laurilla Aleroyla." Two are especially worth consideration for their nonconformist—and uncompromising—expressions. The first appeared in *Freedom's Gifts or Sentiments of the Free* in 1840. Entitled "The Bloody Banner," it is a two-page account of a vision of a banner glowing red and dripping "reeking gore" into the ocean. "What nation's banner may that be?" she asks, discovering to her surprise that it belonged to the "noble nation" of America. "I know her gallant story," the author continues. "She was taxed by a kingly power—abused by kingly pride—and she revolted. She would not bear oppression." Yet in winning "liberty, peace, happiness, and equal rights to all her people," she nevertheless "has shorn her beauteous flag of all its honors" by drenching it in "the gore of guiltless Africa"—defenseless mothers, helpless children, and shrieking babes. Smith ends by calling for someone to "take away the Bloody Banner of America!"

Her second essay, "The Stranger," was composed for *Star of Emancipation*, a collection organized by the Massachusetts Female Emancipation Society. It is of equal fervor to the first. Smith commences by noting how the name "stranger" is a "holy name," and recounts several images from world history in which the protection of strangers was among the most important commandments and social rules. "Is there anyone in this wide world so lone a stranger," she then asks, "as the escaping slave?" In poetic terms she imagines how that world must appear to a runaway slave and then asks who would be of such compromised morality as to refuse to aid such a fugitive. Smith has her answer: "A Northern laborer!" And similarly, a "Northern yeoman" would betray the fleeing slave, even as he—the yeoman—is "free as the mountain breeze himself, rejoicing in his liberty, protected in his rights." This, she fears, is what America has become, having lost her moral compass. Smith concludes in a manner that should speak for itself:

> Oh what an act is this, to take the helpless "stranger" and give him up a bound and trembling victim, into the hands of his enraged and lawless master!! It is a deed of horror! Such are thy trophies, slavery! and such the offerings thy votaries must lay upon thine altar! Thy morning and thy evening sacrifice is human blood! Thy victim is the guiltless "stranger!"

Although this imagery and its call for social change certainly put her at odds with many people in New England, it was rather common for the Smith family. Laurilla also contributed to women's education directly as a teacher first at the Troy Female Seminary in New York and later at the Hartford Female Seminary, but she never lost interest in cultivating her artistic skills. Eventually the family constructed another building across the street from their home to be used as her studio. (There is another legendary story from the middle of the twentieth century, clearly a misunderstanding of where her studio was located, that suggested she built a log cabin on her own to paint, and that during a flood, she borrowed Hancy's boat to access it.)

The fourth daughter, Julia Evelina (born Julietta Abelinda before her parents renamed her in honor of a novel penned by Fanny Burney), and the fifth daughter, Abby Hadassah, were responsible for what Frances Ellen Burr called "one of the most original and unique chapters in the history of woman suffrage." Like their sisters, they were highly accomplished women. Julia was studious in many subjects, but languages were her forte. She learned French, Latin, and Greek easily. Following Laurilla, she also taught for one year at the Troy Female Seminary. One of her major contributions was a translation of the Bible that took several years to complete and for which she learned Hebrew. Her reasons for doing so and then, decades later, for publishing at her own expense, offer telling insights into her mind and those of her sisters.

In the Introduction of this book, I mentioned in passing William Miller, the preacher who prophesized that the world would end between 1843 and 1844, and whose rise to prominence led to a religious movement attracting thousands of followers. Miller had based his prediction on a reading of the Bible; he believed that it held a code allowing him to calculate the rough date of the Second Coming. Several were proposed, with the final attempt set on October 22, 1844. That day of the Great Reckoning became the day of the Great Disappointment. The Smith sisters participated in the Millerite movement, although it is not precisely clear the degree to which their investment ran in comparison with other believers. One commentator who knew them noted that as the fateful day neared, they renounced attachments to this world by turning pictures around to face the wall, covering the piano, and putting their houseplants in the cellar. Another remarked that they prepared their ascension robes, but it is unclear how seriously this comment should be taken.

Nevertheless, Miller's failure to accurately predict the end inspired Julia to investigate the matter herself and to question if it might have been an error of translation rather than of calculation. She set out to remedy this matter and as a result produced what is arguably the first translation of the Bible by a woman. It was a literal translation; that is, unlike the King James Version that was popular in New England, Smith's attempted a word-for-word accounting absent of any flowery language or stylistic changes to make reading easier for an English-speaking audience. Although this decision makes for difficult passages, it also shows her commitment to both Sandemanian and Millerite tendencies that promoted direct communication between Biblical interpreters and the deity.

There is more to say about Julia's translation, but it took two decades from its completion in 1855 to its publication in 1876, and those years were marked by that most significant act of civil disobedience. The family numbers had begun to dwindle. Zephaniah passed in 1836 and Hannah in 1850. Laurilla followed them in 1857 and Cyrinthia in 1864. Hancy, Julia, and Abby remained at Kimberly Mansion. Then, in 1869 they were asked to pay their property taxes twice in the same year. Their response to that demand offers a glimpse at their ardent intellects and equally vehement spirits. When Julia called upon the tax administrator to explain this second billing, he produced an itemized list of outstanding town expenses.

A voter registry was among these items and the administrator explained that it was necessary to pay someone—a man—to produce a record of the names at the polls so that no one would vote more than once. Julia requested that her name be added to the list. She was denied immediately on the grounds that the poll record was only for voters and therefore only for men. Incredulous that women would be asked to pay for a service that benefited them in no way, she explained in reply, "If they are going on at this rate, I must go to that suffrage meeting in Hartford and see if we cannot do better, for I have no doubt one woman could write down every name in town for half that money."

The meeting in question was the Connecticut Woman Suffrage Association. Attendees included prominent figures of the movement including Susan B. Anthony and Elizabeth Cady Stanton. Both of the younger Smith sisters joined, and Abby became a member of the Executive Committee. Hancy, regrettably, would not live long enough to see her sisters become important figures for that pursuit of social justice; she passed in 1871. It was in that early part of the 1870s, however, that Julia and Abby earned a name for themselves—and the ire of many in the community—for their outspoken and nonconforming views. It began in earnest in 1872, when the sisters learned that their property taxes would be increased and, upon checking into the matter, also discovered that a similar hike occurred for two widows in town but no men. Although they paid that year, they did so reluctantly; as they noted, even though it was not a significant increase, the principle of "unjust in least is unjust in much" applied.

No doubt inspired by the women's rights movements, in early 1873 they joined in solidarity with Rosella Buckingham and four other women and requested they be registered as voters in Glastonbury. The registrar recorded their names and passed them along to the Selectmen, who unceremoniously rejected them at a secret meeting. That same year they attended the meeting of the American Woman Suffrage Association in New York City and returned to Glastonbury more determined than ever to object to taxation without the right to vote. At the time, Julia was eighty-one and Abby was seventy-six years old. When asked in late October to pay the increased taxes again, they refused. On November 5, 1873, the sisters appeared at a town meeting to address the matter. Abby rose and presented what the *Springfield Republican*, reporting days later, called "A Novel Speech for a Town Meeting."

In her speech Abby made clear that they, as women, possessed as much intelligence and capacity for managing their own business as the men. "Is it any more just to take a woman's property without her consent," she asked, "than it is to take a man's property without his consent?" She objected to the way the previous year's payment of two hundred dollars was spent by "the very dregs of society" and raised several other concerns about the behavior of men, and especially those who would come and seize property through force. She also used an occasional lighter touch, comparing the town to a family and stressing the need for equality in the management of its domestic affairs. They were, of course, refused the right to vote (or to have their taxes reduced), but as the *Republican* concluded, her speech must have set the townsmen "a-thinking."

In December the *Republican* noted that the tax collector returned to their home. He did not receive the money, the newspaper noted, "but did get a cat-echism which must have been rather disagreeable, and the report of which ought to furnish matter for serious thought to such men in Glastonbury as have any sense of justice." The tax collector, when so confronted, admitted that they paid the second-highest tax of any person in town and that the man who owed more was able to pay it down in installments or through labor. The newspaper applauded their efforts and urged them on in their resistance. In the years of struggle ahead, the *Republican* would serve as a close ally.

What happened next was described in that same paper as "the Battle of Glastonbury." On New Year's Day, 1874, as Abby herself explained in a letter to the editor, the tax collector arrived with an order to seize property for the payment of the bill. They objected and offered to pay the interest on the bill (a tactic several other male taxpayers employed in town) and asked for another opportunity to address the town leaders, but he refused and marched away with seven of their eight Alderney cows to auction, relocating them at a nearby tobacco shed. The heartbreak of the scene as she described it was striking, for the cows did not cooperate and the one left moaned in sadness. Furthermore, the Smith sisters had tenants living in a cottage on their property who were accordingly deprived of the milk they needed. The *Republican* hailed the sisters in the face of this seizure as standing for "the American principles as did the citizens who ripped open the tea-chests in Boston harbor, or the farmers who leveled their muskets at Concord." In praising "the pluck" of Smith sisters, the newspaper continued, "and they seem to have very much the same quality of quiet, old-fashioned Yankee grit, too." The editors concluded by urging readers to contribute to the Abby Smith Defense Fund set up in her honor.

Soon the *Republican* and other newspapers in the region observed how the townspeople in Glastonbury, who once welcomed the charity of the Smith sisters, now looked upon them coldly. This turn of attitude was reflected in letters to the editors by their detractors, who stopped describing the sisters as harmless eccentrics and treated them as unwanted rabble-rousers. A letter in the *Hartford Courant* suffices to give a sense of the hostility. The author, identified only as "G," criticized them and those newspapers that supported them, accusing both of misrepresentations of Glastonbury and its officers. After reviewing at some length the history of the town's lenity with the entire family, "G" got to the point; he dismissed the Smith sister's "howl about the tyranny of men" as nonsense and declared that "no true woman needs the ballot to strengthen and intensify her proper influence, and few sensible women desire it."

Despite this local resentment, the story of the Smith sister's cows became regional and soon national news. Several newspapers stood in solidarity, and just about an equal number opposed them. Letters of support and of condemnation poured in from all over the country and beyond. The cows were brought to auction and purchased back by the Smiths' tenant (likely with their own money), but this incident launched a yearly campaign that continued for years. Later in 1874, for example, the town seized fifteen acres of their land and sold it to a neighbor. This action, however, potentially violated Connecticut law—which insisted that personal property be sold first—and allowed the

Smith sisters to file a lawsuit. A justice of the peace in Glastonbury decided in their favor, but the Court of Common Pleas reversed the decision. The case made its way to the Connecticut Supreme Court, where first in 1876 and fully in 1880 the case was decided in their favor that the land had been improperly seized. (The case did not, however, grant them voting rights or remove them from the duty to pay taxes.)

During this time both sisters became active members and sought-after speakers for suffrage and women's rights organizations and were interviewed by countless papers across the country—many of which, it should be noted, did a poor job in accurately representing the matter and contributed to folklore around the sisters that lasted well into the twentieth century. (The *Chicago Tribune*, for example, reported that their mother, Hannah Hickok, had a glass cage constructed for herself to which she could retreat for reading in peace.) They would eventually testify on the issue of women's suffrage in front of the Connecticut legislature and later the US Congress.

It was also during this time that Julia published her translation of the Bible in order to demonstrate that women possessed the intellectual capacity to manage themselves—and, indeed, to do what men could not do themselves, as all translations of the Bible previously were done by men in consultation with other men; this translation, incidentally, was known as the "Alderney edition" for some time in honor of her equally famous cows. Julia's work laid the foundation for *The Woman's Bible*, published under the editorship of Elizabeth Cady Stanton. Abby died in 1878, and one year later, Julia married Amos Parker, a man who called upon her following the death of her sister. Although the wedding was reported as a happy one in the newspapers—they were both eighty-six at the time—it is unclear precisely how pleasant the marriage was. She moved with him to Hartford and he sold Kimberly Mansion, but by her own request when Julia herself passed, her body was returned to the family plot in Glastonbury and she was buried between her sisters with her maiden name.

In bringing the story of the Smith sisters to a close, I would draw the reader's attention to an insightful observation made about the entire family. Henry Titus Welles may be known best today as a pioneer of Minnesota, but he was born and raised just down the street from the Smith family, and by his own testimony his father was a close friend of Zephaniah. He remembered the family in his *Autobiography and Reminiscences* and took a special interest in noting that the mother and sisters each died in a pattern of seven years from the previous family member (technically Julia, the last, was eight years from Abby). "They did not seem to have a love of the marvelous," Welles wrote, "nor a desire to be eccentric. But they did have a pride of independence, and arrogated to themselves superior judgment, and were inordinately tenacious of their own opinions." In other words, they did not seek eccentricity per se, but the appearance of eccentricity was the result of their living lives of principle. Surely that says something about the world in which they lived.

12

THE VAGABONDS: THE OLD DARNED MAN AND THE LEATHER MAN

On December 5, 1863, newspapers throughout southern New England reported on the death of the Old Darned Man the previous evening on a road in Sterling, Connecticut. A constant figure who walked "with the ceaselessness of a pendulum" across Connecticut's Windham County, western Rhode Island, and southern Massachusetts, the Old Darned Man had been at his travels, the report explained, for half a century. He was a mystery even then. "The poor, harmless wayfarer had a history," the notice concluded, "but no one was ever able to draw it from him." That did not stop storytellers from trying.

Seven years later, a Providence newspaper—clearly unaware of the earlier reports—lamented that he had not been seen in some time and speculated that his "earthly pilgrimage is over." Aged and unnamed witnesses claimed that he was no less than ninety years old. His real name was Addison, the tale continued, and when he was a young man he was engaged, but learned at his wedding ceremony that his fiancée "had been suddenly taken away by death." This news disordered his mind and he began to wander, wearing only his wedding suit for the remainder of his long years until it and he both grayed with exposure and age. His wanderings followed a route from western New York to northern Rhode Island and back, and as he posed no threat to spectators along the way, he was treated with charitable kindness. He never begged except to ask for yarn or thread to stitch up his clothes—in an older vocabulary, to darn them—so that he might keep true to his intentions and never remove his wedding suit.

This story, which appeared in newspapers throughout the Northeast and as far as the West Coast, is a stellar example of the creation of a folk hero. As compelling as it is, every detail of this narrative is questionable as fact. But the desire to tell his story was strong. Five years later, for example, a Boston newspaper published a lengthy and polished narrative with the hauntingly romantic title "The Man with Part of a Soul." In this version the Old Darned Man was only a spring and summer traveler along the turnpikes of northern Connecticut and Rhode Island. And he resisted all attempts at conversation. An elderly woman, the essay recalls—conveniently not remembering her name—once asked him if he had a soul. "Part o' one, said he; and that was all she (or anyone else) ever got out of him."

Here, too, he was a character of misfortune, who lived in western New York and who, on his wedding day, went to the home of his fiancée to find her suddenly dead. His sadness, his madness, and his vow to remain in his wedding suit forever made him seem a purely fictional invention. Other subtle markers fleshed out his personality: He would change his socks and shoes, he possessed enough wealth to carry money—that is, he was not among the class of itinerant tramps who rose in the 1800s—and he would haggle with people who sold him goods. (There was no attempt to explain how he was both silent and an avid negotiator, but such consistency was not the point of the tale.) The idea remained from earlier stories, however, that the physical mending of his suit was really an attempt to mend his soul.

Stories of the Old Darned Man continued unabated in New England for several decades and eventually worked into the lore of the rest of the country. In 1887, for example, he was declared dead *again* by newspapers from Cleveland to Fresno to Baton Rouge. The notice was brief but beholden to tradition: His mind was unhinged as a young man at the death of his fiancée, and he set about to honor her memory for the remainder of his life by wearing his wedding suit. And in 1899, nearly four decades after he passed, the *Springfield Republican* reignited interest in his story by publishing two lengthy accounts and accompanying letters. Written by S. B. Keach, the first article promised readers that it was a "narrative of fact, not fiction," even as it would seem unbelievable. Keach claimed to have encountered the wanderer often in his boyhood. In this and his second contribution (which drew upon copious letters sent to him), he cleared up the mystery: The Old Darned Man was named Addison Thompson, a man of some means from western New York, who lost his fiancée on their wedding day, and who vowed never to change his suit.

Novel elements emerged in Keach's tale, however. The Old Darned Man walked twice a year from the grave of his beloved to the seashore near Boston through northern Connecticut and Rhode Island and back again. He was fond of strong tea and would ask for it when taken in for the night, but otherwise was silent—except, of course, to request a needle and thread for darning his clothes. He wore the wedding ring meant for his wife on his own hand until "it was almost embedded in the flesh of his finger," and it was that same ring that he gazed upon without pause during his travels.

And perhaps most revealing, Keach received a letter from Elisha Anderson, the last man to see the Old Darned Man alive. Anderson discovered him dying on a road in Sterling, Connecticut, in November 1863 and saw to his burial at the cemetery in Oneco near "the Plains." (Oneco is a village in Sterling where there is a cemetery on Plainfield Pike.) Keach was impressed by the number of people who testified to seeing him and whose parents or grandparents entertained him. He noted wistfully that nothing in P. T. Barnum's museum could hold the attraction of the Old Darned Man's coat should it still survive. And he published a poem composed years prior by Mrs. C. H. V. Thomas, entitled "Only a Beggar," inspired by his story:

> The beggar lay dead by the roadside,
> A pitiful sight to see,

But then, he was only a beggar,

And nothing to you or me.

He was weary and worn with travel,

His feet could no further go

In chase of the beautiful phantom

That beckoned from "long ago."

With eyes like the eyes of the maiden,

Full of gentleness and truth,

Who died on the morn of her bridal,

The love of his long-lost youth,

And left him, so crazed and heart-broken,

To wander alone through life,

Its joys and its pleasures unheeding,

Unheeded its turmoil and strife.

He was bronzed with the suns of summer,

He was pinched with winter's cold,

His fare was but scanty and meager,

He sought no silver or gold,

Nor honors from men; but, still onward,

With eager and restless tread,

Never turning aside one moment

He keeps his tryst with the dead!

How gently the moonlight is falling

On the forehead, white and bare,

And the hands that were clasped in passion

Are folded as if in prayer!

The eyes look above and beyond us,

And beauty we cannot see

Is vouchsafed to the beggar's vision,

But hidden from you and me.

Let him rest in the pauper's corner,

Whose stones are mossy and grim.

For earth, with its show and its honor,
Is nothing now unto him!

Keach, too, could not resist the temptation to speculate on the final days of the Old Darned Man. He imagined two scenarios. In the first, he collapsed and was taken to an institution, where, held against his will by well-meaning doctors, he struggled "like a wild bird" to escape and return to his route home to his lover's grave, but died imprisoned. In a second and more peaceful account, Keach depicted a scene of solitude and tranquility, with the Old Darned Man resting in the woods, a brown thrush singing to him as he closed his eyes, smiled, and passed from this world.

This may have been the end of the story of the Old Darned Man, and although it alone reveals several decades of folk narratives baked in the oral tradition—hence the reason for the many changes along the way—a particular event in 1906 forever altered the course of his tale. That year, the Reverend Charles L. Goodell, a pastor who would become a popular host of a series for NBC Radio in the 1930s, published an article in *Success* magazine that reimagined the entire affair yet again. Goodell drew from the sources he could find and then took poetic license to close the gap of what was missing. (Later that year, Funk and Wagnalls issued a book version, *The Old Darnman*, and advertised it heavily throughout the country.) In this fictional account his real name is Frank Howard, a descendant of a *Mayflower* passenger, who planned to attend Yale and eventually taught school in the seaside town of New London, Connecticut.

In New London he met Josephine Alden, the daughter of a sea captain, and the two fell in love. When he proposed, "Josie" first resisted, fearful that he would die at sea as a sailor, as she had seen the fate of so many young men in that town. But he assured his beloved that he was a scholar and she accepted. Her father sent her to New York City on the ship *Hope On* in order that the same seamstress who made her mother's wedding dress would make hers. The tragic ending is predictable: The ship found itself in a sudden storm and Josephine was lost at sea. The sorrow that ensued claimed Frank's memory and he forever thought each day thereafter was his wedding. He prepared daily for the happy event and waited on his bride-to-be, wandering off to find her when she did not arrive on time. One night, many decades later, he was resting near the side of the road and heard a wagon approach. He leapt with joy at the thought his beloved had arrived and was struck by the thundering horses. With his dying breath, he pledged his wedding vows and ended his pilgrimage.

The popularity of Goodell's story—he republished an anthology with the tale in 1932—revitalized interest in the Old Darned Man, leading Ellen Larned, a local historian of Windham County, to inquire in regional papers for information on the actual man who died in 1863. This request led to another outpouring of recollections and speculations. Initial accounts confirmed the elements circulating before Goodell's contribution, but soon the fictional story merged with and often replaced the earlier ones. In the 1930s, for example, the Federal Writers' Project interviewed Louise E. Dew Watrous of Clinton, Connecticut, whose relative often saw the Old Darned Man. Her tale, however, was a memory of Goodell's book rather than the folk narratives from the 1800s.

New information arose as more people declared having had some familiarity with him. A history of Windham County, for example, included a recollection by A. D. Ayer (who also responded to Larned's call in the *Hartford Courant*) in which the wanderer, who came once a month from April to January, offered to work for his father for a few days in order to access their reading library. He also reportedly admonished Ayer to "beware of the girls" lest the boy suffer the same fate as he. Another contributor testified that the Old Darned Man informed his mother his real name was George Johnson, with sisters in Rhode Island. Another history of Woodstock, Connecticut, identified him as Moses Thompson.

And in 1950 yet another local history of Pomfret and Hampton, Connecticut, claiming to have access to a letter from 1860, called him George Thompson, a native of Taunton, Massachusetts, and a merchant. (*Ripley's Believe It Or Not* elected this name for a profile in 1961.) Several accounts recalled his skill at playing the violin. One located his death on Snake Meadow Hill Road in Sterling. As late as the 1980s, the US Poet Laureate Stanley Kunitz, a native of

Worcester, reimagined an encounter with the vagabond, whose heartbroken days began when his fiancée ran away with his best friend.

So who was the mysterious wanderer known as the Old Darned Man? We may never know his identity or the genuine details about his personality, his travels, and his interactions with people along the way. He was, for certain, a man who traveled the roads of a corner of Connecticut on a regular route, accepting the charity offered to him and wearing a coat that he regularly darned along the way. Anything beyond those few details is speculation or folklore. What is certain, however, is that his story remains an appealing font of inspiration and projection in its mixture of simplicity and eccentricity.

—~—

When it comes to the Leather Man, it is also a formidable task to reassemble the details. Countless other collections and commentaries include him, making it difficult to add anything new. And the fascination is warranted. Like the Old Darned Man, the Leather Man was a mystery in his day, a sign of fortitude and of suffering, and an eccentric who defied the presumed benefits of stable society and civilized living yet posed no active threat to those he encountered along his way. He may well have been a product of changing economic conditions in the later nineteenth century—this was a time in which many people took up the tramp's life by necessity—but he seemed to have chosen a life of wandering. And the gaps of information about him invited rampant speculation, titillating romanticizing, and outright mythologizing.

Although the range of accounts concerning the Leather Man varies greatly, there is general consensus on a few matters. The first is that his name derived from his unusual dress, a heavy overcoat and pants made of leather— estimated at some sixty pounds—which he wore on his travels regardless of the season and patched by hand as necessary. His boots, shirt, socks, and hat were often said to be of leather, but there is less agreement on these particulars over time. Most agree that he began wandering in the 1850s—whether early or late is subject to contention—and covered ground between the Connecticut and

Hudson Rivers. By the mid-1880s, his route was so well established as to be predictable, with a clockwise circuit of towns stretching 365 miles and an average of thirty-four days. Along the way the Leather Man camped in a number of rock shelters, caves, or lean-tos, where he occasionally cultivated gardens and kept freshwater supplies. The locations of many of these shelters are known and visited to this day. He visited several host families on his travels, who would prepare meals according to his patterned schedule.

All accounts agree that he conversed little, and most suggested that he was prone to make grunting noises rather than the sounds of language. He was not, however, regarded as animalistic, even with this linguistic penchant and unwashed body. *Harmless* was one of the terms most frequently used to describe him, and even after Connecticut and New York passed laws in 1879 prohibiting tramping, he was allowed to go about his business. The Leather Man was, furthermore, rarely abused by spectators (many gathered in crowds to see him, especially children), except for a few ugly incidents in 1887 and 1888, when he was assaulted by two men and had his shelter burned by some hoodlums, respectively.

The abuses of the weather, however, were another issue altogether, and he often bore the painful marks of frostbite. He survived the savage New England blizzard of 1888, but fell victim to cancer—he was a tobacco user and exposed to constant sunlight—that first manifested in his lip. He was "arrested" in Middletown, Connecticut, by agents for the Humane Society, who persuaded him to go to Hartford Hospital, where he promptly escaped or was allowed to go free without treatment. He was never again detained. The cancer, however, claimed his life on March 20, 1889. He was discovered four days later by Henry Miller in one of his caves near George Dell's farm in Mount Pleasant, New York, and buried at Sparta Cemetery in Ossining.

Those are the points of agreement, and even they skirt speculation. Other popular but unsubstantiated claims contend that he was born in the 1830s and that he spoke French, giving rise to the assumption that he was French Canadian or from France itself. As for his real name, there is little accord. The name Zacharias Bovelat (or Boveliat) was attached to his admission at Hartford

Hospital in 1888, but that was its first and last appearance. The name "Brown" had an early showing and was followed a year later by "Isaac" (or "E-zek," as the report purported to mimic his speech), but these too did not persevere. Randolph and Rudolph Mossey were names introduced by a writer in 1888 who claimed to have spoken with him, but the source cannot be trusted. And as for Jules Bourglay, the name most often associated with him—so much so that it was inscribed on a tombstone plaque installed in 1953—it was a purely literary invention from 1884.

As with his fellow vagabond, the Leather Man appeared in newspapers after his range had been well established. The earliest records are from the late 1860s, followed by a slow drip of information and then an eruption of interest in the mid-1880s. People sensed the opportunities to weave tales about this eccentric vagabond as soon as he was a fixture in the community. An article from 1870 in the *Port Chester Journal*, for example, pondered that "his story may be a sad one," as if to invite storytellers to the challenge, and in 1873 the *Connecticut Valley Advertiser* supposed that he might have "escaped from some Dime Novel." By 1881 the *Woodbury Reporter* admitted that "his history would no doubt furnish capital for a romance," and much later, in 1885, a contributor to the *New Haven Evening Register* longed for a Nathaniel Hawthorne or Charles Dickens to do justice to his tale.

And sure enough, these pleas were answered. One of the earliest tales, from the *Woodbury Reporter* in 1877, will strike the reader as familiar:

> Twenty five years ago, the person known as the "Leather Man" lived in a thriving village in western New York. He carried on a large and profitable business as a tanner and currier, and was considered a prosperous and wealthy man. He owned a splendid mansion, beautiful grounds, horses, carriages, and servants at command, and all of the world's goods the heart could desire. A sudden change came over him. An incendiary fire destroyed his manufacturing establishment, together with his dwelling; the lady to whom he was engaged died about the same time. These combined losses unseated his reason, and he became a wanderer over

the earth, seeking for the loved and lost of his youth. Twice a year he visits her grave, covers it with flowers, and on his weary round he goes.

The story continues for a few more lines to round out his desire to join his beloved in death, but the connection here should be obvious: These are the motifs of the Old Darned Man story, now stitched onto the Leather Man.

As far as I know, no other commentator has noticed this *direct* connection between these two figures, although a few others—such as *Ballou's Monthly Magazine* from 1882—have nominated the Leather Man as a successor to the Old Darned Man. Such transmission, incidentally, would not be an uncommon practice; to the contrary, it is the heart of folklore. Stories themselves are vagabonds. The elements from popular tales migrate and adapt. And in an era when newspapers and oral storytelling were the predominant means of entertainment, the suturing of narrative components onto different figures was a way to keep favorite themes alive. We know, furthermore, that stories about the Old Darned Man were in circulation after his death in 1863. The Leather Man arrived on the scene, then, with just enough similarity—an air of mystery and unknown motives, patched clothing, a gentle personality, and an endless wandering that exposed him to hundreds of potential storytellers—to inherit the basic ideas. And, better yet, the Leather Man actually had a connection to New York. (A later report in the *Woodbury Reporter*, for example, placed his origins in Poughkeepsie.)

The contributor of the 1877 story in the *Woodbury Reporter* identified only as "A," but Dan DeLuca—the leading contemporary authority on the Leather Man—believes that he was Alexander Gordon Jr., the son of a tanner in Woodbury who often hosted the Leather Man and who, so it is rumored, holds the distinct honor of being one of the few people to oil his suit. (The history of Woodbury also notes that a public watering trough was near the tannery, being an especially inviting location for the vagabond.) This is especially important in considering a story that appeared in *Waterbury Daily American* in August 1884, written by one "W. A. Sailson"—the pen name, DeLuca explains, of Alexander's brother William Augustus Gordon, then a reporter for the *Danbury News*.

In that story, the Leather Man's real name is Jules Bourglay. He is the son of a wool merchant in Lyons, France. Sent to Paris in 1857 to finish his education, he meets "a beautiful and highly accomplished young lady named Laron, the daughter of a wealthy leather merchant." They fall in love and become engaged. Bourglay persuades her father, initially enraged by this agreement, for the chance to prove worthy. A deal is reached: Bourglay will work for one year for the father. If he shows himself to be a good businessman, the marriage could go forward; if he fails, he would leave Paris forever. Installed in the company, Bourglay speculates on leather commodities—but the market crashes, bringing financial ruin. He is thrown out of the business, exiled from his engagement, and soon discovered "wandering the streets in the great city in a dazed and half crazed condition."

Bourglay's father is summoned and the suffering Jules is conveyed to the family home on the Rhone, but he does not recover from his delirium. He is then sent to an asylum and kept two years before escaping and fleeing to America. His relatives petition authorities in New York to search for him. Eventually they discover him, dressed entirely in leather, meandering through Litchfield County "as a travelling plumber, noted for his eccentric behavior, as he never took anything but food or tobacco for his work." When questioned, Bourglay refuses to return to his native land. And in time, he abandons plumbing "and for 18 years he has been wandering around the country wearing his heavy suit of leather, as a penance, I suppose, for his disastrous failure in early life."

The story was an immediate success. It supplanted the Old Darned Man plot, but the two shared enough similarity in their romantic theme of heartbreak to resonate with one another, and elements of the two continued to appear in print over the next half-decade. There were competitors. The earliest attempts—outlines for a story that never manifested—hinted that the Leather Man was the Wandering Jew, a folkloric figure who was cursed to live until the Second Coming for a transgression against Jesus. This character appeared with some frequency in New England popular literature in the 1800s—Hawthorne, for example, utilizes him in "Ethan Brand" in 1850—and the connection with the Leather Man percolated well into twentieth century, appearing in the *Hartford Courant* as late as the 1930s.

No complete story developed from this seed about the Wandering Jew, but others competed for the spotlight. A story from 1883 in the *Yale Literary Magazine*, for example, identified the Leather Man as "Old Sol," who wandered in search of his lost adopted daughter. In 1884, just months after the publication of the Jules Bourglay story, Alfred Emil Hammer published a serial in the *New Haven Daily Palladium* that depicted him as an alchemist, living underground in an elaborate laboratory, searching for a means to resurrect his beloved.

A few years after the Bourglay tale appeared, the *New York Morning Journal* published an article—reprinted in newspapers throughout Connecticut—with motifs hearkening again to the Old Darned Man. In this account, an unnamed reporter claimed to have interviewed the Leather Man, whose real name was Randolph Mossey. He came to America from France in pursuit of his beloved, who had eloped with his best friend. When he hunts down his former comrade, pity holds back his bloodthirsty vengeance, as the man had lost an arm fighting in the Civil War. Mossey learns that his beloved has died, however, and mourns at her grave for two days. He extracts a pledge from her traitorous lover to bury Mossey next to her when he dies. For the remainder of his life he follows the path that she took on the run in a new country, and twice a year he visits her grave. The *New York Times* invoked this story the same year, explaining that the Leather Man came to America after a woman was false to him, and it was briefly given new life in the 1950s when the *Hartford Courant* rediscovered it.

After his death a few other stories blossomed and wilted quickly. One was that the Leather Man was a miser and had hidden his wealth in one of his shelters—a theory that earned occasional mention during his lifetime. One of the more unusual variants of this story appeared in the *New York Daily News*, in which a certain Clematis Sorrell encountered the Leather Man's ghost while searching for the treasure. Building on the long-standing idea that he was a penitent for some crime, the *New York Times* published a lurid tale in which his father owned a leather factory in France and dispatched his beloved on the grounds that she was beneath their class; struck with grief and horror, the young man came to America and forever tried to expiate the sins of his father. And one of the most problematic concoctions, initiated by an amateur historian, was that the Leather Man was an African American or mixed-raced member of a criminal—and fugitive—band associated with the "Barkhamsted Lighthouse" (another popular site of Connecticut folklore based in history). This one lasted for some time, appearing in the *Hartford Courant* as late as 1922.

Like the Old Darned Man, the true identity of the Leather Man may be lost to time. In both we find figures who became folk heroes and whose narratives radically metamorphosed as each new generation put a stamp of their interests and aspirations. Their stories, however, raise larger questions concerning hospitality: the responsibility of hosts, the meaning of a guest, the kindness of strangers, and the kindness *for* strangers. The era of tramps is long past in New England, but the contributions these two eccentrics and their stories made remain pertinent to every situation that calls for the respect of individuals as they travel their own path at their own pace.

13

THE BANDIT: JOHN WILSON

In March 1847, John Wilson, a well-respected physician in the town of Brattleboro, Vermont, passed away. An immigrant from Scotland, he had previously held a practice in Newfane and before that taught school in nearby Dummerston and Brookline. Accounts agree he was unusual in his dress and in his manners. He always wore a scarf around his neck, for example, and grew more reclusive as he aged. As the story goes, he refused to disrobe for the doctor attending his death and left explicit instructions for burial in the clothes he was wearing.

This request was not honored, however, some say by well-intended citizens who wished to give the doctor a proper burial and others say by an undertaker not aware of his desire. A remarkable sight appeared upon the removal of his clothing. The cravat concealed a deep scar on his neck, his garments hid indications of a gunshot wound, and his boot disguised a cork heel that bolstered his actual foot. And these marks, they soon learned, were the telltale sign of a notorious highway robber known as John Doherty, alias Captain Thunderbolt.

The story of the eccentric John Wilson tests the limits of believability. The protests of a few close associates against the claim fell on deaf ears. The New

England public feasted on the possibility that he was a wanted man whose peculiarities masked a dark secret. And that delight has hardly waned; even today people tell stories about his infamy lurking undetected in those sleepy Vermont towns. In order to understand how this impression took hold, we need to follow the circuitous trail of the Thunderbolt legend.

The tale begins in August 1821. Major John Bray and his wife, Sarah, were returning home to Boston from a visit with Governor John Brooks at his home in Medford. They were held up by a young man who aimed his pistol at Bray's chest. Bray surrendered money and his watch and the robber quickly set off. He was arrested, days later, in Springfield, Massachusetts, and returned to Cambridge for trial. This man, Michael Martin, would be found guilty and sentenced to death. He was executed by hanging in December 1821—Bray himself was among those who petitioned for clemency—and died at twenty-seven years of age. Martin's criminal activities spawned their own lore of hiding places and pursuits, but it was the publication of his confession (dictated to F. W. Waldo) that heightened the curiosity and fear of New Englanders.

In his testimony, Martin—who claimed his real name was John—explained that he was originally from Kilkenny, Ireland. He was a troubled youth, inclined toward wrongdoing. In 1816, at twenty years old, he was recruited by a man disguised as a member of the clergy to join him in a life of crime. This man, John Doherty, was the highway robber Captain Thunderbolt, who already had an enormous price on his head. In time Thunderbolt persuaded the young man and christened him Captain Lightfoot, and many pages of Martin's confession explained their dangerous exploits throughout Ireland. They also made clear the principles by which they conducted themselves: always robbing from the rich and never from the poor—or in his words, "to make property equal in this world"—and avoiding taking a life if possible. (When Martin robbed the Bray couple, he refused jewelry offered by the wife on the grounds that he would not steal from a woman.)

Martin described Thunderbolt in admiring terms. He was, said Martin, "an elegant, fine proportioned man, between thirty and forty years of age, about six feet and an inch in height, with an uncommon appearance of muscle and strength." During their crime spree, Thunderbolt was struck by a musket bullet while fleeing lawmen at Doneraile. The bullet lodged in Thunderbolt's leg, and Martin was forced to pry it out with a knife. Martin carefully noted how his partner had used his medical knowledge to survive the incident. Indeed, Martin was convinced that Thunderbolt had "studied physic"—that is, medicine—before he turned to highway robbery, and for a few weeks the two ran a quack medicine scheme. Thunderbolt was, furthermore, shrewd at the "gift of the gab" and skilled at disguises, which he utilized to move undetected, to surprise victims, and to escape speedily.

After a stint in Scotland, the two returned to Ireland in 1818, where the impetuous Martin decided to rob people in broad daylight. His plan went awry, and when he returned to their hideout at an inn, Thunderbolt was gone. The two never saw each other, although Martin once received a letter that his partner had traveled to the West Indies and began an honest life under another name. As for Martin, he made his way to Salem, Massachusetts, and found some employment, but eventually returned to his old business, working the roads from Boston to as far north as Montreal. He was the only person in the United States executed for that crime and earned the alluring title of "the Last Highwayman." And it did not take New Englanders long to speculate that if Lightfoot were in the region, Thunderbolt could be as well. (Martin attempted to escape jail before his execution, for example, and later rumors emerged that he was assisted with tools slipped to him during a visit from his old partner.)

The story now shifts to John Wilson. He was the son of a blacksmith, born in Muirkirk, a village in the south of Scotland. He and his brother Robert immigrated to Boston around 1818. Robert was engaged in the slate import industry and invested in a quarry in Guilford, Vermont. He eventually moved to New Haven and then Woodbridge, Connecticut. John Wilson, according to numerous reports, returned to England briefly in 1819 to import slate and upon his return made his way to Vermont, where he boarded with Peter Willard, a blacksmith. He was, apparently, reclusive from the start—in the words of one historian, "an air of mystery and romance followed him"—and more fantastical accounts depict him as hiding in closets or jumping out of windows when people arrived suddenly. Whether this has any truth in reality, Wilson did take up the unassuming position of a schoolteacher for a winter session in Brookline. While there he was responsible for the design of the new schoolhouse and constructed a round brick building with five windows spaced equally, similar to a popular folk architecture in his native land. It still stands today.

He also dedicated himself to medical studies. An inspection of his letters confirmed that he studied in Edinburgh, and a medical historian contends that he trained at the Medical College in Castleton, Vermont, in order to practice in the state. He did not remain long in Brookline, however, moving to Dummerston and then eventually to Newfane; he was living there when Martin's confessions broke. There are many records in the area of his flourishing practice, including one of his prescriptions for indigestion, and physicians or other people who worked with him often praised Wilson—although, even among them, he was known for antisocial behavior, an oddity made all the more glaring given his ease of conversation. Henry Burnham, for example, recalled Wilson as a "mysterious oracle" and noted that although he was "gifted with rare powers of conversation, which gave evidence of extensive information, he rarely, if ever, sought the society of those who could best appreciate him."

Also remaining are copious records of his real estate and business interests. Wilson did very well for himself, at least early on, and was able to purchase a considerable amount of land. In 1834 he married Abigail Chamberlain, the daughter of one of the proprietors who furnished granite for the railroads, and a year later they had a son. He was, furthermore, able to purchase an electrical machine for his practice and invested in a steam-powered sawmill in Brattleboro around 1836, when he moved to that town. In time he constructed a large house on the Connecticut River and cultivated an inclination for art; at least one of his works, a sketch of another prominent doctor in the area from 1821, survives. As one writer summarized, there were no striking passages in the life of John Wilson.

Wilson's life was not, however, a golden one. His investment in the sawmill proved unprofitable and his wife divorced him in 1838, citing his "intolerable severity" toward her in the case. (Later stories, published long after his death, claim that she knew of his nefarious past and refused to be married to such a criminal.) Reports also convey that he became a heavy drinker as he aged—one defender lamented that rum ended his marriage—and increasingly withdrew from society. When he appeared late in life, so the rumors contend, he was a disheveled phantom of his old and dapper self. He was once robbed by a group of rowdy young men who broke into his home. And his end came, according to his tombstone, when he was only fifty-eight years old. Wilson's son was placed in guardianship with a close friend—his ex-wife had perished years before—and his worldly goods were sent to auction in May 1847.

It was in the middle of that same month when the *Barre Patriot* published an article—"Death of Thunderbolt"—that launched rampant speculation. "We have been informed," it commenced, "that this celebrated English robber, the companion of the notorious Lightfoot, died recently in Brattleboro, Vt." The newspaper would not provide the name of the "skillful physician" who was the alter ego of the criminal highwayman, but that decision did nothing except excite the imagination of its readers. The article also insisted upon events that quickly hardened into Thunderbolt lore. The *Patriot* explained, for example, that he refused to be undressed while on his deathbed and had the wherewithal to hire two men to bury him in his clothes. The request was thwarted by other citizens, and, on removing his clothing, "the cause of this eccentric desire of his was manifest—the withered leg and cork heel, the shot marks, and the scar which witnessed a previous attempt at suicide—precisely as laid down in Lightfoot's description of him." Except, of course, that very little of that was how Martin actually described him.

The *Patriot* also remarked that a dirk and pistol were found on his person and that inspection of his home gave up a number of other weapons along with watches, diamonds, and jewelry packed away in sawdust. Another oddity demanded attention, namely his habit of wearing several layers of clothes, which the newspaper speculated was an attempt at disguise. Taken together, these elements combined into a plausible scenario. Martin had, after all, described his partner as a tall, cultured, and elegant Scotsman who had trained in medicine, was wounded in the leg, and who perfected the use of disguises and guile to move through an unsuspecting community. John Wilson could readily fit that bill. (Rumors also swirled that the doctor had, prior to his arrival in New England, conducted business in the West Indies.)

Newspapers in all six New England states leapt at the chance to reprint this article throughout the summer and it inspired numerous imitators. Some of them suspected a hoax. The *Springfield Republican*, for example, was vociferous in wondering how a report about an "eccentric Scotch doctor" who turned out to be a "far-famed robber" hiding quietly in the midst of people for thirty years could be anything but a "fish story." Letters to editors mocked the incredulity of the entire affair. But others persisted, and by midsummer purported histories and fictionalized serials of the adventures of Thunderbolt and Lightfoot began to appear. The summer closed with a republication of Martin's confession to which a biography of John Wilson was attached.

The publisher, John B. Miner of Brattleboro, was a clever editor. (He had reason to be—estimates suggest that the original publication of Martin's confessions sold twelve thousand copies.) He noted in his introduction that the press had stirred up "feverish excitement" among the public by intimating John Wilson was Thunderbolt, and, although the "circumstances and coincidents" were plentiful, he would leave it to the discerning reader to decide. Indeed, Miner was insistent that he would neither affirm nor deny the identity. The very title itself left room for ambiguity: "An Account of John Wilson, Who Recently Died at Brattleboro, Vt., Believed by Many to be the Notorious Capt. Thunderbolt." The twelve-page essay, however, left little room for resistance— or more accurately, it made certain that enough suspicion could linger so that readers would grab at any salacious detail.

The dramatic hook was Wilson's eccentric behavior. Wilson was, Miner explained, "one of that enigmatical kind of men—about whom much is said, and little known—about whom much is guessed, and much suspected, but so long as he lived, ending only in guessings and suspicions." Readers learned that Wilson always grew uneasy whenever talk of his past arose and became especially agitated at any invocation of Thunderbolt, once throwing a copy of Martin's confessions into a roaring fire. No specific details were supplied for these claims and blanket statements peppered paragraph after paragraph, all to corroborate Martin's confession. John Wilson, Miner asserted, had indeed been in the West Indies. He was *precisely* the height that Martin detailed and of the same countenance—readers only needed to consult a daguerreotype of the doctor to see the resemblance. His age mapped out as well, as long as Martin's estimate of thirty to forty was closer to thirty and additional calculations could be slightly bent. And the scar upon his leg wholly matched the wound of the Doneraile incident.

The account observed other quirks of behavior: his dreadful aversion to lawsuits and to attending business in courts; his mysterious divorce (and the whispers that she knew of his past); his suspicious intelligence and enjoyment of alcohol; his penchant for sitting near doors to exit quickly and his refusal to stand within a crowd; his deathbed ramblings about Lightfoot and his confessions as he passed in and out of consciousness; and his cache of weapons hidden in his home. There were rumors of a diamond necklace, worth seven thousand dollars, stowed away from the peering eyes of his wife—which when pressed about its origins, Wilson reportedly claimed it was his mother's, despite her being married to a blacksmith. There was his strange fashion—the ever-present cravat, guarding his neck even in intolerable summer heat—coupled with his request to try boots on at home rather than at the store, his three pairs of drawers under his pantaloons, and his adamant insistence that he die with his clothes on. And finally there was his odd aversion to society. What kind of peculiar person, after all, would desire to pass time "in seclusion and study" rather than in the company of those who were, readers learn, talking behind his back about his oddities?

A similar work, *An Authentic Account of Thunderbolt and Lightfoot*, edited by Aaron Bell and published in Boston and New York, appeared the same year and included illustrations of various scenes, including the wounding of Thunderbolt for its cover. As with Miner's pamphlet, this one emphasized that John Wilson was "reputed" to be the robber, but it follows the same pattern: The "good people of Brattleboro and vicinity" were surprised to discover that an "eccentric individual" who served as their physician might be "one of the most reckless and successful highwaymen that ever stained the annals of crime." Here, the rumor of Wilson hiring two men to bury him in his clothes reappeared, even as the account admitted it could be true or false. But it went further still, adding that Wilson's withered leg and neck scar fit a description of the bandit on handbills and wanted posters throughout the United Kingdom.

This second account followed with the stories of crime—and the charming disposition—of Thunderbolt and Lightfoot, concluding that the former disappeared from Dublin thirty years ago, perhaps moving to the West Indies or perhaps "killed in some desperate encounter." It closed with, "But it now seems probable that for the last thirty years he has been an eminent physician, and a quiet, but odd citizen in the State of Vermont. Truly, there is much romance in real life."

Both pamphlets were heavily advertised throughout New England, and the impact was immediate. The public craved for more news and more scandal. And their suppliers readily obliged. In April 1849, for example, the National Theatre in Boston hosted the debut of an equestrian drama—that is, a play that included horses—composed by one of its proprietors, William English, on the exploits of Lightfoot and Thunderbolt. Purely fictional—the robberies were set between Ipswich and Cambridge—and often comical, the play opened to a packed house and lines out the door and then profitably toured eastern New England throughout 1850.

Wilson had his defenders, many of whom were friends whose very testimony complicated the narrative of his reclusive retreat from society. John Morrison, for example, was an associate of both John and Robert Wilson in Boston. Morrison eventually moved to New York, but he and Wilson kept a correspondence. In August 1847, Morrison sent a spirited letter to the editor of the *Boston Post* in which he pushed back against the claim and inadvertently provided other tantalizing information about his friend's life history. Taking a strong stance against the "vile charges" against Wilson, Morrison explained how they met in Boston in 1818, both being Scottish immigrants. Morrison became acquainted with his friend's history prior to arriving in the United States and revealed that he had a child, Maria, outside of marriage. Maria Wilson married a blacksmith by the name of Hugh McKerrow Begg, whom Morrison contacted to inquire further about Wilson.

The *Post* published Begg's response. He had been anticipating the inquiry, as he had recently read the accusation about John Wilson in the Glasgow *Herald*. Begg dismissed it as a "notorious lie," and further noted that Wilson was "loved by every person that knew him" in Muirkirk, where his family still had relations. Morrison did admit that Begg never knew Wilson personally and that the information was gleaned from his wife and others, but he also provided testimony from men in Baltimore and Philadelphia who knew Wilson when he was a young man and who testified to his having a lame leg at the time. (Begg explained that the scar on his leg came from a burn received at the Muirkirk Iron Works.) Morrison raised further objections. Why, he petitioned, would Wilson have traveled to England as an agent for his brother's slate company if he were one of the most wanted men in the kingdom? Why did the lawyer, Larkin Mead, who investigated Wilson's belongings, only note the letters proving his medical studies and not the rumored list of hidden booty? In Morrison's mind, there were too many discrepancies and not enough evidence to add up.

Numerous reports also found that Robert Wilson visited Brattleboro soon after his brother's death. He too refuted the claim and explained that John had been injured and left lame since he was six years old, but various newspapers decided to depict Robert as telling different stories to different people and conveniently offering no examples for support. (It is also worth noting that stories of Thunderbolt the robber occasionally merged with stories of Thunderbolt the pirate, who legendarily operated around New Haven in the late 1700s. Robert Wilson is sometimes brought into these tales, as his house was identified as a secret rendezvous for Thunderbolt.)

Two letters from June 1847, both signed by "F"—likely Brattleboro resident Charles C. Frost, according to local historian Thomas St. John—similarly disputed certain "facts" reported in the newspapers and upheld others. "F," who admitted that he would listen for hours to the Scottish doctor and characterized him as blessed with "ease and grace in conversation," flatly dismissed the notion that Wilson hid jewelry in sawdust and hired two men to bury him. "F" confirmed that Wilson kept a set of weapons, both pistols and swords, and that he would not remove his clothes—including a handkerchief around his neck—but assumed that the motive was only to hide his lameness. He also mentioned in passing that Wilson possessed a set of bagpipes—and a mistress who kept to the outskirts of town! Ultimately, "F" took no stance on the matter of his identity. "Sometimes," he concluded, "I think he was *the* Thunderbolt, and sometimes I think he was not. But the opinion is gaining very rapidly in this place that he was the veritable man."

Perhaps the most convincing evidence in John Wilson's favor was that "Captain Thunderbolt" had reportedly already been captured two decades earlier. In 1823, one year after the publication of Martin's confessions, the *Portland Argus* spun a fantastic tale concerning a certain John Johnson, a barber and recent transplant to the town. Johnson hired out a horse and carriage from the stables of one Mr. McKenney and then disappeared for two weeks. Agents pursued Johnson across New Hampshire and Vermont, arrested him near the Canadian border, and sent him to the jail in St. Albans. He was released before McKenney arrived, and according to the *Argus* he had talked his way out of imprisonment by pretending to be a man of the cloth. These details, as well as his "Herculean frame and dark visage" gave reason for the people of Portland to suspect Johnson was none other than Thunderbolt himself. A grisly thought soon crossed the minds of the citizens—namely, to think how many of their men "passed beneath his razor" in his barber shop. Johnson was, however, soon apprehended in Montreal and returned to Portland, but not before he put up a violent fight.

This narrative continued throughout the summer and autumn of 1823. The St. Albans newspaper corrected the impression that he was let free after conning them and contended, instead, that he was held without evidence for four days and without any sign that McKenney was coming for him. Newspapers in Montreal provided details of the "great force" necessary to take him from the Neptune Inn there, and by November he was convicted of horse stealing and sentenced to two years of hard labor and solitary confinement.

Soon after his trial, the public learned that he was also known as Charles Loring, a convicted criminal in Maryland, who had fled justice for Massachusetts. And throughout all these reports, Johnson was identified again and again as the bandit of the British Isles.

He was not, of course, that man, but publishers never retracted the claim. And while the John Johnson case has no direct link to John Wilson, it does show how ready the public was to indulge in the Thunderbolt story and how easily newspapers of the time could raise their revenues by offering it. So too did nineteenth-century writers continue to flirt with the idea. As early as 1864 Emerson Bennett, the popular dime-novel author, occasionally published fictionalized stories of Thunderbolt and Lightfoot and once noted the possibility that Wilson could have been the robber. From December 1869 to February 1870, the *Vermont Record and Farmer* printed a series, "The Recluse," composed by a Mrs. M. Ritchie; as the title suggests, the narrative revolves around the discovery of John Wilson's true identity and ends with his death in a shoot-out. The editors saw fit to append a note for readers that the real Wilson did not die thusly, but did not deny that he was Thunderbolt.

In 1901 several papers reported that novelist Irving Bacheller was researching the case in preparation for writing a book; it did not materialize, but the turn of the twentieth century saw a spike of interest, as many people in the Brattleboro area claimed to possess items once owned by Wilson, from receipts for his medical advice to a cane that hid a dagger inside. By the 1920s, antique dealer Henry Lawrence had assembled an impressive collection of Wilson memorabilia, which he eventually donated to the library in Brattleboro. In the 1940s, when the round schoolhouse became a tourist destination, rumors swirled that Wilson designed it in such a manner as to see in every direction and therefore have the jump on anyone who tried to ambush him. And in 1954 novelist W. R. Burnett released *Captain Lightfoot*, another fictionalized account that was brought to the silver screen in 1955, starring Rock Hudson and Barbara Rush.

Perhaps not surprisingly, as time marched on, the ambiguities about Wilson's identity gave way to certainties. The reason for this is neatly summarized by a writer for the *Boston Herald*, Elizabeth Ellam, who addressed the Thunder-bolt story at length in 1923. "A live bandit is nothing for a community to brag about," she observed, "but a dead bandit is an asset to that same community and his memory sheds romance and distinction on that part of the land in which he lived." We may never know with absolute certainty if John Wilson was the purveyor of crimes and terror who hid his true identity under the veneer of a peculiar and reclusive Vermont physician, or if he was simply a deeply introverted and eccentric individual who may have suffered from alcoholism as he aged. We can rest assured, however, that the facts in the case of John Wilson readily demonstrate the human desire for mystery.

14

THE WEALTH SEEKERS: EDWARD NORTON, SAMUEL BEMIS, AND PHINEAS GARDNER WRIGHT

Eccentricity and wealth often go together. As mentioned in the Introduction, some commentators argue that wealth is a defining feature of eccentricity, as both allow possessors to impose themselves on others. The pursuit of wealth can also lead to remarkably odd reasoning and quirky behavior. Riches, furthermore, allow people to indulge in activities out of the reach of normal economic means. But the eccentricity of wealth can take many forms, and the desire for money can manifest in very different ways. Another chapter of this book, for example, explores eccentrics who utilized their wealth for the benefit of the public. Timothy Dexter and Frederick Goddard Tuckerman were similarly men of considerable means, but for one wealth fueled ostentation and for the other solitude. In this chapter, I introduce three very divergent personalities who sought wealth in a variety of ways and left legacies that were not soon forgotten.

There are several candidates in New England who could vie for the most unusual idea to get rich, but Edward "Ned" Norton deserves accolades for the way his plans earned him a reputation as an obsessive crackpot decades *after* he passed on. Born in Albany in 1844 and raised in Lewis County, New York, Norton appeared in Colebrook, New Hampshire, and Lemington, Vermont—two small but industrious communities on the upper Connecticut River—in the late 1880s. He remained in northern New England for the rest of his life, which came to a close in 1922. Norton's fame (or perhaps infamy) came much later when, in the 1970s, an amateur historian learned of his decision to mine Monadnock Mountain in Lemington for gold. In an attempt to spin a good tale, this writer and those who followed depicted Norton as a man so monstrously obsessed with his desire to find something that was not there that he neglected his family and society and spent his days toiling fruitlessly in the empty bowels of the earth. This is not, however, an accurate representation of his motives, and the full story is even more engrossing.

Norton debuted in newspapers in 1884, gathering lumber to build a house in Lemington. It was ready in 1886. At the time, he made a living as a fishing and hunting guide, especially on the Connecticut Lakes and in the surrounding Canadian woods. He also tried his hand at maple sugaring and became a proficient trapper; over the decades his impressive catch of foxes, deer, and fishers, as well as his success at catching suckers, secured him minor acclaim. He also married and raised a family of several children, one of whom died of typhoid in 1896. By the mid-1890s Norton was regarded as a taxidermist of considerable skill and took other odd jobs to supplement his living as a sportsman, including work at the Balsams Grand Hotel in nearby Dixville Notch. None of these jobs, however, singled him out as a man possessed of anything but a desire to make ends meet.

Newspaper reports associated with Norton suggested that he was, to use the colloquial expression, quite a character. In 1891, for example, editors of the *Vermont Watchman* noted their Lemington correspondent with a puckish salute for his frugality; Norton had written them with a handmade envelope cut from birch bark and sealed with spruce gum. "If nature had provided any substitute for a postage stamp," they quipped, "Ned would have found and used it." Over the decades he penned several letters to editors with advice concerning deer hunting—he was insistent, for example, that deer should not be skinned in the woods by a hasty hand—or commentary on the Connecticut River Lumber Company, or complaints about hunters from New Hampshire encroaching on Vermont game. A tantalizing and all-too-brief notice in 1904 insisted he was "on the war path" again, that time concerning an issue with the directors of a local school, but no details fleshed out his bombast.

Norton did indeed mine Monadnock Mountain for a few decades, and the site continued to be called "Norton's Mine" long after he ceased working there. The name remained, for example, in state geological surveys in the 1930s and 1960s, and even today hiking guides demarcate trails that will lead to the abandoned shafts. But Norton was not the first person to believe Monadnock would be a viable source of income. In 1891 the *Essex County Herald* introduced a certain Henry Marshall from Colebrook, who claimed to have discovered a silver mine on the eastern side of the mountain. Marshall, it appears, may be the one to have become obsessed. In 1894 the same newspaper noted that he sold his store in Colebrook, moved back in with his mother, and continued "blasting out gold and silver at the base of Mt. Monadnock, where he has been working for two or three years."

As a man earning a living predominantly from the wilderness rather than the vibrant lumbering, farming, tourism, and mill industries in the area, Norton did look for ways to enrich himself from natural resources. One newspaper from 1889, for example, reported that he discovered a limestone quarry with the potential to prove profitable, but it's likely Marshall inspired Norton to try his hand at mining. (If the accounts are accurate, both men set up on the eastern slope of Monadnock with Marshall working the base and Norton much higher up.) In 1892 a brief notice updated readers that Marshall continued to dig his silver mine and Norton claimed to have discovered a gold-bearing rock. The two men would jockey positions over the next decade, and local newspapers obliged the competition, reporting that one or the other was confident he would soon "strike it rich" or observing when one opened his mine and the other did not. Marshall eventually disappeared from the public record, and his mine received no credit in local lore, so it is plausible that Norton simply outlasted his rival.

The idea that Norton was obsessed with gold needs tempering. While newspapers continually identified Marshall's relentless pursuit of silver, Norton clearly changed his expectations as his mining operations evolved. At the turn of the twentieth century, he was optimistic that he had struck a rich amount of nickel ore. Whatever he found, it was enough to keep him sustained for some time. In 1903 he commenced construction on a road to the mine and was still at work on it in 1905. That same year, the *Herald* again wished him well, hopeful that his "pluck and perseverance under discouraging circumstances" would finally pay off—a hint, ever so slight, that the community rooted for rather than mocked or worried about him. But the good wishes never materialized into material gain. The only treasures he took from the mountain—which, according to scientific reports, contained mostly feldspar and quartz—were enough mineral ore to add to paint for his house in 1904.

It would be unfair, then, to characterize Norton as neglectful of all other activities in his pursuit of wealth. Throughout the frustrating decades of mining, he continued other gainful employment. As late as 1904, for example, he was still at work leading parties safely to and from the Connecticut Lakes. As he aged, he showed up in newspapers more for his visiting or hosting relatives or serving as a juror than for digging Monadnock. And when he passed, newspapers in western New York remembered him only as a well-known guide. There is, simply, no evidence that he lost perspective on his life as later writers depict him. Norton certainly exhibited eccentric tendencies, but he was not one-dimensional, and in the larger context of trying to get by on limited finances, his hopes of becoming rich are decidedly common. What makes him unique, then, is that unlike so many of us, Edward Norton did something about that desire.

—◆—

Samuel Bemis, our second example, did achieve great wealth in his lifetime, although his circumstances at birth were not promising and certainly not of privilege. He was born to unwed parents in 1793 in Putney, Vermont, at a time when such parentage would have been a scandal. His father, who would marry (and abandon) several other women, was a clock- and watchmaker, and Bemis learned this trade as a young man. An apocryphal story suggested that he walked from Vermont to Boston to pursue employment, but more plausible accounts contend that he found his way to Cambridge, where his father had a shop, via Keene, New Hampshire. The skills of a clockmaker suited Bemis's intelligence and interest in mechanics, and this in turn parlayed into his becoming a dentist and dental surgeon in the early 1820s. One of Bemis's credited innovations was improvements to false teeth, adopting them in such a manner as to allow practical rather than mere cosmetic use. This career made him considerable wealth and with it he invested in properties in Boston and Baltimore.

Years later Bemis began an annual summer pilgrimage to the White Mountains, a budding site for tourism—albeit in a much different sense than today, for then it was an activity generally restricted to the upper classes. This was an age when such outings were thought to be a way to restore and improve one's health, and Bemis himself would claim that to be his motive. In the 1830s he became a frequent visitor of the Mount Crawford House, owned by the pioneering guide Abel Crawford and managed by his son-in-law, Nathaniel Davis, after 1851. Bemis's friendly relationship with these two hoteliers resulted in his lending them money and effectively holding the mortgage on their property. When Davis became ill and unable to pay the debts, Bemis gained the land and continued to acquire more in Crawford Notch. Some estimates suggest that he eventually owned six thousand acres in the area; many of the geographical features still carry his name today. He continued his practice in Boston, however, until he finally retired to New Hampshire in the 1860s.

Bemis's inventiveness found further expression in the construction of his own house near the Crawford estate. It was built entirely of granite stone quarried from the nearby area and still stands today, operating as an inn. His restless mind turned to other activities as well. In the 1840s he purchased one of the first cameras—or perhaps *the* first—available in the United States, and with it established an impressive library of daguerreotypes of landscape scenes in Boston and the White Mountains; he may have been the first person to snap an image of the Old Man in the Mountain. With the purchase of the Crawford

House, Bemis also had access to a well-established orchard. He tended to the apples there, and his cultivation received accolades, including a silver medal from the Massachusetts Horticultural Society—no small accomplishment given that the fruit was produced in the White Mountains.

Bemis was well regarded by those who knew him. Lucy Crawford, the daughter of Abel, described him in a reminiscence as a "kind and humane" man. An obituary from New Hampshire—he died in 1881—similarly explained that he was "much esteemed by the people." And an account written by the popular journalist and amateur folklorist Samuel Adams Drake depicted a respectful personal encounter. This book, *Heart of the White Mountains*, re-creates a conversation between Bemis and the author, in which the aged man comes across as affable, thoughtful, and charming. (It was, furthermore, this work that hailed Bemis as "Lord of the Valley" for the vast expansion of land he owned; Drake estimated a thirteen-mile stretch all in his possession.) Yet despite these salutations, Bemis garnered a reputation for being both an eccentric and a mysteriously reclusive figure. Tour guides written after his passing directly identified him as such—one called him an "eccentric old patriarch"—as did a few obituaries. It is worth considering, then, how this impression came to be and whether there was any truth to it.

It does appear that Bemis exhibited hoarding behaviors that far exceeded Yankee frugality. As one biographer summarized, he seemed incapable of disposing of even the most inconsequential items. He reportedly once removed the watch papers—the decorative papers that protect the inner mechanics of a watch—before melting down the watches for use in his dental practice. Drake similarly described the room in which Bemis entertained them as having "no counterpart in this world, unless the famous hut of Robinson Crusoe has escaped the ravages of time." It was, Drake continued, crammed full of, among other things, antiques, dentistry furniture, bottles of chemicals, a portable furnace, "and a variety of instruments or tools of which we did not know the use." The sight led his companion to compare it with a sixteenth-century alchemist's laboratory.

Bemis never married. Rumors arose that it was not by choice and that his reclusive behavior was the result of a broken heart. The source of this story, however, was a speculative article in the *Boston Globe*, "The Mountain Hermit: Life and Career of an Eccentric Old Man," that appeared a month after he died. Its author consulted two men to inquire about the "very eccentric, wealthy, ingenious hermit" whose life had been a mystery. One of these was Captain James Mead. The other was Frank George, who leased the Crawford House from Bemis in the 1870s. The story they provided contended that Bemis had moved permanently to the area in 1840, boarded with Nathaniel Davis at the Mount Crawford House, and took an interest in Davis's young daughter—an interest that developed into love over the years. In their tale, Bemis offered to pay off all of her father's debts and give her ten thousand dollars directly if she would agree to marry him. She refused, and Bemis continued to pursue her for some time, all to no avail. When his rejection became evident, so offers the *Globe* writer, he "grew more and more peculiar." There is no corroborating evidence for this tale, and it has all the hallmarks of a folkloric motif attached to other hermit stories, so it must be taken with a grain of salt.

There are also other questionable claims, especially concerning dates, that make this account less than punctilious, but the story is amusing. Others like it depict a man who was kind if approached in the correct way and a terror if imposed upon, who expected everyone to think as he did—he was once surprised to discover that people did not equally enjoy the taste of stale fish—and who was suspicious that associates wanted to steal his wealth. A later anecdote, however, has at least a kernel of truth in it. Bemis prepared a will in 1858 that left his wealth to his legal counsel, William Sohier. Toward the end of his life, he wrote a new will, bequeathing virtually all of his monies and properties to George Morey, his caretaker. As the *Globe* narrated the story, Bemis did so out of spite when Sohier, doing his due diligence, once inquired as to why his client requested a considerable sum of cash, thereby offending Bemis's sense of independence.

This somewhat humorous anecdote proved prescient of trouble, as Bemis's will was contested by Sohier and by several relatives. The lawsuit lingered on for years and became known as the "famous Bemis will case" in newspapers throughout the country. During the process Bemis's status as an illegitimate child was discovered, which prohibited the relatives from having any recourse. (It also led to wild speculation by some that the shame of this fact manifested in his "singular manner.") Sohier eventually lost the suit and Morey received the inheritance, but when one reads between the lines of certain news accounts, it is clear that Bemis's competency was also called into question. This likely fueled the public perception that he was a paragon of eccentricity.

—◦~—

Lastly, Phineas Gardner Wright—known as "Gard" to many—did not have the title of eccentric thrust upon him, but actively courted it in his lifetime, and he did so by drawing attention to the final chapter of existence. He was born in Fitzwilliam, New Hampshire, in 1829, the third of four children. A few years after Wright was born the family left for Woodstock, where his mother was from, and eventually made it to Putnam, Connecticut. In 1849 his father left for California and died in Stockton, presumably during the gold rush, leaving his mother a widow for a quarter of a century. Wright never married but remained close to his relatives. His younger sister died in her early twenties, and his older sister married a local blacksmith who was taken prisoner and passed away in Georgia during the Civil War. His brother moved to Niantic, Connecticut, and Wright supported his mother and bereaved sister (and likely her many children) as they aged; a newspaper report from the early 1890s, for example, remarked that his sister was the housekeeper at his home.

Many commentators assumed that his family was poor given his father's excursion to California, but Wright's grandfather was a well-respected physician in Fitzwilliam, so it is unclear precisely what their circumstances were when they moved to Connecticut. An interview with Wright in 1907 also suggested that he came from impoverished circumstances that led him to seek employment as a railroad worker and brick carrier as a young man (a report a decade later added millworker to his list of jobs), but the point of this claim was to promote the perception that he was a self-made man of considerable means—a rags-to-riches story—and not necessarily an accurate comment on his family's history. The same interview explained that he made his actual fortune in real estate and mortgage deals, and estimates in various accounts ranged from $125,000 to $250,000.

Wright may have cultivated an image of being thrifty to a quirky extreme. Anecdotal evidence from a local history book depicted him as hiding his wealth under a veneer of poverty, riding around in a dilapidated wagon, picking up garbage for his swine and discarded hay for his horses, and wearing a brimmed hat with a cord around it that used to serve as a bathrobe belt. An interview in 1908 further observed that his house was a "modest cottage" on one of the main streets of Putnam. But these images of a cheapskate conflicted with other reports. He apparently kept, for example, a vast collection of postcards from around the world, and his first appearance in newspapers throughout the country occurred in 1892, when he, an "enterprising bargain hunter" and a "proud and happy old bachelor," purchased a range of memorabilia of the author Louise Chandler Moulton at auction. That is, Wright seems to have appreciated a deal, but he did not deprive himself of enjoyable expenditures.

Nowhere is this more apparent than in the investment he made for the after-life. In 1903 he began preparation of his "tomb," as one trade magazine called it. The structure was—or rather is, for it still stands in the Grove Street Cemetery in Putnam—imposing. It consists of a massive monument with a carved image of Wright's face and his shoulders and chest. His name forms a halo above the bust, and below is a stark notice of his birthplace and date (and, as added later, the same for his death). It is, however, another inscription on the stone that propelled him into the annals of eccentricity: GOING. BUT KNOW NOT WHERE. Belowground was also quite a marvel. According to several reports, Wright had a hole dug almost twice the size necessary for a single coffin and then lined the walls and floor with bricks. He did this, reportedly, so that he would have the room he needed. Estimates for all of these luxuries again ran wild from $1,500 to $4,000. And on top of that expense, he provided headstones for family members who were not buried there (such as his father) or who were buried elsewhere in the cemetery (such as his sister) in order to keep the family together.

The unique inscription made national headlines, but so did Wright's decision to send the giant stone back to Worcester Monument Company to alter the whiskers on his face. A newspaper report from 1904 explained that he had changed his living appearance and hence thought it only proper for the stone to reflect his new look, but by 1905 the reports changed to become more richly textured tales. One popular narrative suggested that Wright—then overtly identified as an "eccentric character"—had a dream in which spirits visited him and warned the whiskers were too long. In another, the dreamland vision explained that he could not enter heaven—presuming that was where he was going—if the beard were parted or parted erroneously to his face. Another trade journal delighted in telling a tale of his rejecting three previous and expensive stones until he finally settled on the fourth one, which convinced him that passersby would stop and admire.

The strange expression—going but know not where—was irresistible to editors. Newspapers around the country made mention of it and regularly checked in as Wright passed milestone after milestone in aging. He reveled in the attention and when asked early about its meaning, he replied that he "had friends in both places." In a later interview with the *New York Herald*, Wright delivered a more philosophical, yet no less bold appraisal. "Them's true words," he said, "but they ain't many folks what's got the honesty or courage to say the same thing." The frank assessment also inspired, according to Wright himself, hundreds of replies from people who approved or disapproved, and especially from "theologians" who were appalled by his flouting the risks and who sent "abusive letters" in response. Wright's need for the stone, however, did not come immediately. When he turned eighty-one in 1910, a Norwich newspaper celebrated the good news, and in 1914 the same newspaper gleefully informed the public that he had no use for his "famous monument" and was well on his way to one hundred. Finally, in 1918, at age eighty-nine—and one of the oldest citizens to have lived in Putnam in its history—he left this world to wherever he was heading.

There is little doubt that Wright was in on this joke and enjoyed the celebrity of nonconforming. The *Norwich Bulletin* characterized him as good-natured and prone to a wholesome laugh and who planned to enjoy himself while he lasted. His impish sense of humor also may have motivated comments that by today's standards are certainly questionable. In explanation of his bachelorhood in an interview in 1907, Wright bemoaned that he had been disappointed in love forty years earlier and had forsaken women since that fateful day. He claimed to have composed poetry on their perfidy, and debated adding another inscription to his stone that would read "Never beat by a man, but by a woman." His advice for making money, delivered in another interview in 1908, started out helpful and then quickly turned cringeworthy: "strict attention to details, not trying to know too much, and consistently suspecting all women."

It is, to reiterate, impossible to tell if these problematic comments reflect an actual misogyny or an attempt at comic sentiment that does not carry well a century later. But there is something that may help explain these comments that other biographers have missed. In 1904 a newspaper reported that Wright paid four hundred dollars to erect a headstone at the grave of Sarah Gage in Woodstock. Gage, the account noted, was Wright's "sweetheart." And a quick examination of the 1900 federal census reveals that she was listed at his dwelling as his housekeeper, his sister having died five years prior. Gage was a divorcee who lost her own daughter in 1892. We will never know quite what happened in that relationship, but it is plausible that it was deserving of regard. And to finish the speculation, yet another interview in 1908 characterized Wright as disappointed but willing to "get hitched up" should the right woman come along. This never happened, and his niece, who cared for him in the final years, presumably inherited the bulk of his wealth.

It should not be surprising that a character as colorful as Wright garnered a number of anecdotes about him. A more troubling one suggests that bricks kept disappearing from the Bundy brickyard when it was owned by the mill magnate George Morse Sr. Wright, who was a young man and employee there, was accused of the theft. Although no one could prove his guilt, he also could not prove his innocence, and as a consequence he was sentenced to attend Sunday school during the summer and attend barefoot. That odd detail echoed in other stories from his adulthood in which he reportedly went barefoot in the summer, although he suggested it was for health reasons. In another tale that appeared regularly in early newspapers, Wright left a gift for the undertakers and gravediggers at his tomb; usually this consisted of gin or whiskey or cigars. Later reports lost sight of the intended recipient and insinuated that Wright wanted to be buried with such a trove himself, and soon thereafter he was on the record denying the matter altogether.

Finally, there is a hint of an epic story that was regrettably lost to the sands of time. The gist was that Wright enjoyed a bout of drinking with the boys in the town, and one night they decided to prank him. He drank too much, passed out, and awoke in a coffin filled with ice. Since that day, the story concludes, he continued to keep a "little brown jug" under his buggy, but filled it up in Webster, Massachusetts, rather than in town. (This folkloric tale may have been the impetus for a much later yarn appearing long after his death that he kept his money in Boston so that his neighbors would not know his financial business.) For all of these tales hinting at vices, Wright made good on his intentions to aid the Congregational Church in Putnam in his will. Whether that charitable act influenced where he went remains open to further investigation.

15

THE BENEFACTORS: GEORGE BECKWITH, JOSEPH BATTELL, AND ISABELLA STEWART GARDNER

George Beckwith was identified as an eccentric even by those who cared for him lovingly. His daughter, in her memorial essay, celebrated his "eccentric habits"—or "oddities," as she called them elsewhere—as essential to his being. The *Waterbury American* likewise praised him in similar terms:

> Eccentricity with Mr. Beckwith was no assumption for the purpose of securing ephemeral reputation for talent, but an inborn, inherent attribute of his nature. In facial, moral and physical development, eccentricity was apparent. His laugh was eccentric, his language and gestures were eccentric, his pose was eccentric, in fact the whole "make-up" of the man was compounded of eccentric ingredients.

The *New Haven Journal and Courier*, in lamenting his death, agreed that no citizen was more widely known in the community—and perhaps the country—"for his oddities and eccentricities," while the *New Haven Register* dedicated a lengthy article entitled "An Eccentric's Death." Just what made him such a unique figure?

There are clues to be found in a book written by his daughter soon after he died in 1880, *One True Heart: Leaves from the Life of George Beckwith*. It is an idealized account but remains insightful into the nature of this unusual man, who inscribed his business cards with a quote from Thomas Paine's *Rights of Man*: "The world is my country, to do good my religion." Born in Berlin, Connecticut, in 1810, Beckwith made his name in New Haven and the surrounding area. He was well-known and well regarded for decades for an almanac that he produced starting in 1848 and for his work in a number of reform movements. His almanac became extremely popular, with an estimated fifteen thousand subscribers in the year of his death. It contained, as one would expect, information on the weather, the seasons and calendrical events, phases of the moon, eclipses and related natural phenomena, and the tides. Beckwith himself calculated many of these, drawing upon his keen abilities in mathematics and interest in astronomy.

Beckwith's Almanac, however, provided ample other information from court activities to a chronicle of events in the communities surrounding New Haven, then all of Connecticut and much of the nation. Short essays appeared, as did some poetry, and entertaining lists of sayings or other bursts of wisdom. It was a major contribution to readers, witnessed by the concern of many who used it—sailors especially—that it would close after his death. It did not; the almanac continued under the direction of his daughter and his granddaughter into the 1930s, serving as a reliable source of knowledge for almost a century. In reading through its pages, one catches glimpses of Beckwith's intelligence and admiration for the sagacious, but as a whole the almanac is profoundly sober, almost in complete juxtaposition to the personal spirit of its editor.

Beckwith's eccentricities were found, then, not in his almanac but in his personality and personal appearance. "He always wore an old white hat," wrote the *New Haven Register*, adding that his "clothes . . . looked as if they had been handed down from preceding generations; a blue ribbon in the button hole of his coat, and when he wore shoes he selected the largest and roughest kind of brogans. His hair looked as if it had never been combed. He looked upon shirts with a nicely polished bosom with infinite disgust, and collars, cuffs and neckties he considered an abomination." His daughter confirmed that he refused to wear stockings and often shoes, and he preferred to walk barefoot except when it was too cold to do so. While these fashion oddities are amusing in their portrayal of what New Englanders found odd in the nineteenth century, I would not want to imply that society has yet progressed admirably so as not to judge people by their clothes. And by all accounts, a very busy mind was underlying Beckwith's inattentiveness to his dress.

His daughter recalled, for example, how he would often come home late at night, having forgotten to eat all day while absorbed in his work (in addition to his almanac, Beckwith taught school for many years—an advertisement from 1839 welcomed all men who were "not too old to learn"—and also served as a surveyor and civil engineer for the town of Bridgewater). Material life, she detailed, became unimportant to her father once he committed to a path of knowledge and helping others. Wealth meant even less to Beckwith and his ragged dress mirrored, as yet another obituary lauded, his decision to give liberally to the needy rather than to spend it on the vanity of his own appearance. He seemed to have a good sense of humor about these commitments as well. In the final almanac he prepared, handed to the printer the day of his death, Beckwith recorded the arrest of one Isaiah Simmons for burglary in the neighborhood around his house in New Haven. The thief did not break into his home, however, presumably on the grounds that he knew there was nothing to steal. "Blessed be nothing," Beckwith concluded.

In addition to his support for those with little, Beckwith also earned his eccentric reputation for participating in causes that challenged the status quo. He invited the boys of an African American woman, a fellow member of his Baptist faith, to study at his school, and when he was threatened by the outraged parents of white students, he encouraged them to see the threat through and withdraw their sons. In the 1840s he signed petitions to abolish property qualifications and to support African American voting rights. (He also argued for the need to prove one's ability to read and write before voting, but this conviction needs to be understood in the wider context of his desire to educate all people.) And in 1845 Beckwith was a leading proponent on a petition to grant woman suffrage; his family claims that this was the *first* petition of its kind in Connecticut. His dedication to the temperance movement was unfaltering. His death occurred, in fact, when he suffered a heart attack at a temperance meeting, which his daughter regarded as the noble act of dying at his post with his harness on.

Many anecdotes illuminate Beckwith's eccentric behavior, but I would like to highlight two that speak to his genius and perspicacity. The first is a remembrance of him when he was employed as a clerk just after he moved to New Haven. In his leisure moments, so it was told, he would take a piece of chalk and draw mathematical problems on the pavement outside the store, alternating between a deep focus on the figures and an engagement with curious onlookers who were willing to learn. The second regards his distaste for handshaking, which he characterized as "a hollow, useless ceremony," pointing to how often men would do this before trying to fleece each other in business. There were, however, four types of people with whom he would shake hands: the old man, whose habits were fixed; the "crazy man," to get rid of him; the drunken man, to avoid a conflict; and the "colored man," in solidarity. Quirks such as these and the general generous tenor of Beckwith's life led one paper to conclude that "there were many traits in his character which it would be good for us all to copy"—no small endorsement for an eccentric, indeed.

It is reasonable to say that Joseph Battell, another peculiar benefactor, was generous to a fault. He was born into privilege in 1839 in Middlebury, Vermont. His mother was the daughter of US Senator Horatio Seymour. His father was a successful lawyer and a scion of a merchant family in Connecticut. Battell's sister, Emma, married John Wolcott Stewart, who would become governor of Vermont and serve in the US Congress. And in his seventy-five years on the planet, Battell owned and edited a newspaper, served as a state legislator, wrote novels, bred Morgan horses, rescued thousands of acres of woodlands from lumbering, and donated much of that vast share for parks and perpetual forests or to Middlebury College. He, too, was called an eccentric throughout his life, but in a much less polite or celebratory way, and often by his political adversaries.

Some of the criticism was in response to the opportunities that wealth provided him. Battell followed his father to Middlebury College, but does not appear to have formally graduated; instead, illness took him away at the close of his undergraduate career and he recuperated at a farmhouse in nearby Ripton, a town nestled in the Green Mountains. (Years later he purchased considerable acreage in this area, notably around Bread Loaf Mountain, and transformed the farmhouse into a palatial inn.) Entitlement allowed him the opportunity to tour Europe while the Civil War engulfed the United States, and youthful indiscretion made him tone deaf concerning the sufferings of other young men. In a work written at the time, for example, he recorded his stay at a boardinghouse in London with some American friends, where they spent an evening singing, including "The Star-Spangled Banner." He was taken aback when one of his female companions "felt it her duty to hint a strong doubt of my patriotism because I had not returned before this to get shot." His response to the challenge, however, was simply to observe that his supper was a good one, fortified with Vermont maple syrup.

This work, *The Yankee Boy from Home*, is a travelogue published in 1864. It is, to put it diplomatically, dull and indulgent; the preface, for example, relates his own advice to the book as it heads out to presumably wide readership, and many pages are stocked with heavy-handed poetry. With its unending commentary about parlors and coffeehouses and which cities smell unpleasant to Battell, it offers a tedious display of elitism, although such works were not uncommon by wealthy trendsetters of the time. There are copious intimations of his carousing with women, but nothing truly scandalous. And to be fair, the book occasionally shows glimpses of Battell's interest in nature and preservation of resources that would mark his mature adulthood.

There are few signs of eccentricity in *Yankee Boy* per se, except for an interlude spanning four chapters, "Whisperings of an Old Pine." Presented as if an old pine tree in Vermont narrated the tale directly to the author, it recounts an interaction between the tree and two sisters, Ellen and Bertha, and their romance with a young man, Kenneth. The story is rambling and unrelated to the travelogue. The entire work was apparently so embarrassing to Battell's family members that they tried to stop its publication and distribution. An article in the *Portsmouth Herald* from 1938, for example, mentioned attempts by his brother-in-law, Governor Stewart, who was willing to purchase every copy for fifty dollars to remove it from the market.

If Battell's first literary outing bordered on self-indulgence, his second attempt skirted impenetrability. In 1901 he published *Ellen or The Whisperings of an Old Pine*, expanding upon the idea of those four chapters in his earlier work. And what an expansion! *Ellen* was more than eight hundred pages long, consisting of two parts about four hundred pages each. An advertisement promised a third part, but it did not materialize. Instead Battell brought out an expanded second edition in two volumes; the first, released in 1903, was more than six hundred pages long and the second, released in 1908, added almost one thousand more. Brevity, clearly, was not his interest.

Ellen is a masterpiece of eccentricity. Again framed as a conversation between the old pine tree and a young woman, the subject matter expanded far beyond romance to include all of Battell's intellectual interests including Euclidian geometry, plane trigonometry, calculus, Copernican and Ptolemaic astronomy, motion, elasticity, gases, electricity, sensation, music, and theories of mind—often with accompanying diagrams. Battell spends a considerable number of pages to argue against scientifically accepted wave theories of sound and in favor of dismissed corpuscular theories (dating from the 1600s). Although there are many striking passages relating the beauty of nature and Vermont specifically, *Ellen* reads like a meandering textbook written in dialogue.

Readers may wonder why anyone would tolerate such a ponderous work as *Ellen*. To be precise, not that many people tolerated it. Neither edition sold well, nor did a condensed version entitled *The New Physics—Sound*, despite heavy advertising throughout the Northeast. But Battell's influence on other spheres of life impacted the reception of *Ellen* so that people were compelled to be aware of it. In 1888 he purchased the *Middlebury Register,* and from the 1880s through the early twentieth century, he served as a state legislator and ran, albeit unsuccessfully, for governor. Battell's tremendous wealth allowed him to purchase—and later donate—an astonishing number of acres of wilderness. Some estimates suggested fifty thousand acres were in his possession at one time; Battell himself remarked that he quit counting after twenty-five.

His generosity, however, was not without criticism even in its day. Battell was a man possessed by certain opinions, and he was not afraid to draw upon his money and status to advance an agenda for society. He became, for example, a proponent of the temperance movement but went far beyond the normal work of someone like Beckwith. As a legislator, he led the charge for state prohibition, and, when that failed, he advocated strict licensing and regulations. When an entire block burned in Middlebury, he offered to rebuild it on his own dime, but only if the town accepted his conditions of allowing no "liquor saloons" to exist there—ever. This offer made national headlines and provoked responses by citizens and rival newspapers that referenced him in unflattering terms such as a *czar* or *monarch.*

Battell was also willing to utilize his wealth as a vehicle—pun intended—for his passionate campaign against automobiles, which he regarded as a threat to nature and his beloved horse. (Battell was a breeder of Morgan horses, including for the federal government, and wrote several well-received books about them.) He did everything possible to limit the use of automobiles. In 1910, for example, he offered to personally finance the highway roads in Middlebury if the town selectmen would take no state monies and agree to his conditions regarding their usage. The offer was turned down. Under his editorship, the *Register* frequently reprinted articles from all over the nation detailing gruesome automobile accidents and fatalities.

As a case in point, on a random page taken from the November 4, 1910, edition, there was a story about an automobile death in St. Louis, two articles on serious injuries in Connecticut, a report on a death in Atlanta, another report on a trial in New York for vehicular murder, and a poem written against the "Red Demon," the automobile. Likewise, several of Battell's conservation gifts were tied to stipulations concerning roads and automobiles. His donation of Camel's Hump Mountain to the state, for example, came with the directions that it be renamed Mount Ethan Allen and that strict restrictions prevent access by motor vehicles or at least exclude them from roads used by horses to reach the summit. These conditions were met with resistance by many citizens who, while grateful for the donation, were alarmed at his attempts to dictate the land use in such a way.

As early as 1910, rival newspapers and political opponents tossed around the term "eccentric" in an effort to unseat him during an election. The Vergennes *Enterprise and Vermonter* held nothing back in asserting that "our old eccentric friend" desired "to once more impose upon the good nature of the people of Middlebury, inflict his fanatic ideas upon the lawmakers at the capitol and place the people of Addison County in a most embarrassing position." The editorial continued, labeling Battell a dictator and a man "afflicted with self-importance to such an extent that he would have laws to satisfy his own impractical ideas" and took umbrage with voters feeling "indebted to their public benefactor for a few paltry dollars." The recommendation urged voters to free themselves from bondage to such a peculiar personality. It went unheeded, however, and Battell returned to the legislature.

The term reappeared in full force upon news of his death in 1915. Battell frequented Washington, DC, and the southern states during the winter, and as he never married, he traveled alone. On February 7, the *Evening Star* reported the strange case of a man claiming to be from Vermont but otherwise suffering memory loss and found wandering Union Station. Police reached out to a Vermont senator, who identified the man as Battell. He passed days later, and his body was returned to his beloved state.

A flood of commentaries followed Battell's death, many referencing the "unique character" or "peculiarities" or "pronounced eccentricities" of "one of the most picturesque characters" in Vermont. Several were, put simply, uncharitable for a typical obituary, perhaps in reflection of people finally feeling free of his yoke, but others remained supportive. A farewell in the *Vermont Phoenix*, for example, agreed that he was an eccentric who held on to strange theories, but also wished "other wealthy men might be afflicted with eccentricity if it would influence them to leave their property for the benefit of the nation, State, town and college" as Battell did.

———

The terms of eccentricity were applied to Isabella Stewart Gardner long before her final years, sometimes as a salute and sometimes as condemnation of her originality. Born in 1840 to a wealthy merchant family in New York, she enjoyed a privileged life in Manhattan and on Long Island. She spent her teenage years in Paris at a boarding school where she befriended Julia and Eliza Gardner, daughters of an equally wealthy and influential Boston family. Julia introduced her classmate—known to many as "Belle"—to her brother, John "Jack" Lowell Gardner. They married in 1860 and she was often referred to simply as "Mrs. Jack" in the newspapers of the day. And with this union, Gardner entered into a life that very few of us can comprehend: at once utterly free from material wants and simultaneously constricted by social expectations, especially in the domestic domain delegated to women.

The Gardners gave birth to a son, known affectionately as Jackie, in 1863, but their boy succumbed to pneumonia in 1865. She then suffered a miscarriage and was informed by doctors that she would not—and should not attempt to— bear children. Depression followed this discouraging news. In those days medical advice recommended travel to regain health and stamina, so she and her husband set off for a journey through Europe that lasted a year. Her strength and will to live returned, and when she returned to Boston, Gardner exhibited signs of being unapologetic for the person she was. Soon after their homecoming, Jack Gardner's brother committed suicide and the couple "adopted" the three nephews who remained.

In the decades that followed, the Gardners continued to travel and were routinely welcomed by elites wherever they went. In Cambodia, for example, they were entertained by King Norodom. In Italy they were guests of King Umberto and Queen Margherita, and Gardner was granted a private audience with Pope Leo XIII. Together they began to collect art and associate with artists ranging from the world famous to the struggling. Gardner initiated collections of jewelry and rare books—and admirers. (One associate quipped that if she would agree to convert to Catholicism he would become a priest simply to hear her confessions.) This brought the negative attention of rivals as well, especially for those who considered her to be too flirtatious or too willing to risk the risqué.

In 1898, tragedy struck when Jack died suddenly. Rumors of another breakdown arose. But instead of collapsing, Gardner commenced work on the creation of a museum to hold the extensive art collection she and her husband shared. She purchased land in the "Emerald Necklace" of Boston, specifically in the swampy area of Fenway, where she oversaw—and often literally participated in—the construction of the Italian-style palace then called Fenway Court and now the Isabella Stewart Gardner Museum. She lived on the fourth floor and opened her doors to the public in a celebration of tremendous fanfare on January 1, 1903. News of this palace and of its owner's originality became a national affair.

Such is the basic sketch of Gardner's life. Important as it is to understand the decisions she made and the attitudes she conveyed, her depiction as an eccentric—if not outright provocateur—followed her daily and defined her public identity. She was a regular in society and gossip columns throughout the Northeast and especially for the New York magazine *Town Topics*, which followed her career voraciously and oscillated between outrage and treating her as Boston's most cherished institution. But it would be erroneous to think of Gardner as a professional celebrity, the sort of which has existed since the rise of reality television. While both possess an ample supply of self-assurance, the professional celebrity is beholden to the media in a way that the eccentric is not. The professional celebrity requires scandal to stay relevant; the eccentric celebrity goes about living a determined life on one's own terms. And in the case of Gardner, the truth of the matter was often a rich confirmation of an even more fascinating and determined character than the one the media invented to sell papers.

Gardner, after all, found a way to express her unique personality at a time when membership in high society required adherence to the norms of what the literary satirist Cleveland Amory called the "Proper Bostonian," which meant access to wealth, an impressive family ancestry, and patrician sensibilities of decorum and gentility. She possessed all of these qualities and parlayed them into powerful statements that challenged rather than upheld convention. She befriended several people involved in the struggle for women's rights, and recent biographers have begun to explore her role as an icon and supporter of the gay subculture in Boston when homosexuality was regarded as criminal behavior. Her fondness for artists, dancers, and musicians derived from a serious commitment to people who existed in countercultural spaces. In these ways she was far more bohemian than Boston Brahmin.

Gardner's wealth and status protected her (at least partially) from attacks on her reputation, which were lobbed at her by opponents and those intending to maintain the status quo. The frequent depiction of her as someone abnormal was, at least partially, a way to reiterate what was considered normal. Or they just criticized her looks. In the numerous essays, articles, and books written about Gardner—including those championing her—it is striking to see how often commentators found a reason to allege that she was not conventionally attractive; descriptions of her figure and sense of fashion routinely accompany this questionably significant piece of information.

Admittedly, a few of these accounts were relevant to her biography—for example, the shock produced in 1888 when John Singer Sargent painted a depiction of Gardner in a black low-neck dress, which resulted in her husband removing it from view—but as noted in other chapters, the policing of women by reducing them to mere appearance is a common practice in dismissing eccentrics or misfits. I have no intention of dignifying this trend, although I invoke it to call attention to the ways her eccentricity often pushed against rigid norms concerning women. Gardner's flamboyant dress—whether Paris fashion or the elaborate costumes she wore at events or simply her willingness to show more skin than was deemed appropriate—ignited ire and jealousy precisely because she could seem so comfortable in that skin.

The classic tales of her eccentricity underscore her willingness to challenge society by caring little what strangers thought about her. One prominent story, still circulating in newspapers today, is that she led a lion on a leash down Tremont Street—or sometimes Beacon Street or around Boston Common or through all of Fenway. Other versions reported that she did so whenever she wanted to incite the public. Still others suggested that she kept lions in her basement at Fenway Court. Sometimes the lion in question was a vigorous beast and at other times an old, toothless shell of a creature. Confirmation of any of these "facts" is virtually nonexistent, but that has hardly stopped the propagation of these stories. Their origins seem to lie in a few incidents at a zoo—really more of a circus—erected on the old site of the Boston Public Library after it relocated to Copley Square. Gardner was an avid lover of animals and visited the zoo when a lioness gave birth to cubs. From the most reliable accounts (although not perfectly reliable) it seems that she did convince their keeper to allow her to take two very young cubs home for a few hours and that the same keeper once allowed her to walk a tame three-year-old lion named Rex on a leash around the hall of the enclosure. Once the kernel of truth was released into the public, the stories went wild.

Tall tales, while entertaining, are never just entertainment; as with all folklore, these stories also convey values about who and what is acceptable to the people who tell them. Hence the lore that built up around Gardner— that, for example, she drank beer and smoked cigarettes as would a man; routinely received guests while perched in a potted mimosa tree; insisted her coachmen drive to her door (and on the sidewalk) so that she never had to step in snow; piloted a locomotive in order to reach a party on time; scrubbed clean the steps at the Church of the Advent during Lent; and attended an evening at the Boston Symphony wearing a headband with the message, "Oh you Red Sox"—all have origins of varying degrees of accuracy, but they share a common factor of scandal. While amusing, they also admonish audiences to recognize the limits of the normal.

People can spend time tracking down the veracity of each claim and gossip—the mimosa tree story is untrue, for example, but the Red Sox story is only one legitimate example of her loyalty to the team that became her neighbor in Fenway—and there is a certain degree of enjoyment in the pursuit. (It is, incidentally, absolutely true her will held explicit instructions regarding her museum in order to guarantee that Gardner's vision remain forever as she intended, as were the sizeable donations she bequeathed to charities.) But to a certain degree, the stories concerning Gardner ultimately resist capture and fossilization because she herself resisted capture and courted scandal to use as capital for her own devices. She understood and manipulated the press as readily as the media utilized her to sell papers and magazines. In hailing her eccentricity and in seeing it as a kind of resistance—albeit one that ultimately may have reaffirmed the very norms of the society she challenged—we should recognize that something is lost when every element of that unique nature is categorized and depleted of its mystery. Or as Gardner herself would say, "Don't spoil a good story by telling the truth."

16

THE CASTLE BUILDERS: WILLIAM GILLETTE AND ANTOINETTE SHERRI

In the pantheon of New England eccentrics, William Gillette and Antoinette Sherri hold a place of distinction. They are, arguably, better known today than some of the classic figures discussed elsewhere in this book, in part because they are attached to two physical locations well-known to tourists, Gillette Castle State Park in East Haddam, Connecticut, and Madame Sherri Forest in Chesterfield, New Hampshire. Gillette and Sherri are not the only people to construct "castles" in New England, but they have both been painted with the brush of unusual habits that has escaped others. Sylvester Beckett, Thomas Plant, and John Hays Hammond Jr., for example, whose castles still stand in Cape Elizabeth, Maine, Moultonborough, New Hampshire, and Gloucester, Massachusetts, are often credited as Renaissance men rather than misfits, and the grandeur of the mansions at Newport historically inoculated their owners from the charge of eccentricity.

Why did Gillette and Sherri emerge as the quintessential eccentrics of this group? One plausible reason is that before they were castle owners, they were involved in the theater and a budding celebrity industry that lifted them beyond the norms of everyday life. Furthermore, both revolutionized their respective arts and became successful by challenging the theatrical conventions of their day. Away from the stage, Gillette preferred an introverted life and Sherri that of opulence—and as this book has shown several times, tendencies to the reclusive or to the flamboyant quickly garner the label of eccentricity. All of these factors add up to unique lives, and while neither perfectly fits the eccentric's role, their stories are rewarding and captivating.

It is impossible to detail the astonishing litany of contributions of William Hooker Gillette in the space allotted—the defining biography, written by Henry Zecher, clocks in at over seven hundred pages, and even the recent and elegant book on Gillette Castle by Eric Ofgang approaches 150 pages—so the focus here is only on his reputation for eccentricity. Gillette defined New England aristocracy. Both parents hailed from illustrious Connecticut families and he was raised at Nook Farm, an upper-class community in Hartford that served as an intellectual and artistic haven as well as a neighborhood welcoming to social reformers. He took to the stage early, joking later in life that "predestination and insubordination" led him to the theater against the wishes of his family and the expectations of his day, which discouraged such activity as beneath the elite.

Gillette's career began in earnest in his twenties. His theatrical debut occurred in 1873 and by 1875 he was a regular on the stages from New York to Boston. His manner of acting was itself "eccentric" in that it did not rely upon explosive emotions and abundant histrionics that marked popular drama at the time. Instead Gillette was subtle, sophisticated, and alert to the possibilities of a more realist style. His skillfulness as an actor dissuaded any chance that he would be ignored or pushed aside, and along with a handful of other like-minded performers, Gillette established a new path and a renewed respectability for the craft.

Similarly, as a playwright, Gillette improved upon and cultivated the expectations of his audiences to produce works that raised the bar of what theater could provide. He was certainly not avant-garde and he remained faithful to the performing genres that people enjoyed, such as melodrama and farce, but

Photograph of William Gillette,
c. 1918
LIBRARY OF CONGRESS

Gillette infused these all-too-often clichéd forms with wit, wordplay, and intelligent surprise. Gillette advised as much in his introduction to *How to Write
a Play*, a collection of letters from European dramaturges. "The impression
has always prevailed with me, " he opened, "that one who might properly be
classed as a genius is not precisely the best fitted to expound rules and methods
for carrying on of his particular branch of endeavor." He was referring, on the
surface, to the writers brought together in the volume, but the statement offers
a poignant glimpse into his own genius.

In 1909 the *Connecticut Valley Advertiser* ran a brief article noting that Gillette
had purchased land in Hadlyme (a village straddling the towns of East Haddam

and Lyme) with the intentions of constructing a "bungalow." In 1914, construction began, and in 1919 the dwelling was essentially completed, proving the initial description a spectacular misnomer. Gillette oversaw much of the design, construction, and decoration of his "Hadlyme stone heap," and although newspapers such as the *Hartford Courant* called it a castle early in its appearance, he rejected the term. Nevertheless, the finished building was intricate and at times even puckish, reflective of the mind that conceptualized it (and who, prior to the castle, was fond of a houseboat named *Holy Terror*, designed specifically for him and called an "aquatic freak" by the *Brooklyn Eagle*). Consisting of twenty-four rooms spanning nearly fourteen thousand square feet, it was a steel-framed structure reinforced by fieldstone walls and oak beams and moldings.

The castle was multistoried, boasting an actual tower, as well as a conservatory, an art gallery, and a library. Gillette was an inveterate fancier of mechanical technologies and a person whose enthusiasm for potentiality led him to experiment with his possessions. Trick doors, trapdoors, secret rooms, hidden passages, and well-placed mirrors allowed him to escape unwanted company or to prank his welcomed guests. Very little metal was used; the doors, numbering forty-seven, were hand carved and designed with a unique latch. Similarly, Gillette's infamous liquor cabinet was secured by a pressure panel. On the outside he would eventually construct a railroad track that traversed the perimeter of his estate—complete with a tunnel—for a miniature engine and railcars that he himself conducted.

It may seem odd to readers aware of Gillette's fame that a few paragraphs have passed without mention of the role that made him famous—Sherlock Holmes—but in many ways, that is the least essential ingredient of his eccentricities. After all, his portrayal of Holmes on stage and in the plays he wrote (with the blessings of Arthur Conan Doyle) established the defining features of the detective, imitated or cited by virtually every actor to enliven the character since Gillette. It makes more sense, therefore, to focus on Gillette's reluctance to give interviews or his abiding love of cats as symptoms of eccentric behavior than his mastery of Holmesiana or his innovations to it that became mainstream.

With regard to those habits, the first testifies to Gillette's penchant for quietude. The desire may have bordered on the eccentric, or it may simply have been a case of an introvert capable—as so many introverts are—of turning it up on the performance stage and dwelling with an inward energy elsewhere. Gillette was called a recluse at times, but that term hardly seems fitting for a leading actor whose hospitality was renowned. Nevertheless, folklore developed regarding Gillette's tight lip with reporters. A story was told, for example, that the producer Alf Hayman bet a reporter he would pay a dollar for every word Gillette spoke in an interview. His cost was a mere two dollars, as Gillette's reply to the request for the interview was, "I won't." This is a variation on the anecdote of Calvin "Silent Cal" Coolidge, another taciturn New Englander (and a visitor to Gillette at the castle), who in response to a guest betting she could get him to say three words demurred, "You lose." These humorous folk stories have a basis in reality, but more important, they demonstrate how eccentricities attached to people often are exaggerations wrought by storytellers rather than the eccentrics themselves.

Gillette Castle
PHOTO BY CAROL M. HIGHSMITH, COURTESY OF THE LIBRARY OF CONGRESS

That said, Gillette's admiration for the feline was very real, even as it became an endless source of tall tales. Some stories, for example, suggested that Gillette, whose wife Helen died in her late twenties when he was only thirty-five, promised her that he would never remarry and filled his home with four-legged companions instead. Others exaggerated the numbers of cats he kept at his castle. The *Evening Star*, for one, featured Gillette in a lengthy article published in 1936. Written by the theater critic Ward Morehouse, the entire essay was designed to suggest that the once brilliant actor had, at age eighty, gone "serenely out of it," retired to "his feudal castle," and there, "in his fortresslike retreat Mr. Gillette is a recluse, surrounded by . . . numberless yellow cats." The idea caught on, but more attentive articles tempered the implications that he was obsessive about them. An article from four years earlier, for example, noted that only three cats—Ann, Louise, and Joseph—were awaiting Gillette's return.

Many commentators have linked Gillette's connection to cats—and to cat decorations that graced the castle—with his own sense of independence and aloofness, but he praised them for their comedic brilliance and sense of humor. To miss this point is to neglect Gillette's own mental acuity and comic genius which, when needed, could be rallied to make a point. Gillette once advertised two cats in the Deep River *New Era*, the newspaper that served both sides of the Connecticut River after the *Valley Advertiser* ceased publication (and that featured the castle in its summer travel guide for decades). Those wishing to adopt the felines had to apply in writing and state their qualifications. "We want to be sure," wrote Gillette, "that they do not go to stupid boobs who do not know what a cat is." That abrupt yet penetratingly earnest statement—about two cats at that—is precisely the sort of incongruity that marks both comedy and eccentricity.

That sensibility would return in Gillette's will, in which he seemingly decried the thought that his castle would end up in "the possession of some blithering saphead who had no conception of where he is or with what surrounded." This comment, too, has sometimes been misunderstood as a statement tinged with aggression or viciousness. In the full request Gillette imagined the torment he would face should he have a "continued consciousness" after death and have to deal with someone boorishly ruining his beloved estate. Gillette's thoughts on the afterlife were not to be taken seriously here, so what the statement offers is both a genuine and honest wish that something important be cared for—and who among us would not hope for the same?—and the makings of a riotous comedy. (That no one yet has conceived of *The Odd Couple* with the ghost of Gillette and a resident saphead is a shame.)

Another testimony to Gillette's genteel nature was his treatment of the local community in Hadlyme and the surrounding towns. By the standards of his time, he was fiendishly wealthy and unquestionably famous, thereby possessing all the ingredients for a monstrous relationship with those who did not command a similar clout. Yet time and again newspapers mentioned in passing his polite regard and interactions with those who built his castle or who continually furnished it with supplies. Gillette was a private man, then, but not antisocial. Stories abound of his inviting workmen to tea or assisting farm laborers or performing other acts of generosity and humble demeanor. These stories, not surprisingly, also launched folklore of their own, a narrative meant to demonstrate his magnanimity, as for example the well-known tale of his switching roles with his Japanese butler when the latter's brother, the mayor of Tokyo, paid a visit.

These memories linger in the area. In the summer of 2017, after I spoke to residents about unrelated folklore of the lower Connecticut River Valley, an older gentleman struck up a conversation about Gillette. He knew the story of the mayor of Tokyo, but was proud to share another concerning a friend of his, now gone, who had worked in his youth for a poultry farm that supplied eggs to the castle. Although the gist of the story concerned the smuggling of corn mash to the estate—recall Gillette's alcohol was elaborately guarded during prohibition—the storyteller assured that his friend and others in East Haddam were treated by the actor with the highest regard. In the final assessment, then, Gillette's most prevalent eccentricity may have been his respect for fellow human beings regardless of their class.

It is difficult to call Antoinette Sherri a New Englander—and extremely hard to qualify her as a Yankee in the traditional sense of the word—but she certainly was an eccentric who adopted New England as her home and whose story has increasingly attracted the attention of people in the region. She is perhaps now best known for Madame Sherri Forest, a nearly five-hundred-acre preserve in Chesterfield, New Hampshire, named in her honor and incorporating the site of the ruins of her chateau, but in her day Sherri was a forceful personality made stronger by wealth, fame, and a willingness for the outrageous. Her story bristles with an endless hint of scandal and a whiff of the salacious and concludes with a sad turn to the pathetic. It is a complicated tale, made all the more so by the sheer lack of corroborating evidence and the recourse taken to changing names.

The woman who would become Madame Sherri was born in France around 1878. According to the *New York Times* her maiden name was Antoinette Bramardi (or Bramare in other sources), but she adopted the stage name "Antonia DeLilas" as a cabaret performer. The man who would become her husband was born in the United States and changed his name as well, albeit to outrun his past. He first appeared in 1908 as Tony Macaluso, identified as a young man (either seventeen or nineteen) and witness in a case against Carl Fisher-Hansen, a successful New York lawyer accused of extorting fifteen thousand dollars from Joseph O'Brien, a Philadelphia-based decorator. Fisher-Hansen was in possession of incriminating letters written by O'Brien to Macaluso, and although the newspapers of the time were reticent to explain in detail, it is readily surmised that they were of a sexual nature. (O'Brien, in his testimony, rejected the argument that there was anything immoral in them.)

Macaluso lived in New York in conditions described as stylish and wore, as the *Evening World* noted, a collection of diamonds, but it is unclear if he possessed money on his own or was the recipient of a benefactor's largesse. The earliest reports mentioned that he was a theater actor or otherwise involved in vaudeville or cabaret; he was, for example, among many performers invited to a wedding of two gender impersonators that took place in 1908. Macaluso brought the initial case against O'Brien with Fisher-Hansen as his counsel, but later provided testimony to a grand jury that led to his lawyer's arrest. When Macaluso appeared at the trial, however, he reversed his claims and Fisher-Hansen was acquitted. A year later Fisher-Hansen was again arrested for bribing Macaluso in the previous case. Macaluso, charged with accepting a bribe, fled the country, made his way to France, and eventually met and married Bramardi.

The two returned to the United States in 1911, settling in New York, and apparently concocted an elaborate tale to throw off any investigations into the matter. Newspapers from New York to DC ran a story about a young man, Andre Riela, the son of a man attached to the Italian Embassy, who left the United States three years prior for his education but abandoned those pursuits when he met a certain concert singer, Mademoiselle DeLilo, who convinced him to start a life in the performing arts. The two wed in secret against the family's wishes, although one version of the tale concluded with reconciliation. This story was a cover for Macaluso's identity, but it also helped explain why the couple had access to wealth (presumably from Macaluso's questionable past and the couple's success in Europe) that would have attracted attention. It also demonstrated the depths to which they were willing to utilize mendacity for their advantage.

The ruse worked until 1912, when the couple reported the theft of twelve thousand dollars' worth of jewelry—pearl necklaces, pearl earrings, and five rings—by a young artist, Christo Jancoff, who was employed as their valet. The detective sent to interview the couple recognized Macaluso and arrested him on the spot for the warrant three years prior. Riela admitted to the false identity and in an attempt to clear his name spun another rich tale of arriving in Paris desperate and poor, working his way into the theater as a dancer, making some fortunes, and then winning big at Monte Carlo. In a similar vein, the couple wove an elaborate story that Bramardi was a descendant of Italian nobles and that the jewelry was a gift from "crowned heads" throughout Europe. Macaluso was eventually released and the charges dropped for insufficient evidence, but the couple, both employed in cabaret, decided to change the stage names that had become liabilities.

In 1910 Otto Hauerbach's comedy *Madame Sherry* premiered on Broadway. It was still popular in 1912 and became the obvious inspiration for the couple, who adopted the names Andre and Antoinette Sherri. Earlier commentators have been amused by this call, but few have recognized the homage that the name served to the couple's own circumstances. *Madame Sherry* tells the story of Edward Sherry, a playboy who fools his wealthy Uncle Theophilus into fronting money for the Sherry School of Aesthetic Dancing in Manhattan by pretending to be a faithful family man. When Theophilus unexpectedly shows up, Edward puts into action an elaborate scheme requiring his housekeeper to pose as his wife and pupils at the school to pose as their children. Other mistaken identities, love affairs, and ribald deceptions ensue until the happy ending.

In 1916 the couple again fell into scandal when Elvira Martine, a five-year-old daughter of one of their employees, was removed from their custody. Apparently the couple attempted to become her adopted parents. They were, however, deemed unfit for the task. During this incident reports detailed their life of affluence, working as dancers at some of the elite clubs in New York. Sherri and her husband continued to perform for some time, and Macaluso turned to writing and producing shows. The Andre Sherri Revue was popular in New York throughout the 1920s, so much so that it toured the country with stops in Chicago, Denver, Salt Lake City, San Francisco, and New England, including Newport and Narragansett. But eventually the couple decided to make a living in millinery and costume design. They opened a studio in New York, and into that place in 1917 walked another person who would become integral to the story of Madame Sherri, Charles LeMaire.

LeMaire was a young man and a performer who saw the couple when they toured Salt Lake City. They welcomed him as an apprentice, and he quickly honed his considerable talents. In 1918 LeMaire joined the military for the First World War, but he did not see action and returned to work for Sherri. His timing was fortuitous, as one of the couple's major clients was

Florenz Ziegfeld and the *Ziegfeld Follies*. (Ziegfeld himself would later sue Macaluso for using one of his songs in a revue.) In 1921 LeMaire designed costumes that were not only a hit for Ziegfeld's show, but so impressive that they warranted an ovation for their creator. Madame Sherri was called to the stage, but she did not take the credit and instead hailed her apprentice, catapulting him into fame. (In his lifetime LeMaire earned seventeen Oscar nominations, winning three of those awards, and was often celebrated as the most significant costumer of the century.)

Sherri's generosity toward LeMaire would be repaid throughout her life. Macaluso lost his sight in 1922 and died suddenly in 1924. Commentators have speculated that his death was caused either by syphilis or a poisoning from bathtub gin, but evidence is scant and he himself reported in an interview in April that he lost his vision in an operation and was regaining it slowly. (In the same interview Macaluso praised Madame Sherri's abilities in costuming and she showed off a twenty-nine-carat diamond.) Following her husband's death, Sherri continued to live as a socialite in New York—a newspaper from 1929, for example, featured her dress at the Beaux Arts Ball—and summered in New England. LeMaire paid for many of her excursions and purchases.

Sherri began to visit Chesterfield, New Hampshire, where her associate Jack Henderson also summered and where, according to rumors and locals with some memories of events, he entertained friends from New York with parties that spanned the decadent to the outright libertine. A few reports implied that Henderson was a bootlegger, but this may simply be a misunderstanding of the ease with which liquor could be had by the wealthy during prohibition, especially for those in the northern region of the Connecticut River, a major smuggling route from Canada. Regardless, the extravagance bordering on the illicit certainly echoed Sherri's tastes and led her to seek out her own property in which to enjoy her eccentricities and desires.

In 1929 Sherri purchased a farmhouse in Chesterfield and several hundred abutting acres. With this investment she commenced an ultimate indulgence, the construction of a chateau that would become known as Madame Sherri's castle. Akin to Gillette, she reportedly oversaw the erection of the castle, much to the chagrin of the local workers who quarried stones and built the mansion and to the stonemasons from Fitchburg, Massachusetts, whose talents made the structure a work of art. The building was impressive. Constructed on a foundation of stone arches and an imposing stone staircase, the chateau included sweeping balconies, a grotto, a pond and garden, and a living room with a live tree growing out of the roof. It was decorated with glitzy markers of the theater as well as other ostentatious displays including, if the reports are to be believed, a massive chair known as the Queen's Throne. Sherri did not, however, occupy the castle as her dwelling. She continued to live in the adjacent farmhouse and there, too, swirled rumors of her increasingly unusual behavior and an oscillation between bouts of reclusive introversion when alone and explosive extroversion when entertaining guests.

Unfortunately, much of the information about her life in Chesterfield and in Brattleboro, Vermont (the closest town across the river), is limited to innuendo, rumors, and the memories of residents rather than well-documented reports, so how much is true and how much is a narrative reaction of Yankee resistance to New Yorkers dominating a town—one of the oldest tensions in the history of New England tourism—is unclear. Most reports imply that there was little genuine rapport between residents and Sherri and vice versa. It does not appear that she was an interloper per se, but she did not attempt to ingratiate herself with the local community and rumors depict a rather spotty record of regard for workers and others who cared for her welfare. Perhaps no item better symbolized the gulf separating the two than her possession of a 1927 Packard, a luxury automobile that defined excess and that would have very deliberately been out of place in the area, a certain marker of both opulence and outsider status.

Sherri's permissive habits boiled over with scandal. These included, again according to the locals who would speak about them, such things as wild parties lasting throughout the entire evening or culminating with noisy returns to the castle in the early morning hours; chauffeured tours and expensive dinners in Brattleboro accompanied by a gang of adoring young men and women who often flouted or abused social mores if not actual laws; and shopping outings in

The ruins of Madame Sherri's Grand Staircase
KASEY GUMINIAK AND EVAN HELMLINGER

which Sherri decorated her body with outfits considered outlandish or risqué by the community. Rumors persisted that she kept a pet monkey as a fashion accessory and that she traveled into town during the summer literally wearing nothing but a fur coat. Local workmen served her needs, furthermore, but were not invited to her soirees. Surely their witness to her castle and property generated ample tall tales about the activities that unfolded there.

Late in his life LeMaire admitted that he was responsible for Sherri's prosperity as her benefactor. In time, however, LeMaire curtailed the plenitude—he had his own family, after all, and lived on the West Coast. Sherri attempted to maintain her luxurious lifestyle—again, rumors purport that she sought to turn the castle into a nightclub and was denied a permit—but by the 1950s, her financial circumstances were in rapid decline. The castle was burglarized in the 1940s while she visited New York City, initiating a string of misfortunes to Sherri and her property. Within a decade the aging Sherri converted to become a Jehovah's Witness and was invited to live with two other members of her church in Quechee, Vermont. While she was there the property was again vandalized and burgled, and in 1959 she essentially abandoned the castle for good. The following year, Sherri became a ward of the state, tended to by a couple in Brattleboro. In 1961 the town sued her for outstanding bills related to her care.

Sherri had lost the castle by this time, of course, and it seems that LeMaire himself made the final decision to let it go through a foreclosure suit. In October 1962, fire struck the building, tearing through the grand structure and reducing it to a foundation, fireplace, and stone staircase. According to reports of people who knew her, Sherri slipped into dementia and died in 1965 at a nursing home in Brattleboro, reportedly on the same day that her property was sold to Ann Stokes, who cared for it until 1998. That year, the Society for the Protection of New Hampshire Forests purchased the estate. The grounds have been under the Society's aegis ever since and continue to be a popular recreation site. As for Sherri, she was buried in Brattleboro. Since her death folklore has taken its course, and numerous legends have grown about her activities and her wild lifestyle, prompting people to seek further information about her eccentric life. But LeMaire left a cautionary summary for anyone who wished to uncover all the mysteries of this indomitable woman. "Do not believe in any of the tales you might hear," he advised. "She was a different person to each one who knew her."

17

THE GREAT AMERICAN
TRAVELER: DANIEL PRATT

He appeared like a sudden flash of lightning in the Boston newspapers in the 1850s, his title already bestowed: Daniel Pratt Jr., the Great American Traveler. Although he was, in the blunt assessment of *Appleton's Cyclopaedia of American Biography*, a "vagrant," Pratt also was an engaged observer conversant with the major ideas of his day. He was a frequent contributor of letters to newspapers, the editor of his own journal, a regular feature on college campuses throughout the Northeast, and a habitual candidate for the office of president of the United States. He was perhaps a sufferer of untreated mental illness that contributed to his unusual behavior. In his time Pratt was subject to endless jokes, pranks, and outright inhumane treatment. The time for a reassessment is long overdue, especially for one that treats him as a figure deserving of sympathy and respect.

There is no authoritative source on Daniel Pratt. He wrote an autobiography in the mid-1850s, but it does not remotely encapsulate all of his eccentric contributions to the world. Instead it is necessary to piece his life together from recollections that span decades. These accounts often contain more conjecture and exploitation than fact, so any reconstruction must be treated as temperamental at best. It is certain, however, that he was born in Prattville, Massachusetts, a section of the city of Chelsea near its border with Everett. As the moniker suggests, this area was named for his family, originating with the settler Thomas Pratt. Daniel Pratt was the fourth so-named in a generational line stretching to his great-grandfather and claimed to have been one of eleven children. He was born in 1809. Ruminating on his childhood, Pratt recalled several close calls with injury or death, leading an aunt to predict that if he were to survive into adulthood he would "become an uncommon great man."

Pratt apprenticed to become a carpenter, but apparently did not take to it—many reports accused of him of being too lazy to work—and simply disappeared for nearly a dozen years. During this period, so the story goes, he developed his penchant for travel and crisscrossed the roads of much of the country, living by the hospitality of strangers. Some reports suggested that he sojourned as far as California, walking on foot or hitching rides along the way. Others contended that his travels were largely imaginary or at least exaggerated. Regardless, this reputation garnered his nickname, the Great American Traveler, which Pratt readily adopted. Sadly, all the reports agreed that when he returned to New England from his first voyage, he did so mentally unwell. (There were early rumors that his mind had been unhinged by a broken love affair, but that story did not stick.)

In 1851 Pratt began to deliver speeches in public, both invited and uninvited. Boston was his base of operations at this time—the office of *The Traveller* newspaper at 31 State Street was a favorite spot—and he was not alone. A newspaper article from 1854, for example, listed Pratt among other well-known characters in Boston Common, all competing for the affection of growing audiences. One of these other eccentrics, George Washington Frost Mellen, a chemist and abolitionist, befriended Pratt and worked with him on a publication that became the *Gridiron*, a newsletter praised as being "full of fun and philosophy." The friendship soon dissolved, however, and then transformed into a bitter rivalry, instigated (as the *Boston Herald* explained) by citizens who fomented the hostility for their amusement.

Pratt and Mellen decided to run against each other in the presidential election of 1852. As absurd as this may sound to readers today, it pays to recall that in the 1850s, the United States was a much different landscape. The organized and voting states were generally in the eastern half of the country (California was admitted only in 1850), with large swaths of territories in the central and western part. Additionally, there were numerous political parties vying for control. The 1852 election, for example, saw the victory of Democrat Franklin Pierce against Whig Winfield Scott, but other candidates vied from five other parties, with the Free Soil Party making a reasonable show. Finally, nominations to a presidential campaign by acclamation—that is, people making their choices known by voice—was not uncommon. Pratt and Mellen were often "nominated" in such a manner and did not quite recognize that the vote was a jest played on them by the crowds.

Following the obvious defeat in the election, Pratt turned his attention to traveling regularly and lecturing along the way. This decision may have been the product of necessity. With no other consistent source of income, he lived by charity, and in a world where charity was hard to come by, he was at the mercy of audiences who wanted entertainment for their donations. By traveling from place to place, he could, at least initially, survive by being on the move before he outstayed his welcome. Indeed early newspaper articles expressed excitement upon his arrival, with large crowds forming to witness a new show. From a glimpse at the topics of his lectures, it is clear Pratt was a rapacious reader, and while his talks were often rambling or confused, they were inspired by a thirsty intellect. He was, furthermore, a poet who delighted in inventing new words and an able singer who composed original songs.

An advertisement in the *New York Times* from 1853 stylized him as "Professor" Daniel Pratt, but that sobriquet did not gain traction. It testified, however, to the expanding range of locales he visited on his tours. The sheer number of towns and cities whose newspapers covered his arrival is stunning. Regular haunts included Bangor, Boston, Burlington, Concord, Lowell, Manchester, New Haven, New London, Providence, Portsmouth, Springfield, and Worcester, but he also appeared in western towns such as Pittsfield and Rutland;

eastern towns such as Laconia and Augusta; up and down the Connecticut River at Lancaster, Hartford, and Middletown; coastal cities from Stamford to Portland, including Newport, New Bedford, Salem, and Gloucester; and nearly every well-populated municipality in between.

When Pratt was not in New England, he was spotted in New York, New Jersey, and Pennsylvania, and occasionally in Chicago, Minneapolis, and Richmond. On several occasions Pratt claimed to have visited every state, numerous territories, and reservations. In a letter written in 1856, for example, he mentioned seeing Fort Kearny (an outpost along the Oregon Trail in Nebraska) and California, during which time he broke his collarbone in a buffalo hunt, rendering him incapable of manual labor thereafter. By 1859 he boasted three hundred thousand miles under his belt—and that was nearly thirty years before his death.

His lectures spanned scientific topics to the arts to social conventions to his favorite subject, contemporary politics. The titles alone demonstrate the range—and the reasons why editors were unable to resist covering them in their pages. In the course of thirty years, Pratt offered lectures entitled—again just to name a few—"The Economy of Creation," "Perfections of the Constitution of the United States," "Circumstances," "There Is No Room In The Inn," "Tact," "Presence of Mind," "The Ingenuity of the Rising Generation," "The Life of the World," "The Harmonious Vocabulary Laboratory of Government," "The Fundamental Basis of Government, with Sentiments and Poetry," "The Geological Creation," and—a tour de force late in his career—"The Political Situation in Prussia and Mahometan with a Glance at the Solar System, and Remarks upon Blaine as a Poet." He became known for advocating ideas of equilibrium into his lectures, although the meaning of that term was nebulous and protean, and as the titles hint, he spiced his lectures with poems and songs.

Previous commentaries on Pratt periodically included excerpts from his lectures in order to mock their idiosyncrasies, frenetic leaps of logic, and potentially schizophrenic language. I caution against this derisive tendency to make a sport of his pronouncements. Virtually all accounts of Pratt in his day confirmed that he was serious in his presentations, even when he enjoyed the playful pomp and circumstance that could accompany them. And while it is true that the one factor uniting his earliest lectures with his final ones was a tendency to talk about himself as a prominent intellectual and cultural figure—and in a repetitious way—it is also worth noting that in doing so Pratt was, in effect, inventing a self-congratulatory way of speaking that is the hallmark of celebrities and politicians today.

Indeed these lectures continually fueled his presidential ambitions, not only because he was met with support from crowds, but also because he went around and talked to people about politics at a time when reaching out to voters in such a populist manner was not the norm. When Stephen Douglas took his campaign against Abraham Lincoln on the road, an idea then considered improper, his critics rebuked him as having nothing on Pratt's long-standing practice, and newspaper editors often criticized legitimate politicians on the grounds that their ideas were no more sober than Pratt's—and usually less honest.

In the early days Pratt's lectures were festive events, with estimates of several hundred to several thousand in attendance. Prominent citizens and organizations habitually sponsored celebrations in his honor, in which "dignitaries" greeted him as the keynote speaker. He subsisted on these talks, always passing around his stovepipe hat for donations. As his fame grew and he became a folk hero of sorts, attendees customarily presented him "gifts." Newspapers reported that among these were such illustrious presents as Santa Anna's arms, Myles Standish's sword, and the hat that George Washington wore when he crossed the Delaware. He was often awarded medals, military caps, honors—over time he was called Colonel, Major, and eventually General—and diplomas, frequently with degrees that parodied his circumstances, such as a "G.A.T." or "C.O.D."—that is, Cash on Delivery.

One of Pratt's gifts, an inscribed pitcher presented to him at Grove Hall in Dorchester in 1854, turned up during a police investigation in Boston in 1870 with the implications that it was stolen or hocked. Other reports noted the lengths he would go to protect his clothing against young thieves and instigators. And again, this was more for necessity than honor, as Pratt claimed so few possessions. Reporters commented on his wearing the same overcoat for years, for example, and one once ridiculed him for having so many theories, including the grand idea of not changing his shirt for months.

Many records of these events survived. In a recollection from 1911, for example, Albert Davis recalled "the strangest entertainment that Providence has ever had," when Pratt lectured at Franklin Hall a half century earlier. Davis wrote:

He would lecture in a perfectly serious way, dodging all sorts of missiles aimed at him, and whenever he gave a performance, or lecture—for it was neither one or the other but both—everyone attempted to have fun with him . . . When he made his appearance on the stage, so thick was the tobacco smoke that it was almost impossible to distinguish him, and he had spoken but a short time when the fun commenced in the shape of torpedoes, balls of wet paper, etc., which flew thick and fast around poor Daniel's head. In spite of it all, he kept on speaking but the audience was so enthusiastic that he finally proposed a song to pacify them. This proposal had the desired effect, the whole audience joining in the chorus while Daniel sang, "Roll On, Silver Moon," then a great favorite. After this he read a poem, dedicated to him by a General of the army of the Potomac, which terminated with the following couplet:

Then raise to his memory
A monument of brass
For none like him has spoken
Since the days of Balaam's ass.

As the event drew to a close, the attendees presented Pratt with "a mammoth cane, the head being about the size of a foot-ball." Pratt was, reportedly, so struck by what he took as an act of generosity that he choked up with emotion and could not project his words of gratitude. This display of emotion drew the audience closer to the platform and, perhaps because he felt threatened by the crowding—for he was often subject to physical harm and mobbing—he opened the window and called for the police.

The *Waltham Sentinel* reported a very similar incident in 1873 at Rumford Hall. Pratt was invited by the "M. Y. O. B. Society," who printed and distributed programs announcing the "renowned lecturer" and greeted him with an escort and musical procession to the building. Women were excluded from this talk. Pratt entered the building underneath a triumphal arch decorated with herring and codfish and to the sounds of "The Rogue's March" (a song played when dishonored soldiers were stripped of their rank, made subject to corporal punishment, and exiled). After his introduction, Pratt "commenced a 'lecture' second to no other ever listened to in Waltham, in point of oddity and ludicrousness."

The band continually interrupted his speech, but he shouldered on, demonstrating an adaptability that led him to dance along at times. Others interrupted in order to read regrets from distinguished figures unable to attend. One "luminary" did appear, however: Dr. David Livingstone himself (the actual Dr. Livingstone was in Zambia nearing the end of his life), who greeted Pratt with gusto. The attendees then presented Pratt with a pocket watch of enormous proportions, followed by a "beautiful bouquet" that turned out to be a cabbage. He was ushered out to the tune of "Auld Lang Syne." Again, Pratt took all of this in stride, especially since the foolishness was accompanied by a dinner, a room for the evening, donations, and a railroad ticket away.

Such was his life when things went well, and when they went especially well, he might have received an additional clean shave or an article of clothing or an umbrella. Pratt's inability to gauge social cues and to fully understand intentions, however, could land him in compromising situations, such as a time when his audience locked and abandoned him in a small dark room or when a cabal of boys decided to pummel him with firecrackers. He often found that his hat returned empty from its rounds, and occasionally was so ill-treated by his audiences that he declared the city to be among the worst places on Earth. Lynn, Massachusetts, held that dubious honor in 1883, for example, when no one showed him hospitality during a severe rainstorm.

A more serious incident occurred in Newport in 1869 when he was forcibly removed from the city and in New Haven the same year when students were not around to protect him.

Perhaps no rejections were more severe than two that have become legendary. The first took place in late 1857 when, according to numerous newspapers, Pratt secured an audience with the Virginia governor Henry Wise. After listening to Pratt for an hour, Wise dismissed him as an agitator and advised him to leave the state before he was ridden out on a rail. (As the story evolved over time, Wise's threats of violence became more immediate as he literally ordered Pratt out of the state.) Pratt replied that Wise's hostility was fomented by jealousy that he would one day be president or by Pratt's personal belief that African Americans were as good as whites.

The second incident borders the unbelievable. In 1862 several papers told a story that Pratt visited the 14th Massachusetts Regiment in Washington, DC (The incident, if it occurred, may have taken place in 1861 when the regiment was stationed there.) He overstayed his welcome, and in order to rid themselves of him, the soldiers planted a counterfeit correspondence with Jefferson Davis in his pockets while he slept. The following morning he was arrested as a spy for the Confederacy, sentenced in a trial to execution, and led blindfolded to his death. A dozen blank shots were fired at him, whereupon he was released, terrified, and fled the scene.

Pratt's rebellious spirit and resistance to traditional intellectual authority were especially welcome on college campuses, and he claimed to have visited fifty in his lifetime. The Ivy League schools in New England were perennial favorites, and their literary magazines and alumni newsletters are replete with memories of his public addresses and burlesque displays that erupted with them. Campus administrators and professors were far less welcoming and often had Pratt ejected from the grounds or threatened with arrest. His admirers among the students, however, regularly composed odes in his honor or repeated those that Pratt composed for himself. A particularly popular one on campuses ran as follows (with numerous variations):

Let Shakespeare stand behind the door,

Let Byron woo the muse no more,

Let Milton moulder in his tomb,

But give the Great American Traveller room!

Undergraduates were among his most vocal supporters for the presidency and routinely closed out his visits to campus with a nomination by acclamation, but again, it is difficult to ascertain how much of that practice was a sincere display of camaraderie and how much was subtle mockery.

Pratt actively announced his candidacy for president in newspapers starting in 1852 and every four years thereafter until at least 1876, and his obituaries assume that he continued to run in the two other elections before his death in 1887. When asked once whether he would promise to serve only one term, Pratt made clear that the mess the country was in could take eight years to straighten. He published his platforms, and, although they were ridiculed at the time, they included such ideas that the national debt should be paid, that banks should loan money to poor people in order to stimulate the economy, and that slaves should be freed and educated. (Pratt also spoke to African Americans and encouraged them to vote after the Civil War.)

In his earliest campaign Pratt associated with the Know Nothing Party, which tended toward anti-immigration stands in order to promote American industry, but he did not stay with them religiously. Indeed he fell into a brief public scandal when his old rival G. W. F. Mellen accused him of plotting secretly with the Pope to overthrow the government—the Know Nothings were virulently anti-Catholic—leading Pratt to accuse Mellen of treason. He attended both Democratic and Republican conventions. And as the election and reelection of both Abraham Lincoln and Ulysses S. Grant loomed, Pratt withdrew from the campaign in order to guarantee their success.

These acts of nobility were not, however, without consequences. Pratt came to believe—and express in public—that they entitled him to some considerations, and he often visited Washington to secure them. In a biography of White House nurse Rebecca Pomeroy, Anna Boyden recalls an incident in which Pratt, "a half-crazy unfortunate," accosted President Lincoln and demanded that he consider "it was *my* vote that made you President." In another account in the *Brooklyn Eagle*, Pratt traveled to visit Lincoln with every expectation that he would be well received and to offer his services to debate anyone in the service of the president, as well as to debate Lincoln himself in a friendly game of wits.

It did not go as planned. Six weeks later the *Eagle* reported that the wires carried a message that "a crazy man had got into the White House" and attempted to explain to Lincoln that he (that is, Pratt) had been elected to the office in 1856. When the encounter turned sour, Lincoln ordered his guards to expel Pratt, who, as he was seized and dragged away, yelled at the President the lines from Shakespeare's *Julius Caesar*, "And you too, Brutus?" (In a separate article, the *Eagle* mentioned—and not without a hint of schadenfreude—that during his visit Pratt harangued Congress, and noted that his speeches were as coherent as half the members of that body "with the additional advantage they do no harm, and cost nothing for printing.")

Pratt's political ambitions were attuned to the issues of his day, and as they evolved so also did his interests. He attended, for example, abolitionist meetings in the 1850s and 1860s and was allowed five minutes at a suffrage convention in Concord, New Hampshire, in 1868. Transcripts of these meetings survived detailing his comments and the unwarranted laughter they produced. But in the late 1860s and 1870s, a very unusual connection arose in this context. Preserved in an 1868 letter from the social reformer William Lloyd Garrison to Susan B. Anthony and Elizabeth Cady Stanton is Garrison's exasperation that the two advocates for women's rights were traveling with "that crack-brained harlequin and semi-lunatic, George Francis Train," whom they also supported for president. Train, Garrison asserted, "is on a par with the poor demented Mellen, and Daniel Pratt, the Great American Traveler."

Train was an eccentric who skirted mental illness, but he was also an entrepreneur whose great wealth allowed him tremendous influence. And as a financier for *The Revolution*, a women's rights newspaper founded by Anthony and Stanton, he held particular sway. This was also a time when the New York–based National Woman Suffrage Association (led by Anthony and Stanton) was caught in a rivalry with the Boston-based American Woman Suffrage Association, headed by, among others, Lucy Stone. This tension led to a situation that is almost impossible to believe.

As the *Princeton Standard* recorded it, in January 1869 Stone decided to enlist Pratt as a candidate to oppose Train. "Mr. Pratt opened the campaign at the recent Boston Convention," the report continued, "and accompanied Mrs. Stone from there to Providence, and thence to Concord, at each of which cities he addressed the large and enthusiastic Convention which had met to greet him and his travelling associates." Such a decision as this speaks more to the travails of early suffragists than it does to faith in Pratt's oratorical powers and electoral chances, but it surely would have inspired his desire to continue pursuit of the highest office.

As time wore on, the novelty of Daniel Pratt wore off. His lectures became less celebratory and more predatory against him. The newspapers that gleefully welcomed him in the 1850s and 1860s grew tired of his exploits in the 1870s and 1880s and routinely characterized him as a bore or a nuisance and knowing that he would read their pages, resorted to direct appeals for him to stay away. By these later decades, Pratt was so well-known throughout the country that his name held proverbial reference, often in a negative way, and he was featured as a character in several fictional stories, plays, and an opera. He was also the butt of a joke that traversed the nation, the gist of which had him meet a newspaper editor or college president or a local folk character and introduce himself with pomposity as the Great American Traveler, to which his unimpressed host would dismissively reply, "Well, travel!"

Pratt certainly enjoyed some pleasures in his life—when the tradition of Antiques and Horribles parades, a procession mocking political figures, took off in New England, he was routinely elected to positions of prominence—but his life was often marred with disappointment that few reports were willing to notice. His attempt to find a wife by advertising in newspapers, for example, was often met with teasing, especially as many women wrote to accept his offer but never included their address. In 1872 many newspapers reported that he had been reduced to selling peanuts at a stand in New York City, and while he was back on the lecture circuit in early 1873, there is no reason to suspect this rumor was unfounded.

He had occasional reason to winter at Rainsford Island, the site of an alms-house and quarantine hospital in Boston Harbor. In 1871 he was arrested for vagrancy in Manchester, New Hampshire, but managed to talk his way out of jail. In 1878 he was arrested in Revere for stealing sixty dollars from a purse. Taken to jail, Pratt found no solace, as none of his admirers posted bond for him. The transcript of his trial reads with the sorrow of a man who oscillated between confusion and regret for his desperate state. (Pratt was eventually released thanks to help of a charitable lawyer, and after reviewing the case the *Portland Daily Press* excoriated the police for amusing themselves at his expense.) And in July 1868 he was despondent enough to attempt suicide by throwing himself off a ferryboat into the East River, while "at the same time waving the American flag." When he was rescued, he gave as his reason simply "a lack of appreciation of genius by the people generally."

Pratt was not a blameless man by any means, and he could exhibit quite a temper when audiences stiffed him. But he was also more than capable of a generosity to others of which he himself was often deprived, and he drew upon his circumstances as a means to call people to ethical practice. He greeted 1859, for example, with a New Year benediction to readers of the *Lowell Daily Citizen*: "I wish my aged parents and brothers and sisters and the rest of the human family a happy new year, and may all the wrongs and grievances of the past year become the incentives to a more right action and duty to each other in acts of kindness, charity, benevolence, and hospitality." And in 1857, concerned that in his travels he met too many Christians who quarreled with each other, he reminded them that "benevolence, charity and hospitality has a good influence in every place; in short, love to God and man."

Pratt died in June 1887 following a paralytic fit on the streets of Boston and admittance to the city hospital. Newspapers throughout the country published his obituary. A considerable number reprinted one of the poems composed (perhaps by himself) in his honor early in his career:

Oh! where is a man so lazy and fat,
Who has not heard of Daniel Pratt,
Who gathers his wings, and flies away
To the parts of earth where the light of day
Shines but a little, or not all,
On the course of the falling waterfall!
I ask you, friends, what mighty mind
Has not seen unfurled upon the wind,
That glorious banner that springs, like a cat
Into the air, for Daniel Pratt?
There never was, and there never will be
Such a mighty man, to stand like thee.
Oh, most magnificent Daniel Pratt,
Above the throne where Plato sat.

References to Pratt lingered well into the first quarter of the twentieth century. Today this man who claimed to speak to over two million people in the course of his lifetime has become merely a footnote in collections of oddities, reflecting a legacy of abuse he carried while he traveled the country. It is time for a reassessment of Daniel Pratt; this chapter hardly scratches the surface. In his days genuine sympathy for him was demonstrated by only a few brave reporters or critics of the cruelty played upon him. And despite his rambling writings and incoherent speeches, Pratt made one thing clear: that so-called normal people can exhibit some of the most vicious, inhumane, and uncharitable behavior toward anyone who refuses to conform. His perseverance in the face of these trials seems worthy of commendation, so we should let him have the final word, taken from a letter in which he urged a better government for the people: "A dead fish can go with the current, but it takes a live one to swim against it."

18

THE VISIONARIES OF THE ORDINARY: JOSEPH PALMER, WILLIAM HENRY HARRISON ROSE, ELIZABETH TASHJIAN, AND WILLIAM JOHNSON

The ability to see the extraordinary in the everyday and the miraculous in the mundane is not solely the prerogative of eccentrics, but far too often so-called normalcy requires a sedate temperament that squelches risks of the imagination. There are, thankfully, ample notables in the history of New England eccentrics who dared to defy the demand that life be rendered boring—those women and men whose appreciation for ordinary things proved visionary in their times, even as their determination often earned the title of "obsessive." The debt we owe their wisdom—and with it, a reminder to look for beauty in things readily overlooked—may be difficult to calculate, but that should not stop us from trying. In this chapter, accordingly, we encounter several people whose eccentricities were a testimony to human ingenuity and insight.

Joseph Palmer has enjoyed minor celebrity for at least a century, although his tale stretches back into the mid-1800s. He holds the distinction of being one of the few people—if not the only person—persecuted for the outrageous crime of wearing a beard, and in doing he so made a unique contribution to the history of New England eccentricity. He was born in 1791, the youngest of fourteen children, to a veteran of the American Revolution who owned land in a place called "No Town" near Leominster, Massachusetts. Palmer inherited this farmland and began his own family there, and if a very late story is to be believed, his marriage apparently stirred some controversy as the couple literally published their wedding banns on a tree rather than in a newspaper, church, or civil institution.

According to an interview with his son, Thomas Palmer, the family moved to Fitchburg, Massachusetts, in the 1830s. Trouble began soon thereafter, as Palmer wore a very full and lengthy beard, flouting the social norms of his day. Storytellers in the twentieth century frequently exaggerated this feature, some claiming that he was the *only* man in New England or even the United States to adorn his face with whiskers. This is untrue—even his son names a person who lived in a nearby town—but facial hair was generally regarded as inappropriate or potentially sinful and certainly a marker of nonconforming individuals. Orson Murray, for example, was a contemporary of Palmer who lived in Brandon, Vermont, and published the *Vermont Telegraph*, a reform newspaper, and he also was criticized for his beard and its signal of radical beliefs. Another group—American Jews—likewise kept to their tradition of long beards, and despite being a Baptist, Palmer earned the nickname "Old Jew Palmer," a point that says as much about burgeoning anti-Semitism in New England as it does about his unusual style.

Palmer was singled out and ridiculed by the people of Fitchburg and surrounding towns for his beard, and a memorable (if apocryphal) tale records that the local pastor once refused him communion, whereupon Palmer took matters into his own hands, drank from the cup, and declared his love of Jesus to be stronger than anyone else's in the room. Another incident that led to his fame occurred at a hotel in Fitchburg in 1830. Palmer left the building and was seized by four young men armed with scissors and razors who intended to shave him. He defended himself with a jackknife and injured two of his assailants, but was then himself arrested for assault. He refused to pay the fine and was jailed in Worcester, where he remained for over a year, adamant that he would not admit to guilt for self-defense. Palmer kept a diary of his abuses and secreted out letters to local newspapers. These reports brought sympathy to his case.

A folkloric version of his release depicts the jailor physically removing him in a chair and depositing him outside the prison in order to rid Worcester of a gadfly, but in all likelihood the fine was either dismissed or paid, and he returned to Fitchburg still brandishing his whiskers. At this point several commentators close their tale, but there is another chapter of Palmer's life equally as impressive. He was interested in reform movements, especially abolition and temperance (and his months in jail certainly laid groundwork for prison reform), and his resolve strengthened after his release. But Palmer's most ambitious undertaking came in the early 1840s, when he and his wife associated with the commune known as Fruitlands in Harvard, Massachusetts. This utopian experiment, the brainchild of Amos Bronson Alcott and Charles Lane, intended to become a self-sustaining community that upheld Transcendentalism, practiced vegetarianism, and prohibited both stimulants and animal labor. Begun in earnest in June 1843, it failed within seven months and one cold New England winter.

As several historians have noted, the residents of Fruitlands were better philosophers than farmers. Palmer was the only experienced one among them, and his efforts likely kept the demise of the commune from occurring much earlier. Palmer purchased the property after it failed and welcomed guests there, including Ralph Waldo Emerson (who held the original deed for Alcott and Lane) and Henry David Thoreau. Louisa May Alcott, the daughter of Amos, lived at the commune and in her story based on Fruitlands, *Transcendental Wild Oats*, praised Palmer through the character of Moses White.

Palmer died in 1873. His story might have slipped into obscurity at that point, but in 1883 his son erected a monument at his grave with an image of

Palmer's face and the inscription "Persecuted for Wearing the Beard." The *Fitchburg Sentinel* noted this event and concocted the idea that by wearing a beard Palmer violated the Massachusetts Blue Laws—again, an erroneous statement, but one that added to the story. In 1884 the *Boston Globe* published an extensive interview with Thomas Palmer, who secured canonical anecdotes about his father for decades. And in 1910 Clara Endicott Sears purchased the Fruitlands property and restored it as a museum and tourist attraction. Five years later, in a book about its history, she popularized Palmer's story, setting the stage for a revival of interest that included stints in *Reader's Digest*, *Life* magazine, and numerous books, all finding ways to laud this champion of individualism.

William Henry Harrison Rose earned his reputation as an eccentric simply by committing himself to a common activity long after it had fallen out of fashion. He was born in 1839 and died in 1913, living the entirety of his life at his family farm in Rhode Island where Exeter, South Kingston, and North Kingston intersect, accompanied only by his sister, Elsie Marie Babcock Rose, who outlived him. But it was weaving, not farming, that made Rose "an anachronism," as Isadora Safner admiringly called him in her well-researched book about his life and the nearly 250 patterns he designed. Rose continued the ancient tradition of hand weaving at a time when industrialization rapidly advanced to provide such goods to consumers. With his skillfulness and shrewd business acumen Rose managed to compete against that tide and earn accolades that lasted far beyond his lifetime.

Rose was the descendant of a long line of families who were influential in New England history. His grandfather was equally skilled and an apprentice to "the Prince of Narragansett weavers," Martin Reed. Hand weaving was already in decline when Rose entered the world, but he pursued this craft diligently and in a manner that earned the nickname "Weaver Rose." (His other nickname, "Quaker Billy," testified to his steadfast faith and his family history, as Rhode Island had been accepting of Quakers when other colonies in New England shunned them.) Rose was proud of his family heritage—he once shared a gruesome story about an ancestor who fought in the Great Swamp Fight during King Philip's War—and no stranger to patriotic impulses; one of his dogs, for example, was named Pulaski after the military leader in the American Revolution.

It was this appreciation for the past and for his family heritage that inspired Rose and his sister to maintain the craft of their ancestors. Rose was not bullishly nostalgic; he did utilize machine-made threads and yarns in order to spare the demanding time necessary to produce them by hand, but he was otherwise dedicated unswervingly to the art and transformed his home into a workshop. Alice Morse Earle, the social historian, mentioned Rose in three of her books written at the turn of the twentieth century. In *Home Life in Colonial Days*, she described his weaving loft, in which "a veritable atmosphere of the past still lingers." Earle's conception of the past in this case went further back than pre-industrial America. "There are piles of old and new bed coverlets," she wrote in 1898, "woven in those fanciful geometric designs, which are just as the ancient Gauls wove them in the Bronze Age, and which formed a favorite bed-covering of our ancestors, and of country folk today."

In addition to three looms—one built by Rose himself—all of mid-century design, the loft housed several spinning wheels and a seemingly countless display of weaving tools, many of which were constructed when Narragansett was a center of the industry. His yard, likewise, struck the visitor as unique with its low stone wall covered in bleached shells and terminating boulders at each corner, and dotted periodically by a birdhouse. In the late nineteenth century tourists began to visit Rose, and he capitalized on the idea, as it meant the opportunity for selling his wares. (One local rumor suggested that among his clientele was Edith Carow, the wife of Teddy Roosevelt.) When callers arrived, Elsie would summon Rose from the fields by blowing on a cockleshell, and he would dutifully make his way to the house and his potential customers.

I have been reticent throughout this book to ascribe eccentricity to someone based on his or her physical appearance, but contemporaries of Rose made such frequent mention of it as a condition of his unique lifestyle that it would be irresponsible not to address it. One writer, the same who marveled at the cockleshell, described him as "an old man, with long white hair and flowing white beard and bare feet," who, carrying home the scythe needed in the fields, appeared as "the most picture perfect of Father Time I have ever seen." Earle, in a passage from *In Old Narragansett*, saw fit to describe his pale and delicate skin, "suffused at times with that semitransparent flush which is seldom seen save on those whose life is wholly indoors." She too mentioned his preference for walking barefoot, as did others who recalled their encounters with him. In remembering him more than two decades after his death, the WPA guide to Rhode Island called him "anything but conventional, as Narragansett Pier and neighboring resorts measure conventionality." Here as well, his bare feet and long beard drew comment, as well as his old clothes and his love of snuff.

Rose was no recluse. In addition to his welcome of tourists, in 1912, he founded the Colonial Weavers Association with a small group of admirers at his home and served as its first officer. The organization did not live beyond his years, but his efforts and handiwork inspired artisans throughout the twentieth century, many of whom honored him with occasional tributes and articles featuring his contributions. Rose himself seemed to have a good sense of humor—or at least an amused sensibility—when he wrote a short poem honoring the profession, published in the *Providence Journal* in 1905 and preserved here with his original spelling:

come ye Patrones Proud and Lowley
Rich and Raged, Every Man
Come and Fork over what you owe
The poor old weaver Man.
We are rite Anxious to Receive it
Oh, we Sadley Nead the Chink,
Every Dollar Bright Believe It
To Pay for Weaving Warp and Wullen.
Pray Dont hesitate ye byers
Of the Weavers Pittance Think

Send o Send the Silver Shiners
Quickly Cash us or We Sink.

Rose died in his sister's arms. She herself passed in 1926. And in 1931, sparks from a passing train engine ignited a fire in the area that burned the Rose homestead to the ground. Although this incident signaled a certain end for an eccentric man once called "a being from the Ages Long Since Gone," in honoring the past Rose paved a way for a future ripe with possibilities.

Elizabeth Tashjian resisted the moniker of eccentric throughout her life. "I'm not eccentric at all," she once insisted in an interview, "I'm original." Despite her sensible distinction and protest, she was celebrated in national media more for her quirkiness than for her artistry, and her story is compelling precisely because of what it says about eccentricity in a media saturated and celebrity culture. She was born in New York City in 1912 to Armenian immigrants. Her father was a rug dealer and her mother was reportedly from an aristocratic background; they fled the violent period that saw the collapse of the Ottoman Empire. Tashjian's parents divorced when she was young, and she was raised by her mother, who took every care to see that her daughter was well educated. She graduated from the National Academy of Design and the New York School of Applied Design for Women and began her career as an artist.

In 1950 Tashjian and her mother moved into a mansion in Old Lyme, Connecticut. Old Lyme had been a renowned community for artists since the turn of the twentieth century and articles from local newspapers in the 1960s occasionally mention her work or participation in exhibits around her adopted town. Her mother passed in 1959, and Tashjian inherited the mansion that they shared. It was there, in 1972, that she made headlines throughout the region by opening the Nut Museum on the grounds of her home. At its opening, this museum—dedicated, as the name suggests, to the edible nut—occupied two rooms of the mansion and included specimens of nuts from throughout the world as well as a small collection of artistic works made with or about nuts. Tashjian had plans to construct a walnut-shaped building to house the artifacts, but the funds for this endeavor never materialized, and over three decades her house transformed by degrees from a personal residence to a place where, as she explained to a Bridgeport newspaper, "whimsy can try its wings."

Tashjian's attraction to the nut began early; she told stories of seeing beauty in them as a child and incorporated them into her artwork as early as the 1930s. The museum grounds displayed from its inception a looming nutcracker of gigantic proportions, and Tashjian often joked that her home brokered peace between nuts and nutcrackers. As the decades passed, she continued to expand the collection at the Nut Museum with original works made by her—sculptures, paintings, and masks—as well as donated and acquired items, including jewelry, toys, and a Nativity scene made of nut carvings. Commentators often praised Tashjian's role as sole curator and tour guide, but they have tended to pass over another important feature of the museum, namely its admission price of one nut. People from throughout the world brought unusual and cherished nuts, prompting Tashjian to ask them to share their stories. Similarly, groups of school-children—the "nutkins" as she called them—and other organizations such as the Brownies habitually donated their own artistic renderings in nut. Tashjian was the elemental force behind the museum, then, but it also became a place for a rich enactment of community and gift exchange that, at least initially, fostered unique understandings of the guest–host relationship.

By the late 1970s the Nut Museum was known throughout the nation thanks to being featured in newspapers and tour guides. In 1981 Tashjian commenced her role as a minor television celebrity with an appearance on *The Tonight Show*. Johnny Carson was so enamored that he invited her back weeks later and gave her twenty minutes of airtime. She would appear several times again and was also invited to David Letterman's *Late Night*, where she was hailed for her perspicacity and wit rather than mocked. Future stints included *The Chevy Chase Show*, *The Roseanne Show*, *The Howie Mandel Show*, *The Howard Stern Show*, *Good Morning America*, *To Tell The Truth*, and *National Geographic* magazine as well as countless radio interviews and local television broadcasts the world over. In these interviews and at the museum, Tashjian routinely wore either a gold wedding dress that belonged to her mother or a purple robe belonging to her grandmother, accented with a belt of black walnuts. She did so to call attention to the historical origins of nuts in Asia Minor—that is, Armenia—and would jest that the Garden of Eden surely was located there. On more than one occasion Tashjian disputed that Eve would have tempted by so paltry a thing as an apple and concluded that it must have been a nut that lured her and Adam into disobedience.

As might be expected, the regional press could not help but embellish her stories with nicknames ranging from "Kernel Sanders" to the "Nutmegger" (a play on a term for someone from Connecticut), but the "Nut Lady" eventually became her best known sobriquet. Tashjian did not relish this name; she herself preferred to be called a "nut culturalist" or a "nut visionary." She numbered among her associates equally formidable individuals such as the playwright Richard Hepburn (the brother of Katharine Hepburn, both of whom lived in Old Saybrook just across the Connecticut River) and his son, the artist Mundy Hepburn. And while she never married and once described herself in an interview with the *Hartford Courant* as an "abstinence achiever," she was well aware of the potential for sexual innuendo among the items in her collection and often impishly played up the comparison. She did not hesitate, for example, to note how the coco de mer in her collection—rumored to be the largest in the world—resembled human buttocks or breasts, but she also produced a series of paintings in the mid-1970s of female heads based on nut shapes and declared that it was a contribution to women's liberation on the grounds that the images shattered stereotypes of sexual objectification.

Despite its popularity and the charm of its owner, the Nut Museum was never financially successful. Attempts to court nut companies as sponsors never succeeded and as early as 1978 the *Courant* reported the threat of its closing. In 1983 the same newspaper listed four adversaries of Tashjian's vision: taxmen, vandals, sign stealers, and squirrels. She herself admitted that her willingness to appear in the media (not owning a television herself) was an attempt to attract donors and publicity, or as she once summarized, she and the Nut Museum garnered "fame but not fortune." The museum was, furthermore, seasonal and always limited to certain days and times, and even when the admission fee rose from one nut to one nut and a few dollars that increased over the years, it could not survive on its own. Tashjian's fortunes declined with the museum and when she was in her early nineties, she was essentially indigent.

These circumstances led to a closing chapter stained with plaintiveness. In 2002 a social worker discovered Tashjian collapsed and in a coma at her home. Doctors did not expect her to survive, but she pulled through two weeks later. She also discovered, quite to her anguish, that her home had been put up for sale to redress her debts and that she was bound for a nursing home as a ward of the state. Thankfully her collection was rescued through the efforts of local citizens and a professor at Connecticut College, Christopher Steiner. Tashjian was declared incompetent by the state, and, to be fair, reports did conclude that she exhibited signs of dementia, but she remained physically robust and adamant about her restoration to her home. This struggle led to a final recognition of Tashjian as an abiding symbol of elderly rights and artistic independence. Local and regional newspapers, especially the *Hartford Courant*, rallied around her, and in 2005 Don Bernier released a laudatory documentary film entitled *In a Nutshell*.

Tashjian never reclaimed her home, and regrettably her celebrity was not enough to secure support from any of the media outlets that enriched themselves with her appearances. She did live long enough to see a retrospective exhibit of her work at Connecticut College and at the Lyman Allyn Art Museum in New London before she died in 2007. "Roadside America," the online site for tourist destinations, continues to maintain a webpage dedicated to her and the museum, which includes artwork, interviews, and recordings of Tashjian singing two of her original songs, "Nuts Are Beautiful" and "March of the Nuts." Her passing was covered by newspapers through New England, New York, and the nation, and she was hailed as an avant-garde artist whose ability to see the remarkable in the common was both an important act of social commentary and a life philosophy well worth emulation.

William "Bill" Johnson was another "colorful individual" whose obsessive genius was underappreciated by government officials in his day. Born in Berwick, Maine, to dairy farmers, Johnson set out to make a living in Boston as a piano tuner but returned to his home state in 1976 when he purchased a historical building, the Barnard Tavern, in Kennebunk. He married and then in the early 1980s purchased Libby's Colonial Tea Room on Route 1 in Wells, Maine, a building that would eventually be listed on the National Register of Historic Places. And akin to Tashjian, Johnson also would, over the decades, turn his property into a work of art and a stage for his unique performances of skillful storytelling.

The property, now known as the Johnson Hall Museum, reflected his career as an auctioneer, a lover of history and preservationist, and as he himself admitted, a hoarder. When he passed in 2014 and auctioneers assessed his collection, they reported without exaggeration hundreds of thousands of items ranging from tiny trinkets to literal buildings and from genuine antiques to pop culture kitsch. Reporters often marveled at the dwellings he had shipped to the property from all over New England: an eighteenth-century blacksmith shop; a nineteenth-century schoolhouse; an icehouse; a soda fountain; a parsonage; a Baptist church; a Socony service station; a Spartan trailer; jail cells; barns; a shack from the Sandy Cove nudist colony; and a railroad depot from South Berwick that his mother used to take to Boston, accompanied by railway cars.

Commentators frequently claimed that Johnson's collection was unorganized or eclectic to the point of being impossible to categorize, but interviews with regional newspapers, *Yankee* magazine, and an episode of the television series *American Pickers* demonstrate a method at work: Johnson was an unequivocal admirer of Americana (especially items reflecting life in Maine or New England) that could provoke a tale. And tell tales he did. Indeed, according to reports, he often called the tours of the property and the extensive collection that he gave to visitors "show and tell," and even a cursory glimpse at Johnson in videos posted online by tourists reveals a raconteur brimming with boyish charm—a man ready to break into song at any number of the many musical instruments at his disposal or even to invite a stranger onto the dance floor for a moment of connection. His desire for anecdotes was equally uncontainable and reflects, as the *Boston Globe* once surmised, his "biggest eccentricity," namely that "he has assigned himself the duty to show off things he thinks are worth being seen. He calls himself 'the keeper,' and he looks for things that are threatened." Those that were threatened, Johnson delivered from oblivion and reinvigorated with new energy and purpose in his collection and with it his endless store of tales to disarm visitor hesitations.

Johnson seemed willing to engage in a certain style that begged for recognition. In media appearances he frequently wore suspenders and tied his long gray hair into a ponytail or hid it under a pith helmet or adventurer's hat. The *Portland Press Herald* once compared him to Archie Bunker, noting that Johnson would sometimes wear a pin emblazoned with "Archie Bunker tells it like it was." And he had a vanity license plate announcing "A Bunker"—on his silver 1937 Buick LaSalle, recalling the line from the theme song to *All in the Family*. And although Johnson was routinely depicted as a joyful, welcoming eccentric, his homage to Bunker should not be overlooked, as it implied an equal willingness to demonstrate the indelible and gruff resistance to authority that is bred in the bones of many Yankees.

That contrarian impulse erupted in 2012 when Johnson became entangled in a controversy with the local government. He had already been featured in *Yankee* and on *American Pickers*—the latter of which also showed him to be secure and grounded in his convictions, as he was cooperative but not submissive in the face of celebrity and did not readily sell from his collection—when he sought to add a 1915 tin garage to his property. This required a permit, of course, and with it a renewed site plan, but Johnson had removed two dead maple trees that abutted Route 1. The town insisted that he obey zoning ordinances and replace the trees with a sizeable hedge buffer, a recommendation he interpreted as a demand to shield the entire property from view.

As the museum survived based on word of mouth and the curiosity of pass-ersby, any attempts to hide it would have produced a serious negative impact for attracting visitors. And so, in 2012, Johnson made news from Portland to Boston in his struggle against bureaucracy. For their part, officials played the role of stodgy town officials perfectly. "We can't grant waivers," argued one of them, "just because someone is a colorful character." According to John-son himself, they threatened a thousand-dollar daily fine at one point, which, predictably, only garnered sympathy from those tourists and outsiders who learned of his plight and set him on the path of becoming a folk hero.

It is remarkably easy, of course, to idealize eccentrics and to vilify local offi-cials as dunderheads who fail to see inspired madness when it conflicts with petty ordinances and an inflated sense of consistency in matters regarding waivers. And no one can deny that eccentrics can be notoriously difficult peo-ple, especially when they veer toward the cranky rather than the groovy. But that is precisely the challenge of eccentrics: to demand respect for the integrity and for the unique and unusual demands of every individual and to refuse to allow authority—however minor—to get away with discouraging people who hear a different drummer.

Johnson died in February 2014, fittingly doing what he loved: attending an auction in Wells. He was only seventy-three years old. His widow, Jo—an accomplished ophthalmologist—eventually decided to auction a considerable amount of his collection as well as the Barnard Tavern in order to invest money in the Johnson Hall Museum. Today it is a stunning estate, albeit one removed of the overflow of Americana, and a popular rental destination for weddings and related events. Tours are no longer available of the remaining collection, but many of the buildings remain and form the backdrop of a provocative scene. And in the remembrances of Johnson, one from Dan Meader, the gallery director who oversaw the auction, is telling. Johnson, he explained, appreciated value in things beyond their material and financial worth and "saw beauty in whatever that type of collectable was." His was the eye of an eccentric, then, and with it the perception of a visionary.

19

THE LEGENDARY ECCENTRICS: CHARLES DUNBAR, TOMBOLIN, AND TOM COOK

It should be obvious by now that all of the eccentrics whose stories appear in this book became legendary to some degree, so in giving that title to this final chapter, I do not mean to take anything away from the subjects of the earlier portraits. Here, rather, *legendary* has a very specific meaning, of eccentrics much more closely attached to folklore than to history. The "facts" surrounding these men are inevitably hazy because they may simply be products of the imagination and an active oral tradition. These tales involve feats that transcend the limits of everyday life and yet, in a strangely profound way, reinforce the importance of the mundane and the common as a place we all share, even in our longing for its transformation into something extraordinary. I close the book with the stories of these legendary eccentrics, then, because they poignantly remind us of the endless need to reenchant the world.

The first of our legendary eccentrics brings a speculative connection that may prove erroneous—but nevertheless remains tantalizing. In his journals in

1850, Henry David Thoreau introduced his uncle, Charles Dunbar, who "grew up to become a remarkably eccentric man." That Thoreau would nominate anyone as an eccentric surely says something about that person's character, but the comment here was meant as a compliment of sorts as Dunbar was, in the words of the preeminent scholar Walter Harding, "Thoreau's favorite relative." Dunbar was a lifelong bachelor who lived with the Thoreau family on and off from 1830 until his death in 1856, albeit with long breaks during which he would essentially disappear. Dunbar was, however, instrumental in the fortunes of the Thoreau family, for in 1821 he discovered a deposit of graphite in Bristol, New Hampshire, and with a partner, Cyrus Snow, began a company to manufacture pencils. Two years later Thoreau's father, John, went to work for the company and took it over when both Dunbar and Snow abandoned the pursuit. Thoreau himself worked at his family pencil company for his adult life.

Two early biographers of Thoreau, Henry Stephens Salt and Franklin Benjamin Sanborn, agreed that Dunbar was an eccentric with a vagabond's tendencies, and Sanborn, who knew Dunbar personally, confirmed that he was "an amusing guest." He was, apparently, a skillful magician and juggler. Thoreau relished writing about Dunbar's card tricks in another journal entry, twice mentioned that he could toss a hat high into the air only to catch it on his head, and remarked that he could also "swallow his nose." Similarly, Sanborn introduced the idea that Dunbar, when dining at an inn, could swallow knives and forks and make plates disappear, returning them to the applause of onlookers after the innkeeper agreed to nullify the bill. Dunbar apparently suffered from narcolepsy—his nephew called them "cat naps" in a letter to his mother—and in Walden Thoreau notes that his uncle would fall asleep shaving and had to resort to keeping busy sprouting potatoes in a cellar in order to keep the Sabbath.

In an insightful entry about his uncle's charming disposition, Thoreau recounted an episode in 1853 in which the two discussed important people of their time. With the conversation at a close, the two retired to bed. Sometime thereafter, Thoreau heard Dunbar arouse, "and he called out, in an earnest, stentorian voice, loud enough to wake the whole house, 'Henry! Was John

Quincy Adams a genius?' 'No, I think not,' was my reply. 'Well, I didn't think he was,' answered he." This would be the second time that Thoreau characterized his uncle's booming voice. In the earlier entry from 1850, he noted that Dunbar's "lungs were proportionally strong" and added an unusual tale. "There was a man who heard him named once," Thoreau recalled, "and asked if it was the same Charles Dunbar whom he remembered when he was a little boy walking on the coast of Maine. A man came down to the shore and hailed a vessel that was sailing by."

This observation has long passed without comment, but there is a reasonable chance that it is connected to a minor cycle of folklore in New England. Richard Dorson, the distinguished folklorist, collected a series of stories published in the *Yankee Blade*, a Boston paper, in 1847. Anonymously published and entitled "Tough Stories Or, Some Reminiscences of 'Uncle Charles,'" they do not overtly name Dunbar, but the resemblances are uncanny. "One of the oddest and most eccentric geniuses that ever fell under out notice was 'Uncles Charles,'" the tale began, "an old, grey-headed man, of about three score and ten, who resided some years ago in a little village with a big name, about twenty miles from the Capital of Maine." If this were Charles Dunbar, the age works out, as he would have been sixty-seven years old. Augusta had become the state capital by then, and although it is difficult to reach any shore town from there within twenty miles, Dunbar was known to travel throughout Maine, New Hampshire, and Vermont during his sojourns away from the Thoreau household. It is plausible, then, that this is evidence of his wandering.

The most significant connection, however, is the first story told about "Uncle Charles," in which a conversation in a tavern turned to the strength of the human voice. "Someone remarked to the company that Uncle Charles could 'holler' as loud as any person he ever heard." The old man agreed with this assessment and told a tale about the time he was in Augusta before there was a bridge. He missed the ferry across the Kennebec River. "The Captain thought if I hollered the ferryman would hear me," Uncle Charles continued. "I did so once or twice, *just as easy as I could*,—but no answer. I then just let out my voice, and cuss me, if I didn't make a *roar!*" His companion begged him not to try again for fear of alarming the entire village. The ferryman came, fearful that an earthquake or cannon had erupted, and reported frightened horses and broken glass on the other side of the river. The anecdote ends with a man in Gardiner, some five miles south of Augusta, reporting to Uncle Charles that he heard his voice clearly down there as well.

The tall tale aspects are, of course, not true, but the heart of this story concerns an eccentric man of nearly seventy with a booming voice and a penchant for exaggeration in storytelling. And the similarities between Uncle Charles and Charles Dunbar do not end there. Uncle Charles, for example, next told a story about falling through the ice of a frozen pond and walking on the bottom—presumably holding his breath—until he could find another hole near a landing. He survived but earned several bumps on his head, as he kept hitting the ice above him while navigating the path to safety. This improbable tale echoes several comments that Thoreau offered throughout his journal, such as in his first entry, when he declared that Dunbar was "celebrated for his feats of strength."

In another entry from 1853, Thoreau reported a man telling a tale about Dunbar's ability to jump back and forth over the yoke of an oxcart while it was moving. And in 1856, following Dunbar's death, he noted that people were sharing stories about his uncle, and especially his tremendous dexterity and his prowess at wrestling in which no man could beat him. Thoreau added his own tale, stating that Dunbar claimed to have lost all the teeth in his head by age twenty-one, but he grew a second pair. And finally, in 1859, Thoreau related a story passed on to him through a chain of storytellers that Dunbar was able to plant a twelve-foot ladder in the ground and then run up one side and run down the other without effort.

The evidence remains circumstantial, then, but there is a very good chance that the Uncle Charles tall tales were inspired by the real Charles Dunbar and introduced to the wider public either by the anonymous author of the essay in the *Yankee Blade* or, as Dorson speculated, by stories that formed in the oral tradition as a short-lived phenomenon. The real Charles died in Hampstead, New Hampshire, and was buried in Haverhill, Massachusetts. On the day of his burial, Thoreau remarked that his beloved uncle was born the year of a great snowstorm and died the year of one as well. His was, Thoreau offered with profundity, "a life bounded by great snows." It is a fitting observation for a man—and perhaps a legend—who was anything but boring and normal.

Our second eccentric offers an intriguing example of mistaken identity and the influential power of folk narratives. In 1892 Elizabeth Ward published her reminiscence, *Old Times in Shrewsbury*, a loving study of the town in Massachusetts. Therein she identified "an eccentric individual" who lived in Shrewsbury around 1740 known only as Tombolin. Observing that New England pioneers had very few opportunities for fun, Ward proposed that one source of entertainment was to follow the tradition of the "ancient Britons" in creating rhymes about notable events or people. Tombolin, she continued, had clearly been regarded as such a figure to the local community given the number of comic rhymes composed around his antics.

The songs about him were nearly extinct, Ward lamented, lingering only as fragments in the memories of elderly residents, but one song remained relatively complete:

> Tombolin was a Scotchman born,
> His shoes were out and his stockings torn,
> The calf of his leg came down to his shin;
> I'm a nice good figure, says Tombolin.
> Tombolin had no breeches to wear,
> So he got his mother to make him a pair,
> Flesh side out and wool side in;
> They're warmer so, says Tombolin.
> Tombolin wanted new stockings to wear,
> So he got his old grandmarm to knit him a pair;
> For want of a needle she knit with a pin,
> They're delicate wearing, says Tombolin.

Tombolin, his wife and her mother
All went over the bridge together;
The bridge broke down, they all fell in;
"The deuce go with you," said Tombolin.

Ward's recollection inspired further mention of Tombolin as an eccentric character living in Shrewsbury in three touring guides: Stephen Jenkins's *The Old Boston Post Road* from 1913, Porter Sargent's *Handbook of New England* from 1917, and George Francis Marlowe's *Coaching Roads of Old New England* from 1945. All of them cite the second stanza of the song as evidence of Tombolin's oddities and popularity as a subject of rhyme in the town.

How, then, to explain the following recording of a five-stanza rhyme sung by Viola Marsh Coolidge of Ludlow, Vermont—a town roughly one hundred miles from Shrewsbury—in 1930?

Tombolin was a Scotchman born;
His shoes worn out, his stockings torn;
His shirt was ragged, his spencer thin.
"This is my best suit," said Tombolin.
Tombolin had no breeches to wear.
He bought a sheepskin to make him a pair—
The flesh side out, the wool side in.
"They are charming and cool," said Tombolin.
Tombolin and his wife and his wife's mother,
All got into one bed together;
The weather was cold, the sheets were thin.
"I'll sleep in the middle," said Tombolin.
But his wife's mother said the very next day,
"You will have to get another place to stay;
I can't lie awake and hear you snore;
You can't stay in my house anymore."
Tombolin got into a hollow tree,

And very contented seemed to be;
The wind did blow and the rain beat in.
"This is better than no house," said Tombolin.

The answer is relatively simple: Tombolin never existed. He was a figure of folk ballads popular in New England throughout the 1800s and likely before then. Coolidge, whose version was collected in Helen Hartness Flanders's *Vermont Folk-Songs and Ballads*, recalled that she learned it from her father, who was born in 1800. In 1810 a broadside was published in Boston that contained two songs, "Tom Bolin" and "The Maid of Boston," and sure enough, the opening stanza depicts

Tom Bolin was a Scotchman born,
His shoes worn out, his stockings were torn
His jacket was short, his shirt it was thin,
This is my summer dress, says Tom Bolin.

Fourteen stanzas follow, incorporating most of the events that appear in Ward and Coolidge's songs. Likewise, another broadside, *Dame Durden and Tom Bolin*, reprinted the song in the 1830s. In 1935 the *Springfield Republican* published an article by Flanders, who had received another version from Amos Eaton of South Royalton, Vermont, which his mother used to sing to him. It neatly echoes these longer versions.

To complicate matters nicely, in 1876, there appeared *Mother Goose's Pocket of Pleasure*, a rhyme book published in Boston with the following song concerning two kittens and the mother cat:

The two gray Kits
And the gray Kits' mother
All went over
The bridge together.
The bridge broke down,

They all fell in,

May the rats go with you,

Says Tom Bolin.

And with just a little more digging, one can find a folk song collected in Ireland by Sam Henry in the 1930s, concerning:

Bryan O'Lynn was a Scotchman born,

His head it was bald and his beard it was shorn.

O'Lynn, akin to his American cousin Tombolin, contrives various schemes in the remaining stanzas to clothe himself, and the rhyme ends with his plummet into a river with his wife and mother-in-law when a bridge collapses. He was, however, pleased with the adventure—"We'll go home by water," says Bryan O'Lynn. Variant names appear in other collections, including Brian A'Linn, Byran O'Lin, Tommy O'Linn, Tom O'Linne, Thomas o' Linn, Tam o' the Lynn, Tom-a-lin, Tommy Linn, Old Tumble Lynn, Tom Bolyn, Tom Boleyn, Tom Bowlin, Tom Robin, Byran O'Flynn, John Barney Flynn, and even Harry Trewin. Folklorists have traced the ballad to the late 1500s, when it served as a comic satire upon the Scottish. The ballad's tune and its premise (of a foolish or eccentric character who compensates in a humorous way for lacking some important item) may have even inspired the great Scottish poet Robert Burns's "Duncan MacLeerie."

The question, then, is how this figure of international folk song became associated with a town in the heart of Massachusetts. An earlier history of Shrewsbury, published by Andrew Henshaw Ward (Elizabeth Ward's fraternal uncle) in 1847, provides the answer. Elizabeth Ward had mentioned a place in the town called "The Tombolin," and later travel writers noted it was frequently called "Tombolin Hill," located on the road to Northborough, the adjacent town. In Andrew Ward's history, he invoked a similar location, "Tomlin Hill" or "Tomlin Place," which was also known as "Tomblin" or "Tombolin." (Tomblin Hill still divides Shrewsbury from Northborough.) The name was taken, however, not from Tombolin the folk character but from an original settler, Isaac Tomlin, born 1732 from a family originating in Westborough, another town adjacent to both Shrewsbury and Northborough.

The pieces now fit together with little effort. A site settled by Isaac Tomlin at the rough intersection of three towns became, over time, fertile ground to localize a popular folk ballad about Tombolin. Unaware of the rich tradition of the folk song, residents in Shrewsbury adopted him as a cherished eccentric. And in addition to adaptations of the ballad, it is also clear that Shrewbury residents invented other songs about him. Elizabeth Ward offers only a glimpse, citing a single line—"All that she saved was her tea-kettle lid"—about an incident in which the first Tombolin house, nestled on the road to Westborough, burned to the ground, prompting them to relocate to the hill that eventually bore their name.

That Tombolin was a popular figure is indisputable. In 1812, for example, the *National Aegis* of Worcester (another municipality adjacent to Shrewsbury) published a poem, "To Tombolin," that was unrelated to the ballad but nevertheless paid homage to him. A newspaper in New London, Connecticut, similarly published an independent poem, "Tom Bolin and the Whale," in 1846, continuing his fantastical and eccentric adventures. And throughout the first half of the nineteenth century, the schooner *Tombolin* was a visitor to Newburyport and advertised widely. All of these examples testify to the popularity of the character in New England and, ultimately, to his international origins.

Our final example, Tom Cook, basks even more in the aura of folklore. The stories of his life are so remarkable as to raise the question of whether he really existed or was simply a character thought to have once lived. He was, however, reportedly born on October 6, 1738, to Cornelius and Eunice Cook of Westborough, Massachusetts, and family genealogies written in the late 1800s do indeed include all three of them. Similarly, the diaries of Ebenezer Parkman, a pastor in Westborough, both record marrying the couple and an incident on August 27, 1779, in which "the notorious Tom Cook" visited him. "I gave him what admonition, instruction and caution I could," Parkman continued, "I beseech God to give it force!"

When Tom Cook died, reportedly at the age of ninety, heading to Boston, he was already infamous and often cited in newspapers throughout New England. Some commentators claimed that he would work during the haying season for farmers in need of assistance, and yet others suggested he occasionally took up the role of a butcher, but Cook was predominantly known for his criminal activities, being a thief of the highest order. Parkman does not overtly identify him by an illicit occupation, but he seems to have engaged in some furtive events that warranted a broadside in his honor, "The Devil and Tom Cook," which appeared in 1826 in the *New England Galaxy*, a popular magazine:

> Tom Cook, he was a noted thief,
> I've heard old people tell,
> In petty larceny did he
> Most other thieves excel.
> Where Tom was born, or where he died,
> I cannot now find out;
> So, gentle reader, on these points
> We must remain in doubt.
> Tom often from the rich would steal,
> And then the poor supply,
> Promoting, like true democrat,
> Complete equality.
> At a poor widow's he, one night,
> Requested he might stay
> Till morning, as he was much tired,
> Then for her kindness pay.
> She owned she had nothing to eat,
> Or to her children give;
> Says he, "your wants shall be supplied,
> As surely as I live."

He hastened to a neighboring mill,
And quickly there did steal,
And bring into the widow's cot
A heavy bag of meal.
On hasty pudding they did feast,
Tom, widow, children four;
The slept till morn, when on his way,
He left the widow's door.
The widow was a woman, so
She quickly spread the fame
Of Tom Cook's present, all around,
Not knowing whence it came.
The miller heard the news full soon,
And raised the hue and cry;
And ere the sun was down, poor Tom
Was safe in custody.
They took him to a bar-room, where
A crowd all gaping stood
Of "sovereign people," whom Burke calls,
A "swinish multitude."
Tom walk'd and talk'd among the crowd,
Declaring, without fail,
The devil soon would take him off,
Nor let him go to jail.
Beneath his dread-nought, old coat, he
Had of gun-powder store,
Which, while he walk'd and talk'd, around
He scatter'd on the floor.
Then from the fire-place suddenly
A burning coal he took,
The powder touch'd—the room was filled
With sulphur-scented smoke.

Tom disappear'd, the night was dark—
The folks were sadly scared—
So he was far away, before
They to pursue him dar'd.
Full many more there might be told
Of Tom's fam'd tricks so clever;
Which for the present are deferred.
And, probably, forever.

Other accounts from this time told stories about Cook laden with the unbe-lievable. One tale, again from 1826, imagined an unnamed clergyman who came to counsel Cook while he was in jail as an elderly man of seventy. Cook proclaimed that he was a better man than most considered him, as he had never robbed from the poor and "exercised much prudence and philanthropy in my calling." When pressed to review his misdeeds, Cook decided to make amends by giving advice to the young. His advice, however, was not repentance. Quite the contrary, he encouraged young people who wished to follow his profession the good sense of keeping stolen goods on hand long enough that "he can sell to the owner without being suspected."

Later in the same year, the *Galaxy* again indulged readers with stories of his wily nature. Cook, the essay ruminated, was not above taking a retainer from the wealthy who did not want him to steal, and further explained that several families around Boston would treat him to lunch or cider on a consis-tent schedule to keep his hands off their other goods. The tale also introduced another feature of his character: that Cook would never lie. In the specific case, he bargained with a man and promised not to steal a horse from the entire—and again unnamed—town in exchange for a regular payment. When a horse went missing, Cook was accused. He protested that the pasture was not in the township, and when shown the error of his ways, the horse was promptly returned under cover of darkness.

But perhaps the most charming tale in this collection was of Cook tying a rope around a tree and splicing it in such a manner that no end could be found, giving the unholy appearance of an endless form. It first became a point of fascination for those who discovered it and then a source of fear that a witch had been at work; in a nice homage to another eccentric in this book, Moll Pitcher was directly named as the likely culprit. When the crowd grew large enough and distracted, Cook robbed them all and made off without detection. Finally, by 1828, stories were circulating about Cook's deceiving his way into the estate home of a judge (given the pseudonym Deacon Snooks) through an alibi and then, in confronting the wealthy owner, bargained for a regular meal.

These early stories do not locate Cook with any specificity. Toward the end of the nineteenth century, when local historians commenced in earnest to detail nearly every town in New England, Cook appeared in several. A history of Brookline, Massachusetts, from 1874, for example, confirmed that he operated there until he made the mistake of stealing a goose for himself, and, in cooking it at a schoolhouse, alerted a perceptive squire of his activities. (Cook reportedly accepted a public whipping rather than imprisonment on Castle Island in this case.) A history of Sudbury from 1889 identified a barn in which Cook stopped for the night. And in both of these, the impression arose that, as the Brookline history summarizes, "He had many eccentricities, among which was a habit of stealing from the rich to give to the poor."

The eccentric Tom Cook was, however, welcomed home in a lengthy passage in a history of Westborough written by Harriette Forbes in 1889. Several interesting elements appear. In "The Devil and Tom Walker," the Evil One was only a ruse. In Forbes's account, however, Cook was actually in league with the Devil, either by his own will or by his mother's, who reportedly begged that Cook's life be spared when he was dying at the age of three. Forbes proffered the tale of the day that the Devil came for his due and Cook, thinking quickly, asked the satanic agent for time to put on his suspenders. When the Devil consented, Cook threw them into the fire and forever released himself from the clutches of the diabolical. In great detail Forbes then explained his many crimes, how he was beloved by children for the toys he would bring them, and how he was known as "the honest thief" throughout New England but himself preferred to be called "the leveller," as he leveled wealth and poverty.

Tales of Tom Cook continued into the twentieth century, and even today Westborough residents post comments online about passing by the house believed to be his home. We might pause and debate if stealing from the rich for the charity of the poor is deserving of the title of eccentric, but few can dispute that even if Cook was a purely fictional invention, the ethical questions and conundrums he raises are common to the human experience, and his story, to quote Forbes yet again, asks us all to consider how best to respond to a man "whose wrongs, in his own eccentric way, he was to endeavor to right." This legacy—and that of all the storied eccentrics who enliven our world—calls attention to what is normal, what is weird, and why we divide up the world in the way that that we do.

ACKNOWLEDGMENTS

I am grateful, first and foremost, to my favorite eccentrics—my family—for their inexhaustible enthusiasm and encouragement: Winnie, Cellina, Antonio, Angeline, and Salvatore.

I could not have a better conspirator in the accursed share than my friend Ray Huling. Ray's selfless contribution of time and attention to these pages made this book possible.

I once joked that I would sell my soul for a good editor. Having worked with Evan Helmlinger at Globe Pequot Press, I may be in serious trouble. His patience, keen advice, and thoughtfulness are a testimony to the ideal practices of his profession.

I am thankful that Chris Dobbs, Executive Director of the Connecticut River Museum (CRM), is both a friend and a visionary leader. I am equally thankful to Amy Trout, the museum curator, for her advocacy and admirable attention to details. And I am thankful to the dedicated staff—Suzanne Burns, Helen Davis, Caleb Lincoln, Joan Meek, Kendall Perkins, Liz Sistare, Phyllis Stillman, and Jen White-Dobbs—as well as all the volunteers who make the CRM one of the best educational institutions in New England.

I appreciate all those who bolstered this project: Michelle Anjirbag, Ibby Carothers, John Coston, Meredith Dias, Eliza Donhauser, Alex Foulkes, Lori-anne Panzara Griswold, Wick Griswold, Michael Lee-Murphy, Randy Melick, Linda Rilley-Blue, Molly Turner, Porntip Twishime, Dave Williams, Gary Williams, and Stacy Winchell. Mark Griswold deserves special thanks for keeping the conversations and the mind well lubricated.

No book of this sort would be possible without the tireless efforts of town historians, historical societies, and librarians throughout New England. I am especially indebted to Maggie Humberston, Betsy McKee, Jim Moran, and Judy Moran at the Longmeadow Historical Society; Phil Wooding at the Southington Historical Society; Bob Montgomery at the *Bristol Press*; and Ann Thompson at the Essex Public Library for their assistance.

I am thankful for the support of colleagues in the Communication Department at the University of Massachusetts, Amherst, and the Lyme Academy College of Fine Arts. And, finally, I am grateful to all the students in my folklore classes who offered ideas, suffer my lectures, and inspire me with their endless eccentricities.

BIBLIOGRAPHY

Introduction: Let Us Now Praise Eccentric Folk

Botkin, Benjamin, ed. *A Treasury of New England Folklore*. New York: Bonanza Books, 1965.

Brague, Rémi. *Eccentric Culture: A Theory of Western Civilization*. South Bend, Indiana: St. Augustine's Press, 2002.

Knapp, Samuel Lorenzo. *Life of Lord Timothy Dexter*. Boston: J. E. Tilton and Company, 1858.

Marcus, George. "On Eccentricity." *Rhetorics of Self-Making*. Edited by Debbora Battaglia. Berkeley: University of California Press, 1995.

Weeks, David, and Jamie James. *Eccentrics: A Study of Sanity and Strangeness*. New York: Villard Books, 1995.

The Lord: Timothy Dexter

Columbian Museum, September 25, 1801.

Currier, John. *History of Newburyport*. Newburyport, 1906.

Dexter, Timothy. *A Pickle for the Knowing Ones, or Plain Truths in Homespun Dress*. www .lordtimothydexter.com/index.htm.

Gazette of the United States, August 3, 1794.

Greenfield Gazette, May 12, 1806.

Holmes, Oliver Wendell Sr. *Over the Teacups*. Boston: Houghton, Mifflin and Company, 1891.

Knapp, Samuel Lorenzo. *Life of Lord Timothy Dexter*. Boston: J. E. Tilton and Company, 1858.

Livermore, Arthur. "Arthur Livermore, Chief Justice of New Hampshire." *Proceedings of the Grafton and Coös County Bar Association* 3 (1898).

"Lord Dexter." *Newburyport Herald*, July 1, 1803.

Todd, William Cleaves. "Lord Timothy Dexter." *The New England Historical and Genea-logical Register* 40 (1886).

The Secret Keeper and the Seer: Joseph Moody and Horace Johnson

"Attempt on the Life of Horace Johnson!" *Hartford Globe,* June 6, 1907.

Botkin, Benjamin, ed. *A Treasury of New England Folklore.* New York: Bonanza Books, 1965.

"Dire Prophecy by Horace Johnson, Connecticut Seer." *Boston Globe,* September 3, 1893.

Dorson, Richard. *Jonathan Draws the Long Bow.* Cambridge: Harvard University Press, 1946.

Hartford Courant, February 20, 1860.

Hartford Courant, February 17, 1864.

"Horace Johnson, Hale and Healthy." *Hartford Courant,* May 13, 1908.

"The Last of the Ceres." *Hartford Courant,* April 23, 1870.

Moody, Charles. *Biographical Sketches of the Moody Family.* Boston: Samuel Drake, 1847.

"Old Uncle Horace, Weather Seer, Dies." *The Sun,* January 21, 1917.

"A Visit to the Prophet Who Predicted the 1888 Blizzard." *New York Times,* July 16, 1916.

Woodwell, Philip McIntire. *Handkerchief Moody: The Diary and the Man.* Portland: Colonial Offset Printing Company, 1981.

The Unruly Women: Mary Webster and Hetty Green

Atwood, Margaret. *Morning in the Burned House.* Boston: Houghton Mifflin Company, 1995.

Drake, Samuel Gardner. *Annals of Witchcraft in New England.* Boston: W. Elliot Woodward, 1869.

Hutchinson, Thomas. *History of the Colony and Province of Massachusetts Bay.* Salem: Thomas Cushing, 1795.

Judd, Sylvester. *History of Hadley.* Northampton: Metcalf and Company, 1863.

Mather, Cotton. *Magnalia Christi Americana.* London: Thomas Parkhurst, 1702.

———. *Memorable Providences.* London: Thomas Parkhurst, 1690.

Records of the Court of Assistants of the Colony of the Massachusetts Bay 1630–1692. Boston: County of Suffolk, 1901.

Sifakis, Carl. *Great American Eccentrics: Strange and Peculiar People.* New York: Galahad Books, 1984.

Slack, Charles. *Hetty.* New York: Ecco, 2004.

Warner, Charles Forbes. "Picturesque Hampshire: A Supplement to the Quarter-Centennial Journal." 1890.

The Hermits: John Smith and English Jack

Barber, George Warren. *History of the Hermit of Erving Castle*. Andover: Warren F. Draper, 1868.

Congregationalist and Boston Report, January 26, 1876.

"Eating Live Frogs." *Jackson City Patriot*, October 3, 1890. [Reprints *Chicago News*.]

English Jack. "The Lonesome Life." http://whitemountainhistory.org/uploads/English_Jack_Poem.pdf.

"Erving's Hermit Actor." *Boston Globe*, October 9, 1892.

"Grand Autumn Excursions." *Saturday Morning Citizen*, August 31, 1889.

"Heart of the Mountains." *Boston Herald*, July 22, 1894.

"Hermit of the White Hills." *Boston Herald*, July 20, 1902.

"Hill Hermits Bitter Enemies." *Boston Herald*, August 20, 1905.

"In the White Mountains." *Boston Herald*, August 3, 1890.

"A Live Frog-Eater." *Times-Picayune*, March 22, 1879. [Reprints *New York Star*.]

Lowell Daily Citizen and News, July 15, 1878.

Mitchell, James. *The Story of Jack the Hermit of the White Mountains*. Boston: Press of the Standard Printing Company, 1891.

Nason, Elias. *Gazetteer of the State of Massachusetts*. Boston: B. B. Russell, 1874.

Smith, G. P. "Dead to the World." *Worcester Daily Spy*, October 18, 1893.

Smith, John. *The Hermit of Erving Castle*. Erving: Lyndon Crawford, 1871.

Springfield Republican, September 13, 1888.

Vermont Phoenix, March 27, 1874.

"The White Mountains." *Hartford Courant*, July 7, 1879.

"White Mountains." *New Hampshire Sentinel*, August 2, 1877.

"White Mountains, Farewell!" *Springfield Republican*, October 7, 1895.

The Healers: Elisha Perkins, Sylvester Graham, Robert Wesselhoeft, and F. C. Fowler

"Cold Water Cure." *Boston Medical and Surgical Journal* 34 (1846).

"Concerning Dogs." *New Haven Register*, January 31, 1885.

Connecticut Valley Advertiser, September 16, 1882.

Emerson, Ralph Waldo. *Journals*. Boston: Houghton Mifflin Company, 1911.

Fessenden, Thomas Green. *Terrible Tractoration!* London: T. Hurst, 1803.

Fowler, F. C. *Life: How to Enjoy It and How to Prolong It.* Moodus: 1896.

Graham, Sylvester. *A Lecture to Young Men on Chastity.* Boston: George Light, 1838.

———. *Lectures on the Science of Human Life.* London: Horsell, 1849.

———. *The Philosophy of Sacred History.* London: Horsell and Caudwell, 1859.

———. *A Treatise on Bread and Bread-Making.* Boston: Light and Stearns, 1837.

"Great Year on the Track." *Boston Herald,* March 8, 1891.

Haygarth, John. *Of the Imagination, as a Cause and Cure of Disorders of the Body.* Bath: R. Cruttwell, 1801.

Holmes, Oliver Wendell Sr. *Homeopathy and Its Kindred Delusions.* Boston: William Ticknor, 1842.

"A Mammoth Deer Park." *Bridgeton Evening News,* May 22, 1893.

"Patent Address." *Connecticut Courant,* November, 1796.

Perkins, Benjamin. *Cases of Successful Practice with Perkins's Patent Metallic Tractors.* London: J. Johnson, 1801.

———. *The Efficacy of Perkins's Patent Metallic Tractors.* London: Luke Hansard, 1800.

———. *New Cases of Practice with Perkins's Patent Metallic Tractors.* London: G. Cooke, 1802.

———. *The Influence of Metallic Tractors.* London: J. Johnson, 1798.

Perkins, Benjamin, ed. *Experiments with the Metallic Tractors.* London: J. Johnson, 1799.

Spaulding, J. A. *Illustrated Popular Biography of Connecticut.* Hartford: Case, Lockwood and Brainard Company, 1891.

"Sylvester Graham." *Boston Medical and Surgical Journal* 45 (1852).

Thacher, James. *American Medical Biography.* Boston: Richardson and Lord and Cottons and Barnard, 1828.

Walsh, James Joseph. *Psychotherapy.* New York: D. Appleton and Company, 1913.

Wesselhoeft, Robert. *New-York Tribune,* April 16, 1845.

———. *Some Remarks on Dr. O. W. Holmes's Lectures on Homeopathy and Its Kindred Delusions.* Boston: Otis Clapp, 1842.

The Settler: William Blaxton

Amory, Thomas Coffin. "William Blaxton." *The Bostonian Society Publications* 1 (1886).

Blackstone, John Wilford. *Lineage and History of William Blackstone.* Frederic: John Wilford Blackstone Jr., 1907.

Bliss, Leonard. *The History of Rehoboth.* Boston: Otis, Broaders, and Company, 1836.

"Boston's First Settler." *Kansas City Times,* May 24, 1886. [Reprints *Boston Post.*]

Drake, Samuel Adams, ed. *A Book of New England Legends and Folk Lore.* Boston: Roberts Brothers, 1884.

Hawthorne, Nathaniel. *The Scarlet Letter*. Boston: Ticknor, Reed, and Fields, 1850.

———. *Twice-Told Tales*. Boston: American Stationers Company, 1837.

Hopkins, Stephen. "An Historical Account of the Planting and Growth of Providence." *Collections of the Rhode Island Historical Society* 7 (1885).

Mather, Cotton. *Magnalia Christi Americana*. London: Thomas Parkhurst, 1702.

Motley, John Lothrop. *Merry Mount, a Romance of the Massachusetts Colony*. Boston: James Munroe and Company, 1849.

Newman, Sylvanus Chase. *An Address Delivered at the Formation of the Blackstone Monument Association*. Pawtucket: James Estey, 1855.

Sanford, Ezekiel. *The Humours of Eutopia: A Tale of Colonial Times*. Philadelphia: Carey, Lee and Carey, 1828.

"William Blackstone." *Worcester Aegis*, December 24, 1828.

The Poets: Sarah Helen Whitman and Frederick Goddard Tuckerman

Baker, Noelle. *Sarah Helen Whitman's Literary Criticism: A Critical Edition*. Dissertation, Georgia State University, 1999.

England, Eugene. *Beyond Romanticism: Tuckerman's Life and Poetry*. Provo: Brigham Young University, 1991.

Golden, Samuel. *Frederick Goddard Tuckerman*. New York: Twain Publishers, 1966.

Kunce, Catherine. *The Correspondence of Sarah Helen Whitman and Julia Deane Freeman*. Newark: University of Delaware Press, 2014.

Mazer, Ben, ed. *Selected Poems of Frederick Goddard Tuckerman*. Cambridge: Belknap Press, 2010.

Momaday, N. Scott, ed. *The Complete Poems of Frederick Goddard Tuckerman*. Oxford: Oxford University Press, 1965.

"Sarah Helen Whitman." *New-York Tribune*, June 29, 1878.

Ticknor, Caroline. *Poe's Helen*. New York: Charles Scribner's Sons, 1916.

Varner, John Grier. *Sarah Helen Whitman, Seeress of Providence*. Dissertation, University of Virginia, 1940.

Whitman, Sarah Helen. "Conversations with Goethe." *The Boston Quarterly Review* 3 (1840).

———. *Hours of Life and Other Poems*. Providence: George Whitney, 1853.

———. *Poems*. Boston: Houghton, Osgood and Company, 1879.

The Mesmerists: John Bovee Dods and Phineas Parkhurst Quimby

Bangor Weekly Register, March 23, 1820.

Deep River New Era, April 6, 1950.

Dods, John Bovee. *Bangor Weekly Register*, November 16, 1820.

———. *The Philosophy of Electrical Psychology*. New York: Fowlers and Wells, 1853.

———. *Six Lectures on the Philosophy of Mesmerism*. Boston: William Hall and Company, 1843.

———. *Spirit Manifestations Examined and Explained*. New York: De Witt and Davenport, 1854.

Dresser, Horatio, ed. *The Quimby Manuscripts*. New York: Thomas Crowell Company, 1921.

History of Penobscot County, Maine. Cleveland: Williams, Chase and Company, 1882.

"Latest from Dr. Dods." *Age of Progress* 2 (1855). [Reprints *Spiritual Telegraph*.]

Quimby, George. "Phineas Parkhurst Quimby." *New England Magazine* 6 (1888).

Quimby, Phineas Parkhurt. *The Complete Collected Works of Dr. Phineas Parkhurst Quimby*. Manchester: Seed of Life Publishing, 2012.

Quinn, Sheila O'Brien. "How Southern New England Became Magnetic North: The Acceptance of Animal Magnetism." *History of Psychology* 10 (2007).

Sibley, John Langdon. *History of the Town of Union*. Boston: Benjamin Mussey and Company, 1851.

The Fortune-Tellers: Moll Pitcher and Mary Scannell Pepper Vanderbilt

Boston Traveler, July 12, 1879.

Cadwallader, M. E. *Mary S. Vanderbilt: A Twentieth Century Seer*. Chicago: The Progressive Thinker Publishing House, 1921.

Drake, Samuel Adams. "Coast Rambles in Essex." *Harper's New Monthly Magazine* 56 (1878).

Funk, Isaak. *The Psychic Riddle*. New York: Funk and Wagnalls Company, 1907.

Hoey, Ellen Mary Griffin. *Moll Pitcher's Prophecies; Or, the American Sibyl*. Boston: The Eastburn Press, 1895.

Jones, Joseph Stevens. *Moll Pitcher; or, the Fortune Teller of Lynn*. Boston: William Spencer, 1855.

Lewis, Alonzo. *History of Lynn*. Boston: Press of J. H. Eastburn, 1829.

"Lynn." *Commercial Bulletin*, May 8, 1869.

"The Modern Job, or the Philosopher's Stone." *The Token and Atlantic Souvenir*. Boston: Charles Bowen, 1834.

"Moll Pitcher." *Newburyport Herald*, December 2, 1830.

Moore, William Usborne. *Glimpses of the Next State*. London: Watts and Company, 1911.

Reichel, Willy. *An Occultist's Travels*. New York: R. F. Fenno and Company, 1908.

"A Second Dis DeBar, Lawyer Calls Medium." *Brooklyn Daily Eagle*, June 11, 1907.

Skolfield, Diane Jackman. "Camp Etna's Most Famous Medium." www.campetna
.com/mary-vanderbilt.html.
Whittier, John Greenleaf. *Moll Pitcher: A Poem.* Boston: Carter and Hendee, 1832.

The Prophet: William Sheldon

Federal Writers' Project of the Works Progress Administration. *Massachusetts: A Guide
to Its Places and People.* Cambridge: The Riverside Press, 1937.
Lowell Daily Citizen, May 27, 1871.
Proceedings at the Centennial Celebration of the Incorporation of the Town of Longmeadow.
Hartford: Case, Lockwood and Brainard Company, 1884.
Sheldon, William. *Aerial Navigation and the Patent Laws.* Boston: Thurston, Torry, and
Company, 1850.
———. *Millenial Institutions: Being a Comment on the Fortieth Chapter of the Prophet Eze-
kiel.* New York: 1833.
———. *The Millennium: The Good Time Coming; with a History of Experiments on the Odic
Force.* Springfield: Samuel Bowles and Company, 1862.
———. *Observations on the Theological Mystery, the Harmonial Philosophy, and Spirit Rap-
pings.* Hartford: Case, Tiffany and Company, 1851.
———. *The Seventh Vial: Consisting of Brief Comments on Various Scriptures; and of Obser-
vations on Divers Topics.* Springfield: George Wilson, 1849.
Springfield Republican, April 21, 1909.
Springfield Republican, August 2, 1862.
"William Sheldon." *Springfield Republican,* May 25, 1871.

The Reformers: The Smith Sisters

"The Battle of Glastonbury." *Springfield Republican,* January 6, 1874.
Dexter, Franklin Bowditch. *Biographical Sketches of the Graduates of Yale College.* New
York: Henry Holt and Company, 1907.
Freedom's Gifts or Sentiments of the Free. Hartford: S. S. Cowles, 1840.
"G." "A Plain Statement of Laws and Facts." *Hartford Courant,* January 24, 1874.
Koontz, Laurel. *Bible Translators, Educators, and Suffragists: The Smith Women, a Nine-
teenth-Century Case Study in America about Power, Agency, and Subordination.* Disserta-
tion, Georgia State University, 2013.
"A Novel Speech for a Town Meeting." *Springfield Republican,* November 11, 1873.
Sampson, Emily. *With Her Own Eyes: The Story of Julia Smith, Her Life, and Her Bible.*
Knoxville: University of Tennessee Press, 2006.
Smith, Julia. *Abby Smith and Her Cows.* Hartford, 1877.

——. *The Holy Bible: Containing the Old and New Testaments; Translated Literally from the Original Tongues*. Hartford: American Publishing Company, 1876.

"Smith, the Woman and Tax-Payer, Again." *Springfield Republican*, December 12, 1873.

Stanton, Elizabeth Cady, Susan B. Anthony, and Matilda Joslyn Gage, eds. *History of Woman Suffrage*. Rochester: Charles Mann Printing Company, 1886.

Star of Emancipation. Boston: Massachusetts Female Emancipation Society, 1841.

Welles, Henry Titus. *Autobiography and Reminiscences*. Minneapolis: Marshall Robinson, 1899.

The Vagabonds: The Old Darned Man and the Leather Man

Ayer, A. D. "The Old Darned Man." *Hartford Courant*, July 20, 1906.

Boston Herald, December 5, 1863.

Botkin, Benjamin. *A Treasury of New England Folklore*. New York: Bonanza Books, 1965.

Bowen, Clarence Winthrop. *The History of Woodstock, Connecticut*. Norwood: The Plimpton Press, 1926.

C. B. "The Leather Man." *Yale Literary Magazine* 48 (1883).

"The Darned Man." *Providence Evening Journal*, December 19, 1870.

DeLuca, Dan, ed. *The Old Leather Man: Historical Accounts of a Connecticut and New York Legend*. Middletown: Wesleyan University Press, 2008.

Goodell, Charles. "The Old Darnman." *Success Magazine* 9 (1906).

Griggs, Susan. *Early Homesteads of Pomfret and Hampton*. Abington, 1950.

Kansas City Times, December 28, 1887.

Keach, S. B. "Darned Man's Wedding Suit." *Springfield Republican*, February 19, 1899.

——. "More about the Darned Man." *Springfield Republican*, May 28, 1899.

Kunitz, Stanley. *Passing Through: The Later Poems, New and Selected*. New York: W. W. Norton and Company, 1997.

Larned, Ellen. "The Old Darned Man." *Hartford Courant*, July 18, 1906.

Lincoln, Allen, ed. *A Modern History of Windham County, Connecticut*. Chicago: The S. J. Clarke Publishing Company, 1920.

"The Man with Part of a Soul." *Christian Era*, September 30, 1875.

McCain, Diana Ross. *Mysteries and Legends of New England*. Guilford: Globe Pequot Press, 2009.

"Old Leather Man Quaint Connecticut Character." *Hartford Courant*, April 2, 1922.

Owens, James. "He Was Connecticut's Mystery Man." *Hartford Courant*, June 29, 1952.

"Queer Wanderers." *Ballou's Monthly Magazine* 55 (1882).

"A Wanderer of the Past." *Hartford Courant*, August 7, 1933.

The Bandit: John Wilson

Bell, Aaron, ed. *An Authentic Account of Thunderbolt and Lightfoot*. Boston: 1847.

Bennett, Emerson. "A Narrow Escape." *The Railroad Telegrapher* 27 (1910).

———. "Thunderbolt and Lightfoot." *New York Ledger*, January 2, 1864.

Burnett, W. R. *Captain Lightfoot*. New York: Alfred Knopf, 1954.

Burnham, Henry. *Brattleboro, Windham County, Vermont*. Brattleboro: D. Leonard, 1880.

"Captain Thunderbolt." *American Repertory*, August 28, 1823.

"Captain Thunderbolt." *Portland Argus*, August 12, 1823.

Caverly, Charles. "John Wilson." *American Medical Biographies*. Edited by Howard Kelly and Walter Burrage. Baltimore: The Norman, Remington Company, 1920.

"Death of a Notorious Outlaw." *Springfield Republican*, May 25, 1847.

"Death of Thunderbolt." *Barre Patriot*, May 14, 1847.

Ellam, Elizabeth. "Story of the Bandit Thunderbolt, Who Died in Brattleboro." *Boston Herald*, April 8, 1923.

Martin, Michael. *The Life of Michael Martin*. Boston: Russell and Gardner, 1821.

Miner, J. B., ed. *Confession of Michael Martin, or Captain Lightfoot*. Brattleboro: J. B. Miner, 1847.

"The New Drama of Mike Martin." *Boston Herald*, April 9, 1849.

Ritchie, Mrs. M. "The Recluse; or, A Legend of Brattleboro." *Vermont Record and Farmer*, December 1869–February 1870.

St. John, Thomas. "Dr. John Wilson, Captain Thunderbolt." www.brattleborohistory .com/cemeteries/dr-john-wilson-gravestone-1847.html.

The Wealth Seekers: Edward Norton, Samuel Bemis, and Phineas Gardner Wright

"The Bemis Will Case." *Hartford Courant*, July 9, 1883.

Bermudes, Robert Jr. "Ultimate Success Is Certain: The Life and Art of Samuel A. Bemis." *The Daguerreian Annual 2006*. Philadelphia: Print.Net Incorporated, 2006.

"Bound to Have It Satisfactory." *The Reporter* 41 (1908).

Campbell, Catherine. "Dr. Samuel Bemis: Renaissance Yankee." *Historical New Hampshire* 41 (1986).

Essex County Herald, April 13, 1894.

Essex County Herald, April 15, 1892.

Essex County Herald, April 29, 1904.

Essex County Herald, December 6, 1889.

Essex County Herald, June 16, 1905.

Essex County Herald, October 23, 1891.

"Death of Samuel A. Bemis." *Portland Daily Press*, May 5, 1881.

Drake, Samuel Adams. *Heart of the White Mountains*. New York: Harper and Brothers, 1882.

Gifford, William. *Colebrook, "A Place Up Back of New Hampshire."* Colebrook: The News and Sentinel, Inc., 1970.

Griggs, Susan. *Early Homesteads of Pomfret and Hampton*. Abington, 1950.

"Has Tomb All Ready." *Carlisle Evening News*, September 3, 1908.

"Is 81 Years Old." *Norwich Bulletin*, April 9, 1910.

Jordan, Charles. *Tales Told in the Shadows of the White Mountains*. Lebanon: University Press of New England, 2003.

Kilbourne, Frederick. *Chronicles of the White Mountains*. Boston: Houghton Mifflin Company, 1916.

"Louis Chandler's Birthplace." *Harrisburg Daily Independent*, August 25, 1892.

"The Mountain Hermit: Life and Career of an Eccentric Old Man." *Boston Globe*, June 8, 1881.

"No Use for Monument Yet." *Norwich Bulletin*, April 6, 1914.

Philips, David. *Legendary Connecticut: Traditional Tales from the Nutmeg State*. Willimantic: Curbstone Press, 1992.

"Removes Part In Beard On His Tomb." *The Vicksburg American*, March 7, 1907. [Reprints *New York Herald*.]

Successful American 8 (1903).

"Tomb Is Ready for Him." *Duluth News-Tribune*, April 26, 1908. [Reprints *New York World*.]

"Tombstone Whiskers Bad." *Evening Star*, August 12, 1905.

Vermont Watchman, August 19, 1891.

"Whiskers Don't Match Bust." *Baltimore Sun*, October 30, 1904.

The Benefactors: George Beckwith, Joseph Battell, and Isabella Stewart Gardner

Amory, Cleveland. *The Proper Bostonians*. New York: E. P. Dutton and Company, 1950.

Battell, Joseph. *Ellen or The Whisperings of an Old Pine*. Middlebury: American Publishing Company, 1901.

———. *The New Physics—Sound*. Middlebury: American Publishing Company, 1909.

———. *The Yankee Boy from Home*. New York: James Miller, 1864.

Beckwith, George. "Chronicle of Events." *Beckwith's Almanac* 34 (1881).

"An Eccentric's Death." *New Haven Register*, July 13, 1880.

Ewell, M. L. Beckwith. *One True Heart: Leaves from the Life of George Beckwith*. New Haven: Henry Peck, 1880.

Hurd, Jay. "Mrs. Jack—Art Collector, Muse, Mentor, and Mascot: Isabella Stewart Gardner and the Boston Red Sox." *The Cooperstown Symposium on Baseball and American Culture 2013–2014*. Edited by William Simons. Jefferson: McFarland and Company, 2015.

"John Quincy Wrote Poem in House." *The Portsmouth Herald*, July 15, 1938.

"Joseph Battell." *St. Albans Daily* Messenger, August 20, 1910. [Reprints *Enterprise and Vermonter.*]

"Joseph Battell's Offer." *St. Albans Daily Messenger*, February 4, 1903.

"Memory Is Affected." *Evening Star*, February 7, 1915.

"Mr. Battell's Will." *Middlebury Register*, April 2, 1915. [Reprints *Vermont Phoenix.*]

St. Albans Daily Messenger, February 17, 1903. [Reprints *Burlington Clipper.*]

St. Albans Daily Messenger, June 16, 1910.

Shand-Tucci, Douglass. *The Art of Scandal: The Life and Times of Isabella Stewart Gardner*. New York: Harper Perennial, 1997.

"Sudden Death of George Beckwith." *New Haven Journal and Courier*, July 13, 1880.

Tharp, Louise Hall. *Mrs. Jack: A Biography of Isabella Stewart Gardner*. New York: Peter Weed Books, 1965.

Watertown Daily Times, July 19, 1880.

The Castle Builders: William Gillette and Antoinette Sherri

"Cabaret Producer Here Blind; Sight Returning." *San Francisco Chronicle*, April 8, 1924.

Connecticut Valley Advertiser, September 10, 1909.

"Gillette Deserts Cats, Castle for Farewell in Sherlock Holmes." *Minneapolis Star*, February 27, 1932.

Gillette, William, ed. *How to Write a Play*. New York: Dramatic Museum of Columbia University, 1916.

Morehouse, Ward. "Gillette, at 80, Vigorous Master of Big Estate." *Evening Star*, February 2, 1936.

Ofgang, Erik. *Gillette Castle: A History*. Charleston: The History Press, 2017.

"Returns with a Bride." *Washington Post*, December 16, 1911.

Stanway, Eric and David Fiske. *Madame Sherri: The Special Edition*. Fitzwilliam: Emu Books, 2014.

"Tony Macaluso, Witness against Hansen, Is Found." *Evening World*, April 7, 1908.

"Two Salomes to Wed." *Indianapolis News*, August 18, 1908.

Zecher, Henry. *William Gillette, America's Sherlock Holmes*. Middletown: Xlibris, 2011.

The Great American Traveler: Daniel Pratt

"Birds of a Feather." *New York Times*, April 12, 1854.

Boyden, Anna. *Echoes from Hospital and White House*. Boston: D. Lothrop and Company, 1884.

"Daniel Pratt." *Harvard Advocate* 11–12 (1871).

Davis, Albert. "Some Yesterdays of the Stage." *Americana* 6 (1911).

Garrison, William Lloyd. *The Letters of William Lloyd Garrison*. Cambridge: The Belknap Press, 1981.

"The Great American Traveller." *Waltham Sentinel*, January 10, 1873.

"The Great American Traveller at Washington." *Brooklyn Daily Eagle*, March 21, 1864.

"Melancholy." *Buffalo Daily Republic*, August 7, 1856.

"A New Know Nothing Journal in the Field." *Boston Herald*, September 27, 1854.

"A Poor Jest." *Portland Daily Press*, October 16, 1878.

Pratt, Daniel. "Brief New Year's Address." *Lowell Daily Citizen and News*, December 31, 1858.

———. "To All Denominations." *Manchester Daily Mirror*, January 26, 1857.

"Pratt En Route for Washington." *Brooklyn Daily Eagle*, February 13, 1864.

"Pratt on Perpetual Motion and Political Economy." *Daily Eastern Argus*, September 24, 1866.

"Pratt Versus Lincoln." *Brooklyn Daily Eagle*, March 31, 1864.

Princeton Standard, January 8, 1869.

"Unappreciated Genius." *Boston Herald*, July 16, 1868.

Wilson, James Grant, and John Fiske, eds. *Appleton's Cyclopaedia of American Biography*. New York: D. Appleton and Company, 1888.

The Visionaries of the Ordinary: Joseph Palmer, William Henry Harrison Rose, Elizabeth Tashjian, and William Johnson

Allen, Mel. "The Johnson Wells Museum in Wells, Maine." https://newengland.com/yankee-magazine/living/new-england-environment/antique-collector.

"Antique Collector's Beloved Treasures on the Auction Block." *Newburyport News*, July 6, 2015.

"An Ax to Grind Over Trees?" *McClatchy Tribune Business News*, June 30, 2012. [Reprints *Portland Press Herald*.]

"Bill Johnson, Founder of Johnson Hall Museum in Wells." *McClatchy Tribune Business News*, February 3, 2014. [Reprints *Portland Press Herald*.]

"Charming, Off-Beat Museums Serve Local, National History." *Hartford Courant*, November 18, 1990.

Earle, Alice Morse. *Home Life in Colonial Days*. New York: The Macmillan Company, 1898.

———. *In Old Narragansett*. New York: Charles Scribner's Sons, 1898.

Federal Writers' Project of the Works Progress Administration. *Rhode Island: A Guide to the Smallest State*. Boston: Houghton Mifflin Company, 1937.

Fitchburg Sentinel, June 18, 1883.

Hall, Eliza Calvert. *A Book of Hand-Woven Coverlets*. Boston: Little, Brown, and Company, 1914.

Lang, Joel. "The Nut Lady Isn't Nuts." *Hartford Courant*, March 9, 2003.

"Museum Faces Tough Nut." *Hartford Courant*, June 2, 1978.

The Nut Lady's Homepage. www.roadsideamerica.com/nut.

"Oddball Maine Museum Runs Afoul of Town." *Boston Globe*, August 5, 2012.

"Persecuted Joseph Palmer." *Boston Globe*, December 16, 1884.

Safner, Isadora. *The Weaving Roses of Rhode Island*. Loveland: Interweave Press, 1985.

Sears, Clara Endicott, ed. *Bronson Alcott's Fruitlands with Transcendental Wild Oats*. Boston: Houghton Mifflin Company, 1915.

Sternberg, Alan. "The Nut Lady." *Hartford Courant*, July 10, 1983.

"Woman 'Goes Nuts' Over Nuts." *Bridgeport Post*, September 24, 1975.

The Legendary Eccentrics: Charles Dunbar, Tombolin, and Tom Cook

"Anecdotes of Tom Cook." *Natchez Newspaper and Public Advertiser*, August 9, 1826. [Reprints *New England Galaxy*.]

"Dame Durden, and Tom Bolin." *Harris Broadsides*. Brown Digital Repository. Brown University Library. https://repository.library.brown.edu/studio/item/bdr:270147.

"The Devil and Tom Cook." *Old Colonial Memorial*, April 8, 1826. [Reprints *New England Galaxy*.]

Dorson, Richard. *Jonathan Draws the Long Bow*. Cambridge: Harvard University Press, 1946.

Flanders, Helen Hartness. "New England Folksongs—'Tom Bolin' in New Version." *Springfield Republican*, January 20, 1935.

Flanders, Helen Hartness, and George Brown. *Vermont Folk-Songs and Ballads*. Brattleboro: Stephen Daye Press, 1931.

Forbes, Harriette. *The Hundredth Town: Glimpses of Life in Westborough*. Boston: Rockwell and Churchill, 1889.

Forbes, Harriette, ed. *The Diary of Ebenezer Parkman*. Worcester: Oliver Wood, 1899.

Harding, Walter. *The Days of Henry Thoreau*. Princeton: Princeton University Press, 1982.

Henry, Sam. *Songs of the People*. Athens: University of Georgia Press, 2010.

Hudson, Alfred Sereno. *The History of Sudbury*. Boston: R. H. Blodgett, 1889.

Jenkins, Stephen. *The Old Boston Post Road*. New York: G. P. Putnam's Sons, 1913.

The Journal of Henry David Thoreau. www.walden.org/collection/journals.

Marlowe, George Francis. *Coaching Roads of Old New England*. New York: The Macmillan Company, 1945.

Mother Goose's Pocket of Pleasure. Boston, 1876.

Salt, Henry Stephens. *Life of Henry David Thoreau*. London: Walter Scott, 1896.

Sanborn, Franklin Benjamin. *Henry D. Thoreau*. Boston: Houghton, Mifflin and Company, 1892.

Sargent, Porter. *Handbook of New England*. Boston: George Ellis Company, 1917.

Thoreau, Henry David. *Walden*. www.walden.org/work/walden.

"To Tombolin." *National Aegis*, December 30, 1812.

"Tom Bolin, and the Maid of Boston." *Isaiah Thomas Broadside Ballads Project*. www.americanantiquarian.org/thomasballads/items/show/242.

"Tom Bolin and the Whale." *Morning News*, November 5–6, 1846.

"Tom Cook." *Jamestown Journal*, August 2, 1826.

"Tom Cook." *Nantucket Inquirer*, June 14, 1828.

Ward, Andrew Henshaw. *History of the Town of Shrewsbury*. Boston: Samuel Drake, 1847.

Ward, Elizabeth. *Old Times in Shrewsbury*. New York: The McGeorge Printing Company, 1892.

Woods, Harriet. *Historical Sketches of Brookline*. Boston: Robert Davis and Company, 1874.

INDEX

Abbott (servant), 76

Adams, John, 5, 13

Adams, John Quincy, 135, 242–243

Agassiz, Louis, 35

Albany (NY), 174

Albert (Prince), 126

Alcott, Amos Bronson, 229

Alcott, Louisa May, 229

Alden, John, 78

Alden, Priscilla Mullen, 78

Allen, Ethan, 2

Allentown (PA), 64

American Civil War (1861–1865), 22, 45, 47, 94, 158, 180, 189, 221

American Revolutionary War (1775–1783), 2

Amherst (MA), 60, 90, 94

Amory, Cleveland, 195

Anderson, Elisha, 149

Andover (MA), 42, 100

Anthony, Susan B., 141, 222–223

Archer-Gilligan, Amy, xi

Atwood, Margaret, 32

Augusta (ME), 216, 243–244

Ayer, A. D., 152

Bacheller, Irving, 171

Bangor (ME), 25, 100, 107, 215

Bar Harbor (ME), xii

Barber, George Warren, 42

Barkhamsted (CT), 159

Barre (VT), 165

Barrett, Elisha, 98

Battell, Joseph, 188–193

Beckett, Sylvester, 199

Beckwith, George, 185–188, 191

Begg, Hugh McKerrow, 169

Begg, Maria Wilson, 168

Belfast (ME), 105, 107–108

Bell, Aaron, 167

Bellows Falls (VT), 36–37, 39

Bemis, Samuel, 176–180

Bennett, Emerson, 171

Berlin (CT), 186

Bernier, Don, 236

Berwick (ME), 237

Bishop, Sarah, 41

Blackstone, Lorenzo, 81

Blaxton, John, 76

Blaxton, Sarah Fisher Stevenson, 76

Blaxton, William, 71–81

Block Island (RI), 22

Blood, Henry Ames, 13

Boston (MA), 2–3, 17, 22, 24–25, 29, 34, 44, 46, 49, 51, 59–60, 64–65, 67, 71–72, 75–77, 80–81, 86, 90–91, 94, 99, 102, 114–115, 118, 125, 143, 148–149, 162–163, 167–168, 172, 177, 179, 184,

193–196, 200, 213–215, 217, 223–224, 230, 237–239, 243, 247, 250, 252

Botkin, Benjamin, ix, 18

Boyden, Anna, 222

Bradford (VT), 41

Bradstreet, Simon, 29

Brague, Rémi, x

Braintree (MA), 73

Brandon (VT), 228

Brattleboro (VT), 64–65, 161, 164–167, 169, 171, 210, 212

Bray, John and Sarah, 162

Bridgewater (CT), 187

Bristol (CT), 97

Bristol (NH), 242

Britt, Bill, 41

Brookline (MA), 253

Brookline (VT), 161, 164

Brooklyn (NY), 37, 52, 99, 104, 116, 202, 222

Brooks, John, 162

Buckingham, Rosella, 141

Burkmar, Lucius, 105–107

Burlington (VT), 215

Burney, Fanny, 139

Burnett, W. R., 171

Burnham, Henry, 164

Burns, Robert, 248

Burr, Frances Ellen, 139

Byfield (MA), 17

Byron, George Gordon (Lord), 86, 88, 221

Cambridge (MA), 162, 168, 177

Cape Elizabeth (ME), 199

Carson, Johnny, 234

Castleton (VT), 164

Charlestown (MA), 2, 71

Chelsea (MA), 214

Chester (NH), 4–5

Chesterfield (NH), 46, 199, 206, 209–210

Chestnut Hill (MA), 41

Civil War (1861–1865). *See* American Civil War

Clay, Henry, 104

Clinton (CT), 152

Colchester (CT), 26, 67

Colebrook (NH), 174–175

Concord (MA), 94, 143, 213, 223

Concord (NH), 222

Coolidge, Calvin, 203

Coolidge, Viola Marsh, 246–247

Cook, Cornelius and Eunice, 249

Cook, Tom, 249–254

Coperthwaite, William, xi

Cornwallis, Charles, 138

Corpus Christi (TX), 125

Crawford, Abel, 177–178

Crawford, Lucy, 178

Crawford Notch (NH), 47, 49, 52, 177

Cumberland (RI), 75, 81

Danbury (CT), 156

Dartmouth (MA), 34

Darwin, Charles, 68

Davis, Albert, 218

Davis, Andrew Jackson, 127

Davis, Jefferson, 220

Davis, Nathaniel, 177, 179

Deerfield (MA), 122

Dell, George, 154

DeLuca, Dan, 156

Dexter, Elizabeth Lord Frothingham, 2

Dexter, Nancy, 2–3

Dexter, Samuel Lord, 2–3

Dexter, Timothy, 1–14, 173

Dickens, Charles, 155

Dickinson, Emily, 83, 90

Dimond, John, 112
Dirth, Samuel, 44
Dixville Notch (NH), 174
"Dr. Baggs," 24
Dr. Seuss, 83
Dods, John Bovee, 99–106
Douglas, Stephen, 217
Dorchester (MA), 217
Dorson, Richard, 18, 243–244
Dow, Lorenzo, xi
Doyle, Arthur Conan, 202
Drake, Samuel Adams, 178
Drake, Samuel Gardner, 32
Dummerston (VT), 161, 164
Dunbar, Charles, 241–243

Earle, Alice Morse, 231–232
East Haddam (CT), 199, 201, 205
East Hampton (CT), 21
Eaton, Amos, 247
Eddy, Mary Baker, 105
Edward VII (Prince), 131
Ellam, Elizabeth, 172
Emerson, Ralph Waldo, 17, 60, 93, 95, 229
Endicott, John, 73, 78–79
English Jack, 47–55
English, William, 168
Erving (MA), 42–44, 47
Etna (ME), 116, 119
Everett (MA), 214
Exeter (RI), 230

Fall River (MA), 101
"Farmer Beebe," 24
Fessenden, Thomas Green, 58
Fisher-Hansen, Carl, 206–207
Fitchburg (MA), 210, 228–230
Fitzwilliam (NH), 180

Flanders, Helen Hartness, 247
Flora (enslaved person), 119
Florida (NY), 99
Forbes, Harriette, 253–254
Fowler, Enanntha, 69
Fowler, Frank Chester, 66–69
Fox Sisters (Margaret and Kate), 116
Franconia (NH), 49
Franklin, Benjamin, 59
Franklin, William, 59
Frost, Charles C., 169
Fuller, Margaret, 133
Funk, Isaak, 117

Gage, Sarah, 183
Galvani, Luigi, 57
Gardiner (ME), 244
Gardiner, Christopher, 79–80
Gardner, Eliza, 193
Gardner, Isabella Stewart, 193–197
Gardner, Jackie, 193
Gardner, Julia, 193
Gardner, John Lowell, 193
Garrison, William Lloyd, 222
George, Frank, 179
George, Norman, 89
Gorges, Robert, 72, 80
Gillette, Helen, 204
Gillette, William Hooker, 199–205
Gilray, James, 59
Glas, John, 135
Glastonbury (CT), 134–137, 141–144
Gleason, Cynthia Ann, 99
Gloucester (MA), 199, 216
Goethe, Johann Wolfgang von, 88
Goodell, Charles, 151–152
Gordon, Alexander Jr., 156
Gordon, William Augustus, 156
Graham, John, 60

Graham, Ruth, 60

Graham, Sylvester, 59–63

Graham, Sarah Manchester Earle, 60

Grant, Ulysses S., 51, 221

Green, Edward, 35–37

Green, Hetty Howland Robinson, 33–39

Green, Ned, 33, 36–37

Green, Sylvia, 33

Greenfield (MA), 2, 91–92, 94–95

Guilford (VT), 163

Hadley (MA), 28–31

Hadlyme (CT), 201–202, 205

Hamilton, Alexander, 2–3

Hammer, Alfred Emil, 158

Hammond, John Hays Jr., 199

Hampstead (NH), 244

Hampton (CT), 152

Hampton Beach (NH), 4

Harding, Walter, 242

Hartford (CT), 21–23, 25–27, 49, 58, 98,
    115, 120, 122, 134, 139, 141, 143–144,
    152, 154, 158–159, 200, 202, 216,
    235–236

Harvard (MA), 229

Hauerbach, Otto, 208

Haverhill (MA), 98, 244

Hawkes, Eva Van Cortland, xii

Hawthorne, Nathaniel, 16, 20–21, 65,
    78–79, 84, 93–95, 114, 155, 157

Hawthorne, Sophia, 65

Haygarth, John, 58

Hayman, Alf, 203

Henry, Sam, 248

Hepburn, Katharine, 235

Hepburn, Mundy, 235

Hepburn, Richard, 235

Henderson, Jack, 209

Hirst, Mary, 16, 19

Hoey, Ellen Mary Griffin, 115

Holden, Joseph, xi

Holmes, Oliver Wendell Sr., 13, 35, 58,
    64–65

Holyoke (MA), 46

Hooker, Isabella Beecher, 133

Hopkins, Stephen, 77

Houdini, Harry, 117

Howland, Abby, 34

Howland, Sylvia, 35

Hudson, Rock, 171

Hutchinson, Thomas, 31

Hydesville (NY), 116

Ipswich (MA), 168

Jacobs, Sarah, 89–90

Jancoff, Christo, 207

Jefferson, Thomas, 2, 5–6, 13

Jenkins, Stephen, 246

John J. Cisco and Son, 37

Johnson, Horace, 21–26

Johnson, Jo, 239

Johnson, John, 170–171

Johnson, William "Bill," 237–239

Jones, Joseph Stevens, 114

Judd, Sylvester, 29–30, 32

Keach, S. B., 149, 151

Keene (NH), 46, 177

Kennebuck (ME), 237

Kidder, Guy, xi

Kimberly, Eleazer, 136

Kipling, Rudyard, 83

Knapp, Samuel Lorenzo, x, 3–6, 11

Kunitz, Stanley, 152–153

Laconia (NH), 216

Lake Pleasant (MA), 116

Lamont, Richard, 24
Lancaster (NH), 216
Lane, Charles, 229
Larned, Ellen, 152
Lawrence, Henry, 171
Leather Man, 153–159
Lebanon (NH), 195
LeMaire, Charles, 208–209, 211–212
Lemington (VT), 174
Leo XIII (Pope), 193
Leominster (MA), 228
Letterman, David, 234
Levant (ME), 100–101
Leverett (MA), 44
Lewis, Alonzo, 112–113, 115
Lincoln, Abraham, 217, 221–222
Litchfield (CT), 137, 157
Little, Maggie, xi
Little Compton (RI), 60
Livermore, Arthur, 4–5, 8
Livingstone, David, 219
Longfellow, Henry Wadsworth, 93–94
Longmeadow (MA), 121–122, 128, 130, 132, 256
Lonsdale Company, 81
Loring, Charles, 171
Louis XVI (King), 3
Lovecraft, Howard Phillips, 83
Lowell (MA), 47, 98–99, 123, 215, 224
Ludlow (VT), 246
Lyme (CT), 202
Lynn (MA), 111–112, 114–115, 219

Macaluso, Tony, 206–209
Malden (MA), 1, 13
Manchester (NH), 215, 224
Mansfield (MA), 115
Marblehead (MA), 112

Marcus, George, x
Margherita (Queen), 193
Marlowe, George Francis, 246
Marshall, Henry, 175–176
Martin, Michael, 162–167, 170
Martine, Elvira, 208
Mather, Cotton, 30–31, 74–75, 122, 124
Mather, Increase, 122, 124
Mead, James, 179
Mead, Larkin, 169
Meader, Dan, 239
Medford (MA), 162
Mellen, George Washington Frost, 214–215, 221–222
Mesmer, Franz, 98
Middle Haddam (CT), 21
Middlebury (VT), 69, 188–189, 191–192
Middletown (CT), xii, 23–24, 154, 216
Miller, Henry, 154
Miller, William, xi, 140
Miner, John, 166–167
Mitchell, James E., 50–52
Moodus (CT), 66–68
Moody, Charles, 18
Moody, Joseph, 15–21
Moody, Mary, 17
Moody, "Father" Samuel, 15, 17–18
Moody, "Master" Samuel, 17
Moore, William Usborne, 117
Moore, Willis, 23
Montague (MA), 47
Morehouse, Ward, 204
Morey, George, 179–180
Morrison, John, 168–169
Morse, George Sr., 183
Morton, Thomas, 73–74, 78, 80–81
Motley, John Lothrop, 79–80
Moulton, Louise Chandler, 181

Moultonborough (NH), 199

Mount Pleasant (NY), 154

Murray, Orson, 228

Nantucket (MA), 99

Narragansett (RI), 118, 208, 230–232

Nashua (NH), 99

New Bedford (MA), 34–35, 99, 117, 216

New Haven (CT), 66, 155, 158, 163, 169,
  185–188, 215, 220

New London (CT), 59, 68, 151, 215, 236,
  249

New York City (NY), 44, 99, 119, 125,
  141, 151, 211, 224, 233

Newburyport (MA), 18, 13, 114, 117,
  249

Newfane (VT), 161, 164

Newman, Sylvanus Chase, 80–81

Newport (RI), 199, 208, 216, 220

Newtown (CT), 135

Niantic (CT), 180

Norodom (King), 193

North Kingstown (RI), 230

Northampton (MA), 29–30, 61

Northborough (MA), 248–249

Norton, Edward, 173–176

Norwich (CT), 23, 56, 182

Noyes, John Humphrey, xi

O'Brien, Joseph, 206–207

Ofgang, Eric, 200

Old Darned Man, 147–153, 156–159

Old Lyme (CT), 233

Old Saybrook (CT), 97, 235

Oneco (CT), 149

Orange (MA), 42. 45

Osborne, Ben, 51–52

Ossining (NY), 154

Paine, Thomas, 186

Palmer, Joseph, 228–230

Palmer, Thomas, 228, 230

Parker, Amos, 144

Parkman, Ebenezer, 249–250

Pawtucket (RI), 99

Pepper, George, 117, 119

Pepperrell, William, 19

Perkins, Benjamin, 57–59

Perkins, Elisha, 55–59, 68

Philadelphia (PA), 1, 13,57, 60, 99, 169,
  206

Pierce, Franklin, 215

Pitcher, Moll, 11, 111–115, 253

Pittsfield (MA), 215

Plainfield (CT), 56

Plant, Thomas, 199

Plummer, Jonathan, 11

Poe, Edgar Allan, 52, 84, 88–90

Pomeroy, Rebecca, 222

Pomfret (CT), 152

Portland (ME), 48, 98, 102, 107, 170, 216,
  224, 238–239

Portsmouth (NH), 190, 215

Power, Anna Marsh, 85

Power, Nicholas, 85

Power, Nicholas (captain), 85

Power, Susan Anna, 85

Poyen, Charles, 98–99, 102, 105

Pratt, Daniel, 213–225

Pratt, Thomas, 214

Prattville (MA), 214

Preble, Ebenezer, 18

Providence (RI), 41, 75–77, 83–84, 86–89,
  99, 115, 119, 147, 215, 218, 223, 232

Provincetown (MA), 101

Putnam (CT), 180–182, 184

Putney (VT), 176

Quechee (VT), 212

Quimby, George, 108

Quimby, Phineas Parkhurst, 105–109

Quincy (MA), 73

Quinn, Sheila O'Brien, 102

"R. Rho," 24

Reed, Martin, 230

Rehoboth (MA), 75, 78

Reichel, Willy, 117

Reichenbach, Carl von, 129

Renaissance Community, xi

Republic of Nayaug, xi

Revere (MA), 224

Revolutionary War (1775–1783). *See*
    American Revolutionary War

Ridgefield (CT), 41

Rinn, Joseph, 117

Ripton (VT), 189

Ritchie, Mrs. M., 171

Robinson, Edward Mott, 34

Rockland (ME), 101

Roosevelt, Edith Carow, 231

Rose, Elsie Marie Babcock, 230

Rose, William Henry Harrison, 230–233

Rush, Barbara, 171

Rutland (VT), 215

St. Albans (VT), 170

St. John, Thomas, 169

Safner, Isadora, 230

Salem (MA), 27, 72, 77, 163, 216

Salinger, J. D., 83

Salt, Henry Stephens, 242

Salt Lake City (UT), 208

Sanborn, Franklin Benjamin, 242

Sandeman, Robert, 135–136

Santa Anna, Antonio López de, 217

Sanford, Ezekiel, 78

Sargent, John Singer, 195

Sargent, Porter, 246

Saugus (MA), 115

Scales, William, xi

Scott, Winfield, 215

Scugle, Tibby, 42

Sears, Clara Endicott, 230

Seekonk (MA), 41

Sevengala (Sol Weinberger), 97–98, 104

Sewall, Hannah, 17

Sexton, Anne, 83

Seymour, Horatio, 188

Shattuck, Louise, xi

Sheldon, William, 121–132

Shelley, Percy Bysshe, 88

Sherri, Antoinette, 199–200, 206–212

Shrewsbury (MA), 245–246, 248–249

Sifakis, Carl, 33

Sigourney, Lydia Huntley, 128

Simmonds, Bill, 50

Simmonds, Mary, 50, 52

Simmons, Isaiah, 187

Slack, Charles, 33, 36

Smith, Abby Hadassah, 133–145

Smith, Cyrinthia Sacretia, 133–145

Smith, G. P., 51

Smith, Hancy Zephina, 133–145

Smith, Hannah Hadassah Hickok,
    133–137, 140

Smith, John, 41–47, 50, 52–53

Smith, Julia Evelina, 133–145

Smith, Laurilla Aleroyla, 133–145

Smith, Philip, 30–31

Smith, Zephaniah Hollister, 135–136, 140

Snow, Cyrus, 242

Sohier, William, 179–180

South Berwick (ME), 237

South Kingstown (RI), 230

South Royalton (VT), 247

Southington (CT), 97, 256

Sorrell, Clematis, 158

Springfield (MA), 28, 44, 46, 51, 121–122, 124, 131, 142, 149, 162, 166, 215, 247

Stamford (CT), 216

Standish, Myles, 73, 217

Stanton, Elizabeth Cady, 141, 144, 222–223

Steiner, Christopher, 236

Sterling (CT), 147, 149, 142

Stewart, Emma Battell, 188

Stewart, John Wolcott, 188

Stillman, Wilbur, 24

Stokes, Ann, 212

Stone, Lucy, 223

Stowe, Harriet Beecher, 65, 88

Sudbury (MA), 253

Suffield (CT), 60

Swampscott (MA), 116

Taft, William Howard, 23

Tashjian, Elizabeth, 233–236

Taunton (MA), 99, 101, 152

Tennyson, Alfred (Lord), 92–93

Thatcher, Charles, 46

Thomas, C. H. V., Mrs., 149

Thompson, James, 137

Thoreau, Henry David, 41, 229, 242–245

Thoreau, John, 242

Ticknor, Caroline, 84

Tipu Sultan, 138

Tombolin, 245–249

Tomlin, Isaac, 249

Train, George Francis, 222–223

Trout, John, 67

Troy (NY), 139

Tuckerman, Edward, 90

Tuckerman, Edward (son), 92

Tuckerman, Frederick (son), 92

Tuckerman, Frederick Goddard, 83–84, 90–95

Tuckerman, Hannah (daughter), 92

Tuckerman, Hannah Jones, 91–93

Tuckerman, Samuel, 90

Tuckerman, Sophia, 90

Turner, H. H., 45

Twain, Mark, 51, 83

Twin Mountain (NH), 52

Tysdal, Fanny, 43

Umberto I (King), 193

Union (ME), 100–101

Van Buren, Martin, 65

Vanderbilt, Edward Ward, 118–119

Vanderbilt, Mary "May" Scannell Pepper, 115–120

Vanderbilt, Minerva, 118, 120

Varner, John Grier, 84–85

Verdirome, Sal, xi

Very, Jones, xi

Victoria (Queen), 45, 131

Voorhis, Robert, 41

Waldo, F. W., 162

Walsh, James Joseph, 55

Waltham (MA), 219

Ward, Andrew Henshaw, 248

Ward, Artemus, 51

Ward, Elizabeth, 245–249

Warner, Charles Forbes, 29

Washington (DC), 23, 192, 220–221

Washington, George, 5, 7, 12, 57, 115, 217

Waterbury (CT), 156, 185

Watrous, Louise Dew, 152

Webster (MA), 184

Webster, Daniel, 104

Webster, Mary Reeve, 28–32

Webster, William, 28

Weeks, David, 9–10

Welles, Henry Titus, 144–145

Wells (ME), 237, 239

Wells, Horace, 25

Wesselhoeft, Robert Ferdinand, 63–66

Wesselhoeft, William, 63–64

Westborough (MA), 249, 253–254

Westerly (RI), 24, 41

Westport (NH), 46

Weymouth (MA), 72–73

White, Lucy, 19

Whitefield, George, 20

Whitman, John Winslow, 86

Whitman, Sarah Helen, 83–92

Whittier, John Greenleaf, 113–114

Wilbur, David, 41

Wilkinson, Jemima, xi

Wilks, Matthew, 36

Willard, Peter, 163

Williams, John, 122, 124

Williams, Roger, 75–77, 85, 87

Williams, Stephen, 124

Willis, Nathaniel Parker, 128

Wilson, Abigail Chamberlain, 164

Wilson, John, 161–172

Wilson, Robert, 168–169

Winthrop, John, 72

Wise, Henry, 220

Wollaston, Robert, 73

Woodbridge (CT), 163

Woodbury (CT), 155–156

Woodstock (CT), 152, 180, 183

Woodwell, Philip McIntire, 16, 18–19

Worcester (MA), 77, 87, 153, 182, 215, 229, 249

Wordsworth, William, 91

Wright, Benoni, 41

Wright, Phineas Gardner, 180–184

York (ME), 15, 17

Young, Alse, 27

Zecher, Henry, 200

Ziegfeld, Florenz, 209

Ziegler, "Wild Bill," xii

ABOUT THE AUTHOR

Stephen Olbrys Gencarella is a tenured professor in the Communication Department at the University of Massachusetts, Amherst. He is also the resident folklorist for the Connecticut River Museum in Essex, Connecticut, and has been a visiting professor at the Lyme Academy College of Fine Arts. He is the cohost of *Fermented* and currently developing a series on the folklore of the Connecticut State Parks for iCRV Radio. He holds a joint PhD from the Folklore Institute and the Department of Communication and Culture at Indiana University and has published numerous articles in academic journals. He serves as a board member and officer of the Connecticut Eastern Regional Tourism District. A native New Englander, he lives in Lyme, Connecticut, with his wife Winnifred and their children Salvatore, Angeline, Antonio, and Marcella.